PRAISE FOR

Mary Kay Andrews and *Hissy Fit*

"[A] sharp Southern treat. . . . A fascinating peek into the luscious world of designer home furnishing, sure to make readers drool with envy." —*Publishers Weekly*

"Readers who enjoy books set in the South that deal with love, friendship, and getting even will find themselves laughing out loud at this latest novel by Andrews."

—*Library Journal* (starred review)

"Andrews's descriptions of antique furniture and heart-pine flooring are so lush and appealing that they will seduce even the decorating-challenged. Throw in the idyllic Southern setting and the humorous, often scintillating banter, and you've got yourself another winning read." —*Booklist*

"Laced with humor and a sense of place that oozes the aroma of magnolia blossoms." —*Atlanta Journal-Constitution*

"Andrews is at her best in this thoroughly satisfying story with the right blend of mystery, romance, and sharply funny writing."

—*Orlando Sentinel*

"A truly rollicking tale. . . . If you are interested in interior design, Southern manners, heartache, romance, or just a well-told story, *Hissy Fit* is for you." —*Charlotte Observer* (North Carolina)

"[A] Southern-fried romp. . . . The furnishing descriptions are scrumptious and the love story's sweet." —*Entertainment Weekly*

© 2003 Greg Foster

About the Author

MARY KAY ANDREWS is a former journalist for the *Atlanta Journal-Constitution*, and is the author of *Savannah Blues* and *Little Bitty Lies*. She lives in Raleigh, North Carolina. Visit her at www.marykayandrews.com.

Hissy Fit

Hissy Fit

Mary Kay Andrews

Perennial

An Imprint of HarperCollinsPublishers

First Perennial edition published 2005.

The Library of Congress has catalogued the hardcover edition as follows:

Andrews, Mary Kay
    Hissy fit / Mary Kay Andrews.—1st ed.
        p.   cm.
    ISBN 0-06-056464-4
    1. Young women—Fiction. 2. Southern States—Fiction. 3. Rejection (Psychology)—Fiction. 4. Revenge—Fiction. I. Title.

    PS3570.R587H57 2004
    813'.6—dc22

                                                                    2004042898

ISBN 0-06-056465-2 (pbk.)

05 06 07 08 09 ❖/RRD 10 9 8 7 6 5 4 3 2

Acknowledgments

Many thanks go out to many folks for their invaluable assistance and advice with this book. Frank Garson of Atlanta and Kathy P. Reynolds of VF Intimates patiently explained the bra business to me. Dianne and Patrick Yost of the *Morgan County Citizen* became my Madison tour guides, as did Adelaide Ponder, publisher emeritus of *The Madisonian*. Thanks go to Charles Seabrook of the *Atlanta Journal-Constitution* and Lee Glenn of the Georgia Power Company for trying to educate me about Lake Oconee. Sue Ruby of Savannah gave me interior design advice—and a guided tour of ADAC, and Elizabeth Jackson of Back Roads Antique Salvage told me where to shop for antiques in Alabama, Mississippi, and Louisiana. Any errors of fact are totally mine.

Hissy Fit, more than any of my other books was truly a collaborative effort. Heartfelt thanks and love go to the best agent in the whole damn world, Stuart Krichevsky, and the fabulous Shana Cohen of SKLA, along with the best editors in the whole damn world, Carolyn Marino and Jennifer Civiletto at HarperCollins who midwifed *Hissy Fit* every step of the way. And last, but never least, thanks and unending love to my family, Tom, Katie, and Andy, who have been putting up with my own hissy fits for many years.

Hissy Fit

I

If it had not been for my fiancé's alcoholic cousin Mookie I feel quite sure that my daddy would still be a member in good standing at the Oconee Hills Country Club. But Mookie can't drink hard liquor. She can drink beer and wine all day and all night and not bat an eyelash, but give her a mai-tai or, God forbid, a margarita, and you are asking for trouble.

It was my rehearsal dinner, which the Jernigans were hosting, and I *was* the bride-to-be, so I don't believe I should have been the one responsible for keeping a grown woman and mother of two away from the margarita machine, even if she was one of the bridesmaids.

Nonetheless, I was the one standing there when Mookie went spinning out of control across the dance floor, and I was the one who got sprayed with a good six ounces of strawberry margarita. And across the front of my blue raw silk Tahari dress too.

"For God's sake," snapped GiGi, my mother-in-law-to-be. She of course had neatly sidestepped Mookie, leaving her own pale pink beaded gown spotless. "I told you not to have her in the wedding. You know how she gets."

"Keeley," Mookie yelped, lunging at me with her half-empty glass. "I am sooooo sorry. Let me help you get cleaned up."

She proceeded to dump the rest of her drink down my back.

"It's fine," I said, gritting my teeth. "Just a little spot."

Mookie's mother, who is used to this kind of behavior, snatched her up by the arm and started dragging her toward the door so she wouldn't cause any more of a scene, and all the women closed ranks around me, dabbing and fussing until I wanted to scream.

Actually, I'd been wanting to scream for several weeks now.

Enough! Enough parties. Enough presents. Enough luncheons

and teas, enough sappy wedding showers, enough family and friends oohing and aahing over the perfect couple.

A.J. had had enough too. "Can't we just go somewhere and screw our brains out for a couple weeks, then come back and be normal?" he'd asked the night before the rehearsal dinner.

It had been a busy week. I'd already endured the "Sip 'n See Tea," where everybody in the county came by my daddy's house to paw over my wedding loot, and the bridesmaids' luncheon where GiGi let it be known that she thought it was awful my mama hadn't been invited to the wedding. As if I even knew where Mama had been living for the past twenty-some years.

And that was just the solo stuff. That very night A.J. and I had suffered through the "His 'n Her Barbecue Shower" given by one of his former fraternity brothers.

At the time he asked this question, A.J. was modeling the Hot Stuff! barbecue apron and padded oven mitt, which had been a shower gift from his Aunt Norma. To be perfectly honest, A.J. was naked under the apron. And he wasn't wearing the mitt where his Aunt Norma had intended.

I had A.J. backed into the corner with the barbecue tongs, and then one thing led to another, and pretty soon we were rolling around on the floor of his apartment, and my chef's hat came off along with the rest of my clothes, and the next thing you know, A.J. was having one of his attacks.

"Hee-upp! Hee-upp." His whole body arched backward. I pushed him away, not startled really. A.J. gets like that sometimes when he's, uh, in the throes.

"Breathe, baby, breathe," I instructed, slithering out from under him.

"No," he managed, between hiccups. "Don't stop, Keeley." He tried to pull me back down. "Come on. I'll be all right."

"Hee-upp! Hee-upp! Hee-upp." His body jerked violently with each hiccup. I was afraid he'd hurt himself. Hell, I was afraid he'd hurt me. Not to mention that I don't find fits of uncontrollable hiccups much of a turn-on. Not even when the hiccupper is the love of my life.

I scrambled to my feet, ran to the sink, and filled a cup with water. "Come on, A.J.," I said, helping him to his feet. "It's better if you stand up. Come on, sugar, drink some water for Keeley."

"I (hee) don't (up) want any damn hee-uppp! water," A.J. stuttered. But he took a sip anyway.

"Another one," I urged, rubbing his bare back. He caught my free hand and slid it down his belly. The man never stops trying.

"No, now," I said, giggling and moving away. He pulled me back toward him. I held out the cup. "Not until you drink all this water."

He frowned but started sipping.

"Go slower," I said. "You know it's the only thing that works."

"I know what works," he said, getting that look in his eye again. "Come back over here and rub on me again."

But I'd picked up my clothes and was already hurrying into the bedroom to get dressed.

"Hey!" he called after me. "That wasn't the deal."

I pushed the button on the doorknob. "I know," I called through the locked door. "I tricked you."

By the time he found the key to the bedroom door I was just zipping my skirt.

"Aw, Keeley," he said, his lip thrust out in that adorable pout of his. "I wanted us to do it one more time tonight."

I tried to kiss the pout away, but he wasn't having it.

"A.J.," I said, pushing his hands away from the button he was unfastening. "Now, really. The wedding's just a few days away. I have an early morning meeting and a ton of stuff to do. I can't be staying over here fooling around with you all night."

"Come on, baby," he whispered, sliding the zipper on my skirt down while pushing my skirt up toward my waist. "Once we're married, it won't be as much fun as this. We'll be all legal and stuff."

I pushed him away, my feelings hurt.

"You're saying sex with me is gonna be boring? Just because we're married? Thanks a hell of a lot."

"You know what I mean," A.J. said, grabbing for me again. I spun away from him, and got my shoes and my purse. My car was parked outside. I headed for the front door.

A.J. wrapped the apron around his waist and followed me out to the car. His cute white butt glowed in the June darkness. "I don't mean we won't have fun," he said, glancing around the yard to see if anybody was watching. A.J.'s apartment was in the carriage house behind The Oaks, his parents' antebellum mansion. I glanced up too, at the lit-up second-floor window I knew was his parents' bedroom.

"I just mean it won't be forbidden, like it is now," A.J. said. He looked up at his mother's window too, and now he had me backed up against the door of my car. He let the apron drop to the ground, and now he was honest-to-God naked as a jaybird. "Come on, admit it, it's a turn-on, thinking we might get caught."

It was obvious that he was turned on, all right.

"No," I said firmly. "You may be an exhibitionist, but I'm not. Now be a good boy and say good night."

He pressed up against me again. "I'll be a good boy. A very good boy. In your car," he whispered, kissing my neck. "We haven't done it in your car in ages."

"No."

"My car." He worked his knee between mine.

"Hell no." His car was a BMW Z-3 roadster. After the last time we'd done it there I'd needed a chiropractor to get my spine back to normal.

He got a demonic grin then. "I know. Mama's car. The back seat of that Escalade was made for love."

That did it. I mean, there's kinky, and then there's KINKY.

I gave him a gentle push, and he stumbled and fell backward, planting his bare tush on the crushed oystershell of the drive.

"Oww," he howled.

"Night, darlin'," I said. I got in the car, locked the door, and drove off into the inky Georgia night.

Now it was a week later, and the longest damn party in the history of Madison was just a day away from being over. The wedding was tomorrow. One more day and I would be Mrs. Andrew Jackson Jernigan. Keeley Murdock Jernigan.

"One more day," I muttered to myself, as I extricated myself from the clutches of the womenfolk.

"Here," my Aunt Gloria said, thrusting a bottle of club soda at me. "Go in the ladies' room, take the dress off, and dampen it with the soda. Otherwise you'll never get that strawberry stain out of that silk."

"Thanks," I said, shooting her a grateful look.

I was hurrying down the hallway at the Oconee Hills Country Club when I heard it. A faint noise. Coming from a room on the right side of the hallway. It was the boardroom.

I paused outside the door.

"Hee-upp."

"Shhh!" And then a faint giggle.

"Hee-upp. Oh God, do that again."

I froze. A fist seemed to slam into my chest. I felt dizzy. Nauseous. I had to get to the ladies' room. I took two stumbling steps.

"Keeley never does it like that."

Another giggle.

Now I had my hand on the door.

"Hee-up, hee-up, hee-up!"

I flung the door open.

Andrew Jackson Jernigan, the man of my dreams, dressed only in his white tux shirt, black tie, and black socks, was standing, facing me. Facing him was Paige Plummer, my maid of honor, her perky little ass perched on the boardroom's shiny mahogany table, her perky red chiffon cocktail dress hiked up to her waist, her legs wound around my fiance's waist.

"Heeeee." A.J.'s head snapped forward. His mouth slammed shut. "Oh God." He said it differently this time. He backed away from Paige, reached down for his pants.

"What?" Paige turned her head around. Her perky little red lips formed an astonished O when she saw me standing there.

"Oh God," Paige said, hopping down from the table. Paige was an advertising copywriter, but she'd never been a really original thinker. "Oh God, Keeley."

Something came over me. One minute the bottle of club soda was in my hand. The next minute I was flinging it across the boardroom at A.J. He tried to duck, but since his pants were still at half-mast, his reaction time was off. Fortunately for him, the bottle was plastic. Unfortunately, it was full. It hit him right above the left eye, and he went down like a rock.

"Goddamn," he roared.

"Keeley!" Paige cried out.

I was out of things to throw. But that was only a temporary situation.

2

Paige darted around to the far side of the table, searching for her perky little red thong panties. I found them first.

"You bitch," I screamed. "How could you? My best friend. How could you?"

"Now Keeley. We didn't mean anything by it," A.J. said, slowly standing up. His fingers fumbled with his belt buckle. "You know, we've all had a lot to drink tonight . . . you know how it is, baby. You know how I get a little frisky when I have a few drinks." He had the nerve to wink at me.

I took the panties and slapped the wink off his face. "With my maid of honor?"

I wheeled around and faced Paige, who had her shoes in her hand and had been stealthily edging toward the door.

"You're supposed to help me with my veil and hold my bouquet," I screeched. "Not fuck the groom, you scum-sucking slut."

"Hey!" Paige said sharply. "Who are you calling a slut? You're the one who screwed him on your first date."

"Shut up." I hauled off and bitch-slapped her. Right there in the boardroom of the Oconee Hills Country Club, with the oil portraits of forty-some past club presidents, including A.J.'s granddaddy Chub Jernigan, glowering down at me.

"Ooooowwww," Paige howled. She clutched the side of her face. I noticed with satisfaction that her cheek bore the imprint of my palm, and that my palm bore a smear of Paige's CoverGirl foundation.

Seconds later Paige launched herself at me. At five-foot-eleven, I stand a good six inches taller than she does, but Paige had played forward on the state runner-up Morgan County High girls' volleyball team. She was tiny, but I had forgotten about her sports prowess, and more importantly, that she came from a long line of what we in Madison like to call trailer trash.

"Bitch," she shrieked. Her long red nails clawed at my face, and her stocking-clad size six feet kicked at my shins and knees with a force that took me by surprise.

I was trying to fend her off when A.J. stepped between us and clamped my right forearm tightly in his hand. He held Paige firmly by her shoulder.

"Girls!" he said. "Come on, y'all. Be nice, now. Calm down, both of you."

I wriggled out of his grasp. "Be nice? Calm down? You sneak in here with her and bang her on the board table—during our rehearsal dinner? With me and my whole family and my minister in the same building, and you want me to be calm?"

His face softened. He almost managed a tear. "Aw, Keeley. I'm sorry. I didn't mean to hurt you, darlin'. You know I love you more than anything. Me and Paige were just foolin' around. Things got out of hand. That's all. Right, Paige?" He looked over at my former best friend for confirmation.

"Tell her, Paige. We were both just a little drunk. Right?"

Paige's dark blue eyes glittered with malice. "Right, A.J. Drunk and bored. You were bored out of your mind with Keeley. That's why you snuck over to my place last week, in your mama's Escalade. And the week before that, why we did it in your office at the bank."

She gave me a perky little smirk. "Keeley. Sweetie. You've always been so concerned about proprieties. 'That's tacky, Paige. Don't be so low-class, Paige.' But it's like my mama always said. If they can't get it at home, they're gonna go get it somewhere else. And I'm the somewhere else."

"Paige!" A.J. whispered. "That's a lie. Tell her it's all a lie. I never—"

I didn't give him a chance to finish. I wheeled around and grabbed a golf trophy from the elaborate mahogany display case by the door. It wasn't just any golf trophy either. It was the A. J. "Chub" Jernigan Memorial Cup, a huge sterling silver chamber pot–shaped affair, with fancy cursive writing and a bas relief bust of Grandpa Chub on the front.

"Bastard," I cried, hurling the trophy at his head. It missed by a mile, but knocked two club presidents off the wall behind him. I turned around and stalked out of the room.

And ran head-on into my future mother-in-law.

"Keeley!" GiGi exclaimed. "What on earth is going on here? Everybody in the club can hear you carrying on. Have you lost your mind?"

"Mama," A.J. said, hurrying up behind her. "We had a little tiff, that's all. Talk to her. Tell her she's blowing things all out of proportion."

"Keeley?" GiGi said, her voice stern. "Honey, you don't want to be fussin' the night before the wedding. It'll spoil the party."

I looked over GiGi's shoulder. Our guests had followed her into the hallway, and they were all standing there, clumped together, clucking and whispering and staring at me.

"He was screwing Paige!" I cried. "Back there in the boardroom."

"Keeley," GiGi whispered, grabbing me by the shoulders. "Boys will be boys. Now get ahold of yourself. You're causing a scene here."

"He's not a boy!" I said. "He's thirty-four years old, and he's engaged to me."

"Hush," she said, giving me a little shake. "Trust me, that girl means nothing to him."

"It means everything to me," I said. I could feel my rage growing, feeding on itself, out of control.

"The wedding's off," I cried. "Everybody go home."

The whispering and clucking got louder.

"I mean it," I shouted, pushing past GiGi and Mookie and my Aunt Gloria and all the rest of them. "Go home!" I made my way into the ballroom where the band was playing, and I found my father, who was sitting at a table with his golf buddies.

"It's over, Daddy," I sobbed. "The wedding's off. I want to go home."

Daddy stood up, his dear, weather-beaten old face suddenly animated and alarmed. His poker buddies melted away from the table.

He'd unbuttoned his stiff white shirt, and his black tie was rolled up on the dinner table beside his Scotch and rocks. "Off? What do you mean, Keeley? Is this some kind of a joke?"

"Now, Wade," I heard GiGi say. She'd come up behind us. She looked perfect. Completely composed. Not a hair out of place. "Keeley's just a little upset. First Mookie ruined her dress, and then she and A.J. were fussin' at each other, and she's overreacted. Wade, I think maybe you should take her on home so she can get a good night's sleep before the big day tomorrow."

"There is no big day tomorrow," I exclaimed. "I wouldn't marry that two-timing, lying, cheating son-of-a-bitch for all the tea in China."

"Honey," Daddy started.

"I'm serious," I said, my voice trembling. "I wouldn't marry A.J. Jernigan if he were the last man on earth."

"Keeley, angel." A.J. himself was at my side now.

I snapped then. I really did. Maybe it was chemical, maybe it was hormonal. I really couldn't say.

But I pitched a hissy fit.

I did. And after that, nothing was the same.

One minute I was standing in the ballroom at the Oconee Hills Country Club. I was a sober, respectable, thirty-two-year-old professional interior designer with a successful career and the respect of my community.

The next minute I was a deranged force of nature. The sane Keeley Rae Murdock, the one who knew right from wrong, was shocked and appalled. But I was powerless to stop myself.

Our minister, Dr. Richard Wittish, pastor of Madison First United Methodist Church, rushed over to comfort me.

"Keeley," he said quietly, his kind face flushed red with discomfort. "You don't want to do this now. Let's go in the other room. Let's have some quiet time and say a prayer for serenity."

Instead I shook Paige's red thong panties right in his face. The same face that had looked down on me from the church pulpit my whole life. "I don't want serenity, Dr. Wittish," I screamed. "I want to fuckin' kill Paige Plummer and A. J. Jernigan."

"Keeley!" GiGi said, gasping. "Get ahold of yourself."

I snatched up Daddy's highball glass and smashed it against the wall. "No, GiGi, you get ahold of yourself. Get ahold of your cheating, lying, son-of-a-bitchin' son too, while you're at it."

Now A.J.'s daddy, Big Drew, pushed forward. He was tall and distinguished-looking, with a shock of silver hair and a ruddy beef-and-bourbon kind of face. He'd disappeared sometime after the waiters served the appetizers. Outside sneaking a cigar probably. GiGi didn't allow him to smoke at home. "Now, really, young lady," he said, his voice booming across the hushed ballroom. "There's no need for this kind of display."

"How about this kind of display?" I asked. I looked around for something else to throw. And then I saw it. At every place on every one of the round tables in the room, GiGi had placed a little party favor. Each guest had been gifted with a hand-painted Limoges snuff-box with the words "Keeley & A.J." scripted in flowing fourteen-karat gold paint on the lid.

I swept my hand down the center of Daddy's table, knocking the crystal wineglasses and china to the floor, and gathering up six of the snuffboxes.

"Here," I cried, smashing the first box against the polished oak dance floor. "Here's a display.

"And here's another display." I looked around the room for approval. Everybody in the room was frozen in place. My Aunt Gloria stood in the doorway, clutching her hand to her throat in a look of horror I'll never forget.

But I couldn't stop myself. I snatched up the other snuffboxes and flung them against walls, against the windows. I threw one at A.J., and when his mother gasped, I threw one at her too. There was movement in the room now. The band members were hastily packing up their instruments. Men were gathering up their wives, and wives were gathering their pocketbooks, apparently afraid of being my next target, and the waiters were gathering up the glass and china, to keep them from joining the carnage.

Finally Daddy put a stop to my rampage. He stood up and wrapped his big bearlike arms around me and crushed me to him. "Keeley," he whispered, stroking my hair. "Stop this, honey. Come on. It's all over. You don't have to marry A.J. You don't have to marry anybody if you don't want to."

The look on his face nearly killed me. Worry. Fear. Pain. He thought I'd gone berserk. And I had.

"I'm sorry, Daddy," I whispered. I ran out of the ballroom, past the fleeing wedding guests, terrified waiters, my fiance, and my former best friend.

I ran down the front steps of the country club, past the teenaged valet parking attendants who were huddled together, sharing a stolen bottle of beer. It wasn't until I'd gotten to the parking lot that I realized I didn't know where I was going.

I glanced over my shoulder. People were streaming out of the country club. I needed to make a fast getaway. But how? I'd come to the club with A.J. His red Z-3 was easy to spot. He'd parked it in the front row of the lot and left the top down. I walked over and looked down at the black leather interior. For the first time I realized I still had Paige's panties clutched in my hand. I draped them over the steering wheel. His keys dangled from the ignition. How very A.J.

Should I just take the car and leave? And go where? And do what?

I had a better idea. I grabbed the keys and considered the gleaming expanse of freshly waxed red paint.

The valet parking guys were heading out to the lot to start retrieving cars. I had to work fast. My letters were big and bold and scary. The handwriting looked like that of a serial killer. Excellent. I wanted him to fear me.

"Asshole!" I whispered triumphantly, reading what I'd just written in five-inch-high letters. I wrenched my engagement ring off my finger and threw it in the car. "Asshole."

I heard a cough then. I looked around. For the first time I noticed the car parked next to A.J.'s, a big old canary yellow Cadillac, the vintage kind with the fins. A man was sitting in the front seat. He was laughing his head off.

"Ash-hole," he said, laughing again.

"What did you say?" I asked, my voice dripping venom.

"Ash-hole." He repeated himself. "You spelled it wrong."

3

I'd never seen this guy before. He certainly wasn't from Madison. I'd have remembered a car like that. He was in his early to mid-thirties. He had red hair going gray around the sides, and he was good-looking in a sort of outdoorsy way, even though he was dressed in a tux.

"Do I know you?"

"Not really," he said. He pointed at A.J.'s car. "See? You left out an 'S.' So it sounds like you're calling him an ash-hole."

"Mind your own damn business," I snapped, giving my hair an "I don't care" toss.

People were walking to their cars. I had to get out of here. I took a few brisk strides through the lot. Damn. I'd forgotten about my shoes. High-heeled slingback sandals are not exactly made for walking. And my strapless silk dress wasn't either.

I didn't care, I told myself. There was no way I was going back inside to beg a ride from Daddy or anybody else. Not after the spectacle I'd made of myself. I half jogged out of the parking lot and up the two-lane blacktop road back toward town. My apartment was less than two miles away. I can walk a ten-minute mile most days. But most days I don't walk in cocktail attire.

After less than fifty yards my calves were screaming in protest. I could feel blisters forming on the tops of my toes. And I had to keep hiking up the top of my dress to keep my boobs from falling out.

I wasn't wearing a watch, but it was full dark now, so it had to be past nine. Mosquitoes swarmed around my face, and moths fluttered softly in the muggy night air. One of the county road crews had recently mown the grass along the shoulder of the road. The warm green smell would have been wonderful any other night. But tonight grass blades were clinging to my ankles, and my spike heels sank half an inch into the rain-softened earth. I sighed and stepped out of the sandals. I'd make it home faster barefoot.

Cars slowed as they approached me. I could see people craning their necks to look at me, and then look away quickly and speed up before their eyes could meet mine. I was the county's newest freak.

The big yellow Caddy pulled over on the side of the road, forcing me deeper onto the grassy shoulder.

"Hey," I said, pissed.

"Hey yourself," the driver said. "Come on, Keeley. Get in. I'll give you a ride back to town."

How did he know my name? I took another look at the car. It had a white leather convertible top and shiny chrome hubcaps, and real white leather tuck and roll upholstery. It was a supreme pimpmobile.

"Uh-uh," I said. "My daddy taught me never to get in a car with a stranger."

"We're not really strangers," he said. "We were introduced earlier tonight. Back at the party. Before you went nuts."

"I've never seen you before," I said. But really, I thought maybe I had.

"Sure you have. Your cousin Janey introduced us. Come on, Keeley. It's at least two miles back to your place."

A chill ran down my spine. A redheaded stranger driving a pimpmobile. Was this the price for notoriety? Did I have a stalker already? "How do you know my name? And where I live?"

He shook his head impatiently. "Your name is Keeley Murdock. You live above that sofa store in town. And if you don't get your butt in this car right now, I'm just gonna leave you here."

"It's not a sofa store," I said. "It's an interior design studio. And I don't remember meeting you. I don't need a ride. I like to walk. I love to walk."

He shrugged. "Suit yourself. I saw the Jernigan crowd leaving the country club right behind me. They'll be along any minute."

I hopped in the front seat of the pimpmobile. "Hurry up and go before somebody sees me with you," I said.

He pushed the gas pedal to the floor, and the yellow land yacht's rear wheels spurted a shower of dirt. We sped down the blacktop toward town. I glanced over at my driver, and when his lips twitched in a sort of snicker, I hitched up the bodice of my dress again.

"Is that blood?" he asked, pointing at the red stain on the front of my dress.

"No, dammit," I said. "It's just strawberry daiquiri. My aim was off."

He winced.

"What did you say your name was again?" I asked.

"Will."

"Will, what?"

"Mahoney."

I knew that name. I took a closer look at him. He was tall, taller than me even, I thought, and his dinner jacket didn't fit him exactly right. The red hair barely brushed the collar of his dinner jacket. Not a mullet yet, thank God. My reputation might be in tatters, but I do still have some standards.

Will Mahoney had the freckles that usually go with that color hair, and deep brown eyes that took in more than they should.

"Will Mahoney? You're the guy who wants to tear down Mulberry Hill?"

"You have a problem with that?" he aked.

One thing you have to know about Madison, Georgia, is that the place is just run over with historic old antebellum mansions. In fact, our state claim to fame is that when that Civil War boogeyman William Tecumseh Sherman was burning and pillaging his way to the coast during the dying days of the Confederacy, he took one look at Madison and just seized up over how beautiful it was. He put away the matches and had supper instead.

Well, anyway, that's the story.

Mulberry Hill, a big white clapboard pile off U.S. 441, was, to be honest, neither the oldest nor the wonderfullest mansion in town. It had been empty so long, most folks were waiting for it to fall down all by itself.

"It's a historic landmark," I said disapprovingly. "Anyway, what were you doing at my rehearsal dinner? I don't know you, and I'm sure the Jernigans don't either."

"Your mother-in-law invited me," Mahoney said.

"GiGi? I don't believe you. She's the one who started the petition drive to save Mulberry Hill."

"I've had a change of heart," he said. "The house stays put. I even made a donation to the historical society. I'm your mother-in-law's new best friend."

"She's not my mother-in-law," I pointed out.

"Not after tonight, no," Mahoney agreed. He was wide-open grinning now. "That was some floor show you put on back there. No wonder the orchestra left."

So he'd been there. My mortification was complete. I stared out the window at the landscape whizzing past. "I don't want to talk about it."

We were coming into town now, thank heavens. In five more minutes I could be home in my own apartment. I could burn my ruined dress, turn off the phone, and give serious thought to moving to another state.

"Turn right at the next light," I told him. "It's two blocks up."

"I know where it is," Mahoney said. "Glorious Interiors, right? And your aunt runs the business? You live in the second-floor apartment. Nice building. I'm thinking of buying it."

Our building, with its elaborate plasterwork detailing, had been the old Merchant's Mercantile building up until the mid-fifties. My granddaddy bought it from the original owner and turned it into Murdock Notions, which he ran until shortly before he died in the late 1980s.

"Buy our building? Dream on. Gloria inherited that building from my granddaddy. It's been in the family for more than fifty years. She'd never sell. Especially not to you."

"Whatever you say," he said. "I'm not gonna cross a hot-blooded woman like you, Keeley Murdock."

He pulled the car alongside my own five-year-old red Volvo sedan, which was illegally parked in a loading zone. But it was *our* loading zone. The parking space that should, by rights, have been mine, was taken up by one of the bumper-to-bumper cars whose drivers were probably having dinner at the half-dozen new restaurants that have popped up in our revitalized downtown recently.

Our own storefront, with its jaunty black and white striped awning stretching out over the sidewalk, was softly lit. I'd decorated the window myself, earlier in the week, with a gorgeous French Art Deco chaise longue I'd bought at the Marché aux Puces flea market outside Paris, a stack of shiny Hermès and Chanel hatboxes, and an unfurled bolt of Pierre Frey fabric in a luscious gold damask. I'd been thinking French, of course. A.J. and I were to have honeymooned at a villa in Provence this coming week.

"Shit," I said quietly, looking at that window, with all its naked, girlish optimism. The window had to be dismantled, immediately. Right after I found some chocolate to overdose on.

I got out of the car, my eyes glued to that telling window. "Thank you very much for the ride," I mumbled, the picture once more of polite, Southern charm.

"Hey," he said, thrusting something toward me. "Don't forget these."

I blushed. My shoes. The price of those size 11 blue satin Manolo Blahniks would make any career girl blush. I grabbed for them, and muttered another quick thank-you. Which he should have taken as a "Goodbye, get lost."

But Will Mahoney didn't take the hint. He didn't put the car into drive. He didn't leave. He didn't even take his hand away from mine.

He gave me a long searching look.

"Will you be all right? Tonight? I mean . . ."

"I'm fine," I said, forcing a fake smile. "Great. Thanks for asking. Everything's just peachy." I felt a hot tear go rolling slowly down my face.

"You were right about one thing, you know," he said. Just for an instant, I thought he squeezed my hand. I snatched it away from his.

"A. J. Jernigan really is an asshole," Will Mahoney said. "No matter how you spell it."

4

Gloria had a key to my apartment, and she never hesitated to use it. After all, she was technically the owner of the building. And my employer. Technically. That morning was no exception. She didn't even bother to knock on my bedroom door before busting in on me. "Keeley?"

I pulled the coverlet over my head. "Keeley doesn't live here anymore."

"Lucky you," Gloria said tartly. She leaned down and kissed the coverlet approximately in the area of my forehead.

"It's nearly noon, you know. Come on, punkin, I've got hot coffee and two chocolate éclairs. One is supposed to be for you, but if you don't get out of this bed right now, I'll be happy to eat yours and mine."

"I'm not hungry," I said, turning over and managing to wrap myself, mummy-style, in the process. I was amazed that this was the truth. Last night I'd sat and stared at a bag of Hershey's Kisses left over from Christmas and I hadn't been able to eat a single one. I had, however, polished off a bottle of tequila and a pint of Harveys Bristol Cream that I'd found downstairs in the studio.

"Suit yourself," Gloria said. I heard the rustling of a paper bag and peeped out from under the coverlet.

"You look like death," Gloria said, nibbling at the edge of an éclair. "Did you finish off all the liquor in the joint before or after you created that fetching window display?"

Good question. I had to think about that one.

Oh yes. I'd found the tequila in my own liquor cabinet, and being a liquor wussy, I'd mixed it with a quart of orange juice. Sometime after midnight, I'd gotten enough of a buzz off the tequila to go downstairs and rearrange the shop's window display. But the buzz wore off, so I'd rummaged around in the studio's little kitchenette until I found the Harveys Bristol Cream that had probably been in there since my granddaddy's days.

"Both," I said, grimacing at the memory. My head was pounding and my mouth tasted like the inside of a litter box.

"Interesting use of symbolism and metaphor, that window," Gloria said, sipping her coffee. "I thought the wedding gown in the trash can was an effective juxtaposition of the industrial with the sentimental. But I'm afraid some of our older, more conservative clients might be offended by the slashed photos of A.J., not to mention the inherent symbolism in the douche bag you left hanging in that particular vignette."

I felt a stabbing pain in my left eye then. "I'd forgotten about the douche bag."

Gloria nodded thoughtfully. "Where in God's name did you find that thing? I didn't even know they made them anymore."

"It was in the storeroom. I found it a long time ago under some old boxes of Butterick dress patterns and stuff Granddaddy must have packed away after Nanna died."

"Well," Gloria said briskly. "I don't even want to *contemplate* what my papa thought that thing was. If he put it with all the outdated dress patterns he probably thought it was some kind of sewing machine attachment."

"Did you take the window down?' I asked meekly.

"Oh yes," my aunt said. "I got the first phone call about it at eight o'clock this morning. And before I could get my teeth brushed and my hair combed there were three more outraged messages on my answering machine. Two of them were from GiGi."

"Oh."

"She's called your daddy too. Twice."

"Oh. How is Daddy?"

"Considering the circumstances, I think Wade is holding up as best as can be expected. He went out to get the paper this morning and instead he found a registered letter from the board of directors at the country club informing him that his membership has been revoked."

"Oh."

"There was an itemized bill too. Apparently you put a nasty dent in the Chub Jernigan trophy. Not to mention all the china and crystal you smashed."

"Excuse me," I said, bolting from the bed. I barely made it into the bathroom before I blew chow. It took me ten more minutes to get the rest of the tequila and cream sherry out of my traumatized gastric system.

Eventually, while I was making a feeble attempt to mop up the bathroom floor with one of my new monogrammed KMJ towels, Gloria came in and wordlessly shoved me in the direction of the bathtub.

"Hot water," she said, turning on the shower. "Lots of it. Come and talk to me when you're ready. I'll be in the studio."

I ran the shower until the hot water gave out. When my skin was shriveled and scorched pink, I got out and dressed in my rattiest blue jeans and a John Mayer band T-shirt and wound a towel around my wet hair.

Gloria was sitting at her rolltop desk in the tiny alcove we use as an office. We keep a handsome heart-pine farmhouse table in the showroom that we call a desk. That's where we make presentations to clients, show them the fabric swatches and carpet samples and furniture catalogs, but the office is where all the real work at Glorious Interiors gets done.

It seems to me my Aunt Gloria has been sitting at that big golden oak rolltop desk as long as I can remember. It once belonged to the first owner of Merchant's Mercantile, but when Granddaddy bought the place, they discovered it was too big to move without dismantling the whole front door, so it got sold along with the rest of the fixtures.

All the desk's little pigeonholes and drawers are neatly arranged with the business stationery, correspondence, and paid and unpaid bills. Gloria uses a Haviland china teacup as a pencil holder, and ever since I can remember, she's worn those same, simple tortoiseshell reading glasses perched on the end of her nose. She's had the same hairdo too, come to think of it; a sleek auburn pageboy, the ends tucked behind her left ear only, exposing the chunky diamond stud earrings I've never seen her without.

"Who else called this morning?" I asked, settling in at my own desk.

She rolled her eyes. "Paige's mama."

"Shit."

"She claims she's hired a lawyer and is going to sue you for character assassination, not to mention file criminal charges against you for assault and battery."

I laid my head down on the desk and groaned. The cool wood felt good against my cheek, which was burning up.

"I wouldn't give Lorna Plummer or her slutty daughter Paige another thought if I were you," Gloria said. "First off, I happen to know that Lorna still owes Graham Anthony three thousand dollars for the last time he handled a divorce for her. He wouldn't sell her icewater if she was burning in hell. And secondly, I seriously doubt that the sheriff would give those two the time of day."

I managed a smile then. The sheriff of Morgan County, Howard Banks, had been happily married for thirty years, but it was a well-known fact that he'd never gotten over his high school crush on Gloria Murdock.

Gloria kissed her fingertip and planted it on my cheek. "That's it, honey. Smile. See? It doesn't hurt that bad. Try again, okay?"

"I can't."

She sighed. "Well, it's early yet. Do you want to talk about it at all?"

I clamped my lips together and shook my head no. "I'm sorry," I croaked.

"Shhh!" Gloria said fiercely. "Don't you dare apologize. You did what needed doing. I shudder to think what might have happened to you if you'd gone ahead and married into that loathsome Jernigan bunch."

"But you loved A.J. . . . " I started. "Daddy adores him."

"No!" she said, slapping her desktop for emphasis. "We put up with him. For you, Keeley. Wade and I had serious reservations about A.J. from the get-go. I mean, he was just too good to be true. He seemed so charming and sweet, always kissing up to me and calling your daddy SIR, with capital letters."

"You saw through him?" I asked, bewildered. "Why didn't you say something?"

"You wouldn't have listened," Gloria said. "You were tee-totally in love. And we didn't know anything bad about him. Not really. Just that there was something . . . down beneath the surface . . ."

"Slimy," I said, filling in the blank for her. "And I never saw it. I never even had a hint that he was cheating on me. Not until last night. Not until I caught him and saw the two of them with my own eyes. How could I have been so stupid?"

The tears were coming fast and furious now. I was sobbing so hard I couldn't catch my breath. Gloria stood over me, stroking my hair, shushing me like a baby.

"How could he?" I cried. "How could he do that to me?"

"Oh honey," Gloria said, her voice low and sad. "He's a man, that's all. They're all the same, you know. Every sorry last damn one of 'em. They've got different names and different addresses, but it's all just the same damn sorry man."

5

Eventually I stopped crying and went back upstairs and tried to make myself look human. The mirror was not my friend that morning. I dabbed concealer over the dark circles under my eyes, but there wasn't much I could do about their bloodshot condition. I added some eyeshadow and mascara, brushed on some blusher, and dabbed on lip gloss. My long brown hair needed more work than I had patience with this morning. I pulled it back into a ponytail high on top of my head and winced with pain when the rubber band was too tight.

My hair. Good Lord. I had a noon appointment with Mozella at La Place. We'd been working for weeks on an upswept do that was supposed to have emphasized my long neck and the daring back plunge of my wedding gown.

The same twelve-thousand-dollar cream silk satin Vera Wang dress that I'd draped over the shop's garbage can in our window last night.

I'd have to call Mozella right away to cancel. At the thought of it, I bit my lip until I drew blood. Mozella wasn't some backwater spitcurl and Aqua Net artist. She'd moved to Madison from Atlanta a year earlier, after one of her clients at her chic Buckhead salon fixed her up with her newest ex-husband.

Now Mozella was married to a retired anesthesiologist who'd built her a brand-new shop in Madison, and the ex-wife was happily making the fifty-mile drive all the way from Atlanta every month to get her hair highlighted. Nobody does foil like Mozella. And nobody, I mean, nobody, cancels on Mozella without twenty-four hours' notice.

My hands were shaking as I dialed the number at La Place.

Oscar, the receptionist, answered as he always does. "Chess?"

Oscar is Cuban, originally from Tampa, and he's spoken English his whole life, so I think he just does the Ricky Ricardo accent because it makes him feel glamorous.

"Oscar, this is Keeley," I said, taking a deep breath. "I, uh, I am afraid I'm going to have to cancel my appointment today."

"No," he said flatly. "Is not possible."

"I'll pay, of course," I said quickly. "But I really do have to cancel."

"Chust a minute," Oscar said, his voice cold.

"Mozella," I heard him call. "Mozella, somebody is on the phone pretending to be Miss Keeley Murdock, wanting to cancel her appointment. I tole her no. Better you talk to her."

"Give me that, you idiot," I heard Mozella say.

"Keeley? Sugar, are you all right?"

"You heard."

"Well . . . yes."

"Who told you?" I asked.

"Who told me first? You mean last night or this morning?"

"You heard last night?" I don't know why I was so surprised that Madison's kudzu telegraph was already humming with the news of my broken engagement.

"I was comin' in early to do GiGi," Mozella said. "I was gonna open up at eight, just for her. She called around eleven, last night."

"She gave you an earful, right?"

Mozella's laugh was a dry rattle. She was in her early fifties, and she had no intention of giving up her pack-a-day cigarette habit. Not even for her rich new doctor husband.

"You could say that."

"And everybody else in town has given you their version too, right?"

"It's been pretty colorful," Mozella admitted. "But I don't pay much attention to gossip. You know that."

I gasped. Mozella was a world-class gossiper. She knew everybody in town's dirt, and she knew it first.

"So I guess you know I won't be needing that upsweep today," I said finally. "Or the manicure and pedicure."

"Yeah, I know," Mozella said. "The rest of your wedding party already called in and canceled too."

"Even Paige?" I almost choked on her name.

"Oh nooo," Mozella said. "I'm looking out the front window and that's her car pulling up front right now. Her and her mama both."

"Do me a favor, will you?" I asked.

"Try to."

"Snatch 'em bald."

"I wish I could, honey," Mozella said. "But that's kind of bad for business. I'll tell you what. How 'bout if I experiment with Paige's color? Maybe give her a rinse just a little on the orange side?"

"I'll pay double if you do," I said.

"This one's on me," Mozella said. "I never did like the little hussy. Always whining about her sensitive scalp. And she doesn't tip for shit either. And don't get me started on that mother of hers."

"I won't," I said. "Thanks, Mozella. Send me the bill, okay?"

"No bill," Mozella said. "I'll be doing that upsweep on you sooner or later, and when I do, it's gonna be so fabulous we're both gonna make hairdo history."

I blinked back tears as I hung up the phone. Gloria was sitting on the sofa in my tiny living room, clutching a yellow legal pad. It was one of her famous "things to do" lists, I knew.

"I've called the caterer and the club and the florist already," she said, running her finger down the list. "And I'm gonna post a tasteful little note on the church door for anybody who hasn't already heard that the wedding is off." Her voice was as businesslike as if she were discussing a drapery installation.

"You canceled the hair and nails?" she asked, her pen poised above that item.

"Yeah. Mozella already knew, of course."

"Of course."

"Everybody else canceled too, except for Paige and Lorna."

"You think she has a big date planned for tonight?" Gloria asked.

"I don't want to think anything about her," I said. "As far as I'm concerned, she's dead. She does not exist."

"Tell me something, will you?" Gloria said, cocking her head. "How on earth did the two of you ever get to be friends? I mean, I hate to be a snob, but I just never could figure out what you two had in common."

I twisted a strand of my hair around my finger and thought about that.

"We started first grade together," I said. "But we never really bonded until, like, fourth grade, I guess. I remember, she was the first girl in class to get a bra. First to have a period, first to shave her legs. I thought she was so cool."

"I bet she was first in a lot of other ways too," Gloria said tartly.

"Yeah." I laughed, remembering some of Paige's more notorious junior high exploits. "She could get any guy she wanted. And eventually I think she had 'em all."

"Like her mama," Gloria said. "Tramps, both of 'em."

"Lorna didn't seem trampy to me when I was a kid," I said, thinking back on it. "She was so nice to me, you know? After Mama left?"

Gloria nodded, tapping her pencil on the notepad.

We didn't talk a lot about my mother. I'd been seven when she left us. Old enough to remember the usual stuff, how she drank a Pepsi every morning, first thing, how she swept the kitchen floor every night before she went to bed, the sound of her voice, soft and low in nonstop phone conversations with dozens of "girlfriends," and the scent of her perfume, which was Joy. I still have the bottle she left on her dressing table. Only a few drops of the perfume remained in the bottom of the frosted glass bottle, but every now and then, I unstop the bottle and inhale, and think about her.

"You know me, Keeley," Gloria said. "It's no secret that I can think of a lot of bad things to say about Jeanine Murry Murdock. But let's give her credit. Your mama was nothing like Lorna."

"Probably not," I agreed. "But to a kid, Lorna was a mom when I didn't have a mom. She treated us like grown-ups, you know? Let us use her makeup, showed us how to fix our hair. I remember, the first time I ever had shrimp cocktail was when she fixed it for us one night when she had a boyfriend coming over."

"Probably some other woman's husband," Gloria said, pursing her lips. "No telling how many men passed through that house of hers. Your daddy was worried to death you'd see something you shouldn't over there. But he couldn't keep you two apart. You were thick as thieves."

"I know," I said. "And even in high school, when she got really wild, and I was too chicken to do the stuff she was doing, we stayed friends. Even during college, when I went away and she stayed home and went to junior college, we stayed friends."

"Force of habit," Gloria said, arching her eyebrows. "Not always a good thing."

"Hindsight," I retorted, "unfortunately, not always twenty-twenty."

"All right," Gloria said, tapping her list again. "Let's get to work. Who's canceling the party tent and the ice sculpture? Me or you?"

A bell tinkled just then. When we converted Granddaddy's second-floor storeroom into an apartment for me, Gloria had our electrician rig up a system to alert me when somebody opened the door downstairs.

"I left the door unlocked when I came in, but the sign says we're closed," Gloria reassured me. "Why don't you just run down there and get rid of whoever it is?"

"What if it's A.J.?" I asked, starting to panic.

"Don't be silly," Gloria said. "He knows better to come around here. After you took off last night we had words."

"Hello?" a man's voice called up the stairs. "Anybody here?"

"Just a minute," Gloria called back. "Go," she said, nodding at me.

I took the stairs slowly and peeped around the corner into the studio. What if it really was A.J.?

"Hey there," the redheaded stranger said, looking up. He was staring down at my wedding gown, which Gloria had temporarily draped over my drafting table. "Will Mahoney. Remember? Your chauffeur?"

"I remember," I said dully. "Go away. Okay?"

6

"**Keeley!**" **Gloria exclaimed,** sweeping past me.

"Hey there," she said, taking both of Will Mahoney's hands in hers, like some great, lost treasure. "I am Gloria Murdock. Please excuse my niece's rudeness. She's had her heart broken recently, and of course she's never at her best this early in the morning."

She treated him to one of her trademark, megawatt smiles.

My Aunt Gloria would not be called a conventional beauty; not in her prime, which was the seventies, or in the here and now, but she does have a powerful secret weapon: her smile.

Gloria's was the kind of smile that made men want to doff their hats—even if their hat was a greasy ballcap—that made women want to take her to lunch and confide their deepest secrets, and then pick up the tab. I had seen that smile stop dogs from barking and kids from screaming. Gloria knew its power—and she used it shamelessly.

"And you're Will Mahoney, of course," she said, adding a wink to her arsenal.

"You know who I am?"

"Of course. I meant to speak to you last night, but then things got . . . unpleasant."

"Keeley," Gloria said, seamlessly changing the subject, "Mr. Mahoney here has bought the bra plant."

I looked from Mahoney to my aunt and then back again.

"You did?"

Mahoney nodded. "Lock, stock, and patented twin crossover underwires."

The Loving Cup Intimates factory, or the bra plant, as everybody in town called it, had been founded by Jacob and Dora Krichevsky,

Ukrainian siblings from Brooklyn who'd intended to set up a lamp-shade operation down South back before the Depression.

Nobody knew why they'd settled in Madison, Georgia, but they did. Local lore had it that Dora, a full-figured gal, had despaired of ever finding a support garment to tame her double-D bosoms, until one day, while she was hand-whipping silk to the wire skeleton of a shade, she came up with the idea of incorporating horsehair and wire into her own brassiere.

Jacob, who was a bit of an amateur tinkerer, was unwillingly drafted into helping design such a garment, and the rest became lingerie history. At one time Loving Cup Intimates was one of the ten largest bra manufacturers in the country.

Every prepubescent girl in the South dreamed of the day she could purchase that first demure pink cardboard box and become a part of the Loving Cup sisterhood. Up in the attic at Daddy's house, I am sure my own first Loving Cup—First Blush, I believe was the trade name for the training bra—was tucked away with all the rest of my girlhood.

Sometime in the eighties, though, Loving Cup had lost touch with the sisters. The company had changed hands four times, and as far as I knew, the plant was only running a skeleton shift these days, with most of its output being shipped off to Third World countries whose women couldn't afford a Wonderbra.

"I understand you're going to completely revamp the plant," Gloria said approvingly. "Add more shifts, hire more workers. It'll be a godsend," Gloria concluded.

"If you know all that, then I guess you also know I've bought Mulberry Hill."

Gloria's smile dimmed a little. "You know how small towns are. News travels fast. And Mulberry Hill is an important old property to a lot of people in Madison."

He held up a hand. "Let me save you some time, Ms. Murdock. I know you probably heard I was going to bulldoze the place. In fact, I was going to tear it down. But I've changed my mind."

"It's Gloria, not Ms. Murdock," my aunt told him. "Good for you. Is the house back on the market again, then?"

He shook his head emphatically. "Not at all. I'm keeping it."

Gloria clapped her hands gleefully. "Excellent." She gave him a coy look. "I imagine it's going to need some work."

He returned the look. He did it pretty well too. "That's where I thought you two could give me a hand. I want Mulberry Hill to be something special again. Something . . . amazing."

"We're interior decorators, not magicians," I put in.

"Keeley!" Gloria snapped. "Be nice."

"I have a contractor," Mahoney said. "And an architect, and a work crew. They're already at work out there." He glanced at his watch. "In fact, they should be ripping off that shed kitchen at the back of the house, right about now."

He looked up at me, those brown eyes way too observant.

"What I need is an interior designer. I've seen pictures of your work in magazines. I don't know a lot about this stuff, but I liked what I saw. That house out in the country, the horse farm. I liked that a lot."

"Les Morgan's house? Barnett Shoals Farm? You saw that in the October issue of *Veranda*? How sweet of you to mention it. Les was a dream to work with. Very supportive. And open to new ideas."

"And rich," I put in. "Barnett Shoals Farm was a two-million-dollar project. Did you have a budget in mind for Mulberry Hill?"

"Whatever it takes, I guess. We'd be starting from scratch. None of my old stuff is anything I'd want in Mulberry Hill. You've seen the condition the house is in now, right?"

"Not really," Gloria said. "It's been empty for so long, I don't know if I've been in that house since I was a child. Do you have a time frame in mind?"

"Absolutely," Mahoney said. "I need the house done by Christmas."

"Which Christmas?" Gloria asked.

"This Christmas," Mahoney said. "It's only June now. That should give us plenty of time. As soon as we get the framing, plastering, plumbing, wiring, and roofing out of the way, I was thinking we could buy some furniture and stuff and get the painters and those type folks busy."

Gloria laughed and laughed.

"I should tell you, Mr. Mahoney, that Glorious Interiors is just the two of us. Myself and Keeley here. Right now I don't know if we could take on another project of the scope you seem to be entertaining."

"What do you mean?" Mahoney asked. "Are you saying you won't do it?" He shook his head, perplexed. "You're turning me down?"

"What you're asking is impossible," I explained. "Six months to do a whole house restoration? Even if we didn't have all those other jobs ahead of you, it would be impossible. You don't just go out and buy things, you know."

"Why not?" He ran his hands through his dark red hair, making the ends stand up. He badly needed a haircut. This morning he was wearing a pair of faded blue jeans, work boots, and a faded red T-shirt. He hadn't shaved, and his chin was covered with red-gray stubble. He looked more like a truck driver than a successful business owner.

"Because that's not the way it works," Gloria said gently. "Most of what we do for our clients is custom work. Fine furniture, fabrics, wallcoverings, all those things take time. They have to be ordered and sometimes they have to be custom manufactured. When we buy antiques, we only buy the best. Keeley and I travel to auctions in Atlanta, Charlotte, Nashville, and New Orleans."

"Travel all you want," Mahoney said. "I don't mind. I told you I want the best. I just have to have it all done by December."

Gloria sighed. "Mr. Mahoney, we would love to work for you, we really would. I'm sure you'll turn Mulberry Hill into an absolute showplace. But we just can't do it. Not with that time frame. We've been working on Barnett Shoals off and on for three years, and we still haven't finished buying art for the guest house."

"The fabric for the downstairs powder room window treatment has been on back order for eight months," I volunteered. "It's being woven in France, and—"

"That's ridiculous," Mahoney said, cutting me off. "What kind of a way to do business is that?"

Gloria nodded sympathetically. "I know. But it's the way things work. I can recommend another designer here in town, if you like. Traci is very good, and she's just starting out, so she probably won't have the time constraints—"

"No," Mahoney said abruptly. "I want you two. Glorious Interiors. It's you or nobody."

"That's sweet," Gloria said. "But really—"

"Just come out to the house and take a look around," Mahoney said, looking straight at me. "You can do that, right? We could go right now. What do you bill out at—fifty, sixty bucks an hour, something like that? I'll pay you for your time. How about it? It's Saturday, and I happen to know you've had a change of plans."

"Fifty bucks an hour?" My face was starting to burn. I was feeling the urge to start throwing things again.

"Listen, you, you hayseed," I sputtered. "This is not Rooms-to-Go here. You don't just walk in here and start ordering up a house. Like I told you last night, this isn't a sofa store. And Gloria and I didn't just fall off the turnip truck."

"Okay, okay," he said hurriedly. "Cool your jets. I didn't mean to offend you. That's the last thing I want to do. I know you guys are the best. Like I said, I've been doing my research, but obviously I still have a lot to learn about interior design."

He gave Gloria a pleading look. "Put in a good word for me here, will you?"

She laughed. "I think maybe you should just take no for an answer, and walk out of here while you still can, Mr. Mahoney."

He looked at his watch again and frowned. "All right. I gotta meet the crew out at the house and I'm late as it is. We'll talk again. When you're in a better mood?"

I gave him a tight smile. "This is as good as it gets with me."

"We'll see about that," he said. The door tinkled softly as he walked out. A minute later, we heard the deep throb of the Caddy's engine.

Gloria stood at the window and watched him drive away. "Interesting man."

"He's an ignorant swine," I said. "Fifty bucks an hour, my ass."

"I think he's adorable. And I'm dying to see the inside of that house," Gloria said. "There's a lot of potential there."

"What are talking about here?" I asked, standing beside her. "Bra boy or Mulberry Hill?"

"Both," Gloria said.

7

In a perfect world, on what would have been my wedding day, I, the devastated bride-to-be, would have been stretched out on that Parisian chaise longue, with cucumber wedges pressed to my eyes, perhaps mildly sedated with some of the Valium we keep in the office safe for stress-related emergencies.

But mine was not a perfect world. Gloria had put the chaise longue back in the window, and we were out of refills for the Valium. Anyway, the phone kept ringing, and somebody had to answer it, and that somebody, unfortunately, was us.

Gloria took the incoming calls, assuring everybody and their cousin who called that I was fine, just not up to taking calls yet. I did the outgoing calls, to all the assorted people who wanted to be told that their bills would be paid despite the cancellation.

Downtown Madison on a summer Saturday is a busy day. There aren't really enough working farms left in the area to still call this a farming community, but old habits die hard, and one of the habits of small Southern towns is Saturday market day.

The street outside was clogged with traffic, and the other shops on our street stayed busy with Saturday shoppers. All afternoon I watched people strolling slowly past our shop, their eyes darting sideways, as if to catch a furtive glimpse of the train wreck inside our plate-glass window. If I caught their eyes, they'd cock their heads, give a sad smile, or glance quickly away.

At two I switched the office phone over to the answering machine. Gloria put her phone down five minutes later.

"You hungry?" she asked. "I sent most of the reception food over to the Methodists, Baptists, and Presbyterians, but the smoked salmon blinis and the shrimp potstickers won't hold. Elise is bringing some of it over here right now."

"Salmon. Yuck. That was GiGi's idea," I said. "I guess I could maybe choke down a couple potstickers."

She hesitated a minute. "What about the wedding cake, Keeley? What should we do with that?"

My right eye twitched. "Throw it out. Take it to the city dump. I don't care. Just don't make me look at that cake. Please, Gloria?"

She patted my leg. "All right. Elise wants to take it over to the children's hospital. The kids will love that white chocolate frosting."

I gave her a pained look. The chocolate had been A.J.'s inspiration. "It'll be cool, Keeley," he'd said. "Whoever heard of an all-chocolate wedding cake? And it'll drive my mother fuckin' nuts."

If I hadn't been sold on the chocolate idea before, the comment about GiGi sealed the deal. It wasn't that I hated GiGi Jernigan. Not at all. I mean, she's the whole reason I met and fell in love with A.J. It's just that it was always fun to yank GiGi's chain.

The Jernigans had been Gloria's clients for years, even before I joined the business. GiGi was forever fussing with their houses, which included The Oaks on Academy Street, their lake house at Cuscawilla, and the mountain house up in Highlands.

I'd had plenty of dealings with GiGi over the years, of course, but I'd never really spent any time with A.J. He hadn't gone to high school in Madison, because all the Jernigan men went to Brandon Hall, a snooty boarding school in Virginia, and then he'd gone to college at Washington and Lee, where all the Jernigan men went to college before they came back to work at Madison Mutual Savings and Loan, the family business.

The day I went over to Academy Street to measure for the new drapes GiGi had ordered for A.J.'s bedroom was only the second or third time I'd ever met him.

I was standing on the top rung of a stepladder in the bedroom, and it was wobbling because I was trying to measure the depth of the old cornice we were replacing. The door opened, and A.J. came strolling in. He'd been out jogging or something, because he was dressed in shorts and a T-shirt and was dripping with sweat.

"Oh, hi," I said, embarrassed. The ladder wobbled just then, and a minute later he was steadying it and grinning up at me. And looking up my skirt, he admitted later.

Let's face it, Andrew Jackson Jernigan was criminally attractive. Lots of glossy dark hair, his mother's blue-green eyes, and just the slightest bit of lantern jaw—which made him appealingly imperfect. He was as tall as me, which was important; he liked to laugh; and he was easy to talk to.

A month later, when I came back to install the drapes, he had no problem at all getting me into that walnut four-poster bed. And he was as much fun in bed as out of it.

Afterward A.J. had snuck downstairs and swiped half a pan of brownies his mother had baked for some garden club function. We'd eaten the brownies, naked, in that bed, and A.J. had sworn then and there that he'd never taste chocolate again without thinking of me. And sex.

Now the thought of that wedding cake made me want to heave.

Elise arrived a few minutes later, with a foil tray full of food. A complete professional, she wordlessly loaded the food into the refrigerator in the studio's kitchen and left the bill on Gloria's desk.

I was hungrier than I would have believed possible. Gloria heated up a plate of the potstickers, while I poured us a couple of Diet Cokes.

We were just sitting down to lunch when the shop bell jingled again. I looked up in dread. Had Will Mahoney come back to harass us some more?

But the visitor was a skinny brunette dressed in purple hip-hugger capris and a purple tank top that exposed both the silver ring piercing her navel and the tiny rose tattoo on her right shoulder.

"Oh," I said. "It's only you."

"Yeah," she said, opening the door again to toss the butt of her still smoldering cigarette onto the sidewalk outside. "It's only good old Janey. Good to see you too, cuz."

"That's not how I meant it," I said. "It's just been so crazy around here today."

"It's been a zoo," Gloria put in. She stood up and kissed the top of Janey's head.

My cousin Janey gave Gloria an air kiss. "So Glo. You're on suicide watch today? You keeping Keeley away from sharp objects and gas ovens?"

"Janey!" Gloria exclaimed. "That's not funny."

Janey shrugged. "Keeley knows I'm kidding."

"It's all right," I agreed. "We could use some humor around here. Sit down. Have a potsticker. We've only got enough for the Russian army."

Janey plucked a potsticker from my plate and popped it into her mouth.

"Mmm," she managed, in between chews. "You'll never guess who I saw at the Atlanta airport just now."

"What were you doing at the airport?" I asked.

Janey raised an eyebrow. "Remember what day this was supposed to be? Your wedding day? Uncle Beau and Aunt Fran flew in all the way from Sacramento."

"Beau and Fran. Oh no." I moaned. "I completely forgot."

"You sure as shit did," Janey said. "But don't feel bad, because nobody else remembered either. Your daddy called and woke me up this morning and bribed me to go pick 'em up at the airport.

"Anyway," she continued, "you still haven't guessed who I saw at the airport."

"I don't know," I said, dunking one of the potstickers in the soy sauce. "And I don't really care."

"Come on and guess who I saw," Janey insisted. "Please?"

"Not today, Janey," Gloria said, trying to shoot her a warning look.

"Okay, I'll tell," Janey said. "Who did I see getting out of a cab at the airport, just as I was loading Beau and Fran and their kids into the car? A. J. Jernigan."

"Janey!" Gloria said. "Shut up, now. I mean it."

"For real," Janey said. "And he wasn't alone either."

"Janey," Gloria said, yanking her arm. "Time for you to go home." But Janey didn't get it.

"Yeah," Janey went on. "I guess he was using your honeymoon tickets, right? I mean, you don't just cancel a trip to France the day before, right? It was A.J. and—"

I felt the bile rising in my throat. "Excuse me. I don't feel so good," I said. My head was swimming. I clamped my hands over my mouth and lurched toward the bathroom.

"Yeah," Janey went on. "A.J. and Nick Curtis. How weird is that? Taking your best man on your honeymoon?"

8

I clutched the door frame for support. "He took Nick? He took Nick to France with him? On our honeymoon?"

Janey gave Gloria a smug smile. "See? I knew you'd never guess."

I sat back down and held the icy glass of Diet Coke to my forehead. "But Nick is afraid to fly. And he won't eat anything except fast food. He claims he can't go a day unless he has a Whopper."

"Perfect," Gloria said. "He and A.J. will make a perfect couple in the South of France."

"He didn't take Paige?" I said, grabbing Janey's hand. "You're not just making this up? He didn't take Paige to France?"

"Hell, no," Janey said. "I saw Paige coming out of Mozella's right as I was leaving for the airport. Her and her skanky mama. I would have run Paige over too, but I was driving Uncle Wade's new car and I was afraid she'd leave a dent."

"You're sure it was Paige?" I repeated. "She didn't go to France with A.J.?"

Janey gave Aunt Gloria a worried look. "What's with her today?" she asked, jerking her head in my direction. "You sure she didn't take an overdose of Midol or something?"

"Just answer the question one more time," Gloria said.

"Oh. Kay," Janey said, enunciating slowly, as though she were speaking to a mildly retarded foreigner.

"A.J. took Nick to France. Not Paige. Nick. To France. On the airplane. Paige is still right here in Madison. And," she added, grinning wickedly, "she's got some dog-ass-looking orange hair too. Mozella must have been smoking some crack this morning when she got ahold of Paige Plummer."

9

On Sunday I slept.

On Monday, as Gloria said later, "The grits hit the fan."

First thing, our carpet installation guy showed up with a truck-load of one-hundred-twenty-dollar-a-yard custom-milled broadloom and a very worried expression.

"We were supposed to install at the bank this morning, but the guy says no, we can't come in," Bennie said, crunching his cap between his hands.

"Which guy?" Gloria asked. "Somebody at Madison Mutual?"

"The guy," Bennie said. "I go in, show the lady at the reception desk the work order, she calls, some guy in a suit comes out, looks at the work order, and hands it right back to me. I can't repeat what he said. But he sure wasn't gonna let me lay no carpet."

"You can tell us what he said, Bennie," I said. "We're big girls. We can take it."

Bennie looked down at his hat and blushed. "Okay. You're the boss. He said, 'Tell Keeley she can take this carpet and shove it up her ass.'"

"Right," I said.

Gloria sighed. "The guy in the suit, what did he look like?"

"Never mind," I said. "I'm sure it was Kyle. A.J.'s daddy would never use that kind of language in public."

A.J.'s brother, Kyle, was some sort of mid-level manager at the bank. Although he'd always been perfectly polite to me, I'd sensed that he had some long-simmering resentment over his older brother's role in the business. It had always been clear to everybody that in the family flow chart, A.J. would forever be head dog over there, and Kyle would be reduced to sniffing his big brother's butt for the rest of his life.

Gloria looked down at the work order and frowned. We'd been working on a long-needed "freshening" of Madison Mutual's ground floor offices for six months now. The carpet sitting outside in Bennie's truck was worth a lot of money. Our company name was on the invoice Bennie was folding and unfolding.

"They can't just refuse delivery," I said. "Can they?"

"Looks like they did," Gloria said. "I mean, Bennie can't make them let him install it."

"What y'all want me to do with it?" Bennie asked. "That's a boatload of carpet out there, Miss Gloria. I can't do no other installation until I unload that stuff. And I got another job in Eatonton first thing in the morning."

"You can't put it here," Gloria said. "There's no room."

"Anyway, Drew Jernigan authorized us to order that carpet," I said, grinding my teeth at the thought. "He can't up and cancel just because he's pissed off at me."

"I'll have to call him," Gloria said. "Maybe it was all Kyle's idea. Surely Drew understands that this is a professional relationship."

"Maybe," I said, remembering the look of blind fury on A.J.'s father's face at the rehearsal dinner.

But Drew Jernigan wouldn't take Gloria's phone call. His secretary coolly informed her that "Mr. Jernigan is in meetings all day."

Gloria slammed the phone down. "Fine. Bennie, you'll just have to take the carpet over to our warehouse." She handed him the key. "We'll get this straightened out, and I'll call you to set up another installation time."

He handed her the invoice and his work order. "It's a lot of carpet, Miss Gloria."

Not long after Bennie left, we got a call from Annabelle Waites. That would be Annabelle Shockley Waites, of the Shockley Poultry family, married to Walter Waites, who mostly managed his wife's vast inheritance when he wasn't playing golf.

"Oh, hi Keeley," Annabelle said, her voice unnaturally high and agitated. "I wasn't expecting to find you there this morning."

"I wasn't expecting to find me here either," I said.

That really got her flustered.

"I'm calling to tell Gloria we'll have to cancel lunch today," she continued.

"I'm sorry," I said. "Is everything all right? You're not sick again, are you?"

Annabelle Waites was subject to many mysterious ailments, but she was also one of our best clients, what we referred to as a "frequent fluffer." Right now we were about to embark on a serious "fluffing" of the kitchen in her Greek Revival house on West Washington Street. The plan was to rip the "old" kitchen (last remodeled four years ago) down to the studs, bump the back wall out by eight feet, install French doors, and build a new antique brick terrace. Annabelle's cooking consisted mainly of boiling bag rice and Heat 'n Serve frozen entrees, but she'd decided that nothing short of a top-of-the-line six-burner Viking stainless steel commercial range, Sub-Zero fridge, double Gaggenau drop-in burners, twin Asko dishwashers, and a Sub-Zero wine cooler would do for the new kitchen.

"No, I'm not really ill, not per se," Annabelle said, her voice quivering. "It's just that Walter thinks . . . that is, we agree, perhaps, we should hold off on the kitchen, until the stock market settles down a little."

"Hold off," I repeated, letting the words hang in the air, like a stink bomb. "Hold off on the kitchen?"

"Oh no," Gloria said, putting her head down on her desk and banging it gently a couple of times.

"Give me the phone," she said finally.

I handed it over to her. Gloria pushed the loudspeaker button so I could listen in.

"Annabelle?" Gloria cooed. "Is your esophagus acting up again? Or is it those nasty bone spurs on your heels?"

"Gloria, honey," Annabelle said, getting all quivery again. "My feet are just killing me. I can't even stand to put on a pair of stockings, they're so sensitive. Walter thinks I should go back to that doctor down in Jacksonville."

"You poor old thing," Gloria said, clucking sympathetically. "I'm going to come right over there and bring you some of my foot salve. I have it sent over from England, you know. And I'll stop by the Silver Spoon and bring you some of that soup you like too. Now you sit tight, and I'll be over there in a jiffy."

"But Walter thinks . . . the kitchen might be too much for me to undertake, right now, with my feet, and the stock market the way it is," Annabelle's voice trailed off.

"Now, Annabelle," Gloria said briskly. "Wasn't it Walter who said he was tired of those old dark wooden cabinets? And wasn't it Walter who complained that there was never enough room for beer in the old refrigerator?"

"Well, yes, but Walter feels . . ."

Gloria laughed her tinkly little laugh. "Honey, when did we ever let what Walter thinks stop us from getting you what you want? Remember when he said those drapes for the den were too expensive? And we just doctored the bills the teeniest little bit and you paid for them out of your own account? Honestly, men have no idea what it costs to have a decent living environment. Thank the Lord, your daddy left you your own money."

"Daddy did like for me to have nice things," Annabelle said.

"Only the best, that was Arthur Shockley's motto," Gloria agreed. "Walter isn't there right now, is he?"

"Oh no," Annabelle said. "He had a noon tee time."

"Fine," Gloria said soothingly. "Shall I bring some dessert too? Maybe some lemon bars?"

"Well . . ." Annabelle hesitated only a moment. "Nothing too chunky. My esophagus, you know."

"I'll be right over," Gloria said.

She hung up the phone and kneaded the base of her neck with her right hand. "I've got a bad feeling about all this," she said. "First the bank, now Annabelle."

"It's the Jernigans," I agreed. "They're putting the screws to us, is what it is. Walter Waites doesn't give a damn about the stock market, and he doesn't give a damn about Annabelle's feet either."

"But he banks at Madison Mutual, and I think he plays golf with Drew Jernigan," Gloria pointed out.

"This is all my fault," I said. "That's a three-hundred-thousand-dollar job over there at Annabelle's house. And to save it, you're gonna have to go over there and kiss her bony old ass."

"Keeley, if it means keeping Annabelle Waites as a client, I'll not only kiss it, I'll rub her bunions and prechew her lemon bars," Gloria said, picking up her purse.

"Mind the store now," she said, heading for the door. "And don't worry about Annabelle. She'll come around. Especially after I tell her those hand-waxed English kitchen cabinets she wants are being discontinued next month. You know her cousin Becky over in LaGrange just had her kitchen done, and that's what she's got. And if Becky has it, be damned if Annabelle doesn't have to have it. You watch. I'll get Annabelle to write the deposit check today."

"Those cabinets aren't the ones being discontinued," I pointed out.

"Annabelle doesn't know that," Gloria said grimly.

After Gloria had gone, I kept myself busy working on a presentation for our newest clients, Suzie and Benjamin Chin. They were a young couple, both in their thirties, both with busy careers as pediatricians. I'd met Suzie the previous year at a Junior League function. And when she'd heard what I did for a living she seized on me like a tick on a dog.

"Oh God," she'd said, clutching my arm. "Tell me you'll come over and make it all right."

"Make what all right?" I'd asked.

"That house." She moaned. "That awful, hideous house."

The Chins, it turned out, had bought a huge pseudo-Tudor house in Hampton Court, one of the new subdivisions full of faux chateaux that were springing up on the outskirts of town.

The builders of the Chins' house had thrown every bad English country house cliché in the book at that particular property. The exterior had stucco, dark wood half-timbers, exposed beams, oversized wooden shutters, and a heavily metal-studded front door. Inside the ceilings were too high, the wood floors were too shiny, windows and doors were awkwardly placed, and the floor plan was choppy and dysfunctional.

The Chins and their two toddler daughters had more or less been camping out in the house, clueless about how to decorate or make it liveable. With two careers and two young children, they had no idea what their taste was, or how to achieve any kind of cohesive plan.

Suzie and I had spent two happy months together, chatting and window shopping, having long lunches, and getting to know each other before we even began discussing how to turn their mausoleum into a home.

I'd given her stacks of magazines to dog-ear—*House Beautiful, Architectural Digest, HG, Veranda, Traditional Homes.*

She'd given me back a neatly organized file folder. Colors—they liked neutrals, with touches of red and black. Furniture—mostly traditional, although Ben was leaning toward contemporary and Suzie had some ideas about country French. Art—Ben had begun collecting contemporary Southern folk art. Suzie liked watercolor florals.

Ben's contribution had been a carefully thought-out budget. The first year the Chins would spend forty thousand dollars. For this they would like to furnish their family room, buy a good rug for the living room, and get a chandelier for their so-far unused dining room.

I was pulling fabric swatches for their new sofa and love seat when I heard the door chime tinkle.

"Hey, Suzie," I said, holding up a square of dark green chenille fabric. "I'm just thinking about you and your new sofa."

Instead of coming in and sitting down beside my desk, Suzie stood just inside the door, her hands punched down into the pockets of her white lab coat. Her usually sunny face looked troubled.

"Oh Keeley," she said softly. "I don't know . . ."

"What?" I asked. "Is something wrong?"

"Furniture. It's so expensive. And maybe this isn't such a good time. The girls are still so little, maybe it's foolish to spend money on nice things when they are still so messy. You know, grape juice stains and crayon marks on the walls . . ."

"But Benjamin worked out the budget to the penny," I protested. "He isn't saying you can't spend the money, is he?"

"No, it's not that," Suzie said, chewing her bottom lip. "He wants the house to look nice, maybe even more than me."

She gazed out the window, toward the street. "You know, Ben and I are getting ready to build our own office. We've bought the land, over near the hospital, and we're having an architect draw up plans."

"I've done lots of doctors' offices," I said quickly. "We could have a lot of fun with the waiting room. There are some wonderful wall-papers and fabrics, you know, youthful, but not too cutesy."

She fidgeted with the plastic ID badge clipped to her coat pocket. "The thing is, we have to get a construction loan for the new building. And the banker is asking a lot of questions about our cash flow."

I tied the chenille fabric in a tight knot. My face got hot. "I see. Suzie, is your banker somebody at Madison Mutual?"

She nodded, too miserable to speak. "I'm sorry," she whispered. "Ben and I feel terrible about this. We love your work. The children love you. And I still think . . . after things settle down, well, nobody will care about our little design project."

I got up and put an arm around her shoulder. She looked away. "Can I keep the drawings you did?" she asked.

"Sure," I said. "We'll get back to it. Later. Like you said, after things calm down around here."

She squeezed my hand. "This sucks," she said. "We thought, a small town, everybody is so friendly. So nice. But we have to have the money to build that office. So we have to do things that aren't so nice."

I found myself telling Suzie what my own daddy had told me so many times. "You do what you have to do."

"But I don't have to like it," Suzie said.

10

Daddy called at noon on Wednesday. "You're coming tonight, aren't you?"

I tried to beg off. "Oh Daddy, I'd completely forgotten what day this is. I've got a late appointment, and some paperwork to catch up on."

He wasn't fooled for a minute.

"Appointment with who?"

"A new client."

"What's their name?"

"Nobody you'd know."

"You'd be surprised how many people I know. Look, shug, I know you're feelin' kinda down. And I know what's been happening over there. GiGi and Drew and that Jernigan crowd think they can run you out of business. But I'm not gonna stand around and let that happen."

"Now, Daddy . . . I'm a big girl. I can handle this."

"Of course you can. I didn't raise you to just roll over and take it when a bully picks a fight. Anyway. I'm expecting you at six, same as always. Don't be late now, 'cause I don't want my salmon loaf to get dried out."

"Daddy," I tried. "It's been an awful week. I really don't feel like dealing with Aunt Fran and Uncle Beau and the kids."

"You won't have to," Daddy said. "I packed 'em all off to Six Flags this afternoon. Gave 'em money for a motel too. So no more excuses, right?"

"Right," I said.

I should have known my father wouldn't let anything like wide-spread public humiliation change our day-to-day lives. It was

Wednesday, after all, and every Wednesday night, ever since I can re-member, Daddy has fixed me supper.

Daddy doesn't really know how to cook. But after Mama left us, when I was in fourth grade, we had a housekeeper named Juanita who didn't care a lick about cleaning, but loved to cook. Daddy's fa-vorite dish of hers was salmon loaf. He loved it so much that before she quit to go take care of her grandchildren, Daddy took the radical step of learning how to make it.

Aside from Sundays, Wednesdays are Daddy's only day off from his car dealership. So Wednesday nights, Daddy cooks. The menu rarely changes. He fixes Juanita's salmon loaf, which he tops with a lemon-dill sauce, canned LeSueur peas, rice cups, iced tea, and ba-nana pudding.

It wasn't like it was a hardship for me to make it over there that Wednesday night. Our business was a bust. The phone was suddenly quiet. Although she'd managed to coax Annabelle Waites into going ahead with her kitchen project, I knew Gloria was starting to get wor-ried.

I locked up the shop shortly after five, and changed into shorts, a T-shirt, and sneakers. I put my hair in a loose braid down my back, then got my bike out of the storage shed downstairs and set off on the two-mile ride to our house.

Although it had been scorching hot all week, it had rained earlier in the afternoon, and the smell of the rain-washed pavement, along with the rhythm of tires and pedals, were soothing to my harried nerves.

It was good to be outside, good to be away from the deadly quiet of the office, good to feel sweat, good to work the knots out of my legs.

When I walked in the back door, sweating and panting, Daddy was just taking the salmon loaf out of the oven. He had a terry-cloth dish towel wrapped around his waist for an apron, and a rolled-up red bandana wrapped around his forehead.

I kissed him just below the bandana. "What's this? Are you supposed to be Willie Nelson or the Iron Chef?"

"Neither," Daddy said. "I just didn't wanna get sweat on our supper, and I wanted to keep my hair lookin' nice."

He patted the back of his mostly bald head and chuckled at his own joke.

I looked over at the kitchen table, which was set with three places. "I thought Gloria was in Atlanta tonight."

"She is," Daddy said, setting the hot pan on the kitchen counter.

"Then who's having supper with us?" I asked. He took the pitcher of iced tea from the refrigerator and poured me a glass.

I took a long sip and looked around that tired old kitchen, with its harvest gold appliances and worn vinyl tile. Our house had been considered the newest, most modern house in Madison when my parents built it back in the early 1970s. It was just after Daddy started making real money with the car dealership, and he wanted everybody in town to know what a success he was.

Our house had a cathedral ceiling in the entryway, with real marble floors, white wall-to-wall shag carpeting, big picture windows, and a patio out back with a fishpond and birdbath.

I could still remember the house when everything had been shiny and new. He'd let Mama order new dishes from the JC Penney catalog, and even new wineglasses.

My mother loved those dishes. They were heavy stoneware, with hand-painted borders of bright red poppies and yellow stripes around the outside. The wineglasses had little poppy designs too.

When she left, she left all that behind. In fact, as far as I knew (and at seven, I had taken an extensive inventory) my mother had taken along nothing from her old life when she ran off to start a new one with Darvis Kane, the sales manager at Murdock Motors.

And Daddy had pretty much left everything the way it was the day she left. The carpet had long since been replaced, of course, along with some of the appliances, but despite my begging and pleading with him to let me redecorate, twenty-five years later we were still eating off the same dishes, sitting at the same simulated Early American maple dinette set.

I refolded one of the worn gold napkins Daddy had put at each place setting. "So who's the mystery guest?"

"You wanna heat up the peas for me?" he asked, pointing at the can of LeSueurs on the kitchen counter.

"I can do that." I found one of the gold Club aluminum pots and dumped the can of peas in and placed it on the front burner of the stove.

"The rice is done, if you wanna put it in the little cup thingies," Daddy said, pointing to the glass custard cups he'd set out on the counter. "Put some butter on the rice before you put it in there, though," he instructed.

"I know, I know. Now, about that dinner guest?"

"You want a beer?" Daddy asked, opening the refrigerator door. "I bought that import stuff you like."

"The tea is fine for now," I said. "Come on. Quit making me play guess who's coming to dinner."

"New fella in town," Daddy said. He opened the oven door and peered in at the pan of brown-and-serve rolls he was heating up. "Good-looking young man too."

"Oh Daddy, you didn't."

"Didn't what?" He tried to look innocent.

"A fix-up? You're trying to fix me up with a blind date on the week I was supposed to be honeymooning?"

"A date? Hell no. Is that what you think? Now, Keeley, you know me better than that. Have I ever tried to fix you up with a date in your whole life?"

"Oh please," I said. "Remember the advertising guy?"

"I thought he could help you market the business," Daddy said. "And there wasn't a thing wrong with him either."

"He was a spitter. I had to wear a raincoat when I went out on a date with him. And that wasn't the only dog you fixed me up with. What about that creepy Bible salesman you met at Rotary?"

"A little spirituality never hurt anybody," Daddy said. "And he made a good living too."

"He lived with his mother. He didn't even own a car. And when I wore a sleeveless dress to dinner he tried to give me a lecture on the wages of the flesh."

"You're exaggerating," Daddy said.

"He's still sending me religious tracts," I said.

"Well, this fella is entirely different," Daddy said. "Owns his own business. Bought a house here in town. And he said he's already met you. In fact, I think if you play your cards right, he might throw some work your way. From what I'm hearing, you and Gloria could use some new clients."

"What kind of work?" I asked.

The doorbell rang then. Daddy started toward the front door, then paused and took off the apron and the headband. I hustled down the hallway behind him. "Do not try to fix me up with this guy," I whispered. "I know you mean well, but do not do this. Okay?"

"Okay," Daddy said. He gave me a look of appraisal. "Don't you want to wash your face or something? Comb your hair? Maybe put on some lipstick or something?"

"No!" I said emphatically. I took a look in the hall mirror. My hair had come undone from the braid, and what little makeup I was wearing was in a smudge under my eyes.

"I am not fixing myself up just so you can shop me out to the latest weirdo in town," I said fiercely. "I am not that desperate."

The doorbell rang again. "Fine," Daddy said. "Suit yourself."

He opened the front door. Will Mahoney stood there, holding a bottle of wine and a handful of wilted zinnias.

"Will," Daddy exclaimed, giving him a hearty handshake. "Come on in here."

Will stepped inside. He gave me a quizzical look.

"I believe you've already met my daughter, Keeley Rae," Daddy said.

"Oh yes," I said, taking the flowers that he extended in my direction. "Bra boy. How nice to see you again."

I stomped off in the direction of the kitchen. "Daddy?" I called, without turning around. "Can I see you in the kitchen? Right away?"

11

I yanked the kitchen door closed behind me and then turned toward my father. "You can just take the extra place setting off the table, because I am NOT having dinner with that man."

"Now what's wrong with this one?" Daddy asked, exasperated. "He don't spit. He drives his own car, owns his own home and business. And I understand he's in the, uh, uh, bra business. Maybe you could get some free merchandise or something."

"A Loving Cup bra? Daddy, have you completely lost your mind? I wouldn't wear one of those rags to a dog fight. And anyway, this is not about bras. This is about that man. I've already met him. Twice. And I am not a fan of Will Mahoney. Not at all."

Daddy's face fell. "Well, what do you want me to do? I can't uninvite him."

"Fine. I'll leave." I turned and headed for the back door.

"No ma'am," Daddy said, grabbing my arm. He gave me that look. Sharp-eyed, press-lipped. It was the look he gave potential car buyers when the horse trading had gone too far. The look that said Wade Murdock might be a genial, jovial, and an all-around nice guy, but now it was time to get down to business.

"Have I said one word to you about this wedding business?" he asked, his lips barely moving.

"No sir," I whispered.

"Mentioned how much money I spent on caterers and flowers and invitations and dresses and doodads?"

"No sir."

"Have I complained about being kicked out of the country club?"

"No, Daddy."

"That's right," he said. "And I don't aim to start whining about it now. What's done is done. You're my daughter and I stand behind you one hundred percent. But now there's a perfectly nice young man sitting in our living room, waiting for supper. You don't have to like him. You don't even have to go out on a date with him. But I don't think it will hurt you to be civil to a guest in my home, will it?"

"No sir," I said. "I'm sorry. I'll be nice."

"Fine," Daddy said. "Now go upstairs and wash your face. And see if you can't find a hairbrush and a clean blouse in your old bedroom while you're at it."

I slunk upstairs like a ten-year-old under house arrest and flounced down on the sagging mattress of my white canopy bed. I buried my head in the pink and white chintz-covered pillows that had been my first big home decorating project.

At sixteen I'd spent hours and hours painting and fixing up this room. Gloria had helped me choose the fabrics, a Cowan and Tout floral and a Brunswig & Fils stripe, which were left over from a bed and breakfast she'd decorated in Washington, Georgia, and I'd bought the bed all by myself at a yard sale in Greenville. I'd pulled up the wall-to-wall carpet, polished the wood floors, and put down a faded Oriental rug I found rolled up in the attic. I was in the early stages of my Mario Buatta phase. Other teenagers had posters of rockers and movie stars thumbtacked to the walls of their rooms. I had *Architectural Digest* covers.

My face, aflame with shame and embarrassment, matched the pink of the chintz. Daddy was right. I'd been acting like a grade-A brat. It wasn't Will Mahoney's fault that my life was a mess, and he probably hadn't intentionally insulted me with his offer to hire us. I still didn't like him and I didn't intend to work for him, but for Daddy's sake, I would put on a clean—and happy—face.

I scrabbled around in the medicine cabinet of my bathroom and found a nearly dried-up mascara, which I applied to my eyelashes. I unbraided my hair and brushed it until it shone, then pulled it back in a tortoiseshell barrette I found on my old dressing table. Most of the clothes still hanging in my closet were either rejects or relics of my teenage years. I didn't think Daddy would appreciate me showing up at the dinner table in my crop-top Mötley Crüe T-shirt, but I did find a navy blue Oconee Hills Country Club golf shirt I'd forgotten about. The irony was unfortunate, but inescapable.

When I came back downstairs, Daddy and Will were sitting out on the patio, sipping their iced tea and laughing like lifelong buddies.

Will put his drink down and stood up. At least he had nice manners.

He put his hand out in a tentative gesture. "Can we start over?"

I laughed and we shook. "Sure. If you can forget what a little bitch I've been."

"Keeley Rae!" Daddy said sharply.

"Sorry," I said.

"Never should have sent her to school in Athens," Daddy said. "She didn't learn to talk pottymouth like that around here, Will, I can assure you."

"No," I said. "I learned to talk like that on the car lot."

"Never mind," Daddy said. "My salmon loaf's getting cold. Let's go eat."

To his credit, Will was a perfectly acceptable dinner guest. He'd had a haircut, so the fledgling mullet had been banished. Tonight he wore a well-fitting crisp blue blazer over a yellow and white striped dress shirt. Slightly rumpled khaki slacks. No tie, no socks. Good shoes, Italian loafers.

He tucked into the dreaded salmon with apparent relish.

"Keeley," Daddy said, beaming at Will's clean plate, "Will here has bought the, uh, Loving Cup plant."

I pushed some peas around my plate with the tip of my fork. "So I heard," I said, smiling sweetly.

"Gonna make it a top-notch outfit again," Daddy said. "Isn't that right, Will?"

Will took a sip of beer. "I intend to try," he said.

"So, do you know anything about bras?" I asked.

Daddy choked.

"Keeley Rae!"

"Loving Cup is a bra factory," I said. "That's what they make. Bras. It's not a dirty word, Daddy. It's a product. Right, Will?"

"Right," he said, looking from me to Daddy, and then back to me again. "What do you think of our product, Keeley?"

Daddy gave me a warning look.

"Nice," I said, being deliberately vague.

"But you wouldn't be caught dead in one of our bras, would you?" Will asked.

"I guess I haven't seen one in a while," I said. "I don't do a lot of clothes shopping in Madison. And I usually buy lingerie when I'm in New York."

"If you don't shop at Big Lots, you probably aren't seeing Loving Cup products," Will agreed. "Go ahead, tell me what you really think. You can't hurt my feelings. Loving Cup sales numbers are abysmal. I know what the business analysts say. But I'd be interested in hearing a woman's point of view."

"Now, Will," Daddy started. "Keeley here isn't in any position to be telling you how to run your business."

"Sure, she is," Will said. "She's a woman. She's got breasts. She wears bras." He gave me a wide smile. "Don't you?"

"Usually," I said.

Daddy's face was crimson. "Guess I'll clear the dishes and bring out dessert."

He made a great show of clattering plates and silver. "You two go ahead and talk," he said. "I'll get a pot of coffee started."

That left the two of us alone in the dining alcove.

"Your dad is a great guy," Will said, drumming his fingers on the tabletop. "A little old-fashioned, I guess. I didn't mean to embarrass him by talking to you about bras."

"Old-fashioned is an understatement," I said. "He still thinks unmentionables should be unmentioned. How did you two meet, any-way?"

"I was gassing up the Caddy at the Citgo station, and he came over and started talking to me about it," Will said. "We struck up a conversation, and he mentioned that he sells cars for a living, and I told him I'd probably be buying a truck in the near future, and he gave me his card and told me to drop by the showroom. I did, and we struck a deal on a truck, and he invited me to supper."

"You knew he was my father, right?" I asked.

"Right," he said. "Murdock Motors. I figured, gotta be a connection."

"So the truck thing had nothing to do with your wanting me to work on your project."

"I really do need a truck," Will said. "Your father sells trucks. I need an interior designer too. I understand you do that for a living."

"Look," I started. "I promised to be nice tonight. Daddy has taken a liking to you for some reason I can't comprehend, but I don't have time for a new project right now."

"Sure you do," Will said.

"Says who?"

"Says everybody in town," he said. "I heard your boyfriend's family is jerking you around. Business is off. Your father told me so himself."

"He doesn't know as much as he thinks he does," I said quietly, clasping and unclasping my hands under the tablecloth.

"I met your brother-in-law," Will said. "Quite a piece of work."

"Kyle? He's not my brother-in-law."

"Lucky you. He and his father have been giving me the big rush. Seems they think I could be a nice piece of business for them. They even had me over to supper at that house of theirs on Academy Street street last night. That's some house. And I understand you and your aunt are responsible for the way it looks. It's beautiful, Keeley."

"GiGi would rather redecorate than eat when she's hungry."

"Seeing that house made up my mind for me," Will said. "You've got to come to work for me."

I shook my head no. "Don't think so."

"Just come and see it. Please?" His voice was plaintive. "You're the only one who can do this." He glanced over his back at Daddy, who was out in the kitchen spooning Cool Whip on the banana pudding. My father has never heard of the concept of lily gilding.

"I'm not hitting on you, if that's what you think."

I flushed. "That's not what I think, but since you brought it up, why aren't you trying to hit on me? Am I that unattractive?"

He chuckled. "For one thing, you've got relationship issues."

"If you mean A.J., he's no longer an issue," I said, my voice cool.

"We'll see," Will said. He looked down at the tabletop, and with his fingertips, flipped his teaspoon end over end. "I've got relationship issues too."

"Oh?"

He sighed. "This is going to sound crazy. I really wish you would come look at the house, and after that I'll explain everything to you."

"Why not explain now? It's early yet, and as you've so tactfully pointed out, I've got nothing else to do." I crossed my arms over my chest and waited.

"There's this woman," he started.

Daddy put the tray with the banana pudding and the coffee down on the table. "Ain't that always the way?"

12

Will sipped his coffee slowly while Daddy lit into the banana pudding. "Hey now," Daddy said, pointing at me with his spoon. "Come on and eat your dessert. I been cooking all afternoon. If you don't eat this pudding, I will. And you know I'm trying to watch my girlish figure." He jiggled the spare tire under his shirt and chuckled at his own joke.

I obediently dipped a spoon into the banana and cookie parfait and looked expectantly at Will.

"This is going to sound crazy," he repeated. "I'm in love with . . . this woman. She has a very successful career in Atlanta, and probably has no interest in moving to a place like Madison."

"Well, she's a damn fool then," Daddy said flatly. "Why'd anybody want to put up with all that traffic and crime and mess in Atlanta when they could live someplace like this?" He spread his arms out, indicating not just our kitchen but all of Madison and greater Morgan County.

I took another bite of pudding just to keep from having to explain life to my father, who has happily lived his whole fifty-five-year existence within two miles of the place he was born.

"She's a lawyer with one of the biggest law firms in Atlanta," Will said. "She probably likes going to the theater and museums, you know, parties, all that stuff."

Daddy snorted his disapproval. "We got a museum right here in Madison. And when that multiplex opens up this fall over on the highway, she can have her choice of six theaters."

"I think he means she likes live theater," I said gently. "Anyway it sounds like this woman is a confirmed city girl."

Will just nodded. He didn't give any additional information.

"There's something you're not telling me," I said. "And let me just warn you right up front. I have had my fill of lying, cheating, double-dealing—"

"She loves old houses," Will blurted out. "She's nuts for anything old. And I thought maybe. Well, Mulberry Hill was built in 1858."

"You thought if you fixed it up she would come?" It sounded stupid, even to me.

He took another sip of coffee. "It sounds weird when you say it that way."

"It's not only weird, it's the dumbest thing I ever heard," Daddy said. "You don't get a woman to marry you by fixin' up a house, boy." He scraped the bottom of his bowl with his spoon, pushed his chair back, and got heavily to his feet. "If y'all are done, you can clean up the dishes. I got some phone calls to make."

I tried to shoot him a look, but it was too late. He put his bowl and coffee cup in the sink and left me alone with Will Mahoney.

Will stacked the remaining dishes and ferried them over to the kitchen counter.

"Just leave them there," I said. "I'll load the dishwasher later. After you've gone," I said pointedly.

"I'm not going until you agree to take the job I'm offering you," he said, leaning up against the sink. "Might as well let me stay and help."

"What do I have to do to get rid of you?" I asked. "I can't make it any plainer. We're busy. I can't take this job. It's impossible. Even if we weren't busy, nobody could do what you want done over there in six months."

"You aren't that busy. Your asshole ex-fiance and his family have taken care of that. Anyway, you haven't even seen the house," Will said. He craned his neck and looked out the back door toward the patio. "There's still a good hour of daylight left. Come on, Keeley. Just take a ride over there with me. It's an amazing house. Did you know it was used as a hospital for Federal troops wounded in the siege of Atlanta?"

"Every kid who grew up in Madison knows that stuff," I said.

"The doorknobs are all hand-etched silver," he said. "We found 'em in a packing crate up in the attic."

"Why were they up there?" I asked, despite myself.

"For safekeeping, I guess," he said. "People broke in over the years, kids, maybe homeless guys. We found a mattress and a sleeping bag in one of the back bedrooms, and evidence that somebody had made a little wood fire in one of the fireplaces."

"It's a wonder the place didn't burn down," I said.

"The last owners had the sheriff checking on it pretty regular," Will said. "He ran folks off and notified the owners who came out and kept it boarded up."

He smiled then. "We discovered the original parlor mantelpiece was down there in the basement, covered up with old feedsacks. And you'll never guess what we found out in the old smokehouse."

"A side of bacon?"

"Crystal chandelier," he said smugly. "I took it to a place in Atlanta to see about having it cleaned up and fixed. The restorationist says he thinks it might be Waterford."

"That could be," I agreed. "I think the Cardwells—the original owners—were pretty successful cotton merchants."

"Very successful," he said. "I've done some research at the historical society. There are some photos taken back after World War I of the parlor and dining room. Pretty fancy for a backwater place like Madison."

"Photos?" I asked. "Can you tell anything about the way the rooms looked?"

"You can see the flower pattern on the wallpaper," he said, sensing he had me hooked. "I've got copies of everything. Over at the house. I could show them to you."

"Not interested," I said, looking away.

"Thought you said you were tired of liars," he said.

"I'm tired, period."

"Come on," he said. "Just look at the place. No commitments. Just let me show it to you. It's really something to see. This time of early evening, the sun hits the front room, and it gets this, like, golden glow to it. And I've got all the old pieces of wallpaper saved up. I thought you, or somebody, might want to copy them for when we redo the dining room and parlor."

"This is just a look-see," I warned. "No commitments."

I walked out into the hallway and hollered up the stairs. "Daddy?"

He poked his head over the railing. "What's up, shug?"

"We're going to take a ride over to Mulberry Hill," I said. "Just to have a look, that's all."

"It's not a date," Will hollered up at him. "So don't worry."

Daddy walked down three steps and gave him a level look. "What would I have to worry about, son?"

"Nothing," Will said, blushing. "I just didn't want you to think I was hitting on your daughter or anything like that."

"Will Mahoney," Daddy said, shaking his head again. "Pretty summer night like this? If you're not hitting on a good-looking girl like my daughter, you're dumber than you look."

"Daddy!"

"Just making an observation, that's all," Daddy said.

Will had left the top down on the yellow Caddy. I had to move a stack of files from the front passenger seat and kick a huge flashlight out of the way before I could sit down, and then we were off to the races.

"You'll have to excuse my father," I said, running my hand over the leather upholstery. "He seems to think I'm some two-door late model V-8 sedan he has to clear off the lot. He pretty much never quits selling, and he's pretty used to saying whatever comes to his mind."

"That's all right," Will said. "I like that."

"You haven't had to live with it your whole life," I pointed out. "He sure seems to like you."

"I think he mostly likes this car," Will said, patting the dashboard.

"Yeah, that's a possibility. My grandparents always drove Caddies, so he's got a weak spot for the old ones. And he doesn't trust anybody who drives a foreign car."

"I notice you drive a Volvo."

"He took it as a trade-in on an SUV," I said. "Nobody else in town would have it, so I picked it up cheap."

"What about A.J. and that BMW of his?" Will asked, grinning.

"We never discussed it," I said lightly. "What kind of car does your girlfriend drive?"

"I don't really know," he said. He flipped on his turn signal and made a left into a barely marked driveway that had been hacked out of a six-foot-tall boxwood hedge. He stopped the car short of a thick, new-looking chain that stretched across the driveway.

"You don't know?"

"I'm having a new set of wrought-iron gates and a sign made for the entrance here," Will said, pointing to the sun-faded wooden plaque that hung from a rusted-out steel pole on the right side of the driveway. He put the car in park, hopped out, and put a key in the padlock fastening the chain. "Scoot over and pull on through, will you?" he called to me. "I wanna lock up behind us. Now that we've started construction, the house is wide open. I don't want people coming in and helping themselves to my tools and building materials."

I edged the car through the narrow opening in the hedge, and waited until he got back in on the passenger side.

Gingerly, I let the car roll down the driveway. Trees pressed in on both sides.

"I gotta get this underbrush cut back pretty soon," Will said, wincing after a sapling snagged the flesh of his arm. "But I don't want to do too much until I get my landscape designer in to flag the stuff he thinks we should keep."

I raised my eyebrows. "Landscape architect? Who'd you get?"

"Some guy my architect recommended. Kent Richardson."

"La-di-damn-dah."

"You know him?"

"I've seen his work. He specializes in historic preservation projects. Our client at Barnett Shoals Farm used him, but I never got to meet him in person."

Will nodded approvingly. "That's why we hired him. That horse farm project."

"You really are planning on spending some bucks," I said.

"It's got to be done right," Will said.

"Can I ask you a personal question?"

He nodded, not taking his eyes off the drive.

"How'd you get this rich so young? I mean, was your family in this business?"

He grinned. "Dumb luck. I was working at a hosiery mill in Greenville, South Carolina, and we were having problems with the Japanese knitting machines. Every time one broke down, we'd have to send off to Japan and sit around and wait for a replacement part to be shipped. I tinkered around with their designs a little bit, and came up with something better. It did pretty well for me."

"Looks like it," I said pertly, steering the car around a hairpin turn. Suddenly the drive widened out into a broad green meadow. A huge pair of water oaks seemed to mark the end of the drive and the beginning of the meadow. At the far end of what once must have been a rolling emerald lawn, the house loomed, pale white in the gathering purple dusk. Fireflies flickered in the canopy of the trees, and whippoorwills chirped from the high grass. Without thinking, I let the Caddy roll to a stop and put it in park. It would have been sacrilege to drive any farther.

13

Red clover carpeted the meadow, and fat fuzzy bumblebees hovered in the air. The scent of grass and wildflowers wafted up as we neared the house.

"This was all cotton fields at one time," Will said, picking his way through thickets of blackberry brambles. "The house was originally set much closer to the road, but it was moved back, to give it a grander entrance and driveway, sometime in the late forties."

"Before my time, needless to say. But there's still a lot of cotton grown around here," I pointed out. "Have you given any thought to doing that with all this land?"

He laughed. "Not a chance. I've done my research. Cotton's too much work. Too much heavy machinery, investment. I am having the meadow planted with millet, so we can do some dove hunting this fall, and I'm also thinking about doing a little cattle farming eventually."

I glanced over at him. "You? A gentleman farmer?"

"Maybe not that much of a gentleman," he admitted. "And I don't know a damn thing about farming, but I'm a pretty quick study."

"You should talk to Dallas Pope, the county extension agent," I said. "We went to high school together. He won all the 4-H livestock prizes back then, and I think he still raises cattle on the side."

"I'll do that," Will said. We'd been tramping steadily toward the house, but he stopped now, a few yards away.

Up close the house looked more silver than white. The old cypress clapboard walls had shed most of their paint. Seven two-story-tall fluted Corinthian columns swept across the wide porch of the house, curving around on the east side to another porch. The porch stopped abruptly on the west side, where a framework of old joists was all that remained. An elaborate pilaster and pediment arrangement framed what had probably once been a massive carved front door, which had been replaced with one of cheap, nondescript plywood. A pair of divided light windows, each five feet tall, flanked the doorway, some still retaining their original wavy glass.

On the second floor, directly above the front door, hung a small wooden balcony. Its rail was rotted in places, and most of the carved balusters were missing.

"Here it is," Will said, gesturing toward the house, like a prized coon dog. Pride shone in his eyes. "What do you think?"

"Impossible," I murmured, shaking my head.

He frowned. "You haven't even seen it. We put a new roof on this week. My architect found a warehouse full of slate tiles that came off an old elementary school they tore down in Covington a few years ago. It's watertight now."

I pointed up toward the roofline. The cornice boards were missing in places, and pigeons fluttered in and out of gaping holes under the eaves. "You've got some tenants."

"That's being taken care of," he snapped. "Are you always this negative?"

"All right," I said. "Show me the house. I promise to try to keep an open mind."

He pulled a ring of keys from his pants pockets and stepped up a set of cracked concrete-block steps to the front porch.

"Careful," he said, stepping gingerly on a zigzag route to the door. "Some of these boards are nearly gone. I've got somebody coming in this week to start ripping the whole porch off, but we've got to stabilize the foundation first."

I took a closer look at the aforementioned foundation. Crumbling three-foot-high red brick piers seemed to be the only thing holding the house off the ground.

"Is it safe to go in there?" I asked. "You forget, I've been in a lot of these old houses around town. My aunt broke her ankle stepping through a rotted board at the old Lively place out on the highway a couple of years ago."

"I've had workmen in and out for weeks now, and nobody's had any injuries," Will said, fitting the key in the front door. He opened it with a flourish. "Come on. I never would have taken you for such a sissy."

I scrambled up the steps and tiptoed across the porch. "Nobody calls Keeley Murdock a sissy."

Still, I took a good long look at the floorboards once I stepped over the threshold of Mulberry Hill.

My concerns were needless. The floor was heart pine and rock solid.

"Not bad," I admitted, straining to see more in the dim interior.

Will played his flashlight around. "Not bad? That's the best you can do?"

I took the flashlight from him and swept it around the entryway. The old plaster walls were cracked, but mostly intact, which was a small miracle for a house this age.

The ceilings were high, probably twelve feet, and had a treatment I'd never seen before, four-inch heart-pine tongue-and-groove boards arranged in an intricate parquet pattern.

"Did you have this ceiling stripped?" I asked, walking around with my head turned upward.

"Nope. It was like that when I bought the place. Pretty amazing, huh?"

"We'll want to have the beadboards cleaned thoroughly, and then sealed," I said. "It doesn't really fit with the formality of a house like this, where it's more conventional to have plaster, but—"

"I'm keeping it," Will said. "It's one of my favorite things about the house."

I kept the flashlight moving. The rest of the entryway was what I had expected to find. Twin parlors opened off either side of the wide hallway. Each parlor had a brick firebox, although there were no

signs of any mantels or other moldings or baseboards, or even window casings.

I walked into the east parlor and looked out an awkward boxed bay
window with a view to what looked like a backhoe and a metal construction shed. "This bay probabably isn't original to the house."

"No. The architect said it was probably added on when the house
was moved."

"We could have a new window custom milled," I said, thinking
out loud. "With the four-over-four configuration of the original
windows. Keep the bump-out, put in a nice window seat, maybe box
the whole area in with bookcases."

"Great," Will said. He pulled a small spiral-bound notebook from
his back pocket and started jotting notes.

"There's a place down in Savannah, they sell old cypress boards
salvaged from the river. We can get new millwork to replicate what
was here originally. You said you have some of the old baseboards
and moldings?"

"Down in the cellar," Will said, writing as he spoke. "It's just an
old dug-out root cellar, really, but I can take you down there and
show you."

I'd been in plenty of those old cellars too. They were always full of
spiders, crickets, mildew, and mouse droppings. "No thanks," I said,
repressing a shudder. "If you'll just have somebody gather it all up and
put it somewhere dry, so I can make sketches, that will be fine."

He continued writing while I went through an open doorway into
a large square room adjacent to the parlor.

"Dining room," I mumbled, walking off the room's measurements.
Another gaping firebox stood on the far wall. Three windows on the
opposite wall were tall enough to walk through.

"French doors, maybe? Opening up to this side veranda?"

"Great," Will said, scribbling. "The garden designer said something about a perennial garden out that way."

"With a fountain," I said, nodding. "Definitely a fountain. So you can leave the French doors open and hear the sound of the water trickling."

I aimed the flashlight at the ceiling and frowned. The plaster here was crumbling, revealing large patches of bare wood lathe. A naked black cord dangled from the center of the ceiling.

"The Waterford chandelier should hang here," I said. "Unless you want it in one of the parlors?"

"What do you think?"

"Here," I said. "And we'll find a wonderful table, maybe a set of Irish Chippendale chairs. And a fabulous sideboard. There's an auction house in New Orleans, they put pictures of upcoming items on their webpage. They always have nice things. We'll want some Georgian silver to splash around too. It makes a room so handsome."

"Okay," he said. "That sounds good."

"Unless your lady friend likes French," I said, hesitating. "We can do French, of course, but personally I think a lot of Louie-Louie is going to be too fussy for a house with such masculine bones."

"Masculine?" he said, gazing around the room. "A house can have a gender?"

"Absolutely. And your house is butch. See how all these ground-floor rooms are big and square? What moldings remain are nice, but fairly simple and classical. And the house itself hasn't been tarted up with a lot of Victorian gingerbread."

"Victorian is bad?" he asked, puzzled.

"Not on a Victorian-era house, like a lot of the ones you see in town," I said. "But it doesn't belong on an antebellum Greek Revival house like this one. Lots of times, after the Civil War was over, when people got a little bit of money, they wanted to tack on a lot of scroll-work and doodads, just to keep up with styles and show the neighbors they weren't flat broke anymore."

"But not the Cardwells," Will said. "When cotton went bad, they never really recovered."

"Fortunately for you," I said. I tugged on a door in the wall opposite the windows. "What does this lead to?"

He batted my hand away from the doorknob. "A four-foot straight-down drop."

"Really?"

"It does now. There was a jerry-rigged kitchen wing, but we ripped that off this week."

I went back out into the entry hall and walked rapidly through the west parlor. It was the twin to the other parlor, except that it lacked the bay window.

"Do we really need two living rooms?" Will asked.

"Not necessarily," I said. "Lots of times, in a house of this era, we make one room a formal living room, and the other one functions as a library or study."

"A library," Will agreed. "I've got a storage shed full of books I haven't unpacked since I moved to Georgia three years ago."

"Moved from where?" I asked, running my fingers across a cracked piece of marble on the parlor hearth.

"South Carolina," he said. "And before that, North Carolina."

"And before that?" I asked. "You don't really have a recognizable accent, do you? I know you're not really a Yankee, but you're definitely not a cracker boy either."

"Nashville," he said. "Although I went to school at Georgia Tech. Mechanical engineering, although I took a lot of textile classes too."

"My daddy is a Tech man," I said. "Maybe that's what he likes about you."

"That and the Caddy."

A doorway on the far wall stood ajar. I pulled it open to reveal a narrow rectangular room with the stubs of old water pipes protruding from the floor.

"The bathroom?" I asked. "I haven't seen a sign of another one anywhere."

"Bathroom-slash-washroom," Will said. "There was an old laundry tub in there that the workmen hauled to the dump. This room had the only semimodern plumbing in the whole house. There's not a bathroom upstairs at all."

"We'll have to fix that," I said. "We can probably steal some space from the library and build a nice powder room." I pointed to another door on the other side of the room. "What's that lead to?"

"Originally, it was the maid's room," Will said. "It had been tacked on along with the kitchen wing. The architect's plans call for a pretty sizable addition on the back here. Kitchen, butler's pantry, laundry room, and a breakfast room overlooking a new back porch. With another full bathroom."

"Good," I said approvingly. "Some people would have added on one of those monster ground floor master suites with those hideous garden tub things and a couple of dressing rooms. But that would totally mess up the scale of this house, make it look like you'd slapped a Motel 6 onto the rear."

"Glad you approve," he said, smirking.

"Want to see the upstairs?" he asked.

"Just a quick peek. It's getting pretty dark out."

He led the way up the stairs. A makeshift banister had been constructed out of cheap pine boards. "We've got the original out in the workshed," Will said. "The trim carpenter's making new spindles and refinishing the banister. It's one continuous piece of solid mahogany. Really beautiful."

Another large squarish entry hall stood at the top of the stairs, with two doors on each side. I poked my head in the first room. It had the same generous proportions as the downstairs rooms, and large windows looking out into the now starry sky.

"Nice," I said admiringly, walking inside. I opened what looked like a closet door, but found instead a small room, maybe six feet by eight feet.

"A cradle room," I cried.

"It's not a closet?" Will asked.

"Well, some people call them trunk rooms. But Aunt Gloria always says these rooms were used for the family's babies, when they were still in a cradle, but too young to go in a proper nursery."

"But it could be used as a closet," Will said stubbornly.

"What's the matter? Doesn't your lady friend want any children?"

He blushed. "We haven't discussed it. But I'd like to have lots of kids. What's the point of having a big place like this if you don't have a whole tribe full of kids running in and out?"

"I'd have to agree with you," I said. "There's nothing sadder than putting all this time and effort into a wonderful old house like this, then seeing it run like a mausoleum. We think a home that's full of love and life is the most beautiful home of all—even if the curtains are faded and the rugs are stained, and there's dog pee on the kitchen floor."

"Dog pee?"

"You know what I mean," I said, moving back out into the hallway and into the next bedroom and then the next.

"I'm assuming the architect's plans call for closets and bathrooms for each of the bedrooms?" I asked, following Will back down the stairs.

"Oh yeah," he said. "The landing area will be kept as a big informal seating area, and we'll put a master bedroom wing over the kitchen addition."

"Five bedrooms?" I asked, raising my eyebrows. "Does this woman know what she's in for?"

"The new bedroom wing will balance the addition on the ground floor," Will said, ignoring my jabs. "And I come from a big family. Two brothers and a sister. And they all have kids."

"You'll have room for everybody," I agreed.

The downstairs was now cloaked in darkness. Will shone the flashlight out in front of us as we picked our way to the front door.

He locked the door and jiggled the knob to make sure it was secure, then took my arm and helped me across the rickety porch floor.

"Change your mind?" he asked.

I sighed. "I never should have agreed to come over here and look at this place. Daddy's right."

"About what?"

"Me and old houses. I'm hopeless. A total house voyeur. You know how some people attract stray dogs and cats? I'm that way with old houses. Every old wreck I see, I want to fix up and move into."

"Including this one?" He was steering me through the meadow, his flashlight fixed on the path we'd previously tromped into the tall grasses.

"It's going to be wonderful," I said. "Even if it kills us in the process."

14

"**Let's get** one thing straight," I said, once we were back in the Caddy, tearing down the blacktop toward Daddy's house. "If we take this job, it won't be because we're desperate. Have you got that?"

"Got it," Will said.

I kept my hands tightly folded in my lap. "Glorious Interiors is one of the top design firms in Georgia," I continued. "We've been published in all the major shelter magazines. Gloria is an adjunct faculty member at the Atlanta Art Institute. Most years we turn away more work than we accept. We're a small, boutique design firm, and that's how we like it."

"Certainly," Will said, his expression sober. "You don't have to trot out your credentials for me, you know. I've seen your work. You people are the only ones I've even considered hiring."

I waved all that off. "I don't want you thinking we'll settle for just any old assignment. And I don't want you thinking the Jernigans have got me running scared."

"I think it's the other way around," Will said, grinning. "The way I heard it, A.J. left the country rather than face the wrath of Keeley."

"If we take this job," I continued, ignoring his reference to A.J., "and that's a big IF, I have to consult with Gloria. But IF we take this job, I want you to understand how we work."

He nodded.

"We don't customarily bill out by the hour. Gloria and I will come up with a proposal for the project at Mulberry Hill. We'll present a detailed program with schematics and sample boards for each area of the house. If you approve that, we'll proceed from there."

More nodding.

I sighed. "A Christmas deadline doesn't give us any wiggle room.

It severely limits our choices when it comes to any purchases that would be custom ordered. That's not how we usually work. Not at all. But as long as you understand those limitations, I think there is a possibility that I can change Gloria's mind, and we can take on Mulberry Hill."

"Great," Will said, his face wreathed in smiles. "Perfect. When do we start?"

"Right away," I said. "Assuming my aunt agrees. Can you meet me back out at the house tomorrow morning? I'll need a set of the architect's plans for our files. And then we'll want to measure everything off, photograph the house for our 'before' pictures, and walk the property."

"Tomorrow? Sorry. There's no way I can do that tomorrow. I've got meetings at the plant all day."

"What about the day after that? We really have to get started immediately if we're going to make any headway on this thing."

"Can't," he said. "I'll be halfway to Sri Lanka by then."

"Sri Lanka?" I could feel my eyebrows shoot up.

"To look at a place we may contract out to do our stitching."

"Why wouldn't you do the stitching right there at the Loving Cup plant? You've got sewing machines and all those people there. Half of them aren't even working full-time."

He looked away.

"Hey!" I said, alarmed. "You're not thinking of closing the bra plant, are you? My God, things are bad enough over there. You didn't buy it up just to close it out, did you? What are you, one of those Wall Street scavengers or something?"

His lips pressed together in a thin white line. "I'm not a Wall Street raider. That's not the kind of operation I run."

"What kind of operation do you run?" I asked. "Look. This is a small town. It may look pretty prosperous to you, but there are plenty of people who depend on Loving Cup to make a living. They've been hanging on by their toenails, hoping things would get better, that the assembly line would be geared back up and shifts reinstated. They would hope," I said, my voice betraying my bitterness, "you were going to do that. They would have thought you were going to save the plant and save their jobs."

"I am doing my damndest to keep the plant going," Will said. "But to do that, things have to change radically. We have to make a better product. We have to do it more efficiently, which means some of the manufacturing will have to be done overseas."

"In sweatshops?" I asked, my voice getting shrill.

"With contract labor," he said, the pitch of his own voice now barely audible.

"I see." I opened the passenger door and started to get out.

"You only see what you think you see," he snapped. "Let's make a deal, shall we?"

I turned around to face him. "What kind of a deal?"

"You take care of decorating Mulberry Hill, and leave the running of Loving Cup Intimates to me."

"Fine," I said. "But remember, this is all subject to my aunt's approval."

"Understood. Now. One more thing."

"Yes?"

"You've told me all the reasons you're not taking this job. You still haven't told me why."

The early evening breeze had disappeared without a trace. The air had gotten hot and muggy, and the collar of my shirt was soaked with perspiration. I flipped my hair off my neck and piled it on top of my head, clipping the barrette up high.

"Because it's impossible," I said.

"Fair enough."

"It's going to cost you," I warned.

"The best always does. I don't have a problem with that."

I looked over at our house and sighed. The front porch light was on, but all the upstairs lights were off. Tomorrow was a workday. I was fairly sure Daddy was sprawled out in the recliner in his den, asleep in front of the Braves game. It had gotten too dark to ride my bike back to town, and I hated to wake Daddy up to get him to give me a ride.

"There's something else I need from you," I said, hating to ask.

"What's that?"

"A ride back into town."

He started the Caddy's engine. "Not a problem."

The rush of air felt good now. I hung my head back to let the wind whip through my hair.

"You never told me anything about your woman," I said, suddenly remembering how he'd avoided answering most of my questions about her.

"She's not really my woman," he said.

"Yet you want to spend hundreds of thousands of dollars redoing this house for her."

"For us. And she will be mine. She just doesn't know it yet."

I shivered. "That sounds pretty creepy. You're not stalking her or anything, are you?"

He gave me an annoyed glance.

"Well, what's her name?"

"Stephanie Scofield."

"You said she's a lawyer?"

He nodded.

"How did you meet her?"

"That's not important."

I rolled my eyes. "Look. If we're going to design this house so she'll fall in love with it—and you—I've got to know something about her. Like, what colors does she like? What's her taste in furniture? Is she a collector, or one of those clutter-buster types? Is she outdoorsy? Does she cook? Like to entertain?"

He scratched his neck. "She's blond."

"That's it? That's all you can tell me about her? Come on, Will.

You must know more than that. You're a smart guy. Tell me about her."

We were on Main Street now, but instead of going straight, toward the studio, Will turned the car into the Minit Mart parking lot.

"I need a beer," he said abruptly. "You want anything?"

"Right now?" I asked.

"Yeah. It's hot. I want a beer. Can I get you anything while I'm inside?"

"A bottle of cold water," I said finally. "No. Make that a beer too. Amstel if they have it."

He nodded and went inside.

He'd left the motor running, so I turned up the radio and closed my eyes and let my head loll back on the Caddy's headrest. He'd tuned the radio to a country station, and it was apparently oldies hour because Tammy Wynette was belting out "Stand By Your Man." It was impossible not to hum along. So there I was, humming with Tammy when a car pulled up in the space next to where we were parked. I glanced over and felt my face start to burn.

A short woman with a blue bandana tied over her hair hopped out of the white Toyota. She had her back turned to me, but even with that scarf I knew the car and I knew that cute little butt in those tight cutoff jeans. I sank down in the seat. I was not in the mood for a confrontation with Paige. Not tonight.

But it was too late. The yellow Caddy was impossible to miss.

She turned to get a closer look. Her blue eyes got very wide. "Keeley?" She started backpedaling, and fast. Guess she wanted to get out of slapping range.

Just then Will came loping out of the Minit Mart with a bottle of beer in each hand. He saw me, he saw Paige. And he didn't miss a beat. He swung into the driver's seat, leaned over and kissed me passionately, directly on the lips, forcing his tongue into my mouth.

Startled, I tried briefly to push him away, but he just pulled me closer, almost into his lap.

At last he released his hold. "Miss me, baby?" he asked, giving me a furtive wink. Now I caught on. It was showtime. And Paige was the audience. I nuzzled his neck. "Take me home, lover," I said loudly.

"Disgusting!" Paige snapped. And she flounced off into the Minit Mart.

He waited until she was inside and then eased me off his lap and the car into reverse.

"Not bad for a small-town girl," he said, shooting me a glance. "Or did you learn to kiss like that in New York?"

"None of your business," I said, edging shakily back to my side of the front seat. "Crap! Nobody works the kudzu telegraph like Paige Plummer. It'll be all over town by the time I get home," I said. "Keeley Murdock's got a new man."

"That bother you?"

I had to think about it. "My reputation's already shot. I guess this couldn't make matters any worse. What about you? Won't it bother you to have people assuming we're a couple when we're not?"

"I don't give a damn," he said.

"What if your woman hears about me?"

"She won't."

"Why not?"

"She doesn't actually know my name," he said. "Yet."

15

I took a long sip of beer and considered this new information. "She doesn't know your name?"

"Not exactly," he said. "But that's about to change."

"This isn't some Internet dating service thing, is it? Did you meet her on a porn site or something?"

"Get real," he said, looking annoyed. "There's a perfectly reasonable explanation for all this."

"I'd love to hear it," I said. "How exactly do you know this Stephanie person?"

Will took a swig of his own beer. "About a month ago, I was home watching television. The Braves had a rain delay, and there was nothing else on television. I was channel surfing, and I switched over to APTV—you know, the public television station?"

"This isn't Hooterville, Will. I know all about public television. I never miss *Antiques Roadshow*."

"They were having their fund-raising telethon."

"Lord," I said, rolling my eyes. "I can't abide those things."

"It was that or *The Dukes of Hazzard*," Will said. "So I started watching. You know, just seeing if they'd reach their fund-raising goal. The program that night was called *BarberShop America!* It was like the Super Bowl of barbershop quartet competitions."

"Barbershop quartet contests?"

"Live from Indianapolis," Will said. "Grown men dressed in matching outfits. Women too."

"And you watched this for how long?"

"I kept switching back to the Braves game, but it was a hell of a storm. The public television folks would show some of the contest, then they'd cut back to the telethon, and they had these deadlines. You know, we need to raise twenty thousand dollars in the next fifteen minutes, or you'll never see Masterpiece Theatre again."

"They can keep Masterpiece Theatre," I said tartly. "I am so over all that *Upstairs, Downstairs* crap."

"They had volunteers in the studio, answering the phones and taking people's pledges," Will said. "And the cameras would scan the phone banks, and they kept showing this one woman. Her phone never stopped ringing."

"Let me guess," I said. "Stephanie."

"I didn't know that was her name," Will said. "At the time."

"You couldn't take your eyes off her," I said, my voice all breathy and girly.

He gave me a look.

"She was wearing some kind of red top," he said. "Everything around her looked gray and old, and there she was, like a, a . . ."

"Rose among thorns? Daisy on a pile of cowshit?"

"I called the television station, and when I got through, I told them I wanted to make a hundred-dollar pledge. But the guy who answered was this old guy. So then I called back, and I think I got the woman who was sitting next to her. But I couldn't just hang up, so I pledged another hundred bucks."

"Two hundred dollars, and you still couldn't get her on the line?"

"When I called back the third time, I told the clown who answered the phone that I only wanted to talk to the woman in the red top. He said it was against station policy.

"Then I told him I had a two-thousand-dollar pledge, but I'd only make it to her."

"So they put you through to Stephanie."

He nodded his head, smiling at the thought of it.

"That's when she told me her name. She's a lawyer. Everybody who was answering the phones that night was a member of some lawyer club or something. And I was watching the television as I was talking to her, and she smiled when I told her about the two-thousand-dollar pledge. It got to me, you know?"

I took a swig of beer and nodded, trying to look noncommittal, even though this was one of the creepiest stories I'd ever heard.

"She said it was the biggest pledge anybody had gotten all night," Will said. "And something just came over me. I'm not like this. Not usually."

I nodded again. I glanced casually over at the door to the shop, and wondered how long it would take me to jump out of the car, run to the door, open it, and lock it behind me. I decided not to make any sudden moves, in case it set him off.

"You think I'm deranged," Will said.

"Not necessarily," I lied.

"Don't you believe in love at first sight?" he asked.

"I fell in love with Jon Bon Jovi when I was thirteen," I admitted. "But the most I ever did was skip school to go to Atlanta to buy tickets to the concert. And I was thirteen at the time. I mean, don't you think this is all a little . . . extreme?"

"I've never done anything like this before. Not in my life. Not ever. But sometimes, things just happen. A light goes on in your brain. And it's flashing 'She's the one. She's the one.'"

I laughed. "With Bon Jovi, it was more like my brain was flashing 'OMIGOD. He is so hot. He is so hot!'"

"But you skipped school to buy the concert tickets. That was pretty extreme for a little kid," he said.

"I guess."

"What about A.J.?" he asked. "How did your relationship with him evolve?"

"That's totally different," I said. "I'd known A.J. forever."

"And one day you just decided to date?"

"I don't care to discuss A. J. Jernigan with you," I said, trying to sound aloof. I was damned if I was going to disclose the drapery seduction scene to Will Mahoney. Not that it was in any way comparable to this loony crush he had on a woman he'd never met.

"Doesn't matter," Will said. He took the last sip of beer and tossed the empty bottle in the backseat. "She is the one. I'm not insane. We have a date next week. And if all goes as planned, there will be an engagement by Thanksgiving."

I threw my bottle in the backseat alongside his. The two bottles clinked companionably.

"You really are insane," I told him. "I'd be shirking my professional duty as a licensed interior designer if I didn't tell you so. But tell me something. How in the hell did you get a date with this woman if she doesn't know your name?"

"Very simple," he said. "I called the station's director of development. Told him I'd already pledged twenty-five hundred dollars for the current fund drive, and that I'd round that amount off to an even five thousand if he'd arrange an introduction to one of his volunteers. And then we talked. We're having dinner next Wednesday night at Bones."

"Isn't that called pimping?"

"It's called good business," Will said.

"What if you hate her?" I asked. "What if she has hairy knuckles and thick ankles and halitosis and VPL?"

"She's perfect," he insisted. "And what's VPL?"

"Visible panty line," I said. "You'd think somebody in the intimate business would know about something like that."

"I'm new to intimates," he said. "But I'm a very quick learner."

"It's your money," I said finally. "And it's a free country. But think about all you'll be out if this plan of yours bombs. You've bought an old house, and already spent like twenty-five hundred bucks. And for what? If she thinks you're a creep, or if she already has a boyfriend or something, you're busted. All that effort, and you got nothing."

"That's not really true," Will said. "I'll still have the house, which I intend to restore. And think about all that other stuff."

"What other stuff?"

"All the loot I got for supporting public television. A tote bag, the *BarberShop America!* four-CD compilation. The official *BarberShop America Live!* DVD. And don't forget the stainless steel *BarberShop America!* travel coffee mug."

"Wow. What a bonanza."

He turned to face me, and stuck out his hand. "We've got a deal, though. Right?"

I shook. "Sure. I guess your money spends as good as anybody else's. And the house has wonderful potential. It'll look great in our portfolio."

He handed me a business card. "You can reach me at the office in the morning. Just tell me what time you want to meet the architect over at the house, and I'll set it all up. Anything else you need in the meantime?"

"Don't guess so," I said, opening the car door.

"I'll be back in town on Monday," he said. "Can you have something ready for me by then?"

"A bill," I said. "For our first consultation."

"Fine," he said. "Bring along your proposal too."

He tooted the horn as he drove off in the yellow Caddy.

My mind was a whirl of details as I unlocked the studio door. It wasn't until I was inside, with the door locked behind me that I noticed all the lights were on. The air in the room smelled different. Flowery.

A huge bouquet of lilacs sat in the middle of my desk. And sitting in the chair behind my desk was a tall, elegant man dressed in a black and cream paisley satin dressing gown. His bald head shone in the overhead light.

"Austin!" I cried. "You nearly scared me to death. What are you doing in here this time of night?"

"Slumming," he said lightly. "But let's get down to details, Keeley Rae. Who was that divine hunk of manhood in the yellow pimpmobile out there? And what were you doing swapping spit with him in the parking lot at the Minit Mart?"

"Paige called you?"

"Don't be absurd. Paige knows how thick we are. She called her mama. Her mama called Janice Biggers. Janice called A.J.'s cousin Mookie. And Mookie called me."

"In the space of ten minutes."

He gave me a broad wink. "Actually, it was more like five. I had to cut the lilacs and make myself presentable. So here I am. Now dish!"

16

He calls himself Austin LeFleur, and he owns Fleur, the florist shop right next to ours. Nobody knows or cares whether that's his real name, and he loves being a man of mystery.

Two years ago Austin bought the florist's business from his eighty-two-year-old second-cousin, Betty Ann, and like me, moved into the apartment above the shop. Of course, when Betty Ann owned it, the shop was called Bouquets by Betty Ann, and it specialized in pretty much what you'd expect from a near-blind eighty-two-year-old who chain-smoked three packs of Camels right up until the day Porter Briggs from the Briggs Mortuary drove his ambulance around the block to pick her up after her third, and fatal, heart attack.

Austin and I clicked the same day we met, and have been friends ever since. He has a key to our shop, and I have the key to Fleur. And although he'd only been living in Madison for two years, he'd already firmly established himself in local social circles. He's on the Historic Madison Foundation and the Madison Arts Council, and belongs to my daddy's Rotary Club.

Right now he was fussing with the vase of lilacs on my desk and giving me his famous, all-knowing, once-over.

"You got any food over at your place?" I asked, avoiding his eyes. "It was salmon loaf night at Daddy's. I'm starved."

He gave me an enigmatic smile. "I might. I very well might have a little something over there. Something chocolate, perhaps."

"Good. Let's go over to your place." I headed for the front door.

"Not so fast, sister," he said. "First the dish, and then the dessert."

"There's nothing to tell," I protested. "He's a client. That's all."

"Do you play tonsil hockey with all your clients?" he asked, raising one well-tweezed eyebrow. "Maybe that explains your business success."

"My business sucks right now and you know it," I said. "Anyway, you know all the gossip in this town is blown way out of proportion."

"Are you denying the kiss took place?" he asked. "I wasn't going to say anything about this, but Mookie claims she has a double source. And you know she's usually very reliable about these things."

"Unless she's fallen facedown into a margarita fountain," I said. "Who are you going to believe, Mookie or me?"

He shook his finger and tsk-tsked me. "See, you're still not denying that there was a clinch. Are you?"

"It was nothing," I said, my face getting hot. "We were just yanking Paige's chain. And it wasn't my idea, anyway. I just sort of went along for the ride."

"You rode him?" Austin shrieked and then dissolved into what can only be called a fit of the giggles.

"You know what I mean," I said. "Look, either feed me some chocolate or go home and let me go to bed."

"With whom?"

I turned toward the back staircase. "Okay. G'night."

"All right, all right, all right," Austin said. He stood up and tightened the belt of the dressing gown.

"I like that," I said. "Where'd you get it?"

"It was Betty Ann's," he said. "Frankly forties, don't you think? There are jammies to match, but the top's a smidge tight across the chest, and of course, the bottoms don't *quite* meet a gentleman's needs, if you know what I mean."

"I never saw Betty Ann dressed in anything remotely like that dressing gown," I said. "In fact, I don't think I ever saw her dressed in anything that wasn't one hundred percent polyester."

"It must have been a gift or something," Austin said. "Never been worn."

"Well, if you ever get tired of it, throw it my way," I said, following him through the studio and out our back door. We stepped into the alley and made a quick left. The screen door to Fleur was propped open with a brick, and the inner door was ajar.

"Don't you ever lock up?" I scolded.

"I was just over at your place. Anyway, it's Wednesday night. Nobody's gonna come around and try to knock over a florist's shop. What are they gonna do—pluck my pansies?"

"You should be more careful," I told him. "Don't you read *The Citizen*? Somebody stole a wheelbarrow and a fertilizer spreader from the hardware store last Sunday morning."

"Kids," Austin said airily.

I inhaled deeply as I followed him into his workroom, breathing in the smell of fresh-cut flowers. He'd done the whole place over after Betty Ann went to her maker. Betty Ann's old Pepto-Bismol pink walls had been replaced with a washed green and gold Tuscan villa paint treatment. Austin had installed stainless steel shelves and bins, and painted the old concrete floor to look like aged quarry tiles. Stainless steel buckets of water held bunches of perennials and wildflowers he bought from local gardeners, and a walk-in cooler held the more delicate roses and exotics he imported from around the world. There was nary a gladiolus or a carnation in sight.

He opened the door of the cooler and stepped inside for a moment, coming back out with a white cardboard box. My mouth started to water when I saw the Karen's Bakery logo on the box.

"Gimme," I said, reaching for the box, but Austin held it over my head and walked quickly toward the stairs that led to his apartment.

"Not so fast," he said. "First a little wine, then a little chat, then, maybe, if the dish is high octane, I will share with you."

"Just tell me what's in the box," I asked. "Brownies? Chocolate mousse cake? Espresso bars?"

He turned and waved the box under my nose. "Goo-goo clusters," he said. "Could you just die?"

I moaned. Karen Culpepper opened her bakery and catering shop three years ago, and all of her desserts were my downfall, but her version of a goo-goo cluster, which she only makes very occasionally, is my absolute all-time favorite. Big old clusters of peanuts and pecans, drizzled with warm, bourbon-infused caramel, and coated with dense layers of imported milk chocolate. They probably have eleventy billion calories, but I don't care. Give me a goo-goo any day.

Austin switched on the light in the large airy room that served as his living room/dining room/kitchen.

"You painted again," I said. "It's fabulous."

The last time I'd been up here, Austin had been in his *Miami Vice* mode. The walls had been lime green with tangerine trim on the windows and moldings, and a washed papaya pink on the ceiling. He'd placed huge pots of palms and flowering citrus plants in front of the windows, which he'd swathed in filmy sheers, and all the furniture had been slipcovered with turquoise linen, which he'd sewn himself.

Now it looked like a totally different room. The walls were a glowing, no, make that a *throbbing* red. All the trim had been done up in a sort of baroque old gold treatment, and the pink ceiling had gotten a six-inch border of metallic gold stenciling. Heavy blue velvet drapes were tied back from the windows with thick gold cording, and he'd tossed leopard-print throws over his sofa and loveseat.

"Too slutty, do you think?" he asked, drifting into the tiny kitchenette alcove.

"Not at all," I said. "It's absolutely you. Sort of . . . bad boy bordello?"

"Yes!" he called over his shoulder. "That's it exactly. So, you really like it?" He came out of the kitchen with Venetian glass goblets of white wine, and handed me mine with a tiny lace cocktail napkin. He disappeared again, and returned with a silver tray piled with the goo-goo clusters.

"You're the only person on the planet who could pull this off," I said, taking a sip of the Chardonnay. "Where'd you get all that velvet and leopard print?"

"Promise you won't hate me?"

I quickly sketched a cross-my-heart with my wineglass, and took a big bite of chocolate-covered peanuts.

"The trash!" he whispered dramatically. "I was coming around the square on Sunday, and I saw Porter Junior hauling a big old box of junk out to the curb in front of the funeral home. As soon as he was gone, I pounced. And I found all these yards and yards of fabric. I think the stuff was actually used for skirting around banquet tables or something, because it was all pleated. I just ripped out all the pleats, gave it a toss in the dryer, and voilà!"

I licked the chocolate off my fingers and walked over and touched the drapes. "Probably not banquet tables," I said. "I bet this stuff was used on the platforms that hold the caskets for visitation."

"EEEW," he screeched.

"Who cares?" I said, patting his hand. "It's all about the look, right?"

"Welll . . ."

"And what about the leopard skin stuff? I know Porter Briggs didn't have leopard casket draping."

"It was originally just plain old beige," Austin said, perking up now. "I took some fabric paint and stenciled on the leopard spots."

"You are the bomb, Austin," I said, shaking my head. "I hope you don't decide to quit the florist business, 'cause I'm afraid you'd put me and Gloria straight out of business." I helped myself to a second goo-goo cluster.

"SHUT UP!" he cried, happily fanning himself. "You know I'm just a big ol' DID."

"What's that?"

"Decorator in Denial," he explained, flopping down on the sofa beside me. "Anyway, you taught me everything I know, sis. Look, now, stop trying to kill me with flattery. Let's talk."

I took my goo-goo cluster and dipped it in the wine. Not bad, but a cold glass of two percent milk would have been even better "He's a client. His name is Will Mahoney. He just bought the bra plant, and—"

"The new bra boy?" Austin exclaimed. "He's your client? Why didn't you say so in the beginning?"

"You wouldn't let me," I said. "You just kept on with your smutty assumptions. Anyway, he's bought Mulberry Hill, and Gloria and I have been hired for the design work. It's a huge project, and he's given us an impossible deadline—"

"You've got to get me into the house," Austin said, interrupting. "I would DIE to see that house."

"There's not much to see yet," I started again.

"You'll give him my number, right?" Austin said, ignoring me. "A house like that should be filled with flowers. Enormous blue and white Chinese jardinières full of exquisite cut flowers. And I see tulipieres on the sideboards, and wonderful old cut-glass vases—full of Stella D'Oro roses—"

"Perfect," I said, trying to get in a word edgewise. "The thing is, he's got this loony crush—"

"He's seen me already?" Austin shrieked. "Why didn't you say so?"

"On a woman he's only seen on television."

"Oh," Austin said, setting his wineglass down on the coffee table.

"I'm pretty sure he's straight," I said gently.

"Aren't they all?"

"Not from my perspective," I said. "All the really wonderful men, the ones who like to go dancing, buy good jewelry, and appreciate art and design, are on your team."

"Boy toys," Austin said dismissively. "Either that or withered-up old queens."

I patted his knee. "Don't fret, hon. Someday your prince will come."

He sighed. "By that time my moat will have dried up. There are just absolutely no interesting men in this town."

"Exactly my sentiment," I said.

"Except for Mr. Loving Cup Intimates," Austin said. "You say he's straight. He's rich, he's got a fabulous house, so go for it, girlfriend."

"Not interested," I said firmly. "Anyway, he's in love with a woman he's never met, and I've been hired to design a house to make her fall madly, passionately in love with him."

"You're making that up," Austin said. "Trying to put me off track. If he's so in love with somebody else, why is he necking with you at the Minit Mart?"

"He knows all about the Paige and A.J. incident," I said. "He was at the rehearsal dinner and witnessed my, uh, hissy pitching."

"SHUT UP!" Austin cried. "That was the hottest ticket in town. He got invited and I didn't?"

"The Jernigans did the inviting, not me," I reminded Austin. "And I think GiGi had roped him into contributing to one of her lame-o charities."

"But he still kissed you." Austin can really be annoyingly single-minded at times. He peered at me intently. "How was it? Did he rock your world?"

"No! It was just a kiss. Nothing special," I lied. "And I did not kiss back."

"Liar, liar, pants on fire," Austin taunted. "You should have seen your face when he dropped you off. I saw you through the window. Watching him drive off. You want him, Keeley Rae."

"I want the paycheck we'll get for this job," I said, getting up abruptly. "And that's it. End of story. I am totally over men, as of right this minute. Including you."

He followed me down the stairs, chanting as he went. "Keeley and Willy sitting in the tree . . . K-I-S-S-I-N-G . . ."

I put my hands over my ears and let myself out the back door.

17

Thursday morning I got downstairs early, but my aunt was already at work, as usual.

Gloria had the Benjamin Moore paint deck fanned out on her worktable. She peered down through the tortoiseshell bifocals perched on the end of the nose at the sample cards arrayed before her.

Every now and then, she held a small, clear plastic bottle of sand next to a card, then shook her head sadly.

I tapped my fingernail against the pill bottle. "Just exactly what are you doing?"

She held up the bottle, shifting the sand backward and forward.

"This, my darlin' niece, is a teaspoon of sand from Grayton Beach, Florida. My dear, dear client Bizzy Davis wants me to find a paint color that is an exact match to this, so that when she lies in bed at her house down there, she'll see a seamless stretch of sand, from her bedroom walls, right down to the sparkling turquoise waters of the Gulf of Mexico."

I moved the paint chips back and forth, then tapped one. "This. Cameo."

"Afraid not," Gloria said. "I had the whole damn room painted in Cameo. Bizzy hated it. Said it's the color of dirty white sheets in a cheap motel."

"She's nuts. It's an exact match."

"Of course," Gloria agreed. "She's one ant short of a picnic. One brick shy of a load. All that. But she's the client. And that's a six-thousand-square-foot house down there. So I'm gonna match the damn sand if it kills me. Which it might."

I sat down at my own desk. "I told Will Mahoney we'd take the Mulberry Hill job."

Gloria held up another paint chip. "Albescent. What do you think?"

"Too pinky. Do you think I'm crazy to say yes to this guy?"

Gloria smiled that smile. "Depends on what you're saying yes to."

"The job," I said. "Get your mind out of the gutter."

"A woman my age needs to fantasize. All right. If we're talking about taking on the house project, yes. Absolutely. We need the work. He's got lots of money apparently. So why wouldn't we help him spend it?"

"He's just as whacked as Bizzy Davis," I said. "He's fallen in love with some chick he saw once, on a public television pledge drive. Now he wants me to design his house so she'll fall in love with him. Oh yes. And give up her job at an Atlanta law firm, move to Madison, and become Mrs. Bra Guy."

Gloria wrinkled her brow. "Really? He really told you all that? He seemed perfectly sane when he was here the other night."

"I know. It's impossible."

"Still," Gloria said, holding the sand bottle up to the light. "It's an interesting proposal."

"It sounds like something from a reality TV show. Design a house. Catch a spouse. It's warped."

"But you agreed to do it."

"Yeah," I said, sighing. "He took me out to the house last night, damn him. We walked all through it. You know me. How I am about old houses. I was hooked just as soon as I saw the front door. It could be amazing. After all, he's got the money, and I've got the taste. It's a dream job, in some aspects."

"Except."

"For this nightmarish idea of his. This woman. Her name's Stephanie Scofield. He knows absolutely nothing about her, except that she's the love of his life."

"Research," Gloria said. "Just look at it as a research project."

"He's flown off to Sri Lanka. And he wants a proposal by Monday, when he gets back to town."

Gloria looked over at me. "This is Thursday. Why aren't you already on your way to Atlanta?"

I called Will and arranged to meet his architect at the house later in the week. An hour later, my Volvo and I were on I-20, headed to Atlanta. I'd done a Google search on Stephanie Scofield. I found a handful of mentions of her, in the Atlanta newspaper's society column, the *Atlanta Business Chronicle*, and a slick society magazine called *The Season*.

It was enough to get me started. I knew where her law firm was located, where she lived, and the fact that she was a sucker for high-profile charity events like the Atlanta Zoo's Beastly Feast, the Atlanta History Center's Swan Ball, and the Humane Society's annual dinner dance and auction.

I had photos of her too; a grainy black and white head shot from the Atlanta paper showing her with upswept blond hair and a strapless black dress and long dangly earrings, and one of those standard "grip and grin" photos from the *Business Chronicle* showing her standing in a trim business suit with the other partners in the law firm of Tetlow, Beekner, Carrawan, and Sackler.

Even from those characterless shots, it was easy to see why Stephanie Scofield had attracted my client's attention. She had huge, dinner-plate-sized eyes, an enigmatic, slightly turned-up at the corners smile, and a killer figure.

It was nearly noon by the time I'd navigated through midtown Atlanta to the Wachovia Bank Tower where Tetlow, Beekner had their offices, but by then I'd formed a sort of plan of attack.

There was a florist's shop in the lobby of the bank building. I winced as I shelled out fifty bucks for a vase of deep blue and purple hydrangeas, but I kept the receipt. Will Mahoney would be paying for this little excursion. I scrawled a deliberately illegible message on the accompanying card.

According to the lobby directory, Tetlow, Beekner's offices were on the eighth floor. In the elevator I removed my pearl earrings and necklace, and deliberately ruffled my hair. I shucked my beige linen jacket and tied it by the sleeves around my waist and unbuttoned the top two buttons of my silk blouse. The impromptu changes didn't make me look too much like a real delivery girl, but then again I now didn't look that much like a successful interior designer.

The law firm's receptionist looked up from the magazine she was reading when I cleared my throat a couple times.

"Flowers for Stephanie Scofield," I said.

"Just leave them here," she said, going back to her magazine. Clearly it was no big deal for Stephanie to receive flowers from admirers.

"Can't," I said.

She looked up, raised one eyebrow.

"Delivery to Miss Scofield. Personally. That's what my instructions say. The customer paid extra."

The receptionist looked down at a clipboard on the desk. "Well, she's at lunch right now. So I guess you'll just have to leave them with me. I'll never tell," she added, giving me a conspiratorial grin.

"Can't," I said again. "How 'bout if I just take them back to her office and leave them? That ought to be good enough."

Her switchboard buzzed softly, and she picked up the phone. "Tetlow, Beekner. Oh hi! I was wondering when you'd call. What have you been up to?"

I cleared my throat again. "Just tell me which office," I said. "I'll drop 'em off and get out of your hair."

She frowned. "Down the hall, right at the water cooler, third door on the left. Her assistant's at lunch too. Ms. Scofield is very particular about her office. Don't touch anything in there. Just leave the flowers and go. All right?"

"Sure," I said, hastening down the hall before she could change her mind.

I found her office with no trouble, ducked inside, and closed the door behind me.

I set the flowers on a mahogany credenza behind her desk, then stood there for a few minutes, just taking it all in.

The office itself was what I'd expected. Expensive mahogany desk and credenza, generic reproduction Oriental rug over institutional gray carpet. A separate computer table, expensive leather desk chair and matching burgundy leather wing chair facing the desk. Her desktop was neat, with only one file folder in the out basket, and a bud vase holding a single long-stemmed red rose.

Her credenza was crowded with sterling silver–framed photographs. I studied them carefully. Stephanie in the strapless black cocktail dress, one arm around another woman in a black cocktail dress. Stephanie and a handsome, silver-haired older man, both of them dressed in tennis whites. Was he her father? Senior law partner? Sugar daddy? Stephanie laughing into the face of a towheaded little girl she held in her arms, both of them wearing pink fur bunny ears. Stephanie dressed in red running shorts, a white singlet, and a Peachtree Road Race number pinned to her shirt, her hair wet and her face red. There were three more photos, all featuring Stephanie smooching a tiny black and brown dachshund. So she was a dog lover.

With one finger I slid open the bottom drawer of the credenza. Inside was a black gym bag with a plastic ID card dangling from the handle, reading BodyTeck. Feeling only slightly guilty, I unzipped the gym bag. Sitting on top of neatly folded workout clothes was a clear plastic makeup bag. She apparently liked La Prairie skin products and cosmetics. And didn't mind spending twenty-six dollars for a tube of lipstick. And even though she was clearly a girly-girl, she also played tennis, ran, and worked out at a trendy Buckhead gym. Good to know.

There were gilt-framed oil paintings on the wall opposite her desk. Generic Parisian street scenes, they were reproductions, the kind clueless beginners often chose to lend "elegance and sophistication" to their homes or offices. But they told me something about her; she liked Paris. Or the idea of it, anyway.

I heard voices in the hall outside and froze, for just a moment. Then I opened the door a crack and peeked out. I recognized her immediately, from the photos. Her blond hair was in a ponytail today, and she was wearing well-tailored black slacks and a crisp white shirt under a beautifully tailored jacket. The suit was Escada. The black pumps were Prada. I'd seen them in the latest issue of *Vogue*, and they'd cost four hundred dollars. Bitch. She was down the hall, bent over the water cooler, laughing at something a woman with her was saying.

I ducked out of the office and walked rapidly down the hall. Stephanie Scofield straightened up, looked directly at me, a question in her huge brown eyes. But I walked right past her, gaze straight ahead, around the corner, past the receptionist, and over to the elevator, which thankfully opened its doors just then.

The doors slid shut and I exhaled loudly with genuine relief. I'd boldly gone where others dared not follow. And most importantly, I hadn't gotten caught.

Sitting in my Volvo, in the baking heat of the parking deck, I made some quick notes for myself. Stephanie Scofield liked red. Clothes and flowers. She was something of a Francophile. She liked expensive stuff. Sterling silver, La Prairie, Prada. The art and office furnishings were kind of a puzzle. Maybe her taste wasn't so hot. Or maybe she just hadn't had the time or inclination yet to personalize her office space.

Clearly, there was more work to be done. Clearly, I needed to see where and how she lived. I looked down at my notes. Her address was on a street I wasn't familiar with, named Lombardy Way. I'd looked it up on an Atlanta map, it was a small side street in Ansley Park, a quiet but ritzy midtown neighborhood only a few blocks away.

I passed the High Museum of Art, the Alliance Theatre, and the Fourteenth Street Playhouse on the way to Stephanie's address. Was she a bona-fide culture nut, or was she just interested in a prestige address? I wondered.

The Lombardy Way address proved to be across the street from a back entrance to the Piedmont Driving Club, Atlanta's best-known and most exclusive country club. Number 86, Stephanie's, was the third townhouse in a row of six dark gray stucco townhouses with a vague Spanish Colonial influence. Black wrought-iron grillwork covered the arched front windows, and a black and cream striped awning covered each arched doorway. They'd been built in the 1920s or 1930s, I thought. Each unit was fronted with a little patch of emerald green grass and vividly colored impatiens.

I sat in the Volvo and stared at Stephanie Scofield's front door for a long time, trying to gather the nerve to do something outrageous. In a neighborhood like this, there would be people at home during the day. There would be burglar alarms. Barking dogs.

There would be . . . police.

Somebody tapped on my window. I must have jumped six inches in my seat.

Stephanie Scofield stood in the street, bent down, staring in at me, those saucer-sized eyes shooting sparks, her hands on her hips.

"Hey! Do I know you?"

"Uh." It sounded dumb to me too.

"What are you doing hanging around here? What were you doing in my office earlier? Who the hell are you?"

"I, uh . . ."

She held out a tiny black cell phone, the receiver flipped up. "I'm about to call the cops if you don't tell me what you're up to."

I swallowed hard, tried to think of a logical explanation of what I'd been trying to do. The trouble was, there wasn't any logical way to explain my mission.

"It's about a man," I started. "He's my client. And he thinks he's fallen in love with you. So he's hired me to find out what you like. So you'll fall in love with him."

"Really?" She frowned, twirling the ends of her ponytail absent-mindedly between her fingertips. "Is this guy some kind of freak or something? Did he just get out of prison, anything like that?"

"Nothing like that," I assured her. "He's a successful business-man."

"What's he want with me? Do I know him?"

Sweat beaded on my upper lip. It must have been closing in on ninety, and I'd been sitting in my parked car for at least ten minutes. My blouse was drenched with perspiration.

"Could we talk about this inside?" I asked. "I think I'm about to have heat stroke."

"Okay," she said, looking me over carefully. "You don't have a gun or anything, do you?"

"I'm an interior designer, not a private eye."

18

I heard the barking ten yards from her front door. Actually, it was more like crazed, frantic yipping.

Stephanie jangled her keychain. "I'm coming, sweetie," she cooed. "Mama's home."

She fitted the key in the lock and turned to me, frowning slightly. "How do I know you're really who you say you are? I mean, do you have any ID or something like that?"

The dog on the other side of the door went nuts at the sound of her voice. He was yipping and yapping and apparently throwing himself against the door in an effort to get closer to his "mama."

"I have a driver's license," I said. "And some business cards, if that helps. I don't usually carry my business license on me."

"How do I know you're really an interior designer, and not some well-dressed freakazoid?"

"Listen. My name really is Keeley Murdock. I'm co-owner of Glorious Interiors, over in Madison. Who would make up a story like this? It's too weird to be anything other than the truth."

"How did you find out where I live? Where my office is?"

"Easy. I did a computer search. You're not exactly a hermit, you know. Several mentions in *Peach Buzz*, the *Atlanta Business Chronicle*. And there was that picture of you in *The Season*."

"The one at the Swan Ball? You saw that? Was the French twist too severe, do you think? My hairdresser talked me into it, and I was afraid it made me look too old."

"Not at all," I said. "You have great cheekbones." I could feel sweat pouring down my back. In another minute my silk blouse would be completely melded to my body. "Can we discuss this inside?"

"Well, if you read *The Season*, you can't be too much of a deviant," she said, pushing the door open. "Come on in."

A small brown and black rocket flung itself at her ankles.

"Erwin!" she cried, scooping him up. "Mama's home, angel."

Erwin appeared to be some kind of shrunk-down dachshund. He wriggled in her arms and licked her face all over, an experience Stephanie Scofield seemed to really enjoy. She held his snout tightly and kissed him right back.

She held the dog out to me.

"Erwin, baby. This nice lady is . . . What did you say your name is again?"

"Keeley," I said, backing away an inch or so. "Keeley Murdock."

Erwin's ears perked up. He lurched toward and licked my nose.

Stephanie beamed. "Erwin really likes you. He's very prescient, you know. Most miniature dachshunds are."

"I didn't know that," I said, resisting the urge to wipe the dog spit off my nose. "He looks, uh, very intelligent."

She put her keys down on a hall table and set her pocketbook, a nifty little Prada number, right beside it. "Erwin graduated at the top of his class in obedience school. They have his photo on their website. L'Ecole des Chiens. Do you know them? It's on a farm, out near Crabapple. Very exclusive. Ted Turner's Rottweiler was in Erwin's class." She frowned. "Although, I didn't see Ted at the last class reunion."

"I understand he spends a lot of time at his ranch in Montana," I offered.

"That's right," she said. She gestured toward the living room. "Why don't you sit down? Let me just get us something cold to drink, and I'll join you in a minute. What would you like?"

"Just a glass of water, please," I said. "It's awfully hot outside."

I did a mental inventory of the room as I moved toward the sofa. It was small, with the walls painted a stark white. The carpet underfoot was white, as were the silk taffeta drapes hanging from a gilded cur-

tain rod in front of a deep bay window that looked out on a tiny en-
closed brick patio.

A vaguely French rococo settee was upholstered in tone on tone
white damask, and it faced a couple of bergère chairs in matching
fabric. There was a small fireplace faced in white marble. Hung over
the mantel was a huge gilt-framed mirror. More silver-framed photographs of Stephanie and company were scattered about on ebony-
stained end tables and the coffee table. The only bona-fide painting
in the room hung over the sofa. It was a large gold-framed oil painting of . . . Erwin. Or at least I guessed it was Erwin. The painting
showed a miniature dachshund, seated on a majestic throne, with a
tiny jeweled crown on his head, a scepter clamped between his teeth.

The room and its furnishings had cost money. I scraped the wood
arm of the settee with one fingertip. It was a real period piece, worth
at least ten thousand dollars, I estimated. The bergères were authen-
tic too. I knew the upholstery and drape fabric was an imported
Brunswig & Fils that sells for two hundred and sixty dollars a yard. I
couldn't tell without getting up close, but from where I sat, the drapes
looked like a Jim Thompson silk.

"Here we are," Stephanie announced. She set two ice-beaded bottles of Perrier and two Baccarat tumblers down on the coffee table and
seated herself beside me on the settee, with Erwin nestled in her lap.

I grabbed the Perrier and poured myself a glass, gulping it down
greedily.

"Thank you," I said. "Your home is beautiful. And the painting is
wonderful," I offered. "Is that Erwin?"

"Of course," she said. "It's a Yeardley Frank. She only takes two
commissions a year. And she paints strictly from life, no photographs."
Stephanie tipped the bottle of Perrier down to the dog's muzzle and
let Erwin lap from it, before taking a hearty swig herself.

"They have a Yeardley Frank at the High Museum," she said.
"And one at the Ringling Museum down in Sarasota, though I've only
seen postcards of it. It's called *Dalmatian as Jester*. Do you know it?"

"I don't think so," I said.

"I'm a nut about art," Stephanie said.

"So I see."

"Tell me about your client," Stephanie said, scratching Erwin's ears. "Is he for real?"

"Absolutely," I said fervently. "He's the man who saw you on TV when you volunteered for the public television pledge drive. He made a five-thousand-dollar donation, just so they'd let him ask you out to dinner."

"Oh him!" she said, frowning. "He's your client? What's his name again?"

"Will Mahoney," I said.

"We're supposed to go out this week," Stephanie said. "But I've been having second thoughts. I mean, what if he's this big, hairy creep or something? What if he has bad breath, or hates dogs? What if he's a Democrat, for God's sake?"

"I don't know too much about Will's politics, or his attitude toward dogs," I said. "But I can tell you that he's not abnormally hairy. He's actually fairly attractive, if you like red hair." I thought back to that long kiss in front of the convenience store. "And his breath is fine," I assured her. I left out my rating of his kissing ability, which, if I were being totally honest, would rank him as the best ever.

"Red hair?" Stephanie nuzzled her neck against Erwin's.

"Well, it's not Bozo red," I said. "It's not aggressively red."

"What's he do for a living?" she asked. "Would you call him a successful businessman? I mean, this sounds awful, but so many men can't handle dating a woman like me who's got a high-profile mid-six-figures income. Please don't tell me he's in sales." She grimaced. "I don't *do* commissioned salespeople."

"I guess you'd call him an entrepreneur. He owns a lingerie manufacturing business."

"Lingerie?" she asked, brightening. "Which company? La Perla? Oh God, I just love La Perla, don't you?"

So she was a panty snob as well as a shoe slut.

"La Perla's very nice," I said. "But he owns another company. He just bought it, so he's totally repositioning the product line."

"Well, what's it called?"

I winced as I said it. "Loving Cup Intimates."

"Loving Cup bras? That's his company? My God, my granny wore Loving Cup bras. And cotton hosiery and polyester pantsuits."

"That's the old Loving Cup bra," I said, getting defensive on Will's behalf. "Will is doing a total redesign of the company's product line."

"I should hope so," she said pertly. "But I still don't understand where you come in on all this."

"Loving Cup's manufacturing plant is in Madison. I live in Madison. That's where our design business is located. Will has also bought one of the most beautiful old homes in the county. It's an antebellum plantation, Mulberry Hill. I've been hired to oversee the restoration and decoration. It's a huge job."

"And what has that got to do with me?"

I took another sip of the Perrier. "Will is quite taken with you. I know it sounds crazy, but he's fixing up Mulberry Hill so that you'll fall in love with it, and him. So you'll marry him and move to Madison and everybody will live happily ever after."

She nodded sympathetically. "I have that effect on men. It's almost spooky. They see me for a minute, and poof! They think they've fallen in love with me. I can't tell you how many marriage propositions I've gotten, just standing in line at the bank, or walking Erwin in the park. Total strangers ask me to marry them all the time. Why do you think that is?"

She fixed her huge brown eyes on me. Erwin's were watching me too. They were the same shade of chocolate as Stephanie's. Was that why she chose him? I wondered.

"Keeley?"

"Oh. Well, you're a very attractive woman," I said. "With a magnetic personality. That's what it is. Magnetism." That, a tiny waist, big boobs, and killer legs probably had nothing to do with men falling all over themselves for her.

"Maybe that's it," she said thoughtfully. "So. Will Mahoney sent you to Atlanta to spy on me?"

"Not exactly," I said. "He's out of the country at the moment. Sri Lanka. But he wants a proposal for the design by Monday. And I have to design it so you'll fall in love with it. And him. So I decided to research you."

"Very clever," Stephanie said. "I think research is the key to almost everything, don't you?"

"Absolutely."

"Tell me," Stephanie said. "Since you're such a prodigious researcher, what do you think Will Mahoney's net worth is? Pretax, of course."

19

Erwin's nose quivered with anticipation. Stephanie's eyelids fluttered.

"Net worth?" I said. "Look, he's rich. That's all I can tell you. You don't just fork over eight hundred thousand dollars for a crumbling mansion with pocket change. And you don't lay out the kind of money he has, buying that factory like he did, unless you've got money."

"You'd be surprised," Stephanie said dryly. "I work in mergers and acquisitions. People make deals like those all the time with somebody else's money."

"I don't care about his other financial arrangements," I said. "Glorious Interiors works on genuine American currency. As far as I can tell, Will Mahoney is legitimate."

She drummed her fingertips on the arm of the sofa. "We'll see. I can have a Dun & Bradstreet run on him tomorrow."

I coughed. "Look, uh, the thing is, I have to have a presentation ready for him on Monday. For the house. I'm supposed to figure out all the kinds of things you like. Colors, furniture styles, fabrics, your taste in art, accessories, everything."

She wrinkled her nose. "What if I don't want a stranger poking around in my likes and dislikes? I haven't even met this man. Wealthy or not, I certainly don't want you telling him such personal information without a formal introduction."

"I can tell some things about you already," I said, glancing around the room. "You like neutrals, right? White on white? And good French furniture? A fairly clean palette?"

She fiddled with a thick gold bangle bracelet around her wrist. "What makes you think that?"

"This living room," I said.

She laughed. "It's not actually my living room. It's my step-mother's. She and my father moved down to Boca last year, and I'm renting from them. All of this stuff is Arlene's. The painting of Erwin is the only thing that's really mine."

Dog art. The dream chick liked dog art. At least it was a start.

"Look," I said finally. "I'm not asking for *your* net worth. Or about your preferences in lingerie or anything really personal like that. What do you have to lose here? You've already agreed to have dinner with Will. If you loathe him, you never have to see him again. End of story. But on the other hand, what if there are sparks? What if he really does have the right stuff?"

Her eyes narrowed, then widened. A goofy smile crossed her lips.

Keep reeling, I told myself. Another minute and you'll have the hook set.

"Mulberry Hill could be your dream home," I said softly. "Can't you just picture it? An elegant antebellum mansion set amid gorgeous gardens. It's dusk, and the landscape explodes with the scent of gardenias and night-blooming jasmine. Of moonflowers and exotic orchids. From the road, the only thing visible are the brooding live oaks, and then, a long oak-lined drive crosses a meadow filled with wildflowers, which gives way to boxwood-edged walkways, and then, at the end of that long walk, rises up the pearly white columns of Mulberry Hill, lit from within from the light of hundreds of candles. Oh yes, and who's that answering the door? Look! It's Stephanie. Stephanie Scofield, radiant in, uh, Armani."

She frowned. Had I somehow ruined the mood?

"Why would *I* be answering my own door? Why wouldn't the housekeeper or somebody like that answer the door? And why Armani? I've always liked Gaultier."

I ignored the staffing question. But I'd have a go on the fashion bit. "Leather bustiers are a little too cutting edge for Madison," I said gently. "But what about Ralph Lauren? The couture collection,

I mean. After all he's all about the classics. Like Madison. And for evening, Carolina Herrera, of course."

"Maybe." She stroked Erwin's ears. "Go on. Tell me what else you see."

"Like paint colors? I asked hopefully. "I think we should keep to a historic palette. Maybe a fabulous grisaille mural in the hallway . . . all done in a dreamy blue-green . . . and I'm thinking we have an exact copy made of the Waterford chandelier in the dining room, and hang it in the hallway. Really make a drop-dead statement there."

"I was thinking about my drop-dead jewelry," Stephanie said, pouting. "What kind of jewelry am I wearing with my Herrera ball gown?"

"Well . . . pearls, probably."

The frown deepened.

"Diamonds," I said hastily. "Big, flawless diamonds. And, and, sapphires?" I said, hopefully.

"Rubies," she said firmly. "To go with my red satin ball gown."

"Perfect." I had to get her back on track.

"Now about the floor?" I said. "Marble would be the expected treatment. But why do the expected? The existing floor is gorgeous old heart pine. I really like vernacular materials, and that's Georgia longleaf pine. Why not clean it up, maybe do a lightly stenciled oak-leaf border? Or a checkerboard? Play with period motifs . . ."

She waved her hand, and the gold bangle bracelets made a jarring clinking sound. "Oh, who cares about that stuff? Just as long as everything's top of the line, it doesn't really matter, does it?"

"But it does matter," I said, leaning forward. "Mulberry Hill is one of the last great unrestored plantation houses of the region. We have a once-in-a-lifetime shot at transforming it into something wonderful. Something amazing. Just throwing a lot of money at it isn't the solution."

"Why not?" she asked, shrugging. "I read *Architectural Digest*. Those people spend millions. And it all looks great. We could copy something right out of there. In fact, I saw an issue once, at my dentist's office, and they had pictures of Sharon Stone's San Francisco pied-à-terre. I bet I could find it again. And you could just use the same stuff."

I almost choked. I'd seen that issue myself. Sharon Stone's taste seemed to run heavily to Lucite coffee tables, bizarre African artifacts, and grotesquely oversized sofas constructed of sheet metal and raw foam rubber. It had reminded me of Pee-Wee's Playhouse.

Steady, I told myself. Don't lose her now. Be calm. Be rational.

"Sharon Stone's house is a reflection of Sharon Stone," I said calmly. "And for her, that's fine. But we're talking about Stephanie Scofield's dream house. We're talking about a unique Southern woman. A successful attorney, an accomplished amateur athlete . . ."

Erwin's ears pricked up, and he barked twice.

"And a dog lover," I added. "An elegant, multifaceted woman of many moods."

Stephanie beamed. "Fine. That's perfect. That's what I want."

"What?"

"What you just said. You decorate the house to say all that and it'll be great."

I groaned. "There's nothing else you can tell me about your taste in interior design?"

"Closets," she said firmly. "Walk-in closets. I'd like one of those revolving motorized clothes racks like they have at my dry cleaners. And bathrooms. Lots of bathrooms."

I made a quick note.

Erwin barked again. She dropped a kiss on his snout. "And a doggie door for Erwin so he can come and go as he pleases."

"Anything else?"

"A safe would be nice."

"A safe?"

"For the jewelry," she said.

20

It was getting late. I needed to get back to Madison, Erwin apparently wanted to go for a walk, and Stephanie was getting bored with talking about interior design and restoration.

In the end, I talked her into giving me a guided tour of her inner soul—meaning, her closet.

She opened the door carefully and turned on the light switch.

"Damn" was all I could say.

It wasn't a closet at all, but a full-sized guest bedroom. The wall opposite the door was wall-to-wall mirror. Hanging racks—the kind you see in department stores—filled the perimeter of the room. In fact, it reminded me of a designer salon in an upscale department store.

Everything was sorted by color and style, long dresses at one end, all the way to itty-bitty miniskirts at another end. Wooden cubbies held maybe sixty or seventy pairs of shoes.

"All of this is yours?" I asked, turning to Stephanie, who was lovingly running her hands down a black satin cocktail dress.

"Well, the winter stuff is actually in storage," she said, a trace of apology in her voice. "And I keep the boots in the small closet in my bedroom."

Erwin jumped down out of her arms and raced frantically toward the open door.

"Listen, I've got to take him for a walk before he piddles on the carpet," Stephanie said. "Have you seen enough?"

"Not really," I said. "Can't I look around in here while you take him for a walk? I won't touch anything."

Her furrowed forehead told me she didn't quite trust me in here—despite the fact that her size two clothing wouldn't have fit on my big toe.

"I'll be back in five minutes," she said. "And then you really will have to leave. I've got somebody coming over for drinks at seven, and I haven't even showered yet."

I nodded agreement, and she trotted down the stairs after her dog.

Stephanie's taste in clothing was, luckily, consistent. She liked the big name designers. She liked cool colors—the only exception being red. She liked leather, she liked lush, expensive fabrics, and she liked classic with a touch of hip.

I jotted notes as I flipped through the clothes. Her business suits were fairly conservative, but each one showed a little dressmaker detail. This was good. I could use this. When I was done making notes, I stepped out into the hallway.

"Stephanie?" I called loudly. No answer.

I tiptoed over to the next door off the hallway and turned the knob slowly.

"All done?" Her voice echoed in the tile-floored foyer.

I must have jumped a foot. I snatched my hand away from the doorknob and skittered over to the stairwell. She stood at the base of it, holding Erwin in her arms, looking up at me expectantly.

"Yeah. Great. Wonderful," I babbled, taking a stair with each word.

She held out a hand. "Nice to have met you."

I shook. "Thanks. Listen . . . I know you're supposed to have dinner with Will, Wednesday night at Bones. So it might be better if you don't mention to him that we've met. Or that we discussed Mulberry Hill."

"Why not?"

"Why not?" I couldn't tell her why not, because I didn't really know. Except that he'd made up the rules for this ludicrous mission of mine, and I'd already intentionally broken them.

I cocked one eyebrow in a way that I hoped made me look sophisticated and worldly wise.

"It's never a good idea to tell a man everything you know, is it?"

She beamed. "No. Definitely not. You're right. We'll keep this just between us girls."

The hot bright sky started to cloud up just as I turned the Volvo onto the Interstate and headed east to Madison. Within five minutes it was raining so hard I could barely see a few feet in front of me.

I had to struggle to keep my eyes and my mind on the road. I kept thinking back to that closet, to the neat rows of skirts and jackets and dresses and blouses. I liked clothes myself. I liked how they expressed my outlook, how they could emphasize my good points and hide the bad. But Stephanie Scofield clearly had a fashion fixation. If I could somehow translate that into a design for Will Mahoney's house, success would be mine.

A thought occurred to me that made me giggle. A long time ago, at another famous Georgia plantation house, a woman with a dilemma turned to interior design. Scarlett O'Hara needed a gown, so she'd turned to Tara's green velvet portieres. Now I needed portieres, and then some. So maybe the solution was to literally ransack Stephanie's closet to come up with portieres for Mulberry Hill.

I'd been listening to a politically correct jazz station when I left Atlanta, but the combination of mellow instrumentals and the steady rhythm of the windshield wipers nearly lulled me right to sleep.

When I found myself veering dangerously close to the center line of my lane, I finally resorted to rolling down the windows of the Volvo, allowing cold wet air to blow in on my face. Then I tuned the radio to a country music station, turned the volume up, and sang along with Garth Brooks, and then George Strait, with some Shania Twain thrown in for good measure.

This was much better. As I took the Madison exit off the Interstate, the radio started playing my favorite song of Tricia Yearwood's, another good Georgia gal like me.

The rain sprayed in on me and I bellowed along with the song.

Tricia and I sounded so fabulous together that I hated to hear the song end. I coasted to a stop in front of Glorious Interiors, and home, in the midst of the last chorus of "She's In Love with the Boy."

I glanced over at the doorway of the shop. What I saw there stopped me in mid-warble. There stood A.J., huddled under the black and white awning, his chin tucked down into the collar of an old blue windbreaker. His hair was damp and matted to his head, his skin was sallow, and he had large dark circles under his eyes. He didn't look nearly as miserable as he deserved to be.

Any other time I would have had to circle the block two or three times to find a parking spot. Any other time I could have sailed right past and kept on going. But it was past business hours. Most of the downtown businesses had closed up shop for the night, and the only car parked on the street was A.J.'s Z-3, still sporting my misspelled handiwork.

Slowly I backed my car into the spot right behind his. I caught sight of myself in the rearview mirror. My damp hair was a wild, windblown tangle of knots, and the rain had streaked what was left of my makeup. A.J. was watching me intently.

Fine, I thought grimly. He looked like shit. I looked like shit. At least we were on even ground.

I got out of the car and locked it.

"Hey," he called softly.

"Hey," I said right back, my rapier wit somehow failing me at that exact moment. I wanted to turn and run away, but my legs kept walking me right toward that doorway.

I was hoping that Gloria might come out and rescue me, that she might clobber A.J. with something heavy and blunt, or at least call him some very bad names. But the lights inside the shop had been turned off. Gloria had gone home. I was trapped.

"What are you doing here?" I asked, trying to edge past him to the door. "Aren't you supposed to still be in France?"

He shrugged, and a river of rain ran down his pants leg. "France blows," he said. "We need to talk."

I took my key and put it in the front door lock, deliberately turning my back to A.J. "Send me an e-mail," I suggested, thrusting my hip against the door, which tends to stick in wet weather. "Send it to getthefuckouttamylife.com."

21

I stepped inside the shop and flicked on the lights, and held the door between us. "Actions speak louder than words, A.J. What you and Paige did, at our rehearsal dinner, that said it all for me."

He shoved his foot inside the door. "We were both drunk," he said, his voice pleading. "We were just fooling around. It got out of hand, I'll admit. But I never meant for it to go that far. I swear to God."

I rested my cheek against the cool glass of the door, which was beaded up with evaporation from our air conditioner. "Not that it matters now, but what about all the other times?" I said, my face getting flushed again, thinking of the two of them, naked, in GiGi's car.

"There *was* no other time," A.J. said fiercely, slamming his fist against the door frame for emphasis. "Fuckin' Paige made it all up."

"I don't want to hear this," I said, pushing on the door.

"Just let me come in, please?" he said, pushing back, his voice low. "Don't make me stand out here on the street and beg like a damn dog."

"What's wrong, A.J.? Afraid you'll make a spectacle of yourself?" I asked, laughing at the irony of it. "Like I did? Make a big fool out of yourself in front of the whole town? Listen," I said. "It's over between us. There's nothing you can say, out there or in here, that could possibly change the way I feel."

He closed his eyes and sighed. "Keeley, please just listen to me. I love you, baby. I know you don't believe it now, but I do. And I don't want it to end this way. I don't want you to think that's who I am."

"I know who you are," I said.

"Give me five minutes," A.J. said. "That's all I ask."

This was getting tiresome. I swung the door wide. "Okay. Come on in. Sit down. I'll give you your five minutes. Five minutes for you to tell me how misunderstood you are."

I sat down at my desk, folded my arms across my chest. All business. That was me. Keeley Rae Murdock. Tough chick. Take no prisoners. Kick ass and take names, that was me.

He pulled Gloria's chair over from behind her drawing board and rolled it so that his knees were within a few inches of mine. I rolled my chair back, away from him. No physical contact. Not with A. J. Jernigan. I knew from experience that once he touched me, the tough chick would go whimpering away like a whipped pup.

I narrowed my eyes so he'd know who he was dealing with. "I gotta tell you, A.J., this is gonna be a hard sell. Especially after you and all the other misunderstood Jernigans over there at the bank have been trying to put us out of business."

"Christ," he muttered. "I had nothing to do with that. It was Dad and Kyle. They were pissed, you know, about the wedding. As soon as I got back from France and found out what they'd been up to, I told them to cut it out. I called your carpet installer, and he's gonna lay the carpet at the bank tomorrow. And I'll try to straighten out the other stuff too."

"Annabelle Waites and the Chins?" I asked. "You're gonna call them and tell them that all is forgiven, and it's perfectly fine to do business with Glorious Interiors?"

"Either Dad or Kyle will," A.J. said, nodding seriously.

"No telling who else they trash-talked about us to," I said.

"They're done trashing you," A.J. said, raising his hand as if to swear an oath. "I promise."

"Fine," I said. "Then we're done here." I started to stand up, but he put his hand on my knee.

"Wait. That's not what I wanted to talk to you about."

I brushed his hand aside. "It's your time. Keep talking if you want."

"Don't be like that," he said, grabbing my hand. "You're telling me that because of five minutes—five minutes out of our relationship, when I was shit-faced, it's over? Just like that? You don't love me anymore? You can tell me that with a straight face?"

His blue-green eyes were pleading. I thought I saw tears welling up in them. His fingers squeezed mine until I was numb. "Think about what we have together. All the stuff we were gonna do. All our plans. Our whole life is right there ahead of us. And I don't want a life that doesn't include you. I figured that out in France. Provence? It was the most beautiful place I've ever seen in my life. Better than the travel brochures, and the books you made me read. And it sucked. Totally sucked. I got drunk on red wine every night, and Nick whined about how the French women had B.O. and never shaved their legs. And all I could think about was how much you would have loved everything, and how much better it would have been if you'd been there. Married to me. But because of those five lousy minutes, you're saying it's all over. Done."

Now I was blinking back hot tears of my own. My throat seemed to close up, clogged with the acid bile of the ache that had been festering beneath the surface for days. "It wasn't just those five minutes," I finally managed. "You betrayed me. Don't you get that? The night before our wedding. And with my best friend."

"Paige started it," he said. "She was flirting with me, and she kept getting me drinks from the bar . . . I was slammed, and I didn't even realize it."

I wrenched my hand away from his and held both my hands to my ears. "Don't! I can't stand it. It's so nasty. And it's like the world's tackiest porn movie, and it keeps playing over and over in my head. At night I dream it. When I'm driving down the road, or trying to work, or just watching television, it just keeps playing. And the worst thing is—I'm in the movie. I keep seeing myself, standing out in that hallway, hearing you hiccupping. And I *know who it is, and I know why he's hiccupping* but my hand's on the doorknob, and I hear the two of you talking, whispering . . ."

"I was drunk," he pleaded.

"And I hear you saying, 'Keeley never did it like that . . .' And in the porn movie, I can hear Paige giggling. I can hear the audience sniggering. And everybody's laughing at me. Poor, stupid Keeley. Too dumb to know the punchline. And then I open the door, and there's the punchline. There's the joke. My fiancé, A. J. Jernigan, banging my best friend on the boardroom table at the Oconee Hills Country Club."

"That was the only time," A.J. said. "Ever."

"Doesn't matter," I said. "Once was enough. Even if you're telling the truth, and it was just once, I can't stand it. If you'd loved me, really loved me, it wouldn't have mattered how much you drank that night. It wouldn't have mattered if Paige was coming on to you. Because drunk or drugged or whatever, it wouldn't have occurred to you to do that. Not with her."

"Oh, come on," he said sharply. "Are you telling me you've never been so drunk that you did something totally out of character? Something you totally regretted the next day? Come on, Keeley, I know you better than that. You're thirty-two years old. You've been with other men before. And I never cared. Never gave it a thought. So why can't you cut me a break?"

I stood up fast, and the chair went spinning against the wall. In a minute I was at the door holding it open again.

"No breaks," I said simply. "But I do have a question for you. Just one."

His shoulders slumped, he walked to the door. "What?"

"If that night at the country club was the first and only time with Paige, how did she know?"

"Know what?" he said, his voice sharp.

"About GiGi's car," I said, my tone matching his. "How'd she know you wanted to do it in the backseat of your mama's Escalade?

His face turned beet red.

"Liar," I screamed. I gave him a hard shove, then I slammed the door shut and locked it. I could hear the rain beating hard against the sidewalk outside, and thunder rolled in the distance. A.J.'s car screeched away from the curb and peeled off down the deserted street. I turned off the studio lights and went stomping up the stairs.

I was in the bathroom, washing my face when I heard soft footsteps on the stairs. Hadn't I just locked that door? Startled, I darted into the kitchenette and grabbed the first thing at hand, a pair of kitchen tongs. The footsteps were coming closer, and my intruder was at the head of the stairs.

Adrenaline-pumped, I leaped out from the kitchenette and into the stair hall, brandishing the tongs like a matador's sword.

"Stop!" Austin screeched, shielding himself with a grease-spattered take-out pizza box from Guido's, the joint across the square.

I lowered the tongs and took a deep breath. "You scared the hell out of me."

"Me?" Austin said. "I'm not the one who just verbally castrated the most gorgeous man in Madison." He leaned over and kissed me on the cheek, and he smelled like garlic and anchovies and roses. "And then you jump me with a pair of kitchen tongs? Honest, Keeley, I think I mighta wet myself."

22

"**Jeez-o Pete!**" I cried, letting my weapon drop to the floor with a clatter. "You scared the living crap out of me. You've gotta stop sneaking up on me like this, Austin."

He picked up the tongs and gave me a questioning look. "Or what? You'll tong me to death?"

"It was the first thing I grabbed," I said. "You're lucky my granddaddy's butcher knife was at the back of the bottom drawer."

He followed me back into my living room and dropped down into an overstuffed armchair covered in my favorite blue and white Pierre Frey toile, while I chose the matching chair opposite him.

"So?" he said, raising an eyebrow.

"So. What?"

"I was back in your stockroom when A.J. came in," Austin said, not bothering to apologize. "I heard the whole sad drama. So my question is, do you believe him?"

I picked at a piece of blue braid trim on the arm of the chair. "Doesn't matter."

"Sure it does," he said, his voice cheerful. "If it was just that one time, and they were both drunk, well, maybe it's not that big a deal."

"It's a big deal no matter what," I said. "I can never trust him again."

"Never is a mighty long time," Austin observed.

"Since when did you switch over to A. J. Jernigan's side?" I asked.

"I'm not on anybody's side," he said. "I'm Switzerland."

"You're gay, so you have to be on my side."

He rolled his eyes. "Honey, no offense, but if I had to choose a side to sleep with, it'd be A.J.'s. He may be a liar and a cheat, but honestly, with those blue-green eyes and those shoulders? I could eat him up with a spoon."

"Don't be nasty," I said.

He stuck out his tongue at me, and we both laughed.

"How was Atlanta?"

"I'll never make it as a secret agent," I said. "I got caught spying red-handed."

"She threw you out? Called the cops?" He was loving the intrigue.

"Nope. Actually, she invited me in. I met her dog and cased the joint. So, mission accomplished. Now all I have to do is design a home around a woman who likes dog art, Prada, and shoes."

"You can do it," Austin said, patting my shoulder. "If anybody can do it, it'd be Keeley Rae Murdock. You want some pizza?"

I opened the box and wrinkled my nose. The anchovies and pepperoni and a half-dozen other toppings had congealed into a single unappetizing layer of gunk.

"No thanks," I said, dropping the box on the counter. Instead I opened the refrigerator door and scanned its contents. There was still one foil-wrapped tray of potstickers left over from my canceled wedding reception. I shuddered, took it out, and dropped it in the trash.

"Scrambled eggs, bacon, and toast," I said finally, grabbing a carton of eggs. "I love breakfast for supper, don't you?"

"If you're fixing it, I'll eat it," Austin said. "Just don't take after me with those tongs of yours."

I cracked the eggs into a bowl, added sour cream, some grated cheddar cheese, and some bacon bits, along with salt and pepper. In a minute or two, the smell of bacon frying permeated the small kitchen. Austin popped the bread in the toaster, and five minutes later, we were back in the living room with our supper on a pair of television trays I'd brought with me from Daddy's house when I moved into the apartment.

We ate breakfast and watched *Jeopardy!*, and drank Diet Coke from some crystal wineglasses that had been a gift from one of my daddy's cousins. I'd already started sending back gifts from A.J.'s family, but most of my relatives had been calling to tell me just to keep theirs.

It turns out I was the one doing most of the *Jeopardy!* watching. Austin was mostly just watching me, I finally figured out.

"What? Do I have something stuck in my teeth? It's my hair, isn't it? You know what this rain and humidity does to me. I look like Michael Jackson, don't I?"

He shook his head. "You look fine."

"Then why are you gawking at me? Come on, you're making me nervous."

"I want to ask you something, but I don't know if it's too personal."

"Just ask, then."

"You won't get mad? Never speak to me again?"

"Don't be stupid. What do you want to know? I mean, it's not like the whole town doesn't already know all my business."

"This isn't about A.J. or Paige."

"What's it about then? Come on, now you've got me curious."

He got up and walked to the window, pulling the drapes aside. Rain slashed down. The sky was plum-colored, with streaks from the last light of the day. From across the square, I heard a car backfire.

"I've been wondering . . ." He half turned. "Whatever happened to your mama?"

"My mama?" I looked down at my hands. I always did that when I thought about her. It was one of the things people said I'd inherited from her. Hands. Long, thin fingers.

She could reach a finger down into the olive jar and spear out the last olive, her fingers were so long. She could French-braid my hair in a matter of seconds, taming my long curls into a flat plait down my back. She knew a dozen variations on cat-in-the-cradle, and taught them all to me one time in first grade when I had strep throat and couldn't go to school for a week.

"Never mind," Austin said, his face coloring. "It's none of my business. Forget I asked."

"It's okay," I said, exhaling slowly. "No big deal. She left when I was seven. Ran off with one of Daddy's salesmen."

"You never talk about her," Austin said. "Are you in touch?"

"No," I said flatly. "She just left. No note. Nothing."

"For real?" Austin said, crossing back to his armchair. "No warning? She just up and vanished?"

"I guess," I said. "If she was unhappy, I never knew it. They never fought. Not in front of me, anyway. One night she fixed corndogs and coleslaw for supper. The next day, when I got home from school, she was gone. I still can't look a corndog in the face," I said, laughing at the absurdity of that last statement.

"What did Wade do?" Austin's eyes were sparkling and alive, his voice a melodramatic whisper. He seemed enthralled with what he regarded as an up-close-and-personal installment of *Unsolved Mysteries*.

"He called all her friends, but nobody knew where she'd gone. Then he got worried that maybe she'd had an accident or something. He called all the hospitals all around, talked to the sheriff. They put out a missing persons bulletin, dragged some farm ponds, but nothing came of it."

"What about the man? When did your daddy figure out she'd gone off with this salesman?"

"His name was Darvis Kane. He was Daddy's sales manager. He was supposed to be on vacation in Panama City Beach the week Mama left. He called Daddy's secretary the day Mama left and said something had come up, and he was resigning. He had her forward his last commission check to a post office box in Wedowee, Alabama."

"Wedowee!" Austin rolled his eyes. "Forgive me, sweetie, but *quel scandale! Quel* tacky! They eloped to Wedowee, Alabama?"

"As far as I know. Daddy never told me any of this, of course. He didn't want to upset me. When it was clear Mama wasn't coming back, he took me to a shrink in Atlanta. Poor Daddy. I was like a zombie. I wouldn't cry, wouldn't talk, wouldn't hardly eat. I think he thought he'd have to put me down in Milledgeville, in the junior nut farm."

"What happened next?" Austin asked.

"Time. Gloria moved in with us for a while. That helped a lot. We'd go to movies together, she'd paint my nails and take me shopping. She talked to me about Mama when Daddy couldn't."

"How did they know she ran off with that man?" Austin demanded. "Did she file for divorce?"

"I guess," I said. "Daddy never talked about her, after he figured out what had happened. So eventually I quit talking about her too."

He sighed. "And you've never heard from her? Not in all these years?"

"No," I said.

"And you're not the least bit curious about her? Where she is, what she's doing?"

I laced my fingers together. "I didn't say that. Of course I'm curious. She was my mother, for God's sake. Don't you think I've wondered where she is?"

"GAAAWD," Austin drawled. "I wish I did have to wonder where my mama is. Unfortunately, I know right where she is, just about every minute of every day. Sitting right in front of the twenty-eight-inch Motorola I gave her for Christmas, clipping coupons and watching daytime TV, right down there in Perry, Florida."

"At least you know," I said.

"She calls me every day at four o'clock, to give me the blow-by-blow of who did what to who on Court TV," Austin said. "And to complain about my brother's trashy wife."

"Count your blessings," I said, standing up to look out at the rain. "I couldn't even send my mama a wedding announcement."

Austin followed me to the window. He wrapped his arms around me and hugged me tight. "You think she would have liked A.J.?"

I swallowed hard. "Maybe. Or maybe she could have seen right through him. The way I couldn't. She was quiet, but she was a good judge of character. She used to tell Daddy who he shouldn't give credit to. And nine times out of ten she was right."

"She sounds nice," Austin said. "What was her name?"

"Jeanine," I said, letting it out in a soft stream. "My mama's name was Jeanine."

23

I **was in** a funny mood after Austin went home around nine—emotionally exhausted, but too keyed up for sleep. I tried watching television, reading, I even took a long hot bath, but nothing worked.

At midnight I went downstairs to the studio and sat at my drawing board for a long time, playing with my box of colored pencils. I switched on the CD player, which was loaded with Gloria's idea of good listening. My aunt has wildly eclectic musical taste—everything from show tunes to sixties rock to old school rap to country.

Lately she'd been on a Sinatra kick. With the rain still beating down on the sidewalk outside, I discovered I was in a Sinatra mood my ownself.

With Old Blue Eyes crooning to Nelson Riddle's lush orchestrations, I picked up a pencil and started sketching. At first I was just doing stream-of-consciousness doodles around the edges of my sketch pad. Gothic armchairs, fragments of window treatments, even a small still life of Gloria's coffee mug and a peach she'd left sitting on a paper towel beside it.

Without really thinking about it, I started sketching the front of a house. It was a grand Greek Revival house with seven two-story-tall Corinthian columns, and a pair of rounded porches extending off to each side of the house. I did a thumbnail sketch of a carved pilaster and pediment doorway and a richly detailed front door. I cocked my head and gave the drawing a critical look. No. The house was too grand. It needed a human touch. I sketched a pair of muddy boots hastily discarded by the door, and a battered little teddy bear propped up in a rocking chair. At one corner of the porch, I drew in the tail fins of an old Caddy. Better. But it needed something more. First a head—big, with a muzzle propped on its feet, and ears flopped back.

This dog wasn't any specific breed. It was just a dog. A dog waiting patiently to be fed and petted and loved.

Like the house. Without thinking, I'd sketched Mulberry Hill. Not as it was—battered and abandoned—but as it should be one day. With a family to love it and pet it.

I put my pencil down and went to the bookshelves on the far wall of the studio. We keep fabric samples in woven rush baskets on the shelves, all colorized and sorted by manufacturer and type—florals here, plaids there, solids, wovens, stripes, heavyweight upholstery separated from lightweight drapery sheers.

I pulled out one basket after another, extracting any sample that caught my eye and lit my imagination. When I had three swatches, I knew I'd found my theme color. Yellow. Not gold, not saffron. A clear, sunny yellow. It was a happy, canary color, just what Mulberry Hill needed to make it cheerful and timeless, but contemporary enough to please someone like Stephanie. I took a couple of baskets of yellow fabrics over to the worktable and plunged my hands in— like lowering a dipper into a bucket of sunshine.

With the yellows selected, I branched out into other colors, lots of bright, willow blues—to go with a fabulous Peking blue Oriental rug, which would then cry out for Chinese red accents. I'd seen a photo of just the right rug in the catalog for the upcoming Southgate gallery auction. I found the catalog in the in basket on my desk and quickly leafed through it. Good, it was a huge rug and would work perfectly in the dining room. Nothing looks worse than a dinky rug in a grand room. If I got the rug, I decided, the dining room could go red—Benjamin Moore has a great red called Chili Pepper. And maybe we'd do a glaze finish, if Will was as adventurous as I hoped. And mirrors. I smiled. Stephanie would want mirrors everywhere.

The twin parlors and the dining rooms could go fairly formal— but in an overstuffed, friendly kind of way—nothing that wouldn't stand up to that big dog I'd sketched on the front porch. The memory of that dog made me frown. How would such a beast get along with neurotic little Erwin? Wait. In reality, there was no big dog. My job was to design a house, I reminded myself—not a life.

Back to the dining room. I tapped my pencil against my teeth. A big oval or rectangular table would be de rigueur. But what if we did something different—something unexpected? Maybe two round tables, with leaves to seat twelve apiece? But no. There was only one Waterford chandelier, and clearly the dining room cried out for it. I would just have to find a wonderful table and maybe get more creative with the seating.

I found my mind wandering back to Stephanie's closet. I'd seen a suit jacket there, beautifully tailored in a taupe-colored linen, with black topstitching, cut close and long, with unusual tortoiseshell buttons and self-covered buttonholes. It had that expensive couture look.

What if I turned the look of that jacket around? I doodled around with chair backs, finally settling on a square-backed chair with satiny ebony legs with X-shaped stretchers. The chairs could be custom built, then slipcovered in a variety of fabrics, maybe a Schumacher chintz in deep reds and blues, and for a more casual feeling, something close to that linen, with the black topstitching and tortoiseshell buttons down the back of the chair.

Which gave me another idea. I hunted through a stack of copies of *Veranda* magazines until I found the issue I wanted. The cover shot was of a dining room—with chair backs like the ones I was envisioning. But these had been slipcovered with exquisite heirloom French damask banquet napkins, each embroidered with elaborate monograms centered on the chair front. Unlike the designer who'd done that dining room, I didn't have a stack of a dozen such antique napkins at hand. But there was an antiques dealer in Madison who always had vintage damask linens, and my upholstery woman, Vinh, had a cousin who did amazing hand—not machine—embroidery and monogramming.

Oh yes. Monograms would be just the ticket for Miss Stephanie Scofield.

I was off to the races. Sinatra crooned, and I sketched like a fiend, ripping illustrations from magazines and catalogs, clipping fabric and carpet samples, holding paint swatches up to the light, then up against the fabrics.

For once I didn't bother to consider costs. Time was the only enemy on this job—and I knew that if I had to budget extra for express shipping or custom orders with drop-dead deadlines, Will Mahoney would be more than happy to pay the freight.

I was just sketching the window treatment for the den—a handsome glen plaid in deep golds and greens, when the front door opened.

I yawned and looked up. It was light outside. Gloria stood inside the doorway with a white bakery bag in one hand and her briefcase in the other.

"Good Lord," she said, glancing around at the avalanche of fabrics and wallpaper samples littering the tabletops and floor. "What happened in here?"

I stood up and stretched and caught sight of the clock on my desk. It was eight o'clock. I'd sketched and worked through the night, and never once given a thought to A. J. Jernigan. I'd gotten totally lost in the work. I was exhausted, starved, gritty-eyed, and dry-mouthed. I felt fabulous.

"I'm healed," I told my aunt.

She smiled and handed me the bakery bag. "Praise the Lord and pass the decaf."

24

It was only ten o'clock in the morning, but by the time I pulled into the parking lot at the Loving Cup bra plant on Monday, I'd been working for nearly seventy-two hours straight.

With Gloria's help, I'd assembled sample boards for all the main floor rooms at Mulberry Hill, as well as sketches for the master bedroom suite, one of the guest rooms, and my personal favorite—the upstairs sunroom. In reality it would be a sitting room for the lady of the house—Stephanie—but in my own mind it was just the sunroom.

As I was unloading my portfolio case from the backseat of the Volvo I glanced around the parking lot. Will's big yellow Caddy was there, along with maybe a dozen other cars. I frowned. There were certainly not enough workers to be running even a skeleton shift at the plant.

Still, the grounds looked better than they had in a long time. The crumbling old brick sign out on U.S. 441 had been rebuilt, the bricks painted white again, the familiar Loving Cup cursive logo—with a stylized cupped hand under each word, was outlined in bold gold-leafed letters. Where tall weeds had nearly obscured the old sign before, now were planted neat beds of hot pink geraniums and asparagus fern. A row of watermelon-colored crape myrtles were blooming their heads off along the front drive, and a man on a riding mower crisscrossed the lush lawn in front of the factory, and the smell of fresh-cut grass and flowers—and gas fumes—was particularly sweet.

I smoothed the skirt of my yellow linen suit and tucked an errant strand of dark hair back into my French braid before crossing the parking lot toward the plant's reception area. My stomach twinged. Too much coffee, too little sleep, I told myself. I was *not* nervous.

There was no reason to be nervous. The designs for the house were wonderful. I'd knocked myself out getting everything assembled over the weekend. Stephanie Scofield would love it. Will Mahoney would love it. And Gloria and I would love bringing Mulberry Hill back to glory—and our bank account would definitely love the paycheck.

I pushed open the plate-glass door and entered the reception area—and another era.

Will might have gussied up the outside of the plant, but the reception area was in a permanent time warp, with knotty pine paneled walls, threadbare institutional gray carpet, and a "conversation area" consisting of two orange vinyl–covered sofas facing a boomerang-shaped coffee table. The reception desk was in the corner, and the woman sitting there, her fingers dancing over a keyboard, was unchanged from the last time I'd seen her, when I was sixteen, reporting for my first real job as a summer file clerk.

Her head jerked up at the snick of the glass door closing, her sharp brown eyes giving me a critical assessment behind the steel-framed eyeglasses.

"Miss Nancy!" I exclaimed, "you're still here!"

"And where the hell else would I be?" Nancy Rockmore drawled. "Sailing around the world on a yacht? Climbing Mount Everest?"

She clamped one hand on the edge of her desk and stood with difficulty, reaching out to me with her free arm. "Come here, young'un," she ordered me. "Let me see how you grew up."

I wrapped my arms around her neck and gave her a hug.

"Quit," she said, pushing me away after a minute. She sank back down into her chair with a grunt.

"Your knee still giving you trouble?" I asked. Nancy Rockmore had been born with hip dysplasia, and though she was only in her mid-fifties, had walked with a variety of crutches and canes all her life. Still, she'd worked as the plant's receptionist since graduation from high school, the sole support of her mother, who'd also worked at the plant as a stitcher until retirement.

"Knee, hips, ankles, you name it, they give me hell," Nancy said. "Had both my knees cut on last winter, and now the doctor says he wants to replace my right hip joint again."

"Ow," I said. "Y'all still living over there in Rutledge?"

"Not on the farm," Nancy said sadly. "Mama went in a nursing home in January, so we sold to her cousin's youngest boy, and I've got me a cute little house closer to the plant. What brings you back to Loving Cup? Not hunting a job, I hope. We've been on reduced shifts since last year, and I can't tell you the last time we hired anybody new."

"I've got a job," I said. "I'm an interior designer. Will Mahoney's hired me to work on his house."

"Mulberry Hill," she said, pursing her lips in disapproval. "I heard he's got big plans for the place."

"Very big," I said, grinning. "I've got an appointment to show him the plans this morning."

She glanced at the clock on the opposite wall and then gestured toward the door beside her. "I reckon he'll see you. He doesn't tell me nothing about his personal business, but he did say he had an appointment this morning."

Nancy went back to her typing. I fidgeted a little with the handle of my portfolio.

"Things still aren't any better out here?" I asked, looking around the shabby room. "Business hasn't picked up any since he bought out that last outfit?"

"He spent some money fixing the place up a little, but production's down to nothing. I know the boss is working on some big deal, but if something doesn't change around here pretty fast, we're screwed. You know who our biggest account is these days?"

"Who?"

"Big Lots," she said, hating the sound of it. "We're down to making bras for Big Lots. They sell 'em for four bucks. You know what a four-buck bra looks like?"

I shook my head no.

"Good," she said. "You don't wanna know, either. Go on back. Mr. Mahoney's office is right where Mr. Gurwitz's office used to be. And make sure you knock good and loud before you go in. He thinks I don't know, but he's basically living in that office. So you want to give him time to hide his laundry before you go busting in there."

"Thanks, Miss Nancy," I said. "It's sure good to see you again."

"I heard about your breakup with that Jernigan boy," she said, going back to her typing.

I could feel my face reddening.

"Good for you," she said, nodding for emphasis. "I never could stand any of them Jernigans. And that Paige Plummer? The one summer she worked out here she broke up three different marriages. And one of 'em was the Gurwitzes. Little slut."

She looked up at me again. "I hear you busted up the country club pretty good. Really showed your behind." She grinned broadly and gave me the thumbs-up. "You made us all proud, girl."

What do you say to something like that?

"I'll just go see if Mr. Mahoney is ready to see me now," is what I decided on.

"You could do worse for yourself," she called after me.

I set my portfolio on the floor and took a deep breath before knocking on the battered wooden door with the nameplate that said simply W. MAHONEY.

No answer.

I knocked again. "Will?" I called. "It's Keeley Murdock."

Still no answer.

I looked around. The hallway, with its battered green linoleum floor and scarred pine paneling, seemed deserted. There were other doors, and other offices, but no light shone under any of them. It was a far cry from the summer I'd worked at Loving Cup, when the place throbbed with activity, with phones ringing, type-writers clattering, and the constant hum of machinery from the plant just down the hallway through a set of double swinging metal doors.

I tried the doorknob. It turned, so I pushed on it slightly and peeked inside.

Looking at Will Mahoney's office was like taking a trip in the way-back machine, with the clock stopped sometime in the mid-seventies. Bad burnt-orange shag carpet, a huge pseudo-French Provincial wall unit heaped with books and file folders, weird orange and green striped wallpaper, and an even weirder desk made of aluminum saw-horses topped with a hunk of smoked acrylic were offset by a pair of actually good-looking Knoll armchairs covered in black leather facing the desk.

I stepped inside to get a better look. Now that I was inside, I could hear the sound of water running from the other side of a door set behind the desk. A black rolling suitcase was lying open atop a small ugly orange loveseat, and a suit jacket and rumpled white dress shirt had been thrown across the back of the desk chair. The desktop was covered with lingerie. Black satin bras, hot pink push-ups, underwires in nude lace, complicated corsetières, teeny-tiny silken bandeaus, and yes, several unmistakably homely Loving Cup numbers in serviceable white spandex.

I picked up the underwire bra to get a better look. It was unlike any bra I'd ever seen, and since I'm a C-cup myself, always in search of something that doesn't make me look like something from a Wagnerian opera, I've bought, tried, and discarded a lot of bras.

The fabric was a marvel, silky, lacy, stretchy, all at the same time. The straps were slightly wider than most, but the construction seemed all of one piece. I turned the bra inside out to get a better look at the underwire. It wasn't like any wire I'd ever seen before. It was dense, but with the same silky feel as the rest of the bra. There was no label on the bra, but it looked like my size—32 C.

The water was still running in the bathroom. Impulsively I shed my suit jacket and slipped my arms through the straps. I was bending over at the waist, fastening the bra over my blouse, when the bathroom door opened.

I looked up, startled. Will Mahoney came bounding out of the bathroom in a cloud of steam. His damp red hair stood up in spikes, and a trickle of blood ran down his chin from where he'd cut himself shaving. The only thing he was wearing was aftershave—and a threadbare towel knotted loosely at his hip.

"Well, hello!" he said, wiping water droplets from his eyes. "Are you early—or am I just late?"

"Oh!" I managed. Will Mahoney looked good wet. His shoulders and chest were well muscled, dappled with freckles, and flecked with the same curly red hair going to gray. The towel sagged a little, and I glimpsed tight abs and more of that red hair, just before he had the grace to blush a little and readjust things.

I covered my eyes with my hands and whirled around to face in the other direction. "Oh God. I'm sorry. Excuse me. I'll, uh, I'll go outside. Until you're dressed. Or I could come back later." I was inching toward the door, one hand on the doorknob, when I felt his wet hand clamp my elbow.

"Hang on now," he said, chuckling. "You might want to stay a minute."

"No, no," I said hastily, not daring to look behind me. "I'll give you your privacy."

"Well, okay, if you insist," he said, letting go. "But could I have my bra back before you leave?"

Oh shit. I reached my hands back and tried for the hooks, but they weren't like ordinary bra hooks. I fumbled around, clawing blindly for the catch.

"I'm sorry," I repeated. "I had no right. It's just that, I saw it, and it was so different. I mean, it's an underwire, but there's no wire. And the fabric is so luscious, I just couldn't resist . . ."

"You really like it?" He put his hands on my shoulders and turned me around so I was facing him. He seemed to be oblivious to our bizarre situation—he wearing what was essentially a terry loincloth, me fully dressed, but with a bra fastened over my blouse.

Will gave me a cool, appraising look, ran one finger under the bra strap and lifted it gently. "It doesn't bind at the shoulders?"

"Not at all," I said, surprised.

"How's the fit of the cups?" he asked, his gaze shifting toward my chest. I looked away from his chest, tried not to inhale the scent of his aftershave.

"Perfect, actually," I managed. "Well, as best I can tell, over the blouse and all."

He nodded, thoughtful now. "Why don't you just take off the blouse, then?"

Okay, this was too weird. "I'm not that kind of girl."

He frowned. "I don't mean it like that. You can use my bathroom. Come on, Keeley, please? I just want to see how it fits. It's the proto-type for a new line I'm thinking about."

"Don't you have models for that sort of thing?"

He scratched his belly absentmindedly, and the towel slipped a little lower. I whipped my head around and stared at the office door, so he wouldn't see the streaks of color on my cheeks.

"The fitting models are all beanpoles. This bra is a new kind of minimizer. I haven't seen it on a woman with actual normal-sized breasts yet."

He grinned. "Until now."

That did it. I reached down and yanked the bra upward, and over my head.

"No deal," I said, flinging the bra in the direction of his desk. "Now, get dressed, and let's talk about Mulberry Hill."

"Suit yourself," he said. He turned around and walked slowly to-ward the bathroom door. As he walked, he let the towel slither far-ther down his hips. Just before he closed the door, he yanked it off, giving me a flash of his bare white flanks.

25

Will made a big show of locking the bathroom door. As if.

I put my suit jacket on again—buttoning it all the way to the top. Then I looked around the room for a place to dump the pile of bras. His suitcase was the perfect place. Once Will's desktop was reasonably clear, I spread out the floor plans and the sample boards as artistically as possible.

When he emerged from the bathroom again, Will was dressed in a pair of khaki slacks and a blue oxford cloth dress shirt. A wad of toilet tissue was gummed onto his neck.

"How was the trip?" I asked, resolved to get things back on a businesslike footing.

"Long," he said, sitting down at the desk. "My flight was delayed leaving Miami last night, so I didn't get back here until two this morning."

He picked up the boards and shuffled through them. "Looks like you've been pretty busy yourself," he said, running his fingers over the fabric samples. He held up a swatch of damask to the light. "This is nice. What's it for?"

"It's for the sofas in the east parlor," I explained, pointing to a board with a photograph of the sofa style I'd picked out.

"Is this something a woman would like?" he asked, frowning.

"I like it," I offered. "And I think Stephanie Scofield would love it."

He looked up quickly. "What makes you think so?"

"I've seen her home," I said. "And how she dresses. I even know her dog's name."

"Really?" For the first time he looked impressed. "She likes dogs?"

"Loves 'em," I said.

"What else did you find out about her?" he asked, shoving aside all my hard work. "How tall is she? Is she just as beautiful in person?"

I resisted the urge to gag. He really was totally and hopelessly smitten with this woman.

"She's very attractive," I said. "Probably about five-foot-four." And then I couldn't resist. "Although I doubt that's her natural hair color."

"Who cares?" he muttered. "Tell me more."

I racked my brains for details that would be meaningful to him. "Decent figure." It was a gross underexaggeration, which he would soon find out for himself.

"I think the boobs are man-made. But she does have great legs."

He smiled. "I'm a leg man myself."

I thought ruefully of my own God-given C-cups.

"She's a runner," I added. "And I happen to know she spends a lot of time at the gym."

"Great."

"And at the mall," I added spitefully. "Whoever marries Stephanie Scofield is getting a world-class shopper."

"What does she like?" he asked, stroking the striped silk fabric I'd picked out for the dining room drapes.

"Money."

He pushed his chair away from the desk and went back over to the pile of bras on his suitcase. "So she's ambitious. I like that in a woman. I bought this company because I want to build something here in Madison. And I want a partner, somebody who'll be in it with me all the way. I'm not looking for Betty Crocker, you know."

He picked up the underwire bra I'd so recently discarded and handed it back to me. I felt myself blushing again.

"You saw it for yourself, right, Keeley? This bra is the answer. It's the first new thing to happen in the industry since Victoria's Secret brought out the Miracle Bra in the nineties. I think this little number could be what keeps Loving Cup Intimates afloat. You get it, don't you? This bra is something totally new, revolutionary, really. And we're the only one who has it."

Determined to hide my embarrassment, I ran my finger over the lacy cup of the bra. "What the heck is this, anyway? I mean, it's like an underwire, but different—right? It looks and feels like lace, yet it's pliant and strong at the same time."

He nodded enthusiastically. "You got it. Exactly. I've been researching this since before I bought the company. I hired a marketing company, and they organized focus groups. Think of it. Five hundred women, from all over the country, from all walks of life. And they all told us the same thing. The thing they hate most about being a woman is having to wear bras."

"And panty hose," I said. And Kotex, I thought, but that was a discussion for another day.

"Women said they love having breasts," Will continued, his voice rising with enthusiasm. "But they hate accommodating them. They hate how most bras fit. They hate how the straps slip or dig into their shoulders. They hate how they fasten. I mean, can you imagine men wearing pants with a fly that zips in back? That would never happen."

"No, because men wouldn't put up with the kind of crap they subject women to," I said. But he wasn't really listening. He was on a roll.

"And the women in these focus groups hated, I mean, DE-TESTED, underwire bras. That's when I knew what we had to do to save Loving Cup. We had to invent a better, er, mousetrap."

"Just how much money did you spend on this research?" I asked.

He did some scratching around with a pencil and a notepad. "Five target cities, telephone polling, in-depth interviews, follow-ups . . . maybe two hundred thousand dollars, ballpark," Will said.

"I'd've told you the same thing for free," I said, wincing as I felt my own underwire dig into the flesh of my rib cage. "Underwires are the scourge of modern American women."

"Were," Will said, taking the bra and turning it over lovingly in his hands. "But all of that is fixing to change."

He took the bra and snapped it playfully at my knees. "And this little baby is going to do it."

"Where'd you get it?" I asked. "Sri Lanka? Is that what you were doing there?"

"You're not going to believe it," Will said, crossing his arms over his chest and looking unbearably smug.

"Try me."

"Not Sri Lanka. Not Hong Kong. Not New York. Not even Atlanta. This bra came from right here in little old Madison, Georgia."

I snatched the bra away from him. "You're right. I don't believe you. What? The bra fairy just left it out in your cabbage patch last night?"

"I wouldn't call Dr. Soo the bra fairy," Will said. "Maybe a bra genius, though."

"Dr. Sue?"

"Not like Sue the girl. Although technically, she is a girl. It's spelled S-O-O. Like soo, pig. Her full name is Dr. Alberta Soo. She's a Ph.D. kind of doctor. And she lives right here in Madison."

"Never heard of her, and I've lived here all my life," I said.

"Dr. Soo only retired here about a year ago," Will said. "She and her husband live pretty quietly, not too far from here, actually. They have sort of a farmette. Keep a few chickens, some sheep, and they raise a little cotton, of course."

"Of course?"

"Dr. Soo is a retired textile engineering professor. From Georgia Tech. She's the one who designed this new underwire. Been tinkering with it ever since she retired. Once she had a lightweight, ultrathin wire with the proper tensile strength, she sent it to one of her colleagues over at Tech, and they put some grad students to work on it, figuring out possible applications for it. One of the women suggested they try using it in the design of a new kind of bra. And that's where I come in."

I smoothed the bra out over my kneecaps, bent over to look closely at the fabric. "How on earth did you find out about all this?"

"Same way a blind pig finds an acorn," Will said. "Right after I first bought the plant, I was over here one Sunday, moving stuff into my office. She was driving by, saw me standing in the parking lot, and stopped to say howdy."

"And she just happened to mention that she'd invented this wonder wire," I said.

"Yeah, basically," he said, missing my sarcasm. "I mean, here's this old Oriental-looking lady, dressed in baggy khaki shorts with a bandana on her head," Will said. "At first I thought maybe she was looking for a job on the sewing line. Next thing I know, she's telling me she's a retired professor and she's asking if I was gonna shut the place down. Said one of her neighbors used to work here, and he'd told her we were having hard times. She hated to hear it, because it turned out she'd gotten a little research grant from Loving Cup, back when the Gurwitzes owned it, when she was a grad student at Tech."

"And that's when she sold you the magic bra—in return for a bag of gold coins," I said.

"She'd been thinking about approaching somebody in the apparel business. Used to be there were more than a dozen clothing assembly plants in this area alone," Will said. "We're the last ones left. And it just happens that our plant is down the road from her farmette."

"And she hates underwire bras," I said.

"I wouldn't swear to this," Will said, "but from the look of her, I don't believe Dr. Soo wears foundation garments. She probably only weighs eighty pounds soaking wet."

"So where'd you get the bra?" I repeated.

"I signed an exclusive licensing agreement with Tech," Will said. "Then I found a plant in South Carolina that could spin the wire, and another one in Dothan, Alabama, that could weave the actual lace fabric. That bra you're holding is the first one stitched in the plant in Sri Lanka."

I handed the bra back to him. "If it's made in Sri Lanka, what happens to the plant here? How does this help good old American workers in Madison, Georgia?"

"It will," he said stubbornly. "It's going to save this company."

"All by itself?" I asked, looking around at the timeworn office. "Will, I worked out here, years ago, when Loving Cup was in its heyday. Back then a Loving Cup bra was a status symbol. We were running three shifts a day, and we even had a smaller plant over in the south end of the county. A machine operator working here could make seven dollars an hour. That was big money. But things have changed. The company didn't keep up. The bras you're making now, they're a joke. How are you going to turn all that around—and just like that—overnight?"

"We're going to become a different company," Will said, leaning forward, his eyes glowing with intensity. "Same name, but a whole different product. We'll be smaller, leaner, meaner."

"Smaller than now? How is that possible? This place is a ghost town."

"That's not how I mean small," Will said. "We're going to retool the plant. Completely. We've been making cotton garments all these years. Now we'll switch to MMF."

"MMF?"

"Man-made fabrics. We'll produce and cut the fabric here, but mostly the bras will be stitched overseas."

He saw the unhappy set of my face.

"It's a fact of life, Keeley. We can't compete in the marketplace with a garment made totally here in Madison. But what we can do is this—we can weave the lace here in the States, and we can do the cutting here. Most of the assembly is done in Sri Lanka—but the bras will be sent back here for packaging and shipping. We'll do enough work here to earn a 'Made in USA' label, and we'll get the plant back up and running—and we'll be making a damn good product."

"It sounds like you've got everything all figured out," I admitted.

"Not everything," he said. "Not by a long shot. I've gotta get the financing for the new machinery we'll need, and I'm hoping we'll get some tax incentives from the state to help with that. We'll have to retrain folks for new jobs, and yeah, the ones who can't or won't adapt, those people will be out of luck. And then there's you."

"Me?"

"I need you," Will said. "Need you to get the house rolling. I can't keep sleeping here in the office. I'm getting a crick in my back from the sofa, and Miss Nancy looks at me funny when she comes in every morning. I don't think she approves of me living here."

"She doesn't approve of you, period," I informed him. "She thinks you've got some uppity ideas."

"Uppity." He laughed.

"But if you keep this place running, and her working, you'll have her undying support. She'll take a bullet for you, if she's on your side."

"What about you? Are you on my side? How soon can you get the house livable?"

"You said Christmas," I pointed out.

"I need to be in there sooner," he said. "The old pump house will be ready for me to move in by Friday, sort of as a guest house, you know? They're putting the finishing touches on the roof today, and we'll have wiring and a bathroom by then too. For furniture, I just need the basics. How soon can you get me a bed and a table and some chairs? And some lamps. And a television," he added. "So I can watch the Braves games at night."

"You don't have any furniture of your own?" I asked. "Nothing? Have you been living in that car of yours?"

He sighed. "I had a lady friend. She got a promotion and moved to San Francisco, and that's when we parted company—by mutual agreement. She kept all the furniture and stuff, since I was moving here anyway, and didn't have a house lined up. I kept the Caddy. Now, is that enough information? How about it? How soon can I move in?"

"The end of the week? It won't be anything fancy. I guess I can get a mattress and box spring and bedding delivered by Friday. And I can pull some odd chairs and a table and dresser from our storage locker, to fill in until the real stuff arrives."

"Great," he said. "You're doing great." He gestured at the drawings and fabric samples. "Stephanie's gonna love this. I just know it."

"We'll see," I said, gathering up my stuff. "The rest is up to you. Your big night is Wednesday, right?"

He yawned. "Right. If I can stay awake that long."

26

Gloria wrinkled her nose as I slathered lotion on my face, neck, arms, and legs.

"What is that hideous smell?" she cried. "Surely you're not going to see a client smelling like that."

"It's the latest thing," I said, handing her the tube so she could see. "Deep Woods Off!"

"I take it you're headed out to Mulberry Hill?" she asked, looking up from the auction catalog she'd been marking up.

"Yup. I'm meeting the furniture truck over there in half an hour. With all the rain we've been having, those woods are swarming with skeeters."

I crossed my fingers. "The HVAC guys got the new heat and air unit installed in the pump house yesterday, and the painters were supposed to have finished up last night, and with any luck, the floors will be dry too."

"What did you decide to do about the floors?" Gloria asked.

"I had the old brick pressure washed, and they cleaned up really nice. Just slicked 'em up with a matte-finish polyester."

"Good." She nodded her approval. "What's your client think about what you've done so far? Is he aware of the miracles you've worked on his behalf?"

"Absolutely not," I said. "He's livid that we're three days behind schedule. He wanted to move in on Friday, but the rain delayed everything. Now here it is Monday, and he's been calling me every few hours for updates. Will just takes it for granted that stuff happens like this all the time. He has no idea that it's not the normal procedure to take a nasty old brick pump house and turn it into an adorable guest house in under a week."

"Men," Gloria said.

"Yeah, but in his defense, he's been incredibly busy. He's got some new miracle bra that he's working on, and it's going to take totally re-tooling the plant to get it into production. And then there's Stephanie."

"His dream date," Gloria said dryly.

"We'll see," I said. "I know they had their first date last week, and I haven't had the nerve to ask Will how it went."

"She's crazy if she doesn't jump all over him like a tick on a dog," Gloria said. She smoothed her hair behind one ear. "That Will is just as yummy as they come. Don't you just want to lick him all over?"

"Gloria!" I said, shocked. "Don't be vulgar."

"I speak the truth," she said, winking. "And you know it."

"He's my client, not my john," I said. "Anyway, he has red hair. And freckles. Furthermore, I am officially done with men."

"Right . . ." she drawled.

"I mean it. I'm going to be like you, Glo. Strong, independent, a woman of substance . . ."

"You mean a shriveled up old maid with a healthy bank account? No. I absolutely forbid it. Anyway, what makes you think I'm done with men?"

"Aren't you?" I looked at my aunt carefully. "Are you seeing somebody?"

"None of your beeswax," she said tartly, going back to her catalog. "All I'm saying is, don't judge all men by A. J. Jernigan. And don't overlook the obvious."

"It's not obvious to me," I fired back, gathering up a huge tote bag of stuff I was taking out to Mulberry Hill for the installation. I had my tool kit, with an electric screwdriver, tack hammer, pliers, scissors, measuring tape and yardstick, level, stud finder, and assorted nails, tacks, and other picture-hanging doodads. Plus some hand-sanitizing wipes, paper goods, aspirin, cleaning supplies, a huge can of bug spray, and a bottle of Scotch. Will struck me as a Scotch drinker. Not that I am. Can't stand the stuff.

I'd also packed a cooler with several bottles of water, cheese and crackers, some peaches, a large plastic bag of green seedless grapes, and a bottle of Chardonnay.

"Looks like you're packing for an expedition to Malaysia," Gloria observed.

"I don't want to have to come all the way back into town if I forget anything," I said, slinging the tote over my shoulder. "And you do realize, I'm totally furnishing this place? Will claims not to have any belongings besides his clothes and a few books that he wants to move in with. So that means the works. Dishes, pots and pans, linens, silverware. You should see the trunk of the Volvo. I had to rig it closed with a bungee cord."

"We're billing for all this time, right?" Gloria asked.

"Absolutely. Hourly, plus cost-plus for all the stuff I had to buy. We're going to have a very nice payday this month."

"Good thing," Gloria said. "Our billings are way behind for the year."

"Still? I thought things were picking back up again. A.J. swore he'd tell his daddy and brother to quit trying to drive us out of business."

"We did get the carpet in the bank laid and paid for," Gloria said, frowning. "But it's just slow. Very slow. And it's nothing I can put my finger on."

I sighed. "I can. It's me. People in this town still can't get over the fact that I called off the wedding. And it's so damn unfair. It's not my fault A. J. Jernigan couldn't keep it in his pants."

Gloria got up and walked me to the door. "I'll tell you a little secret. That's how all Jernigan men are. Every damn one of 'em."

My eyes widened. "What's that supposed to mean? You don't mean A.J.'s daddy. I don't believe it. The way people in this town talk? I would have heard something like that. Anyway, GiGi wouldn't put up with Big Drew's foolin' around on her."

"I mean all of 'em," Gloria said firmly. "I kept my mouth shut before, since you were marrying into the family. I really thought maybe A.J. was different. But he's a hound just like all the rest of 'em. A.J.'s granddaddy, Chub? Back in the sixties, when this was still a dry county, there was a place, a roadhouse out there off of 441. It didn't have an official name, everybody just called it BeBo's. I was just a little kid, but my mama said nobody nice would ever step foot in BeBo's. It was where the locals went to drink and dance and whore around. And guess who owned it? Chub Jernigan. And the woman who ran it, her name was Cherie. She was Chub's mistress. Big Drew wasn't any better. You know Angela Baker, that ditzy brunette who used to work the drive-up window at the bank? How do you reckon somebody with only an eighth-grade education kept a job at a bank?"

"Angela Baker used to always give me green lollipops when I went with Daddy to make the dealership's bank deposit," I said. "Are you saying she was screwing around with Drew?"

"Yes ma'am, and she was just the first in a long line. GiGi knew about it too. She only made Big Drew fire Angela after he tried to promote her to assistant manager."

"You're making all of this up," I accused her. "I've lived in Madison my whole life, and I never even heard a whisper about a place like BeBo's. Or about Chub Jernigan. He was on the County Commission, Glo. And so was Big Drew too. And A.J.'s granddaddy was a vestryman at Church of the Advent. There's a stained-glass window in his honor. I've seen it a hundred times."

Gloria gave me a sad smile. "It's not something that gets talked about a lot in polite society, but if you don't believe me, ask your daddy. He eats breakfast every morning of the year, practically, over there with Big Drew and all the rest of the men at Ye Olde Colonial. I bet he knows a lot worse stuff about the Jernigans than I do. Not that he'd ever say a word to you about it."

I felt tears rising in my eyes. It was one thing to catch your fiancé screwing your best friend, but this was too much. Before the wedding debacle, I really liked A.J.'s family. GiGi had been a dream client. She'd treated me like a real daughter. After my first "official" date with A.J., she'd taken me out to lunch at the club and beamed at me across the table. "I couldn't be happier about you two," she'd said then. "A daughter, finally, after all these years."

And Big Drew was funny and sweet and thoughtful. He'd given me a pair of diamond earrings as an engagement gift, and told me they'd been made out of a pair of Chub's old cuff links. The thought made me shudder. I bit my lip and brushed away a tear.

"I'm sorry, honey," Gloria said, giving me a hug. "I probably shouldn't have told you that stuff. It all happened a long time ago. But I figured you'd probably hear about it sooner or later. And it just makes me so damn mad that the Jernigans are still taking this wedding stuff out on us and our business."

"It's okay," I said, pulling in a deep breath. "You were right to tell me. I'm a big girl. It just came as a shock, that's all."

"Thank God you didn't marry into that bunch, after all," Gloria said briskly. "I'm not about to let them drive us out of business. Now, I don't want you worrying about this. I'm sorry I even brought it up. Everything will be fine. This Mulberry Hill job's gonna put us on the map. You wait and see."

The shop's front door opened, and Austin popped his head inside. "Hellooo," he sang out. "Keeley, are you ready to roll yet? Janey's minding the store over at my place, but she says she can only stay till five-thirty 'cuz her Wal-Mart shift starts at six. So let's get going. I cannot *wait* to see what you've done with that old pump house."

Gloria raised one eyebrow. "You've roped Austin into this?"

Austin stepped inside the shop. He was dressed in a pair of immaculate white zip-front coveralls, and he had a white canvas painter's cap perched backward on his nearly bald head. Red Converse high tops finished off the outfit, which he'd accessorized with a red bandana tied jauntily at his throat.

"I roped myself in, Glo," he said. "I'm Keeley's junior apprentice trainee for the day. She's going to teach me all the tricks of your trade. And I am absolutely aquiver with anticipation."

"I told him," I said. "It's dirty, brutal, agonizingly painstakingly awful work. And that's just for the window treatments. But he wouldn't be talked out of it. And I could actually use his help, if we're going to get everything done in one day."

Gloria tsk-tsked. "I'd do it myself, if I could. But I promised to take some wallpaper books and flooring samples over to Mozella this afternoon."

"Mozella? She's going to do the beauty parlor over again?"

"I know," Gloria said, shaking her head. "It's only been a year since we redid the shampoo room and the bathroom. It's fine just like it is. I think maybe she's just feeling sorry for us and is giving us make-work. But if she wants to spend her husband's money, it's not my business to tell her not to."

"Y'all," Austin said, tapping his foot impatiently. "Can you talk this girl chit-chat later? I can hear that pump house just crying out for my artistic license."

"Go on," Gloria said, waving us out the door. "Make magic. And don't forget to take pictures."

The shoulder of the highway at the entrance to Mulberry Hill was lined with a dozen or so battered pickup trucks and cargo vans. New asphalt road had been paved over the old mud road, and huge piles of fresh-cut timber and underbrush were stacked on either side of the shiny black pavement. The shaggy old boxwoods had been closely clipped, and a couple of Mexican workers were putting the finishing touches on whitewashed brick pillars marking the entry to the new drive.

"So this is it," Austin said, craning his neck to see down the road ahead. "I've been by this spot millions of times, and I never dreamed there was a mansion back in here."

"This was a kind of lovers' lane when I was in high school," I said. "But you couldn't drive back in very far, because they had it chained off. Don't expect too much now. There's still a lot of work to be done to the big house."

He squeezed his eyes shut. "Tell me when we're there. I don't want to spoil the surprise."

The Volvo breezed down the nice level road, and I was grateful for all the clearing the landscape designer and his crew had accomplished. I made the sharp turn, the meadow came into view, and I breathed a sigh of relief. Waves of Queen Anne's lace; orange daylilies; scarlet, white and purple cosmos; black-eyed Susans; and other wildflowers I couldn't name spread out before me. The sides of the meadow had been fenced with a simple white fence, and on the right side of the field, a sturdy brown mule munched on a bale of hay that was stacked under one of the water oaks.

"Very nice," I murmured.

"What?" Austin demanded. "Are we there yet?"

"Not yet," I said. "I'm just admiring the landscape. Thank goodness Will had the sense to let it mostly alone."

He raised the fingers of one hand and peeked out. "Oh heaven!" he exclaimed. "Do you know what kind of arrangements I can make with all these little goodies?"

At the end of the meadow the green lawn had been resodded, rolled, and manicured to golf course perfection. A new boxwood hedge marked the transition from meadow to lawn, and the front of the house loomed ahead, its façade covered with a network of bright yellow scaffolding, where workers scraped away at the remains of the old paint.

"That's it!" Austin said, his voice reverent. "Mulberry Hill. It's divine, Keeley."

"Not yet," I said, smiling to myself. "But it will be."

As we got closer to the house, another cluster of cars parked around to the side came into view. More trucks and vans, and a big old yellow Cadillac.

27

Austin jumped out of the Volvo before I'd even turned off the motor. He craned his neck and shaded his eyes with his hand to look up at the worker who was reframing the old balcony over the front portico.

"Divine," he said. "Like out of a Hollywood movie. I keep expecting Scarlett O'Hara to come running out the door in a hoopskirt. It's like Tara or something."

Will strolled up just in time to hear Austin's gushing.

"Better," he said, sticking out his hand to shake Austin's. "The O'Haras didn't have Glorious Interiors on the payroll."

"Austin," I said, setting my tote bag on the ground. "This is our client, Will Mahoney. He suffers from flights of fancy and delusions of grandeur. But he's loaded, so we try to overlook his lesser qualities. Will, this is Austin LeFleur. Austin is the most talented floral designer in Georgia, and he's helping me out with the installation today."

"Oh, Keeley," Austin said. "Stop. You're embarrassing me. I'm just a flower fluffer, that's all."

Will and Austin shook hands and checked each other out. I glanced around the construction site. "Hasn't the truck gotten here yet?"

"Your driver called a little while ago," Will said, gesturing to the cell phone clipped to his belt. "He's running about thirty minutes late."

"The story of my life," I muttered. I hefted the tote bag back onto my shoulder. "Never mind. Let's take a look at the pump house. Have you checked it out yet?"

"Waiting on you," Will said. He turned toward the Volvo. "Does all this get taken inside?"

"Every bit of it," I said. "Plus what's on the truck."

The three of us loaded ourselves down with boxes and bags, and we picked our way through piles of bricks, sand, and lumber, around to the back of the property.

The steady summertime rain had subsided just long enough to make the air as hot and sticky as a wet wool blanket, and a cloud of mosquitoes hovered around my face. My shirt was drenched by the time we made it to the pump house, and my face, where I'd missed applying the bug repellent, stung from numerous mosquito bites.

"Wow," I said, getting my first look at the site in a week. "Unbelievable."

The thick bramble of kudzu, wisteria, and poison ivy that had previously engulfed both the brick structure and the ground around it had been hacked away. A rustic patio of old brick skirted the little house, and a new tin roof gleamed in the sunlight. Will's masons had built a new chimney of stacked rock taken from a creek on the property. Windows that had last week been broken and caked with grime had been stripped, reglazed, and painted, their frames a deep green-black to match the paint on the arched front door. A pair of ancient black cast-iron pots stood on either side of the door, planted with fragrant topiaries of rosemary.

"The pots?" I asked, turning to Will, who was watching me with barely suppressed anticipation.

"Kent Richardson, the landscape designer, found 'em out in one of the sheds," Will said. "He says they were old boiling pots, used to do laundry. He planted them up and put them here. That's okay, isn't it?"

"They're great. The perfect touch."

I tucked a strand of hair behind my ear and shifted my load of gear and pushed the door open. Cool air floated out to greet us.

"Heaven," I said, pushing the door wider to let Austin and Will inside. "If nothing else, you've got air conditioning." I pulled my shirt away from my body to let the air cool me down.

"And fresh paint," Austin said, inhaling deeply. "There's nothing like the smell of fresh paint."

Will felt on the wall for a light switch, and three old black pendant fixtures that had come out of a torn-down Atlanta saloon made the dim room come alive. He set the boxes down against the wall and walked around.

The pump house had originally been nothing more than a one-room brick hut, twelve feet wide by twenty feet long. With almost no time for an extensive remodeling, I'd come up with a plan to divide the long, high-ceilinged room into two areas. The front half would be Will's living and dining areas, with a new double-sided stacked rock fireplace the focal point of the seating area, and the dividing wall between the living area and the only bedroom. We'd fitted a tiny galley kitchen in the left corner of the living area, and behind it, on the other side of the heart-pine dividing wall, was the bathroom and the bedroom. Because the area was so small, only two hundred and forty square feet, and dark, with only four smallish windows, we'd whitewashed the exposed brick walls, but left the brick floors their natural color. After the main house was ready, the pump house would be used as a guest house.

"Not bad," Will said, looking up at the exposed heart-pine ceiling beams. He bent down and ran his hands over the slate hearth by the fireplace. "Not bad at all."

I gave him a sharp look. "Not bad? It's a friggin' miracle. Your foreman should get some kind of combat pay and performance bonus for pulling this off this quickly."

"He has," Will said, straightening up and dusting his hands on the seat of his worn blue jeans. "Let's see how the new bathroom looks."

Even the new door to the sleeping area was old—a weathered cedar number we'd discovered in another of the sheds on the property. Cleaned up and fitted with a heavy black iron doorknob, it swung easily on its new hinges.

Sunlight filtered into the bedroom from the windows near the roofline, and the polished brick floors gleamed with a dull sheen. The three of us stepped inside the room. Will crossed over to another of the cedar doors set into the heart-pine dividing wall and opened it. We'd used more of the heart-pine boards for the bathroom walls.

The room was tiny, but efficient. One of the carpenters had built a primitive heart-pine vanity, with a hammered copper sink set into it. There was a commode, and a shower stall with glass block walls.

"Everything a guy could need," Will said approvingly. He gave me an appreciative thump on the back. "You done good, Keeley."

I nodded my own approval. "I just designed it, Will. Your guys did the work. And even three days past your impossible deadline, they did a fantastic job."

"I could move right in," Austin said.

"Me first," Will said.

"Right. I guess we'll go ahead and start unpacking the kitchen stuff while we wait on the truck. And Austin, if you'll find a stepladder, you could start hanging the drapery rods."

"Draperies?" Will frowned. "I thought this was gonna be pretty basic out here. Why do I need something as fancy as drapes?"

"Not really drapes," I reassured him. "Just a little something for privacy. And to keep the morning sun out of your eyes. Wait until you see. I promise, you'll like them."

While Austin got started on the rods, I moved the boxes and bags of cooking equipment into place. With only three compact cabinets and three drawers, it didn't take long to set everything up.

Will lounged against the wall near the refrigerator, watching me work. When I'd put the last fork and spoon away, he clapped his hands.

"Great. Want to see how the work's coming on the big house?"

I glanced over at Austin, who was just screwing one of the black wrought-iron rod holders into the wall over one of the living room windows. "Go ahead," he called out. "I've got this covered."

The sounds of nail guns and power saws competed with tinny salsa music from a boombox perched on the back of a pickup truck and grew louder as we approached the back of the house. I was amazed at the progress here too. Concrete footings had been poured for the new wing, plywood subfloors had been laid, and yellow pine framing outlined the skeleton of the walls and the high pitched roof. Half a dozen men in hard hats clambered over the two-story addition.

"Where did you get these guys?" I asked.

Will grinned. "They're all laid-off Loving Cup plant workers. Miss Nancy's idea. She said, since I was, quote 'spending so GD much money on my mansion, why didn't I give some of the GD guys a chance to earn a decent paycheck.' She called 'em all up and told 'em to get their GD asses out here. Said if they wanted to show me how hard they could work, this would be the way to do it."

"That sounds exactly like Miss Nancy," I said.

"Come around to the front," Will said, taking my elbow to guide me through a labyrinth of scaffolding. "Careful. The guys are working so hard and so fast, trying to make up time lost because of the rain, they forget to look to see if anybody's down below."

A chunk of two-by-four went whizzing by my head, and I jumped to get out of the way. "GD! I see what you mean."

At the front of the house I noticed for the first time that a newly laid set of brick steps flowed gracefully up to the porch, where the old rotted-out floorboards had been ripped out. New concrete-block underpinnings had been laid, and a mason was lying on his back, applying brick to the concrete veneer. Sturdy new framing was in place, and now the porch extended all the way around to the east and west sides of the house. Two men were busy nailing new floorboards to the support beams.

Will gestured toward the doorway. "That got here yesterday. The guys hung it just before you arrived."

I'd bought the front door online, from an architectural salvage yard in Jackson, Mississippi. It was a nine-foot-tall solid cypress door that had come out of an old convent in Louisiana, and it even had the original ornate brass hinges and doorknobs.

Electricians were busy in the front parlors, snaking rolls of conduit through small holes in the plaster walls. We walked down the center hallway, and Will opened the door that had formerly opened into nothing. Now though, sunlight flooded the hallway, and we stepped out into the newly framed addition.

"Hey, Mr. Mahoney," one of the carpenters called down.

Will looked up and waved. "Good work, Jerry. Keep it up and we'll be roofing by the beginning of the month."

"You're dreaming," I said. But we both knew I was impressed. He started climbing the temporary stairs to the second floor, and I followed behind.

"Speaking of deadlines," I said, "how did your date go last week?"

Will reached the top step and stepped out onto the plywood planking for the second floor. He walked over to the outer wall and looked through one of the window openings. "Hmm?"

"Your date? With the future mistress of Mulberry Hill?"

"You mean Stephanie?" He didn't turn around. "Fine. Great. Fantastic."

I stood beside him and looked out the window. From here you could see the shiny new roof of the pump house, and a couple of other outbuildings that had been reroofed. Everything else was a carpet of green.

"Is she everything you expected?" I asked, digging for details.

"Better," he said.

He was a virtual font of information. I decided to try another line of questioning.

"What did you two talk about? Was it awkward, like a blind date?"

"Not really," he said, shrugging. "We talked about what people usually talk about. Her work. Mine. What we like to do in our spare time. What we're reading. What we like to eat and drink. Like that."

"Let me guess," I said. "Stephanie drinks cosmopolitans."

He turned to look at me and frowned. "Is that some kind of put-down? Anyway, how'd you know?"

"I worked as a cocktail waitress at the country club one summer after graduation," I said. "Stephanie just looks like a cosmo drinker. Girly, kind of."

"And what do you think I like to drink?"

"Easy," I said. "Single malt Scotch. And Sam Adams beer."

He raised an eyebrow in surprise. "How'd you do that?"

"The Scotch was just a good guess," I admitted. "But I was with you when you bought Sam Adams. Remember?"

He looked puzzled. "No. When was that?"

"At the Minit Mart. The night we came out here and you showed me the house? And afterward, you stopped at the Minit Mart for a beer . . ." I felt my face start to burn at the memory of that night, and my discomfort had nothing to do with the hot Georgia sun beating down on our heads. "And we ran into Paige Plummer. She was going into the store just as you were getting into the car . . ."

He scratched his beard and looked over at me, all sweetness and innocence now. "Oh, that night. I remember some of it. I remember stopping at the Minit Mart. And I remember that Paige chick. Oh yeah. I remember kissing you. That was nice. Very nice."

I turned my back toward him, hoping he wouldn't see my flaming red cheeks. "But I'm damned if I remember the Sam Adams beer," he said, chuckling.

28

A faint breeze ruffled the leaves on the limb of an oak tree that stretched toward the house, and I felt my sweat-dampened scalp tingle from the cool.

"Are you seeing her again?" I asked.

"Who, Paige? Why would I want to see her again?" He was being deliberately obtuse.

"I meant Stephanie, of course. Are you going out again?"

"Oh yeah. As a matter of fact, she's coming out here for dinner Friday night."

"Here? Isn't that rushing things a little?"

"I'm not the big bad wolf. Her virtue won't be under assault."

"That's not what I meant, and you know it. What I mean is, it's already Monday. We don't even have your furniture moved in. The paint's just barely dry."

"You'll take care of all that," Will said, patting my shoulder. "It'll be great. And Stephanie's dying to see the place. I took pictures to dinner, to show her. She's a big history buff. Used to come over here for the Christmas Tour of Homes all the time."

"You're hardly tour ready," I snapped, aggravated for reasons I couldn't quite understand. "And do you even know how to cook?"

"I can grill a steak and toss a salad," he assured me. "And I'm great at uncorking wine."

"Better learn how to mix a cosmopolitan," I said.

Just then we heard the sound of tires on the drive, and a horn honking.

"That better be the truck with your furniture," I told him, turning to go down the stairs. "Otherwise you'll be dining off a card table."

Austin already had the truck's cargo doors open and was boosting himself inside by the time we made it out to the driveway.

Manny Ortiz, the driver who does a lot of the hauling and heavy lifting for Glorious Interiors, winced when he saw me. "Hey, Keeley," he called, shoving his red and black Georgia Bulldogs cap to the back of his head. "Sorry to be late. We had another delivery to finish up. And I gotta get right back too. We got two whole-house moves scheduled, and I'm short a guy."

"It's all right," I told him, peering inside the truck, which was jammed with furniture and boxes. "Is this everything?"

He handed me a clipboard with the list I'd faxed over to him. "Everything you asked for. Your aunt had me pick up some pictures from the framer on the way over. So that should do it."

Will stood beside me and poked his own head inside the truck. He looked dubious. "Is all this stuff gonna fit in my little ol' pump house?"

"Easily," I said. "How's your back?"

He held a hand to his spine and grimaced. "Achin' already."

I stepped aside and gestured toward the tailgate. "You're the one with the impossible deadlines. I'd suggest you start with the rugs first. Let's get them laid down, then bring in the bedroom stuff, and the living room sofa last."

Manny grabbed the end of a rolled-up Oriental rug wrapped in brown paper, and he and Will hoisted it onto their shoulders and headed for the pump house. I took three smaller throw rugs, plus a runner, and handed them to Austin, and for myself, grabbed up the boxful of newly framed art, and a carton I knew contained bed linens.

An hour later we'd emptied out the truck and filled up the pump house. Will leaned against the bedroom doorway and watched with detachment as Austin and I tried to set up his bedstead.

Austin stood the heavily carved mahogany headboard upright, and I had the equally heavy and ornate footboard, and was trying to maneuver one of the side rails into place. After two tries, I glared at Will.

"You wanna give us a hand here?"

"And get in the way of bona-fide professional decorators? I wouldn't dream of interfering."

"Get your ass over here," I ordered, "unless you want to sleep on the brick floor your first night here."

After that the setting-up process went a little smoother. The two men got the bed set up, and under my direction even managed to get the box spring and mattress in place with amazing speed and efficiency.

While they moved the dresser and nightstands into place, I made up the bed with mattress pad, sheets, a thick ecru-colored matelasse bedspread, four down pillows, and a brown and black Amish log cabin quilt folded neatly by the footboard.

"That's a wonderful look," Austin said, running his hand over one of the carved pineapple bedposts. "How old is this bed?"

"Not as old as it looks," I admitted. "It's a really good reproduction of a Dutch-Indian planter's bed. It retails for about eleven thousand dollars, but I picked it up at a sample sale at ADAC for not even a quarter of that 'cause it had a scratch on the footboard. Which I just rubbed out with some Old English scratch cover."

"It looks okay. I just hope the mattress isn't an antique," Will said, slapping his hand up and down on it.

"Brand-new, custom-made, top of the line," I said pertly, setting a black and gold tole lamp on one of the bedside tables.

From the bedroom we moved into the living room, while I supervised as the men unrolled a large sisal rug onto the brick floor and then positioned the squashy sofa covered in a tobacco-colored chenille in front of the fireplace, flanked on either side by two mismatched leather club chairs, with a worn antique Sarouk rug between them.

"Now these I like," Will said, sinking down into one of the chairs and rubbing the armrest appreciatively. "These'll do."

"I'm glad you think so," I retorted. "Wait till you see what I bill you for them. They're the real thing, you know. I picked them up at the flea market at Cligancourt."

"Is that around here?" Will asked, furrowing his brow at the sound of the unfamiliar name.

"Cligancourt is in France, right, Keeley?" Austin said. He plopped himself down in the other chair and jiggled up and down on the cushion. "How old?"

"Twenties, probably," I said. "They're getting harder and harder to find."

"Are they supposed to be all scratched up like this?" Will asked. "Not that I mind. I was just wondering if that's how they're supposed to look."

"It's called patina," I said. "And people pay a lot of money to get this beat-up scratched-up look. The new hides just don't have the same beautiful sheen as these old ones."

"Whatever you say," Will said, groaning as he got up. "I hope we're done with the heavy lifting for the day. I've got to check on the progress on the house, then get over to the office for a conference call by four. Anything else you need me for?"

"Not for now," I said.

"I'll check back in with you before I leave for the plant," Will promised.

While Will was gone, I set Austin to the task of hanging the drapes on the rods he'd already installed, and I placed the framed art on the floor, playing with different arrangements of them.

"He's awful cute, Keeley," Austin said, watching Will through the window.

"Will? Austin, you're as bad as Gloria. She's all ga-ga about him too. I just don't see it myself."

"Then you're not looking close enough," Austin said. "Come on, Keeley, what's not to like? He's tall, taller than you, which not many men are. He's got fabulous abs, I saw 'em when he was moving that sofa. He's smart, and he's rich. He's hitting on all the straight-girl cylinders."

"Not mine," I said firmly. "He's not awful. He's just not my idea of wonderful, that's all. Anyway, Will is in love with another woman—which is the whole point of this ridiculous, if profitable, exercise. I'm decorating this place so she'll love him right back."

"And who is your idea of wonderful?" Austin demanded, lifting up the first panel of the heavy canvas drapes and slotting the iron drape rod through the grommets. "A. J. Jernigan? All right, he's also rich and fabulous-looking, but we both know he's a total and complete shit when it comes to women."

"If you don't mind, I'd rather not talk about A.J.," I said, taking the first picture and positioning it in the middle of the wall closest to the fireplace. I pounded the tack harder than was strictly necessary, which bent it flat against the wall.

"Why not? Don't tell me you're still pining away for him?"

"I'm not," I said sharply. "Can we just drop it, please?"

"All right," he said, with an exaggerated sigh. "But will you answer me one question, and be honest?"

"I'm always honest," I said, tapping the next tack a little more gently.

"Hmp," Austin said.

"It's about this furniture," he said, turning from the window and gesturing at the room below. "All this stuff. You just happened to have it all in your storage bin? And it's all fabulous?"

"I have good taste," I said, frowning. "And when I see a good bargain, I buy it and stockpile it. Gloria and I keep two huge storage bins full to overflowing."

"I don't think so," Austin said, pursing his lips. "I think this was all stuff you bought for one particular client: the future Mrs. A. J. Jernigan. Am I right?"

I hung the first picture and straightened it, and with my ruler, marked off the spot for the next picture, and hammered in another tack. Damn. Another one flattened. I really needed to rework my hammering technique.

"You bought all this stuff for you and A.J., didn't you?" Austin asked. "The bed, the dresser, this sofa, those leather chairs. All for your little honeymoon house."

"You're starting to get on my nerves," I warned, reaching into my jeans pocket for another tack. "You may get fired if you don't start minding your own business."

"I was never hired in the first place," Austin said, climbing down from the ladder. He put his hands on his hips and stuck out his tongue at me. "I'm working for free. So you can't fire me."

"Very mature. I could just ignore you," I said. He handed me the next picture.

"Answer the question."

"Yes," I said. "Yes, I bought all this stuff for a house we hadn't even bought yet. Yes, I had everything all planned out. Our beautiful new life together. That bed, the sofa and chairs, everything. I have a whole sketchbook of designs, floor plans, fabric samples. There's a dining room table still on hold at Powers and Sons in Savannah, and a break-front sitting in the storage vault, and a bunch of other stuff I can't bear to get rid of. So yes, to answer your question, this was all stuff that was going in my first house as a married lady. Only my design had one serious flaw. The bridegroom didn't work out. So I didn't get married. Now I have a client who needed furnishings in a hurry. I furnished the furnishings. That's what I do for a living, in case you haven't noticed. There is no hidden agenda, no sublimated longings for another man. Just a simple business transaction. Got that?"

Austin took the hammer away from me and took a tack from my pocket. "I'll nail. You space. You suck at nailing. You suck at lying too."

29

"**Next time** I need help with an installation, I'll hire Manny," I told Austin. But I stepped back, took a look at the wall arrangement, and penciled in the next tack mark.

Will came breezing through the front door and stopped dead in his tracks.

"Wow," he said, walking slowly back and forth. "This is awesome, guys. It really is. Better than I would have ever hoped for."

He rubbed the canvas drapes between his fingers. "Cool. You were right. I like 'em. But I never saw anything like 'em before."

"Desperation is the mother of invention, or something like that," I admitted. "There was no time to find fabric or get anything sewn at our workroom, so I came up with this idea. These are nothing more than painter's drop cloths. I bought the biggest ones they had, went to Farmer's Hardware and bought industrial-sized metal grommets, and banged 'em in with a grommet-setter. Not too shabby, if I do say so myself."

Now Will stopped in front of the art we were hanging, stared and stared again.

"Blueprints? For bras? Where the hell did you get this stuff, Keeley?"

"From the plant." I straightened one of the drawings. It was actually a specification sketch for an early Loving Cup number called The Enhancer. From the look of the thing, I thought it should have been renamed The Enforcer. "You didn't have anything to hang on the walls, so I decided to frame things that would have some meaning for you. Miss Nancy let me go through all the old files and pick out stuff I thought would work."

Will picked up another frame. This one was a yellowing color magazine ad for Loving Cup brassieres—"We Hold You and Mold You Like Mother's Own," was the slogan that year. It had run in the September 1952 issue of *Harper's Bazaar*. A model who looked a lot like Suzy Parker was pictured from the torso up, wearing a Loving Cup bra with bullet-shaped cups and enough strapping and hooks to harness a team of Clydesdales.

He laughed. "This is great. I mean it. What else have you got here?"

"More of the bra sketches, a couple more advertisements, and some old stock certificates for Loving Cup Intimates. I love the scroll-work and detailing on old documents like these. But these are my favorites," I told him, showing him a series of three panoramic black and white photos.

"This one here," I said, pointing to one showing a line of dour-faced women sitting at sewing machines, "is the swing shift. It was taken in 1945. There's a handwritten note on the back that says they were sewing garments with specially made fabric loops. Because it was a war year, they couldn't get metal hooks and eyelets, or even rubber for elastic, so they had to come up with all kinds of design substitutes."

"I'd like to see one of those old designs," Will said, picking the photo up to get a closer look. "I've been looking through the company archives myself, when I get time. It's really fascinating how innovative the designers got over the years."

Austin leaned over my shoulder and pointed at the next photo. "A baseball team? There was a Loving Cup baseball team?" The picture did indeed show what looked like a 1950s-era baseball team, all the members wearing shirts that proclaimed them "The Bombers."

"I didn't know we had a team," Will said, "but I wouldn't be surprised. Every textile mill in the South had all kinds of sports teams. They had regular leagues, and competition was killer. For a small town, a winning mill team was a tremendous point of pride. The whole town would turn out for big games."

"Miss Nancy found one of these old black and white striped baseball jerseys," I told Will. "It's being framed too, but it takes longer because my framer had to build a special shadow box for it."

"I love this one," Austin said, tapping the third photo. It showed a lineup of young girls in ball gowns, each with carefully teased bouffant hairdos, elbow-length white gloves, each holding huge rose bouquets. The girl in the middle, who had a blond upsweep, had a tiny tiara balanced on her head, and a sash proclaiming her "Miss Loving Cup, 1968."

"The bra queen!" Austin exclaimed. "It's my absolute favorite."

"I like this one too," I said. I tapped my finger on the face of the girl on the far end. She was a little taller than the others, but with a regal bearing that was unmistakable, and a thousand-watt smile. "That's Glo."

"Your Aunt Gloria?" Will asked. "Let me see that thing."

He took the photo and studied it carefully. "She was a stunner. Was then. Is now. How come she wasn't named the bra queen?"

"'Cause her daddy wasn't assistant manager at the plant," I said. "It was a very political thing, even then. Gloria said she only entered because the winner got a free trip to New York, and she was dying to go, and my grandfather said no decent girl went by herself to New York City."

Will kept studying the photo. He pointed to another girl, at the far right. She was younger and taller than the others, and tendrils of curls had escaped from her Aqua Net helmet. She was the only one wearing short, wrist-length gloves. "Why does this girl look familiar to me?" he asked, holding the photo at arm's length now. "Is this somebody I've met locally?"

"I doubt it," I said, taking the picture and putting it back in the box. "That's Jeanine Murry. She was fifteen. The youngest girl in the pageant. Gloria was eighteen."

Austin sucked his breath in. "Your mama! My God, you look exactly like her."

Will picked the picture up again. "He's right. You're the spitting image. Same eyes, same nose." He took a tendril of hair that had come loose from my ponytail and tucked it behind my ear. "Same hair."

"Everybody says I've got the Murdock nose," I said, turning away from him.

"She was a stunner," Will said. "I've never heard you talk about your mother. Is she still living?"

"I have no idea," I said, trying to keep my tone light and even. "She left my daddy and me when I was just a kid."

"Oh," Will said. He looked like he'd swallowed a bug.

"It's not your fault," I said, taking pity on him. "But come to think of it, I've never heard you talk about your family either."

"What do you want to know?" Will asked. "My father was an engineer too, but chemical engineering. He retired from Procter & Gamble, and he and my mom live down at Hilton Head. He plays golf, she plays tennis and volunteers at the hospice. I've got two brothers and a sister too, and four nephews and two nieces. Should I go on?"

"Not necessary," I said, conceding defeat. "Anyway, as soon as we finish hanging these pictures, we'll have it wrapped up here."

"I'll get out of your way then," Will said, glad to have an excuse for his retreat. "Just send the bill to the office."

"Don't worry, it'll probably get there before you do," I said.

"Business that bad?"

"It's been better," I said. "Summer's always our slow time."

"Especially since the Jernigans have decided to screw Keeley and her aunt to the wall," Austin piped up.

"Austin," I said, a warning note in my voice.

"It's true," he went on. "And you know it. Ever since you called the wedding off, that family's done whatever they could to screw you over. They're trying to run you out of business, is what they're doing."

"Will's not interested in local politics," I said. "And Gloria and I are doing just fine, thank you."

"Hope so," Will said, his hand on the doorknob. "Remember, Keeley, don't let the ash-holes get you down."

He was gone, and I turned my full attention to glaring at Austin.

"What?" he said, squirming under the heat of my gaze. "What's he mean by ash-holes?"

"Nothing," I said. "Will Mahoney has a very peculiar sense of humor. That's just his idea of a joke. But you are not off the hook with me, Austin. You had no business telling Will about our problems with the Jernigans. That's strictly personal. And my relationship with Will is strictly professional. And that's how I intend to keep it. Okay?"

"Okay," Austin said. "I'm sorry I mentioned it. But it just makes me so mad. Those people think they rule the earth. I hate to see them pushing you around."

"They're not going to push me around anymore," I said firmly.

He nodded understanding, then picked up the next set of pictures and stood away from the wall. "Now where do these go?"

By three o'clock we'd finished with the installation. I left the Scotch on the kitchen counter, along with a note that said, "Welcome Home." Then I took Austin on a quick tour of Mulberry Hill.

"He wants it done by when?" Austin asked, when we were back at my car.

"Christmas." I said. "At first I told him it was impossible. It really was. But I guess I underestimated him. When Will Mahoney sets his mind to something, I think it generally gets done. Look at the house. What he's accomplished out here already is unbelievable. When he says it's going to be done, by God, it gets done."

"Money has that effect," Austin observed.

"It's more than just the money. Somehow he's got all these workers all hyped up about making this house a showplace again. I think they really believe he'll get the plant up and running again too. And I'll tell you something. I'm beginning to believe it myself."

Austin gazed out the window at the wildflower meadow as I threaded the car up the new driveway. "Are you still mad at Austin?"

he asked, in a mock timid voice. "Are you friends with Austin again?"

"Friends," I said with a sigh.

"Best friends?"

"Well, yeah, now. Ever since I crossed Paige off the list."

"Good," he said, smiling widely. "I've got something I want to tell you. I've been waiting for the right time, but I keep getting side-tracked."

"What's this about?"

He took a deep breath. "It's about your mama."

"Oh hell."

"It's just that I love mysteries. Always have. You know, when the other guys on my block were out playing baseball and football, and trying to run each other over with their bikes, I was inside reading Nancy Drew mysteries."

"Not Hardy Boys?"

He wrinkled his nose in distaste. "The Hardy Boys had no style. Now Nancy . . ." He sighed. "That roadster coupe. The chic little frocks. And don't get me started on that Ned Nickerson."

"Okay. So you had a crush on Nancy Drew's boyfriend. What's that got to do with me and my mother?"

He waited. "I'm trying to figure out if this is the best time to talk about this. You're kind of in a pissy mood today, you know."

"I am *not* being pissy," I said, slapping the Volvo's dashboard for emphasis.

He rolled his eyes. "Whatever."

"You started this, now finish it," I said. "Or I really will get pissed."

"All right, all right. The other day, when you told me you had no idea where your mother was, I just started thinking. I mean, as I may have mentioned, I know right where my mother is at. And most of the time, she's standing right on my last nerve cell. Don't get me wrong. I love the old girl, but she makes me crazy. The thing is, we all need our mothers. And you need yours. Good, bad, or indifferent. Especially now . . ."

"Now, meaning what?"

"Now that you've called off this big wedding. You're at a cross-roads here, Keeley. And with what's happened with A.J., and your abandonment issues, it just occurred to me, having your mother around could help matters."

"No." I said it flatly. "She's been gone more than twenty years. I appreciate the thought, Austin, but I'm over losing my mother. And I don't have abandonment issues."

He rolled his eyes again. "Oh please. Take a look at yourself, girl. You have more issues than the *National Geographic*."

We were just passing through the new gates to Mulberry Hill. There was no traffic coming, so I could have pulled onto the county road. Instead I stopped the Volvo, leaned across Austin, and opened his door.

"Out," I said.

"Keeley!" he protested.

"I mean it," I said. "I don't want to hear another word on this subject. You'll have to hitch a ride back to town with somebody else. Maybe one of the Mexican stone masons can stand to hear you jibber-jabber. You don't speak Spanish, do you?"

"No I do not," he said. He closed the door and locked it for effect. "You just don't want to hear the truth, that's all. Denial, denial, denial."

"All right," I said, turning off the Volvo's engine. "Let's get it over with. Right now. Tell me everything you've just been itching to tell me. Then I'm gonna haul your ass back to town, and I don't want to see you or hear from you again for at least the next couple days."

"Tsk. Tsk. Could you cut the air conditioning back on so I don't suffocate out here?"

I turned the motor on, but for lack of anything better to do, cut the radio off.

"Okay," Austin said. "Your mother's full name was Jeanine Murry Murdock, is that correct?"

I nodded.

"Birthdate 1–31–53?"

"How'd you find that out?"

"Research," he said airily. "And she and your daddy were married on 11–27–71?"

"Right."

He bit his lip. "Let me ask you something. When and where do you think your daddy divorced your mama?"

"I don't know. I guess right after she left us. Daddy never talked about it. I just assumed he went off and got a quiet divorce."

Austin swung his head back and forth dramatically. "Negative. I could find no record of a divorce between Wade Murdock and Jeanine Murry Murdock in any county in Georgia. So I searched the records in Florida, South Carolina, North Carolina, Tennessee, and Alabama. Every state that touches Georgia. No record of any such divorce."

I felt a faint buzz in my head. "What's that mean?" I asked.

"I don't know," Austin admitted. "Just that as far as I know, and the law's concerned, your parents are still married."

"On paper."

"There's something else."

I felt a jab of unexpected pain, right around my rib cage. Why was this so hard? I'd written my mother off years ago. After she'd missed my eighth birthday. After she'd missed Christmas. Middle school graduation. Having my tonsils out. My first date. High school and then college graduation. Each occasion had been another reminder that she was gone, well and truly gone. Never coming back gone. "She's dead, then."

"I don't think so," he said. "I can't find any death certificate."

"What did you find?" I asked, my curiosity getting the better of me.

"Mostly dead ends," he said, his voice full of regret.

30

I jounced the car back onto the tarmac and turned a sharp left, toward town.

"I don't want to hear another word," I said, my teeth clenched. "You had no right to do this. Did you?"

Austin's face fell. "I just thought you needed to know. For closure."

"You don't get to decide what I need to know," I said.

The ride back to town was less than five miles, but it seemed to take hours. Austin turned the radio on again, and turned his back to me.

Traffic around the square was heavier than normal. I pulled up to a parking space at the courthouse, across the street from Fleur. "This is the best I can do," I said.

"It's fine," he said, stony-faced. He opened the car door, started to get out, then thought better of it and got back into the front seat.

"You can stay mad at me if you want," he said. "But I care about you, Keeley. I know you think you're over your mama's leaving you. But you're not. You can't be. Nobody could be over something like that. Just think about what I've told you. Okay? I searched the vital records data bases for all those states in, like, two hours on the computer. All that stuff is online now. If I had more information I could really get some answers."

"No," I said. "Look. It's not like I'm some motherless waif. I had Daddy and Aunt Gloria, and they did just fine by me, thank you very much."

"I need the name of the man your mama ran off with," Austin kept up, pretending he hadn't heard what I said. "And there are a bunch of other questions I want to ask you too."

"Goodbye," I said pointedly.

After he'd gotten out of the car, it took a few minutes before I could back out into traffic. I circled the square three times, looking for a parking spot, but it was hopeless. Without thinking about it, I headed the car toward my daddy's house.

The driveway was empty. Monday. It was Daddy's golf day. Before my hissy fit, before I'd gotten him kicked out of Oconee Hills Country Club, Daddy usually played eighteen holes with his cronies on Monday afternoons. He hadn't said anything about it, but I knew he'd switched over to playing the public course over at the state park. This was something else for me to feel guilty about. The state course has more rocks and red clay than greens or fairways, and there was no posh clubhouse, locker room, or grill to repair to with his buddies after a punishing round in the blazing sun. He probably sat on the trunk of his car to change out of his cleats, and stopped at the Starvin' Marvin on 441 for a cold Budweiser on the way back home.

Which would be several hours from now.

I let myself into the kitchen. It was neat and tidy, as always. For a bachelor, Daddy was a bit of a biddy. He never left dirty dishes in the sink, never failed to sweep the kitchen floor, which he mopped every Saturday morning.

The kitchen still smelled like Pine-Sol. When had he gotten into these habits, I wondered. Was that something his mama had done, mopped on Saturdays? Or had it been the practice of my own mother? I'd been such a little kid when she left, I had no idea how things got done around the house back then. I knew Daddy worked at the car lot, and Mama stayed home and did lady things, like cooking and cleaning and making sure I got to school and dance lessons and spend-the-night parties at my friends' houses.

I opened the refrigerator door and reached automatically for the green Depression glass refrigerator jug full of cold water. The refrigerators had changed over the years, but the jug had not. We always had a pitcher of cold water in that green glass jug. Even though

Daddy's refrigerator had an ice and cold water dispenser on the door now, he'd kept that jug refilled, year after year.

In the cupboard over the sink I found a juice glass and poured myself some water. On the bottom shelf of the pantry I found the Porky Pig cookie jar, and helped myself to a package of Nabs. Daddy bought cases of Nabs to keep at the car lot for his customers and salesmen. I think they fed them to me as a baby instead of teething biscuits.

Chewing and sipping, I walked aimlessly around the house. In the living room I toyed with the gold-framed photos Daddy kept displayed on Mama's piano. I had never actually heard anybody play that piano. Now I plinked some of the keys, surprised to find that it sounded as though it was in tune. There was my high school graduation photo, with me wearing the off-the-shoulder drape the studio had supplied all us girls. I'd felt self-conscious about the amount of cleavage that drape revealed, but never said anything about it to anybody. Next to the graduation photo was one of Daddy with his arms around me and Gloria, on his fiftieth birthday, taken a few years ago at the surprise party Gloria had organized at the country club. There was an awful baby picture of me too, in a frilly pink and white dress, with a pink bow Scotch-taped to my nearly bald head.

I plinked the piano some more and wondered about what wasn't there. No photo of my mama. Had there ever been any? I tried to remember. Once maybe, a wedding picture of the two of them. It seemed to me Mama had been feeding Daddy a piece of wedding cake in that picture. Or had I just made that up?

The bookcases that flanked the fireplace were full of old Reader's Digest Condensed Books, my red leather-bound *Encyclopedia Britannica* set, and some tired-looking twenty-year-old hardbacks. I pulled each out by the spine and looked them over. Daddy's reading mostly consisted of the *Morgan County Citizen*, the *Atlanta Journal-Constitution*, *Car and Driver*, *Sports Illustrated*, and the occasional paperback spy novel.

So these would be my mama's books. The titles seemed to run to romances—*Forever Amber*, *The Flame and the Flower*, like that.

I leafed absentmindedly through the pages. A yellowed slip of paper fell out of the pages of *The Flame and the Flower*. Despite all the years that had passed, I recognized her printing, instantly. She always printed my name on the brown bag lunch I toted to school. Keeley Murdock. As though there were another Keeley in my class. We'd had two Jennifers, two Stephanies, a Kirsten and a Kelly. But I was the only Keeley.

The paper was a grocery list, written in pencil on a scrap of lined notebook paper. Nothing exciting, nothing that gave a hint of what my mother's daily life was like back then, or why she'd up and left.

Coffee. Sugar. Haf-'n-Haf (she was a terrible speller), *Clorox, baloney, tin foil, eggs, shaving cream, aspirin, strawberry Jello, pineapple tidbits, cream cheese.*

The baloney would have been for my lunch. I had a baloney sandwich on Sunbeam bread, with French's mustard, every day. Mama cut my sandwich in half on the diagonal, and I always threw the crusts away, because Daddy said eating crust gave you curly hair—and mine was already way curlier than I wanted. The pineapple and cream cheese and Jell-O would have been for one of the congealed salads she liked to make. I never could figure out how something with Jell-O and pineapple qualified as a salad, but in Madison, Georgia, it did.

I smoothed the grocery list with my fingertips. She would have borrowed the paper out of my Blue Horse school notebook, I thought. Driven her red Chevy Malibu over to the Piggly Wiggly, probably while I was at school. After I got too big to ride in the shopping cart, she didn't like to take me with her to the grocery store, because I drove her crazy begging for sugary cereals, candy, ice cream, and potato chips. Maybe she'd stopped off at Madison Drugs after the grocery store, for a Coke over crushed ice, and to hear the latest gossip at the soda fountain.

And then home to unpack the groceries and do whatever else she did all day. What did she do with her time? I wondered. I didn't know if she watched soap operas, like my grandmother. I'd never known her to play bridge, like some of my friends' mothers. She talked on the phone, saw her friends, went to Myrtle Beach for a week with them every summer—no kids, no husbands.

I ran my fingers over the spines of the other books on the shelves, and feeling slightly guilty, shook each one out. What was I hoping to find? An airline ticket? Love letter? I thought about all those birthdays that had passed. Each year, for the week up to and after the big day, I'd raced home from school, hoping to find a card from her. I never got one. After I came home from college, before I moved into the apartment, I'd surreptitiously gone all through the boxes and trunks up in the attic, hoping to find some stash of cards and letters from her that Daddy had hidden. I never found anything.

On the top shelf of the bookcase I pulled out four different volumes of *Echoes*, my parents' yearbooks from Morgan County High. I took the latest one, 1970, picked up my package of Nabs and my juice glass, and climbed the stairs to my old bedroom.

I put the glass down on my nightstand and opened the top drawer of my bureau. The bottle of Joy was hidden under some half slips. I uncapped it, closed my eyes, and inhaled.

The pages of the *Echoes* stuck together slightly, so I used my fingertips to pry them apart. How many times had I gone through this yearbook with her? As a child I'd been fascinated with the idea that she'd been a teenager once. At bedtime I'd beg her to show me the yearbook, point out her friends, her enemies, her favorite teachers. I'd looked in vain for Daddy's picture, until she'd pointed out that he was four years older, and had graduated before she ever set foot inside Morgan County High.

Here was the page of faculty pictures. I smiled at the one of her geometry teacher, Mr. Osier. Somebody (not me! Mama had protested in mock horror) had drawn a mustache and pointy horns on his head. She'd never been any good at math either.

I'd loved the club pictures. Mama had been so popular. Spanish Club, Drama Club, Pen & Palette, Student Council secretary. She'd worn a different outfit in each picture, cute little miniskirts or bell-bottom hip-huggers. In my favorite one, she'd worn an Indian headband and fringed leather skirt.

"Were you in a play?" I'd asked.

"That was just the latest style, that year," she'd said. "I saw Cher wearing an outfit like that on television, and saved up my allowance and bought one just like it at Rich's at Lenox Square Plaza in Atlanta. I was the first girl in school to go native!" And she'd laughed and laughed about that.

I flipped through the pages of senior portraits until I got to hers. Jeanine Marie Murry. Her chin was tilted up in the picture, and her eyes, with their dramatic sweep of black eyeliner, frosted eyeshadow, and goopy mascara, seemed focused on something far away. Beneath the picture was listed a list of her activities and accomplishments, and then, as with every senior, her favorite quote. "Two roads diverged in a wood, and I, I took the one less traveled by." Robert Frost.

Sure did, I thought, slapping the book closed.

I started to put the perfume bottle back in the dresser drawer, but thought better of it. Instead I took it, and the yearbook. Downstairs, I washed out the juice glass, dried it and put it back in the cupboard. Everything was as it was when I'd come in. And Wednesday night, salmon loaf night, I would come back here, sit across the table from Daddy, and talk about the things we always talked about. How, I wondered, could I get to the place where I could talk to him about the thing we never, ever, talked about? Jeanine Murry Murdock and the road less traveled.

31

Wednesday morning I got up and brewed a pot of coffee. I poured two mugs, tucked the yearbook under my arm, went downstairs, and pounded on the back door of the florist's shop.

It was early, not yet seven, and I knew Austin's feet never hit the floor until just after nine, but I had no pity on him, just kept banging away on the heavy metal fire door until he opened up.

He wore a pair of unlovely gray gym shorts, with the satin kimono thrown hastily on, still unbelted. I was surprised to see how trim his bare torso was, even more surprised to see his chest hair was nearly all white, while what hair Austin still had was a sunny blond.

Austin saw where I was looking and quickly belted the robe. He yawned hugely. "So now you know my secret. I touch up my hair, and I'm a religious Abz-Er-Cizer. To what do I owe the pleasure of a visit at such an ungodly hour?"

I handed him the mug of coffee and followed him into the shop and up the stairs to his own apartment.

"It's all your fault," I said, blowing on the coffee to cool it down. "You opened up this can of worms."

He shuddered. "Do we have to talk about worms before I've had breakfast?"

"His name was Darvis Kane," I said, wanting the words out quickly, before I could take them back.

"Who?"

"The man. The one my mother ran away with. His name was Darvis Kane. He was the sales manager at Murdock Motors."

"Ow," Austin said. He took a sip of the coffee. "Okay. This is a start. What else do you know?"

"Not a lot," I said. "Gloria told me some of it. After one of the girls at school spilled the beans. Darvis Kane was her uncle. We were playing dodgeball one day, and I hit her, and she got really mad. And she screamed at me: 'My Uncle Darvis run off with your mama! My mama says your mama's nothing but a little runaround! So don't you be thinking you're better than me.' "

"Nice," Austin said.

"I hit her really hard. It left a mark on the back of her knees."

"Should have knocked the little bitch out cold."

"Yeah, well, that's one of my lasting regrets. It was Paige. All the other kids heard too. Even the teacher. Mrs. Goggins. She made Paige apologize, but she didn't make her take it back."

"*Quel scandale!* But you really had no clue she'd taken off with a man?"

"No. She'd been gone maybe ten days? I really can't remember too clearly. And up until then, I thought she'd gone to the beach with her girlfriends, like she used to do in the summertime. Only this was wintertime. After Christmas, I know. After Valentine's Day too, because I remember Mama bought me Barbie valentines to give away. So it was March, maybe. I didn't believe Paige, of course. But somehow I knew better than to ask Daddy about it. Back then the elementary school was still right downtown. After Mama left I'd walk over here to Glorious Interiors and sit at the table by the window, and color and cut out pictures from *House Beautiful* and do my homework until Daddy came by to pick me up. So I asked her about it."

"What did she say?"

"Just that Mama was having trouble thinking clearly, and she needed some time away from us to feel better about things."

"Did you ask her about this Darvis Kane person?"

"I did. I can still remember the look on her face when I asked her about it. Her lips went all white. 'Who told you about that?' she asked me. 'Who would tell a child such a thing?' After I told her, she took me over to Madison Drugs and bought me a chocolate malted. That was a huge treat. Usually you only got a chocolate malted if you'd made an A on a spelling test. We sat at one of those vinyl booths, and her hands were shaking, she was so upset, but she talked to me. She told me that it was true Darvis Kane had left town. And my mama had gone too. But there was no proof they'd gone off together. And she felt sure Mama would call when she got herself settled someplace. Because she loved me very much."

Austin set his mug down carefully on the marble-topped end table. "She never called, did she?"

"No."

He got to his feet and went over to a table in the corner of the room. A paisley fringed throw had been tossed over the table, and when he lifted the throw, I could see that there was a computer terminal there.

Austin started tapping away at the keyboard. In a minute I heard the modem dialing the phone line.

"Okay," he said, turning around to face me. "First, more coffee. Stat. Second, I need more information about this Darvis Cole."

"Kane. Darvis Kane. I'll bring the pot of coffee back with me. But I don't know anything else about him. Just that he worked for Daddy at the car lot, and he was Paige's uncle."

He kept on tapping, and I walked over to my place and got the coffee, and after a moment's hesitation, a bag of mini Snickers I'd bought half price after Easter, and hidden from myself in case of an emergency that required chocolate. Austin was still working away on the computer when I got back over there.

I poured him a cup of coffee, and he took the bag of candy and gave me a look. "No peanut M&M's?"

I shrugged. "Sorry."

He chewed and thought about things. "Was Darvis Kane an uncle on Paige's mother's or father's side?"

I had to think about that. "On her mother's side. I never knew Paige's daddy. Anyway, Darvis Kane was married to Lorna's sister Lisa."

More tapping. "I need his vitals," Austin said. "Was he from Madison? Any chance he went to school here, something like that? Any family still living here?"

I shook my head slowly. "I just don't know. Lisa and Lorna's maiden name was Franklin. Their family didn't live right in Madison. They lived way over in Rutledge, in a trailer back off the highway. Lorna was the only one who stayed around here.

"Wait," I said, helping myself to another mini Snickers. "Where's your phone book?"

He reached under the table and brought out the Morgan-Madison-Buckhead-Rutledge phone directory. I took it and paged over to the K listings.

"One Kane listed, but it's a LaTasha Kane, and she lives over there on Jeeter Way. She's black. Our Darvis Kane was white."

Austin raised an eyebrow. "You're sure?"

"This was 1979, Austin. My daddy wasn't a racist or anything, but the only black man who worked at Murdock Motors back then was Eddie, the detail man. Anyway, it was a scandal, not a racial incident. I'm positive."

"Who *would* know something?" Austin asked, impatient now.

"Paige, I guess. But there's no way I'm asking her."

"Who else, then? What happened to the jilted sister, after her husband ran away with Jeanine?"

"Lisa? I think she took her kids and moved to Athens, moved in with another one of the sisters. Paige was mad because her girl cousins moved off."

"That's something we'll have to take a look at," Austin said, writing on a yellow legal pad beside the computer. "See if Lisa Franklin and Darvis Kane ever got a divorce. And maybe we can track down the ex. Somebody has to know something about these two. Who else can you think of? Think now, Keeley."

"Maybe Gloria," I said reluctantly. "And Daddy. But I couldn't talk to him about this. Not yet."

"You'll have to eventually," he said.

"Maybe. Once I have some answers," I conceded.

"Oh, you'll have answers," he promised, patting the computer terminal. "All right," he said. "Tell me some more about your mama."

"Like what?"

"Who were her people?" Austin asked, exasperated at my denseness. "I mean, the woman walked off and never came back. How about her family? Did any of them ever hear from her over the years?"

I chewed and thought. "Her only family besides us was her cousin, Sonya Wyrick. She was my mama's maid of honor at her wedding. But I think she and Daddy didn't get along, because the only time she and Mama got together was when Daddy wasn't around."

Austin pounced on this little family tidbit. "She was your mother's only living relative? Why didn't she and Wade get along?"

"Nobody ever came out and said Daddy didn't like her. She just didn't come around that often. She was married and had a couple kids too."

"Sonya. Wyrick." Austin wrote it down on his yellow legal pad.

"She worked as a stitcher at Loving Cup. When she got laid off, she moved away. I haven't heard from her in a long time."

"All right, I'll try and track that down later," he said. He stood up from the computer, stretched, yawned again, and looked at his watch. "Good Lord. It's not even nine o'clock yet. I can't believe my brain is functioning at this high a level this early."

"Coffee and Snickers," I said. "The breakfast of champions. I've gotta go pretty soon. I'm supposed to take some paint samples over to Will, and Gloria and I have a ton of paperwork to catch up on."

"You still haven't told me what your mother was like," Will complained. "I'm just not getting any sense of her. Who was Jeanine Murry Murdock? What was she like before she got married and had you?"

I shook my head in frustration. "She was like any other small-town Southern girl, I guess. She got married when she was eighteen years old, for Pete's sake."

"Before she married your daddy, did she work? Did she go to college?"

"She went to the community college for about a year," I said. "And she worked in a dress shop, right here on the square. The Charm Shop, it was called. A woman named Chrys Graham owned it. It's gone now, but it used to be right over there on Washington Street, where Kathleen Harbin's antiques shop is now. It had a pink awning out front. Mama always loved pretty clothes, and Chrys Graham let her go to Atlanta to the mart with her and do some of the buying. And Mama always did all the window dressing too. In fact, she did the window dressing after she quit working there. I remember she made a Halloween window once, and I helped her make a scarecrow with hay, and we dressed her in the cutest outfit. People came from all over to see Mama's windows."

Austin smiled. "Well, at least we know where you get your sense of style."

That made me laugh. "Yeah, definitely not from Daddy. He's doing good if he remembers to wear brown shoes with green pants."

"Tell me more about the dress shop, about the woman who owned it," Austin ordered.

"I've really gotta scoot in a minute now," I said. But I was enjoying myself, thinking about how happy it had made Mama, all those years ago, fixing those windows. She'd spend hours working on them, bringing props from home, painting backdrops, setting up lights. Then we'd get in her Malibu and cruise past, over and over again, because she wanted to make sure people driving by got the full effect.

"The owner, Miss Graham, let her buy her clothes at a discount, some samples too, because she was a perfect size eight, a sample size. I remember she used to put clothes aside for Mama, even after she quit and got married and had me. One time she got us matching mother-daughter outfits."

"What happened to her, after the shop closed?" Austin asked anxiously. "And please don't tell me she died or moved to North Carolina."

"No," I said. "She's right here in Madison. She works for Kathleen Harbin in the antiques shop, as a matter of fact. Kathleen is her niece."

32

Supper at Daddy's looked like it would be what it usually was; quiet and uneventful. We talked about the car business, about the weather, and sports.

"Braves are gonna make it to the Series this year, shug," he said, as we were putting the dishes in the dishwasher. "Gonna win the whole shootin' match."

"You say that every year," I teased. "And they've only won it once. Don't you ever give up?"

"Nope," he said, handing me the salmon loaf pan. "They've got the talent and the desire. Anyway, I gotta believe in something. Might as well be the Braves."

I dried the pan and put it carefully back in the bottom cupboard where it's always been kept. All during dinner, all during the discussion of new model cars and APRs, and the Braves' combined ERAs, it was on the tip of my tongue. Where is she? Where did my mother go? And why?

"You're kinda quiet tonight," Daddy said, wiping down the kitchen counter. He went to the refrigerator, got out a Budweiser, and held one up for me. I shook my head no.

"Something on your mind? Everything okay at work?"

"It's okay," I said. "Thank God for Will Mahoney. If it weren't for him, and Mulberry Hill, I might be ringing up groceries over at the Bi-Lo."

Daddy took a sip of his beer and frowned. "Maybe I better have a heart-to-heart with Drew Jernigan. What happened between you and A.J., that was just too bad. But it wasn't none of your fault."

"I don't think the Jernigans see it that way," I said.

"Drew's always been a stiff-necked SOB," Daddy said. He paused.

"You know, I had to quit eatin' breakfast at Ye Olde Colonial. It got so bad, I'd walk in, and he'd get up, throw some money down, and walk right out the door. Made everybody damn uncomfortable. So I just switched over to the Waffle House. I like their grits better anyway."

"Daddy!" I hugged his neck. "Waffle House doesn't have biscuits. And all your other friends are over at Ye Olde Colonial. I see them, every morning, when I go to work, sitting around that big table in the window."

"Not all of 'em," Daddy said, grinning despite himself. "Anyway, I was getting in a rut. Time to shake things up a little bit."

I took the damp dishcloth and hung it on the towel rack rod on the back of the kitchen door, just like I did every Wednesday night after supper. "This is all my fault," I said. "I should have just kept my mouth shut at the rehearsal dinner, and gone ahead with the wedding."

"No ma'am!" Daddy said firmly. "You did the right thing calling it off. The only thing you could do."

"It didn't have to be so public," I said. "That's what's got the Jernigans so worked up, I think. I humiliated them. And myself."

I kissed Daddy's cheek. He needed a shave. "And I embarrassed you and Gloria, and now they're taking it out on all of us. I made a big old mess of everything."

Daddy patted the top of my head awkwardly. "Don't you worry about me, or Gloria. We're grown up. And it'll take a lot more than those stiff-necked Jernigans to run either one of us out of this town. You just take care of yourself. Like you been doing."

"A.J. came to see me," I said. "After he got back from France."

Daddy frowned and started to say something. "He was kind of sweet," I went on. "Telling me how much he missed me, and how sorry he was. He says—"

I bit my lip, wondering how much I should tell.

Daddy crossed his arms over his chest. "I wanna hear this!" he said.

"He says it was all Paige's fault. He says he was drunk, and they were just messing around, and it got out of hand. And he claims it was the first and only time . . . they did something like that."

"And you believed him?"

"I kicked him out of the shop. And I told him I didn't believe him. But I just don't know." Tears started welling up in my eyes. "I loved him. And I know he loved me. I just know it. But if he loved me . . . how could he do something like that to me?"

Daddy sighed and handed me a dry dish towel. "Here. Come on now. What do you say we go for a drive? Huh? When's the last time we went for a drive together?"

I mopped my face. "I don't know. We used to go for drives all the time, didn't we?"

He nodded, got the car keys, and I followed him out the door to the big hulking white Chevy Tahoe parked in the carport.

Daddy headed the Tahoe down the blacktop. He didn't say where we were headed, but he didn't have to.

On Sundays, after church, there isn't much to do in a small town like Madison. When we got home from church, we'd change out of our good clothes. Mama would put a roast in the oven, and Daddy would putter around a little bit out in the garage, and then we'd go for our Sunday drive.

Daddy would have brought home a new model car for us to try out. The seats would have plastic over them, and there would be paper mats on the floor, and the new car smell would be stronger even than my mother's Joy perfume.

Our destinations on these trips never varied. We'd take the old Rutledge Road, Highway 12, and turn right when we got to Rutledge. There was a gas station there that stayed open on Sundays, and Daddy would stop and get us all Cokes. Then we'd drive over to Hard Labor Creek State Park.

I would take little tiny sips of my Coke, wanting to save it for our picnic. Daddy would park in the shade, as far away from any other cars as possible, and then we'd take our drinks and our sandwiches, and picnic around the old mill. If it was summertime, I'd change into my bathing suit and swim in the creek, and the two of them would sit in folding aluminum lawn chairs and watch me splashing around. Sometimes Daddy would swim with me, but Mama didn't swim, and she didn't like to mess up her hair, so she always stayed up in the grass, watching and calling for me not to go in any deeper.

I'd ride home wrapped in a big beach towel, and fall asleep to the sound of the two of them murmuring companionably up in the front seat.

I've driven past Hard Labor Creek Park hundreds of times since I've grown up, but to my knowledge, this was the first time I'd gone back since those Sunday drives.

A chain was stretched across the park entrance, and a sign said the park was closed after nine P.M.

"We'll see about that," Daddy said. He got out of the car, went over to the chain, and fiddled with it until it unfastened.

"You lawbreaker!" I said, when he got back in the car. "Won't somebody see us and kick us out?"

"Nah," Daddy said. "I play golf with the park superintendent all the time. This late at night, and the Braves game over with? Little Joe's asleep in the bed."

Daddy steered the Tahoe into the park and toward the lake. "The old mill's gone, you know," he said after a while. "They tore it down when they put in the golf course."

I looked out the window at the passing scenery. "It's all changed," I said.

"Lake's still pretty," he commented. "You used to love that lake. Back then, that was like the French Riviera to us."

"I did love it," I said, remembering. "Daddy? How come we stopped coming? After Mama left?"

He was quiet for a while. "Oh, shug. Everything changed. After she left, Sundays were different. I was still working Saturdays at the lot, so Sunday was the only day I had to get the house straightened up, see about meals for the week, do all the things she used to do all week long. There just wasn't enough time for something like a long drive to the park."

Daddy laughed. "I never realized how hard that woman worked until she was gone, and I was left to do all the things she'd been doing all those years."

I looked over at him. He had a funny half smile on his face.

"She made it look easy," I said. "Even now, I still wonder what she did all day, but of course, I know she was keeping up with the house, and us, and . . ."

We parked under a pecan tree at the edge of the paved parking lot and got out. The grass was already wet with dew, so after a moment of hesitation, I slid out of my sandals and left them in the car.

We found a wooden picnic table facing the lake. "These are new too," I said, sitting down facing the lake.

He sat down beside me. "She never complained," he said suddenly. "We never fought. I thought we were the two happiest people in Madison." He rubbed my arm. "Three happiest. You were happy, weren't you, shug?"

I nodded.

"People keep things to themselves," Daddy said. "Sometimes, when things aren't good, instead of saying something, getting things stirred up, they just keep things to themselves, and keep going along, to get along. But that's all wrong."

He turned to me. "You don't want to be married to a man you can't believe in, do you?"

"What if I love him? What if I want to believe him? Should I give him another chance? That's what I've been wondering. Should I have given A.J. another chance? People make mistakes."

"Messing around with your best friend, when you're getting married the next day, that's more than just a mistake," Daddy said. "That's a character flaw. A big one, if you ask me."

I dug my toes into the wet sand. "Gloria says all the Jernigans are like that. She says Drew and even Chub were runarounds in their day."

"She shouldn't have told you that," Daddy said slowly.

"But it's true, isn't it?"

Daddy looked away. "There's always been talk. I don't like gossip. Never have. And after your mama left, well, I knew everybody in town was talking about us. Nothing I could do about it. But I'm not gonna be the one talking about the Jernigans."

I leaned back with my elbows on the picnic table. I could hear the soft hooting of mourning doves, and frogs croaking over near the edge of the lake. The moon was nearly full, and its reflection seemed to fill the surface of the water.

"You talked about people keeping things to themselves," I said, choosing my words carefully. "Does that include you?"

He nodded, waiting.

"Does it make you mad, still, that she left?"

"Sometimes. Does it still make you mad?"

I laughed. "Austin says I have abandonment issues. He says I'll never have a good relationship with a man until I deal with my feelings about Mama. He says I need closure."

Daddy slapped at a mosquito that had landed on his arm. "Did Austin go to psychiatry school before or after he was at florist's school?"

"I think he watches a lot of daytime television," I admitted. "But even armchair psychiatrists get it right every once in a while. I really do want to know what happened to Mama. I need to know. Why did she leave us? Where did she go?"

"And why didn't she send for you?" Daddy was looking right into my eyes.

My own eyes widened. "You knew?"

"About the suitcase under your bed? Yeah. I found it the one and only time I did any real spring cleaning at the house. I took it out and opened it up. Found your little pajamas, your blue jeans and T-shirt, and your favorite Barbie doll. About broke my heart when I realized why you had it hidden under there."

"I wanted to be ready," I said softly. "I thought she'd pull up in the driveway in her Malibu one day, and honk the horn. And I'd look out the door, and there she'd be, hollerin' 'Come on Keeley, dollar waitin' on a dime!' And out the door I would go, because my suitcase was already packed."

"Whatever happened to that suitcase?" he asked. "I kept checking, and after a couple years, it was gone."

"I grew up some." I put my hand on Daddy's arm. "And I'd heard all the gossip. I knew she left with that man. Darvis Kane. I knew she'd broken not just my heart, but yours too. And I got so I hated her. I told myself if she ever did call or write, I wouldn't talk to her. Wouldn't write back. And if she showed up, I'd tell her right to her face to go to hell."

Daddy shook his head. "We been keeping things to ourselves for a long time, haven't we, shug?"

"Oh yeah."

"I remember the day I looked under your bed, and the suitcase was gone. That night was the first time I slept good after she left."

"Why?"

"You were all I had left," he said, looking away again. "And I thought the same thing as you. I thought she'd come back, take you away with her. And there'd be nothing left for me."

I slid my hand down his arm and squeezed my father's big, callused hand. He squeezed back.

33

We sat in the dark at the picnic table, looking out at the lake, for a long time, until the bugs ran us off, back to the shelter of the Tahoe.

It seemed safe, somehow, to talk there, away from the house and memories of her.

"Gloria says you been asking a lot of questions about Jeanine," Daddy said. "It kind of upset her."

"I know. And I know the two of you were trying to protect me. You guys did a good job of raising me, Daddy. I'm not perfect, but I'm not as messed up as a lot of kids whose parents went through divorce and stuff. But I'm a big girl now, and there are things I need to know about her."

"All right," he said, his voice wary. "I'll tell you as much as I can."

I gulped. "Austin has been doing some research. Online. You can check state databases that way. He did some checking and he says it looks like you two never got a divorce. Is that right?"

"Research," Daddy said, with a trace of annoyance in his voice. "He's right. I never did get a divorce."

"Why not?"

"I didn't know where she'd gone off to."

"Did you even try to find out?"

For the first time he gave me a sharp look. And his voice was pinched, almost angry. "Hell yes, I tried. There was a police investigation, of course, after I reported her missing. At first they suspected maybe I'd done something to her. That's how they think, when a married person goes missing. But after a while the sheriff gave up looking. I'd been at work at the car lot all day the day she left. About a dozen people vouched for me. And there was never any sign of foul play or anything. And Darvis Kane was gone too. There was a lot of talk about that. He'd left a wife and little kids behind too. You know how that looked. Even still, I didn't give up. I wanted to know why. And I wanted to be able to tell you something, even if it was that we were getting a divorce. So I hired a private detective. Spent thousands, chasing down dead ends. In the end I didn't really find out any more than I knew the day she left."

"Nothing? You mean she just disappeared?"

Daddy spread out his fingers on the steering wheel. The dull gold of the wedding band on his left hand shone softly in the moonlight. "Best I could find out. She just walked out, Keeley. And no, there wasn't a note, nothing like that. Believe me, I looked and hunted. I tore the house apart, thinking maybe she'd left some little clue. But there was nothing."

"Did she take a lot of stuff with her?"

Daddy winced. "An overnight bag was missing. She had lots of clothes, so I couldn't be sure of what she might have taken with her. Her closet was full, so it wasn't like she just cleaned it out and took off with everything she owned."

"What about her car? The red Malibu?"

"That's the only thing that detective did to earn his pay. He tracked it down through the VIN number. It turned up in a used car lot in Alabama. She'd sold it for eight hundred dollars cash."

"What about Darvis Kane?"

Daddy's face reddened. "If I could have found him, I believe I would have killed him. For months I kept my shotgun in the car. Eventually Gloria took it and kept it at her house for a long time. She knew what I was thinking. Always has. Even now, sometimes, I'll be someplace like Atlanta, or Birmingham, and I'll look over, and I'll think I see him, walking down the street, or driving in the lane next to me."

"He was married to Paige's Aunt Lisa, wasn't he?"

"That's right."

"Did she ever hear from him over the years?"

"Lisa Kane never would talk to me. Not after the first few days, when it got apparent they'd taken off together. She went around town saying some pretty ugly things about Jeanine. Gloria went out to that trailer of hers, tried to talk to her, but she ran Gloria off. She moved over to Athens to stay with another sister, and after that, I don't know what happened to her."

"You think Mama ran away with Darvis Kane, don't you?"

He held his hands palms up, examining them, like he was searching for a clue there.

"I didn't know what else to think."

"Did you have any idea she was . . . seeing somebody else?"

"Not at the time."

"What about later?"

"Later on, Gloria admitted to me that she'd heard some talk about Jeanine. That she was running with a fast crowd. At the time she didn't want to believe it. Your mama was like a little sister to your aunt."

"And there was never any sign? That she was unhappy? Or wanted out?"

"She seemed . . . restless. She'd go for long drives. Some days she'd leave you with a baby-sitter and just drive around. Said she just wanted some time for herself. She was so young, when we got married, and then when she had you. It was different for me. I'd been in the army, college, seen a little bit of the world. I always knew I'd come back home, start a business and a family. Your mama, I guess she was just finding out who she was, and what she wanted."

"And what she didn't want," I said, not bothering to hide the bitterness in my voice.

He ruffled my hair. "Don't you ever think that. She always wanted you. Always. The day she found out she was pregnant? She drove over to Atlanta, I forget which mall, and bought a bunch of maternity clothes. Had to pin the britches together, they were so big, but she was so proud and excited to be pregnant, she couldn't wait to have everybody know we were having a baby."

"Then why'd she leave me?"

"I wish I knew," he said. "I'd give anything if I could tell you, but I can't. She was good at covering things up. As good as me, it turns out."

"I used to wonder if she was dead," I said flatly. "Sometimes I hoped it. Because that would mean she hadn't meant to leave me."

He looked shocked.

"As far as we can find out, she's not dead, though. Austin did a computer search on that too. There hasn't been a death certificate issued to anybody with her name or date of birth."

"Computers can do all that?" he asked.

"And more. If I had Darvis Kane's date of birth or Social Security number, we could do a search on him. Find out if he's still alive. Maybe even where he is right now."

And Jeanine, I thought. We could find out if she was still with Darvis Kane. But I didn't say it. As it turned out, I didn't have to.

He turned the wedding band around and around while he thought about it. "Some things, maybe, are better left alone," he said finally.

"For you. But not for me."

He nodded. "All right. If you're sure you want to do this, I won't stand in your way. All the old Murdock Motors files are down in the basement at home. You can look through them, see if you can find Kane's personnel file. It oughta have what you're looking for."

"Thank you."

"But I don't want to know anything about that man. Nothing. You hear? I believe you when you say you need answers. I don't understand it, not really, but I believe it. I've got all the answers I need. I've made peace with this, and I don't want it all plowed up again. You do what you have to, Keeley. But leave me out of it."

I said okay. What else could I say? But I didn't believe him. He needed to know, just as much as I did.

We were almost back to the house when it occurred to me that there were a dozen more questions I needed to ask him. But it was too late. His mood had changed. As soon as he started the Tahoe's engine and turned the car away from the park, he'd made just as determined a turn away from our painful past. Cars sped past us on the blacktop. He fiddled with the radio dial, trying to find the rest of the late-night baseball scores from the coast. His jaw was clenched, and he held the steering wheel with such tension, I thought he would wrench it off the dashboard. I'd stirred up something in my father tonight, emotions I'd forgotten he possessed. Later, I told myself. There will be time for more talks later.

He turned into the driveway and shut off the Tahoe's engine. "Quite a night," he said, giving me a rueful smile.

"I guess you didn't know you'd be playing twenty questions when you asked me over for salmon loaf," I said. "Maybe next week I'll have to cook for myself."

"Never," he said quickly. "You're my best girl. Besides, who else would eat my cooking?"

I got out of the car and fumbled in my purse for my own car keys.

He unlocked the back door and stood there for a minute, looking back at me.

"You going right home? Or do you want to go down to the basement and poke around, before I lock up for the night?"

I blinked. After he'd made it clear just how reluctant he was to talk about Darvis Kane, I'd already started planning to look through the files while he was at work in the afternoon. Now here he was, inviting me in, pain or no pain.

"It's been a long night," I said finally. "There's no rush."

34

On Friday afternoon I had a pounding headache. This should have been a sign of unseen forces at work in my life. I should have known it was an omen. I should have gone home and gone straight to bed and stayed there for the next forty-eight hours. Unfortunately I took it to mean I'd spent too much time on a long-distance phone call to New York, where I was trying to figure out why a fancy fabric house there had waited three months to tell me that the silk for a client's living room drapes was on back order and wouldn't be shipped for another three months.

By the time I got off the phone from New York, Gloria was holding up her phone for me, and gesturing for me to pick up the other line.

"It's Nancy Rockmore over at Loving Cup," she warned. "Some kind of crisis over at Mulberry Hill."

"No," I said flatly, waving the phone away. "I'm all crisised out today. My brain is trying to explode."

Gloria pushed the hold button on her phone console. She took the ibuprofen bottle out of her top desk drawer. "Put out your hand," she ordered. I did so. She shook three capsules into my hand, went to the small refrigerator in the kitchen, and came back with a bottle of Diet Coke. "You need caffeine," she said.

I swallowed the pills with a hit of Diet Coke and burped delicately. "My head still hurts," I whimpered. "Can't you deal with whatever's going on over at Mulberry Hill?"

"No," she said, popping three ibuprofens into her own mouth and helping herself to my Diet Coke. "I've got headaches of my own. The cabinet guy just called from Annabelle Waites's house. Her Sub-Zero is half an inch too wide for the slot it's supposed to fit in. And

Annabelle has suddenly decided that she wants the spice cabinet to have glass-front doors instead of the paneled door we'd decided on. She's having some kind of meltdown."

"Oh," I said meekly. I took another, fortifying sip of Diet Coke, then picked up on line two.

"Miss Nancy," I said tentatively, "Gloria says you've got some kind of crisis over at the house?"

"*I* don't have a crisis," she corrected me. "It is four-thirty on Friday. In thirty minutes *I'll* be off work. In forty minutes *I'll* have a Chivas and water in one hand, and the remote control in the other. But my boss, and *your* client, Will Mahoney, now, he has a crisis."

"What now?" I asked.

"He wants to know what he's supposed to serve dinner off of tonight," Nancy drawled. "Seems pretty bent out of shape about it too."

"Dinner?" For a minute there, I had no idea what she was talking about.

"Yeah. Dinner. He's got his boxers all in a bunch about some dinner he's fixing tonight. Some woman from Atlanta he's trying to romance? Sent me clear over to Athens to buy flowers and fancy wine and likker and steaks. You know they're getting seven ninety-nine a pound for a goddamn filet mignon over there? That's a crime and a scandal if you ask me."

"Dinner!" It was all coming back to me now. Will was planning on showing his new home to Stephanie Scofield, the woman of his dreams.

"Men!" I exclaimed, rubbing my throbbing temples with my fingertips. "I bought him eight place settings of china and silver and crystal. Tell him it's all right in the cupboards. If it was a snake, it'd bite him. There are pots and pans and table linens too."

"I think he found all the dishes and crap," Miss Nancy said. "It's the table and chairs that he can't seem to find. I can see him overlooking something like a steak knife or a wineglass. But he's real adamant about not having a goddamn dining room table."

"Oh for God's . . ." I started to say. But then I stopped. My gaze traveled across the office and finally focused on a chunky pine kitchen table and two country French ladderback chairs set on either side. The tabletop was covered with fabric samples and old sketchbooks. I wrinkled my brow. I'd bought the table and chairs at the Scott Antique Show in Atlanta three months ago, to serve as a little dining area in the studio's kitchen, but had intended to have them loaded on the van of furniture for Will Mahoney's pump house. Somehow, they had never made it on the van. Somehow, they were still sitting right here in our studio.

"The dining room furniture is here," I said, my voice meek. "It never got loaded on the truck. Tell him I'll bring it right out there."

"Good," Miss Nancy said. "I've never seen him this worked up before."

I put the phone down and groaned, then looked around for Gloria. Just then I caught a glimpse of her car zooming down the street, away from me and my new crisis.

I picked the phone up again and dialed Manny Ortiz's number and prayed. His sister-in-law, Isabel Saldana, picked up on the third ring.

"Moving by Manny," she said, with only the slightest trace of a Cuban accent.

"Isabel? It's Keeley Murdock," I said. "Is Manny anywhere you can reach him? I've got an emergency delivery this afternoon."

"Keeley!" she said, her voice warm. "That paint color you picked out for the office is fantastic! I don't know how you talked Manny into going with lime green, but you are a genius. It changes everything. So sunny. I don't even mind coming to work in the morning."

"Thanks, Isabel," I said. "I'm glad you like it. But I've got to talk to Manny."

"Oh, but he's not here," she said. "Your aunt sent him to Atlanta to pick up an armoire and some other furniture for Mrs. Waites."

"When will he be back?" I asked, keeping my fingers crossed.

"They only left here at three," she said. "But the warehouse is clear down past the airport, and they had a couple other stops to make too. He's not due back till around eight, I think."

"Nooo," I wailed. "I've got to get a table and chairs moved out to Mulberry Hill right away. How about the other guys? Is Billy around? I think we could fit it into the trunk of my Volvo, if he can come over here and help me move it."

"Oh, Keeley," she said. "Manny took Tim and Jorge with him to Atlanta. And Billy had a soccer game. He just left. I'm the only one here, and I was just picking up my purse to leave when you called. Can it wait till tomorrow? Or Monday?"

"No," I said, "Never mind. It's my screwup. I'll just have to get it out there by myself."

"I'd help you, Keeley, but I have to pick up Maria at day care, and I'm late already."

"It's okay," I said. "It can't be that heavy."

But it was. The table was solid pine, but it felt like solid lead. Once I got it cleared off, I managed to turn it upside down and slide it across the carpet of the studio. But there was no way I was going to slide it across the doorstep, much less across the expanse of concrete sidewalk that lay between Glorious Interiors and my car.

I left the table blocking the doorway and went next door to Fleur. It wasn't quite five, but the lights were off. I tried the door. Locked. Damn Austin. Some best friend he was turning out to be.

I fumed for a while, then tried calling Daddy over at the lot. His receptionist said he was busy with a customer. I knew better than to try to get him away from a hot prospect.

All right. I was just going to do this myself. It wasn't impossible. I'd been moving furniture my whole life. I was young and strong.

Wrong. Young and weak. It took me half an hour to get the table out of the studio and hump it, inch by inch, over to the Volvo. Once I had the trunk up, I had to empty it of the assorted flotsam and jetsam that accumulates in every interior designer's trunk. I stepped out of my high-heeled black mules, took a deep breath, bent my knees, and grasping it by the back legs, heaved the table upward and toward the maw of the trunk.

I heard a tearing noise and looked down. The straight black cotton miniskirt I was wearing now had a four-inch rip up the right seam. While I was looking down I noticed that I had smears of dust across the front of my white silk tank top. My bra strap slipped off my shoulder. No matter. I had the table in the trunk. I adjusted the bra strap and shoved the edge of the table with my hip, to try to wedge it farther in. Another tearing noise. And a matching rip up the left seam of the skirt. I was past caring. It was getting close to six.

By moving the driver's seat all the way forward, I somehow managed to get the pair of chairs stuffed into the Volvo. I went back into the studio, grabbed my purse and keys, and locked up the shop.

With my knees doubled up almost to my chin, I did sixty miles an hour all the way out to Mulberry Hill. At some point in the drive, it occurred to me that I'd left my shoes—my two-hundred-dollar Jimmy Choos—back at the curb in front of the office. I made up my mind to add them to Will Mahoney's bill. This was all his fault. A mile from the turnoff to Mulberry Hill, at the point where Georgia 441 turns onto Old Rutledge Road, I saw flashing yellow lights ahead. Bells clanging. And just as I pulled up to the intersection, the black and white zebra striped railroad crossing bars slapped into place.

I felt the train rumbling toward me before I heard it. "NO!" I cried, slapping the steering wheel with frustration.

It seemed to me that this particular configuration of Southern Railway cars could have qualified for registration in the Guinness Book of Records. Mind-numbing expanses of cattle cars, liquefied natural gas tanker cars, unidentifiable freight cars, and yes, even half a dozen double-decker auto transport cars went creeping past the tracks in front of me.

I eyed my cell phone. I would have called Will Mahoney to tell him that I was on the way with his furniture, but I had no idea what his cell phone number was, or what the number at the pump house was. I had only his office phone number. I tried it now, and listened while his voice invited me to leave him a voice mail message.

"Will," I said, slightly breathless. "This is Keeley. If you're checking your voice mail at work, I just want you to know I'm on the way with the table and chairs. I'll be there in a jiffy, just as soon as this damn train is past me."

Finally, after an interminable amount of time, the bells clanged again, and the crossing bars lifted. The roof of the Volvo just cleared them as I roared across the tracks.

I didn't slow down once I left the blacktop in front of the entrance to Mulberry Hill. I barely noticed that the gates were fully installed, that all the landscaping along the driveway was completed. I didn't slow down until the driveway curved around the front of the mansion and around to the back, and the brick walkway to the pump house.

Will Mahoney stood in the middle of the walkway, holding his cell phone away from his face, glaring at it. I guess he'd been checking his messages.

I pulled the Volvo all the way to the edge of the brick walk. "I'm here," I called to him, throwing the car into park. I hopped out and darted around toward the open trunk.

"Here's your table and chairs," I said breathlessly. "I'm sorry to be so late. I would have gotten here earlier, but I couldn't get a truck. Or any movers. And then the train came . . ."

He flipped the phone shut and tucked it into the pocket of his khaki slacks. He was wearing a soft green short-sleeved sport shirt. It looked nice with his red hair. He looked nice with his red hair. His face was flushed.

"Never mind," he said, cutting me off. "Stephanie will be here in fifteen minutes. Just hurry up and help me get the stuff into the house. And then you'll have to help me set the table."

Will lifted the table out of the trunk with one swift movement. I followed lamely behind, with one of the chairs. He'd set up a fancy stainless steel grill cart on the patio, and the smell of burning charcoal wafted into the treetops. A tray of bacon-wrapped filets stood on a matching bar cart, along with a silver wine bucket and a cocktail shaker. My stomach growled. I hadn't had lunch. Or dinner.

"Where does it go?" Will asked, pausing in the doorway of the pump house.

"In front of the windows," I said, hurrying in behind him.

While he set up the table and chairs, I got the linens and tableware out of the cupboards where I'd stowed them earlier in the week. In ten minutes I had the table set, complete with the bouquet of deep yellow roses I found sitting on the kitchen counter.

"Done," I said finally, gesturing toward the table with a flourish. "And with five minutes to spare."

He'd been loading discs onto the CD player. The music started. Tinkly jazz. He turned around, looked at me again, and pointed and laughed.

"What? You don't like the table?"

"The table's fine," he said. "It's you. You're a wreck."

I looked down at the smears of dirt on my chest, my ripped skirt, and my bare feet. With as much dignity as I could muster, I hitched up the bra strap that was sliding down my shoulder.

"I'll just be going now," I said. "Wouldn't want to spoil your dinner date."

He reached out and hiked up my other bra strap, and shook his head.

"Where'd you get this thing?"

I slapped his hand away. "What? My bra? That's kind of a personal question."

"I mean it. The thing's a disaster. It doesn't even fit you. What kind is it? Hanes? Fruit of the Loom?"

"This is a very expensive bra, I'll have you know," I said, backing away from him. "It's a Bali. And it cost thirty dollars. On sale."

"It's a piece of crap," Will said. "Look at those seam lines."

I looked down. Now that he mentioned it, you could clearly see the stitch lines on the lace cups of the bra through the silk of my blouse.

"And why are you wearing a white bra?" he demanded. "Nobody wears white bras under a white blouse. With your skin shade, you should be wearing ivory. And certainly, with your bust, you need a bra with a leotard back. That's why your straps keep slipping. You should throw that damn thing away."

"Ahem." A delicate cough. We both turned around to see Stephanie Scofield standing in the doorway of the pump house, a symphony in red silk, holding up a bottle of red wine. She looked at me with one eyebrow raised. "Am I early?"

35

Will's face blushed so deeply it was hard to tell where his face stopped and his hairline started. "Stephanie," he said. And that's all he said. He seemed to have been struck dumb by the magnificence of her.

Admittedly, she was pretty magnificent-looking. The dress was an abbreviated sleeveless column of red silk. Her bare arms and legs were tanned a deep, glowing bronze. She'd done her hair up in a deceptively simple-looking French twist. Little gold hoop earrings twinkled from her earlobes, and her strappy red sandals showed off another twinkling gold toe ring.

As for me, I was struck dumb by the contrast in our appearances. She was chic. I was shabby. I didn't have anything near as hip as a toe ring, it occurred to me. At the moment, actually, I didn't even have on a pair of shoes.

She held out the bottle of wine and smiled brightly at Will. "I've brought you a housewarming gift."

Slowly the gift of speech was restored to him. "Great," he said, taking the bottle from her, holding her hand in his. "Welcome to Mulberry Hill." He gestured around the pump house. "Actually though, I guess you'd call this the annex. Until we're done with the work on the main house."

Stephanie looked around and clapped her hands in delight. "It's adorable!" She looked at Will questioningly. "May I?"

"Sure!" he said heartily.

She walked around the room, running her hands over the furniture, exclaiming over the framed photographs, opening and closing the heart-pine kitchen cupboards, even popping her head into the bedroom and the bathroom. Finally she came back and spoke to me for the first time.

"Kelly? This is wonderful. Did you do all this by yourself?"

"Actually," I said, "it's Keeley."

"Right. So sorry. Keeley. I love your work."

"Thank you," I said. I tried to slink toward the door, hoping she wouldn't notice my Elly May Clampett couture. I wanted to go home. I wanted to see if I could find my shoes. I wanted a bath, and I really wanted to throw my Bali bra in the garbage disposal.

"Oh, don't rush off," Stephanie said, grabbing my arm. "Stay and have a cocktail with us." She looked from me to Will. "That's all right, isn't it?"

"No, no," I said, squirming under her touch. "I have to be going. I really can't stay."

"Will," Stephanie said, pouting. "Make Keeley stay for a drink. One little drink."

"Yes," Will said, unenthusiastically. "You should stay, Keeley. For one little drink."

Stephanie was still squeezing my arm. I think the blood flow to my brain was being cut off, because although I clearly intended to go, and I could clearly tell that Will desperately wanted me to go, I ended up agreeing to stay.

"I'll fix us all a drink," Will said. "What will you ladies have?" He looked first at Stephanie.

"Do you happen to know how to mix a cosmopolitan?" she asked. I snuck him a wink. He ignored me.

"I've got all the ingredients right outside on the bar cart," he assured her. "Keeley? How about you? Should I make that two cosmopolitans?"

"Why not?" I said. "Need any help?"

"Not at all," he said. He gave Stephanie a meaningful look. "But I wouldn't mind some company while I do the mixing."

"You go," I said, giving Stephanie a little shove. "I want to slip into the bathroom and clean up a little. I've been moving furniture, and I'm a big mess."

"You look darling," Stephanie said, averting her eyes from my bare feet. "Sort of . . . pastoral."

I darted into the bathroom. The mirror confirmed what I already knew. My hair was sweat-soaked and totally out of control. And I was really, really dirty. Without giving it too much thought, I locked the bathroom door. I peeled off my clothes and hopped into Will's shower. The hot water felt great. I'd already soaked my hair by the time I looked around and discovered the only shampoo in the bathroom was something in a black squeeze tube called Grunge.

It smelled like pine cones. I didn't care. Any shampoo was better than none. I lathered up and quickly rinsed the shampoo out of my hair. Within five minutes I was out of the shower and toweling off. I congratulated myself on spending Will's money on expensive thick white Egyptian cotton towels. I gathered my damp hair into a tight ponytail, then, remembering Stephanie's chic chignon, I twisted the ends around and tucked them back into themselves, sort of a poor man's French twist.

A damp washcloth took care of the worst dust smears on my tank top, but there was no fixing the ripped seams of my skirt. I dressed quickly, hesitating, but then making the command decision to go without the disputed Bali bra. But where to put it? My skirt had no pockets, and my purse was still in the front seat of the Volvo. In the end I swallowed hard, mummified the bra in toilet tissue, and hid it in the bottom of the bathroom waste basket. Thirty dollars, right in the trash, I thought. I consoled myself with the idea of slipping back in here, later, with my pocketbook, and retrieving it.

It felt odd, walking around a strange man's house, with nothing between me and the silk of my blouse, but at least the damn straps weren't slipping off my shoulder. And the underwire wasn't cutting into my rib cage. As I joined Stephanie and Will out on the patio, where cocktail hour was apparently well under way, I wished I had another bra to put on. I wished I had some lipstick, maybe a little eyeliner. And shoes. It was hard to feel like a professional interior designer in bare feet.

"There you are," Stephanie cried, as I padded up to them. "Feeling better?"

"Much," I said.

Will managed to tear his eyes away from his beloved and give me a cursory glance. "Is your hair wet?" he asked, looking puzzled.

"Yes," I said. "I hope you don't mind, but I took a quick shower."

He took a step closer and sniffed my hair. "You smell a little funny. Kinda like . . . a Christmas tree?"

"I borrowed a little of your shampoo, while I was at it," I said. "The Grunge? I'll be happy to replace it, if you'll tell me where I can buy it. I haven't seen that brand before."

"Grunge?" Stephanie said, wrinkling her nose. "There's a shampoo called Grunge? Why would anybody want to wash their hair with Grunge?"

Will took a sip of wine from the long-stemmed goblet he was holding. "Actually, that wasn't shampoo. It's grout cleaner, for the tile. I'm having a little mildew problem in the shower, and the plumber recommended this cleaner." He gave me a helpful smile.

"I can give you the web address to order more, if you like."

I held my hand up to my topknot. Half-dried now, it felt weirdly stiff. "Thanks just the same," I said, smiling back. "I think I'll stick to my own brand from now on."

He put his drink down and handed me a martini glass full of a delicate pale pink nectar. Condensation beaded the lip of the glass. "Cosmopolitan?"

I took the drink gratefully and knocked back half of it in one swallow. I was just barely able to keep from smacking my lips, it was that good. Icy, sweet, tangy, with just the right kick.

"Lovely," I said. I finished mine off and held my glass out for another, which Will poured with a frown. I ignored the frown and enjoyed my cocktail, which reminded me of limeade, with a kick.

Stephanie took a ladylike sip of her own drink. "I just love these, don't you? It feels so grown up and elegant, drinking out of a martini glass." She held hers out toward Will. "Why don't you try one too?"

He shook his head. "I'll just stick to this wine of yours, thanks. Real men don't drink pink."

Stephanie giggled. "You're so clever, Will. Real men don't drink pink. That could be a beer commercial. You should be writing advertising copy instead of selling bras."

I felt oddly defensive on Will's behalf. "What's wrong with selling bras? The world needs a good bra."

Will snuck me an appreciative look. "Not just the world, apparently."

I blushed and crossed my arms over my chest.

"Oh, that's not how I meant it," Stephanie said, recovering quickly. "I just meant, Will, you really have a good head for marketing, that's all. I think the bra business must be fascinating. However does a man get into a business like that?" I swear, she even batted her eyelashes at him.

Will was soaking it all up. "It's not that unusual. There are a lot of men in the business. I got into it through the back door, you might say. My background is in textile engineering. I was working for a company that makes blue jeans. They acquired a company that makes intimates, swimwear, and loungewear, so all of a sudden I was in the bra business. And when I had the ability to buy my own company, Loving Cup was a natural."

"I bet you miss blue jeans," Stephanie said.

"Not at all," he corrected her. "A bra is a fascinating garment."

"Every man I ever met has only had one interest in bras," I said, slurping my way to the bottom of my second cosmopolitan. "And that's in how to get it removed."

Stephanie giggled; Will flushed a little.

"A bra is the most technically difficult garment you can design," Will said. "So there's a lot of engineering involved. Did you know the average bra has between twenty-two and twenty-seven different components?"

"That is fascinating," Stephanie agreed.

"And each one has to be cut to a very exact, specific standard," Will continued. "With a garment as small as a bra, anything that is off by even the smallest measurement will drastically alter the quality of the finished product."

"Wow!" It came out sounding pretty sarcastic. Will frowned and took my glass away. "These drinks are pretty strong, you know," he said. "Absolut ain't no Kool-Aid. I wouldn't want you to get pulled over for driving under the influence."

"I am not under the influence," I said, trying to act dignified.

"Maybe a little tiddly," Stephanie suggested. "Leave her alone, Will. I think she's cute. Now, tell us some more about bras."

"Yes, Will," I said, mimicking her wide-eyed breathlessness. "Please do."

He shot me a look. "I'd better get the coals going if we're going to eat these steaks before midnight."

Stephanie blanched. "Steaks?"

"Filet mignon," Will said proudly. "How do you like yours?"

She chewed her fingernail. "Will," she said quietly. "I don't eat red meat. Don't you remember, last week at dinner, I told you, I haven't eaten red meat since 1996."

"Oh," he said. "Not at all?"

She shook her head. Not a hair on it moved. I wondered how she did that. My grout-cleaner stiffened hair was already starting to come undone.

"Do you have any salmon?" she asked. "Or maybe Chilean sea bass?"

His face fell. "I had my assistant drive to Athens to pick up these steaks."

"I know I told you about the red meat thing," Stephanie said. "Do you have any idea at all about the kind of chemicals they feed cattle these days? Or how cows are slaughtered?" She shuddered.

"I've got a nice Caesar salad prepared," Will said hopefully. "Chilled, poached asparagus. You can eat that, right?"

"Absolutely," Stephanie said, brightening. "I love asparagus. And I can eat the salad, if you'll leave the dressing off."

"And baked potatoes," he added. "With sour cream and chives."

"Baked potatoes?" She looked at him as though he'd just offered her a choice oozing slice of beef heart. "Do you know how many grams of carbohydrates are in a baked potato?"

"I never thought of that," Will said. "Just the salad and asparagus then."

Stephanie gave his arm a loving pat. "Sounds lovely. These cosmopolitans have got me so thirsty. Could I get some water?"

"Sure," Will said. "That's one thing about this old place that you're going to love. The original well is still going strong. We've got the sweetest, purest well water you've ever tasted."

"Well water?" Stephanie's upper lip quivered just the tiniest amount. I'm sure Will didn't even notice. "You mean, like, right out of the ground? Is that safe? Is it even legal? I saw a documentary once, where they showed a droplet of tap water under a microscope. Protozoa! Swarming all over the place! And trace chemicals." She shuddered once again. "I usually drink bottled water. Perrier if you have it."

"Perrier," Will repeated dumbly. "I'm not sure. My assistant did the shopping . . ."

"I think I saw some bottled water in the house," I volunteered. "I'll just run in and get it for Steffie before I take off."

"You're leaving?" Will asked, his voice sounding hopeful. Maybe the evening could still be salvaged, he probably thought. Right after his bride-to-be polished off a big plate of chives and romaine lettuce leaves.

"Big plans for the night," I assured him.

In the kitchen, I opened up the pantry and found the bottled water I'd left for him on Monday, right beside the Scotch bottle. It was just Poland Spring, the cheapest they'd had at the store that day. I took the bottle, and a plastic bag I found under the sink, and went into the bathroom, closing the door carefully behind me. I unscrewed the cap on the Poland Spring bottle and listened while the water gurgled happily down the sink drain. Then I knelt down beside the commode and submerged the water bottle in the bowl. It glugged and glugged until it was full.

I washed my hands in the sink, retrieved my bra from the trash basket, and placed it in the plastic bag. Then I thoughtfully straightened the bathroom, putting out fresh towels and guest soaps. I did want Will to impress his new love.

Out on the patio, the happy couple was just sitting down to their salads. The steaks had magically disappeared. I noticed that the grill had been covered too. Will had apparently decided to forgo his own dinner in order not to offend her. I felt a tiny, grudging sliver of admiration for my clueless, redheaded client, but nothing whatsoever for his date.

I placed the bottled water at Stephanie's place and blew them both a big kiss. "Bon appetit, y 'all."

36

On Saturday morning I watched as a steady stream of customers went in and out of Fleur. It was June, after all, still bridal season. When I saw Austin's green delivery van pull up to the curb at two that afternoon, I locked up the studio and strolled over to the florist's shop.

He was wearing navy cargo shorts and a green and white Fleur Flower Arts logo shirt, and he was picking up the phone when I walked in.

Austin glanced up, blew me a kiss, then started writing things down on an order pad. The shop was a mess, the concrete floor littered with bits of white satin ribbon, lace, leaves, stems, and fallen petals, and the aisles were jammed with flowers; buckets of freesias, orange blossoms, stocks, hydrangeas, lilies, roses, daisies, and exotics whose names I didn't know. Their perfume swirled around me. It was a happy, busy, exciting place, and a sharp aching wave of sorrow hit me so hard it almost knocked me back out the door.

He hung up the phone. "What?" he asked, a look of concern on his face. "What's the matter, Keeley?"

No good trying to make a happy face. "All this wedding shit. It's silly, I know, but it makes me feel so sad. I keep thinking about how my wedding day should have been . . ."

Austin took me by the shoulders and marched me over to the wooden bench behind the counter. "You sit here, little missy," he ordered.

He reached around to the walk-in cooler behind him and fumbled around in one of the tall galvanized buckets until he came up with two cans of Diet Coke. He popped one and handed it to me.

He popped his own, took a drink, and let out a satisfied sigh.

"Do you want to talk wedding shit?" he asked. "Let me tell you about Betsey Forst's wedding. That's where I've been all morning, over at the rectory at First Presbyterian. I finally just told her mama to give me a call when the child's medication kicks in. I had to get out of there before I threw my own hissy fit."

"That bad?"

He shuddered. "Tell me something, Keeley Rae. What is it about a wedding that makes a perfectly agreeable girl turn into a raving, shrieking, lunatic bitch?"

"Betsey Forst was shrieking? That little mouse? I've never even heard her talk above a whisper."

"She was Bridezilla," Austin said. "I kept expecting her head to swivel all the way around on her neck. You know, she actually pelted me with her bouquet? Said the color of the Tineke roses I had shipped in from Ecuador made her physically ill. Do you know I had to get up at five this morning and drive to the Atlanta airport to pick the things up and bring them back here and get them conditioned in time to make up that bouquet?"

"The little ingrate," I said. "So you just had one wedding today?"

"Three! Three nightmare weddings," Austin said, swigging more Diet Coke. "The second one wasn't so bad. Lindsey Winzeler is a doll. But Carolyn Shoemaker. I swear, you don't want to get me started on that one. I *told* her a bouquet made entirely of fruit was a bad idea. But she absolutely insisted. So it's her own damn fault she sprained her ankle. Where do they get these ideas?"

"Martha Stewart," I said helpfully. "It's all Martha's fault. That damn magazine ought to be outlawed. My clients read it too. And they clip out the pictures and want me to find them a chair just like the one in Martha's house in Connecticut. Which is always some one-of-a-kind eighteenth-century hand-carved Jacobean job that costs more than my parents' first house."

Austin nodded agreement.

"You never mentioned how Carolyn Shoemaker sprained her ankle," I pointed out.

He rolled his eyes. "*Champagne* grapes. They were supposed to be little tiny champagne grapes in the bridesmaid's bouquets. Those are the ones the size of English peas. So what does the mama bring in for me to work with? Big old hulking green grapes. And they weren't the freshest. That's what happens when you try to do something on the cheap. But they insisted it would be fine, so I wired them up. What do I know? I'm just a professional floral artist. Anyway, the six brides-maids go floating down the aisle with their rooty-tooty fresh and frooty bouquets. And invariably some of the grapes fall off. And get mashed on that slippery hardwood floor. The next thing you know, little Miss Shoemaker's pump hits one of the suckers, and she goes fly-ing ass over teakettle."

He started to laugh in spite of himself. And then I started to laugh. And pretty soon streams of Diet Coke were shooting out my nostrils. Not so pretty. He had me crying. Only this was good crying.

"I'd love to have seen that," I said, wiping the tears with my shirt-sleeve.

"Call up Billy Howard," Austin said. "He was videotaping the whole thing. I hope he didn't miss the part where the groom reached down to try to help her up and slipped his ownself and screamed FUCK! Right there in front of the entire St. Anne's congregation."

After that I had to get up and get some paper towels to mop the tears off my face. I was already feeling better.

"So, what's up, toots?" Austin asked, sweeping some of the clutter on his workbench into a big trash can.

"I've been playing Nancy Drew," I started.

"No," Austin said. "This was all my idea. I get to be Nancy. You have to be Bess or George. Take your pick."

"Bess was plump and George was probably lesbian," I said. "Not much of a choice, when it comes down to it. Anyway, I talked to Daddy. You know, about Mama."

He patted my shoulder. "Good for you! What did you find out?"

"He hired a private detective, after she left, but all he managed to come up with was the fact that she'd sold her car in Birmingham, for eight hundred dollars."

Austin's face fell. "That's all? He has no idea where she went, or whether she went off with that man?"

"No. But he did tell me I could look in the old employee files to see if I can find Darvis Kane's date of birth and Social Security number."

"It's a start," Austin said. "How was he about the whole thing? Was he angry about you stirring all this up?"

"No," I said. "He says he made peace with the whole thing a long time ago, but he understands why I need answers. But he won't talk about Darvis Kane. He made that real clear."

Austin put down his Diet Coke can. "What are we waiting for? Let's get cracking on those old files."

"They're in the basement at Daddy's house," I said. "And now would be a good time, since he's at the lot all day. I was thinking, I could give you the key, and you could look through the files."

"And what, may I ask, are you going to be doing while I'm knee-deep in silverfish and mildew down in that basement?"

I looked out the plate-glass window of Fleur, toward the square. The big old red brick county courthouse blocked the view, but on the other side of it was another shop, about the same size as this one. The name on the forest green awning said Kathleen's Antiques now, but if you looked closely, you could see where Charm Shop had been painted out all those years ago.

All week long, I'd been thinking about going in to Kathleen's, to see Chrys Graham. Now, it seemed, would be a good time to visit my mother's old friend.

37

Kathleen's wasn't one of those snooty antiques shops where you hold your breath—and your elbows at your side.

The aisles were cluttered with shelves of crystal, china, and silver, and different areas in the middle of the shop had been set up as room vignettes; this one a Victorian parlor, that one a dining room, another a bedroom with an iron bedstead, mahogany dresser, and stacks of vintage bed linens. A huge old window air conditioner hummed noisily from a window in the back, and the room smelled faintly of mildew and lemon-scented furniture wax.

In my granddaddy's time, this had been a drugstore, and it still had the old pressed tin ceiling tiles, beadboard walls, and floor made of tiny black and white hexagonal tiles. The drugstore counter was long gone, of course, but the brass cash register was the original, as was Chrys Graham.

A doorbell buzzed somewhere from the back of the store when I walked in, and through the dim light I spied a petite woman sitting on an overstuffed sofa, looking startled, before she hastily stubbed out a cigarette.

"Hey," she called in her familiar raspy voice. "I'll be right with you, unless you just want to poke around and not be bothered."

I walked toward the back of the store so she could get a better look at me.

She was waving the smoke-filled air around her with heavily bejeweled hands. Chrys Graham had to be in her early sixties, but she was still cute, in a pixieish way, with straight brown bangs that nearly reached the tips of her tortoiseshell glasses, behind which shone a pair of impish brown eyes.

"You caught me!" she rasped. "Promise you won't tell my niece I was smoking in here. Kathleen says I'm a fire hazard."

Silently I held up my right hand in the Girl Scout pledge.

Miss Graham tilted her head and peered at me over the bridge of the glasses, like she thought maybe she could remember who I was.

"Don't tell me," she said slowly. "I know that face, but I just need a little bit of time to put a name with it."

I sat down on the sofa beside her.

She cupped my chin gently between her hands and looked directly into my eyes.

"You're Jeanine's little girl," she said finally. "Keeley Murdock, that's it, isn't it? I'm trying to decide who you look more like— Jeanine or your daddy."

"I think it's the eyes," I told her. "Everybody says I've got the Murdock nose."

"You're your mama, made over," she declared, as though that settled it. "How long has it been since she ran off with Darvis Kane?"

Her directness took me by surprise.

"Ma'am?"

"You did know she ran off with one of the salesmen at your daddy's car lot, didn't you?"

I nodded. At least we had that out of the way.

"It was 1979," I said.

"That's right," she said, nodding in agreement. "The same year they flooded the lake. I remember it, because Georgia Power bought our old family place out there, and I took a two-month-long trip to San Francisco with the money they paid me. When I got back, I heard the news that your mama had taken off."

I looked around the antiques shop. "She used to bring me here with her, you know, when she was fixing the windows. You had a kitten I liked to play with."

"Junior," Miss Graham said. "A calico. I was always partial to cali-cos. Where have you been all these years? Why haven't you been in to visit with me?"

"Maybe I wasn't ready."

"But you're ready now. I heard you got your heart broken. The Jernigan boy. Which one was it?"

"A.J.," I said.

"Never could keep those boys straight," Miss Graham muttered. "GiGi bought all her clothes here, you know, back in the day. Your Aunt Gloria bought a lot of stuff from me too. When I ran the place, the Charm Shop had all the latest fashions. Everybody who was any-body bought from me."

"I remember," I said. "One time you gave us matching mother-daughter outfits. Red plaid jumpers and black blouses."

"That's right," she said, pleased that I remembered. "Your mama was a walking advertisement for the shop. Everything she put on looked like it had been made specially for her. She could have been a runway model, with her looks and style."

She carefully considered my own outfit. I was wearing a sleeveless turquoise blouse, a turquoise and silver bead necklace, and white capris, with a pair of turquoise beaded sandals I'd bought at the Ap-parel Mart on my last trip to Atlanta. She rubbed the fabric of my top between her fingertips and nodded her approval.

"Silk. Good. I can't abide these synthetics. I wouldn't say you had her same sense of style. But you'll do."

"Thanks," I said. "I'm trying to find out what happened to my mother. Where she went."

She shrugged her bony shoulders. "Ask your daddy."

"I have. Right after she left, he hired a private detective to try and find out, but they never really got any answers. With computers and everything now, I thought maybe I could find something out. A friend is helping me."

"Boyfriend?" She grinned slyly.

"Just a friend," I said. "Austin LeFleur. Do you know him? He runs the florist's shop across the square."

"Bouquets by Betty Ann," Miss Graham said. "I know the place."

"Austin did a computer search. He didn't find any record of a divorce. My father says he never filed because he didn't know where she'd gone. And there's no death record that we can find, so I was hoping . . ."

"What? What were you hoping? What kind of mother goes off and leaves a child without so much as a word?"

"I don't know," I whispered. "Was my mama that kind of person?"

"Not when I knew her," Miss Graham said. "She was maybe a little flighty, but she was young yet. Not even thirty."

"Did she talk to you about her marriage? Did you know she was unhappy?"

"Unhappy? Who told you that?"

"Nobody, really," I said. "But I know there were rumors. Before she left. That she was running with a wild crowd. My aunt admitted as much to Daddy, after Mama left."

Miss Graham reached for her cigarette pack. She shook one out and lit it. She inhaled and closed her eyes.

For a minute I thought maybe she'd fallen asleep. Finally she opened her eyes and exhaled loudly.

"I never judged Jeanine," she said. "She didn't ask my advice, and I didn't offer any. I wasn't her mama, and I wasn't any saint. Never said I was. That said, I knew she was up to something she didn't want your daddy to know about. The last three or four months, before she left town, she asked me to pay her in cash, instead of the usual check, which I was glad to do."

"How much money would that have been?"

Her laugh rasped like a wood file. "Not that much. I probably only paid her twenty dollars a window, something like that. And most of the time she took it out in clothes. But those last months, she wanted cash money."

"This wild crowd she was running with," I said. "Who all were they?"

She raised one thinly arched eyebrow. "That was a long time ago, honey. People change."

"But who were they? If I could find out, maybe I could talk to them. Somebody has to know something."

She shook her head slowly. "See, these were people who were sliding around, messing around on the side. Churchgoing, respectable people. It wasn't like they advertised what they were up to. It was all rumors, that's all."

"What kind of rumors? Come on, Miss Graham, it's been more than twenty years. Nobody cares about this stuff but me."

"That's what you think," she retorted. "Anyway, some of 'em are dead. Some of 'em moved on."

"And some of them are still living right here in Madison. Tell me their names. Please?"

She reached for the coffee cup where she'd stubbed out her last cigarette, and flicked a half inch of ash into it.

"Do you remember your mama's cousin Sonya?"

"Sonya Wyrick. But she moved away years ago."

"To Kannapolis, North Carolina," Miss Graham said. "Sonya and Jeanine were thick as thieves back then. Sonya's marriage had just broken up, and she was wild as a hare. Dated every married man in town."

"That's why Daddy didn't like her," I said.

"He was about the only man in town who didn't like her!" Miss Graham said. "I never could understand what they saw in her either. She was a hard-bitten thing, with bleached hair and little skinny legs. Talk was that she left those kids of hers alone at night, while she went tramping around till all hours."

"Shawn and Tanya," I said, suddenly remembering my cousin's names. "One time they spent the weekend at our house. Shawn could spit through his front teeth. And Tanya wore a bra. Daddy was gone to a convention when they came, I think. It was like a big party. We stayed up late and had frozen pizza. And watched scary movies on TV."

"I just bet," Miss Graham said dryly.

"That's all I remember about them," I said. "I think that's the only time they were ever at our house. And I'm pretty sure I never spent the night over there."

"Your daddy wouldn't have allowed it," Miss Graham agreed. "Sonya Wyrick's reputation was not very good around here."

"Who else?" I asked. "You said there was a whole crowd she was running with. But that's the only name I've heard. What about Darvis Kane? Did anybody ever hear from him after they left?"

She stubbed out her cigarette in the coffee cup and stood up suddenly. "I gotta open the door and air this place out. If Kathleen comes back in here and smells this smoke, she'll have my hide."

I followed her to the front of the shop. She picked up a heavy black flatiron and used it as a wedge to prop the door open. Warm air flowed in. She went behind a glass display case filled with old jewelry and bits and pieces of silver, and brought out a can of Glade air freshener, with which she proceeded to mist the entire store.

"That's better," she said, discarding the can in the trash.

"Now it smells like rose-scented cigarette smoke," I said. "What about it? Darvis Kane had a wife and kids. Somebody must know something about him. The two of them didn't just fall off the face of the earth. Just tell me a name, Miss Graham. Please? One name. Somebody who can tell me about my mother and Darvis Kane. I'll be discreet. Nobody else has to know."

"In Madison? Who are you kidding? If a mouse farts in this town, you know it before the smoke clears. Anyway, it's all old history. What if you did find your mama? What would you do? What would you say after all this time? And how does your daddy feel about all this?"

"Daddy understands," I said, putting some steel in my voice.

"And I'll figure out the rest when I figure out what happened to her. Which I fully intend to do."

She sighed loudly. "I have to live in this town, you know. Talk to Sonya. Last I heard, she was still in Kannapolis. Shouldn't be too hard to find, with a last name like that."

"Thanks," I told her.

"You might not thank me, after you hear what she has to say," Miss Graham said, her voice sounding suddenly old and morbid. "Don't say I didn't tell you so."

38

Austin waved at me from a booth tucked into the far corner of the soda fountain at Madison Drugs. He had a huge banana split in front of him, and a spoon poised to dig into it.

"I'm celebrating," he said, before I'd even had a chance to slide into the booth.

"Hey, Keeley," called Vivi Blanchard, who's been waitressing at the drugstore for as long as I can remember. She nodded her head at Austin. "You havin' what he's havin'?"

"What he's havin' is a heart attack, Vivi," I said. "I haven't even had lunch today. Is there any chicken salad left?"

She turned around and opened the door of the refrigerator that stood behind the counter, holding up a half-full Tupperware dish.

"Have you got any ripe tomatoes?"

"Doc brought some in from his garden this morning," she said.

"Good." I could hear my own stomach growling. "Just some chicken salad and tomatoes then. And maybe a couple saltines? And a Diet Coke?"

"There's pie," Vivi said, winking at me. "One slice of lemon chess is all that's left. I'll have to throw it out if you don't eat it. You want me to save it for you?"

I groaned. "Save me the pie and leave the saltines off then."

It was late Saturday afternoon. The soda fountain was mostly empty, except for a handful of Little Leaguers and their dads, finishing off ice cream sundaes.

"Okay," I asked Austin, after I'd greeted the dads and gotten the game results, "what are you celebrating?"

He picked up a file folder from the seat next to him and slid it across the table to me.

"Darvis Kane," he said. "I believe I may have a lead on the whereabouts of the elusive Darvis Kane."

My heart was racing, but I wouldn't allow myself to touch the file folder. Not yet.

"You found the old employee records down in the basement?" I asked.

"Finally! Your daddy didn't make it exactly easy. It took me forever just to drag the file cabinet out from under an old workbench. And it's so dark down there, I had to carry all the old files upstairs in a laundry basket, just so I could read the labels. But I did it. I found Darvis."

Vivi walked up to the table right then, with my chicken salad plate and my drink.

She set everything down, including my check. "Your daddy and them doing okay?" she asked.

"Just fine," I said.

She hesitated a beat. "I'm sorry about what all you been through. That Paige Plummer oughtta be slapped into next week."

"Thanks," I said, hoping that would be the end of it.

"I never liked her. Nor her mama." She lowered her voice, "Come to think of it, all of them Franklin girls was nothin' but trash."

"Well . . . it's all water under the dam now." I was starting to find that clichés were astonishingly useful when one was in a cliché-ridden situation.

Her red curls bounced as she nodded her head in complete agreement. Then she went off to check on the Little Leaguers.

"As I was saying," Austin said. "Just like your daddy promised, I found the file with Darvis's birthdate and Social Security number. I was so excited, I did eighty speeding back to town to get on my computer."

I took a forkful of the chicken salad. "Okay, Nancy, what did you find out?"

"First off," Austin said. "Darvis Kane was a Scorpio. That should have been a red flag right there. Your daddy never should have hired him. You know how Scorpios are. Back-stabbers."

"A.J. was a Scorpio," I said.

"Scorpios are very sexual," Austin said, grinning wickedly. "And manipulative. They exert a sort of malevolent power over others."

"Malevolent?"

"Don't you love that word? You know," he went on. "It was really inevitable that your mother would end up under that man's influence."

"Why?"

"She was born in January, right? An Aquarian. Aquarians are very susceptible to the charms of a Scorpio. They're creative, but fragile in a way. Your mama never had a chance against a man like Darvis Kane."

I pushed a bite of chicken salad around my plate with my fork. "Other than voodoo, what do you have that's concrete?"

Austin opened the file and looked down at his notes.

"Darvis LeRoy Kane. Date of birth: October 30, 1948, in Wedowee, Alabama. Married to Lisa Franklin. Two children. Place of residence, Pine Manor Trailer Court, Lot 9C. Went to work for your daddy in October of 1977, as a salesman. Promoted to sales manager six months later. Employment terminated March 15, 1979."

Austin looked up at me. "Your daddy kept sending his paycheck to Lisa Kane for two months after Darvis ran off with your mama. In fact, he probably would have kept right on sending it to her, except the last one was returned to him with no forwarding address."

"After Lisa moved in with her sister in Athens," I said. "That sounds exactly like Daddy. He felt guilty that his wife had taken those children's father away from them. Even after Lisa Kane went around town saying awful stuff about us."

I cut the tomato with the side of my fork. Red juices and seeds oozed onto the plate. I sprinkled it all with salt, tasted, and then sat back.

"What did you find out with your computer search?"

Austin mashed the banana with a bit of ice cream and tasted it. Next he heaped the whipped cream at one end of the dish and stirred it around with the syrup until he had a syrup and whipped cream soup. He smacked his lips after a couple of bites.

"Darvis isn't dead either," he said. "But Lisa Kane was more determined than your daddy, because she got a no-fault divorce from Darvis in 1982."

"Three years later," I said. "Wonder how she tracked him down?"

"She didn't," Austin said. "The state of Georgia did. And nailed him for back child support payments, to the tune of thirty-five hundred dollars."

I put my fork down. "You're really good," I said, trying to control my eagerness. "So where is Darvis now? Can we talk to him?"

Austin frowned and dabbed at a bit of whipped cream on his upper lip. "I don't exactly know where Darvis is. Yet."

"How'd you find out all this other stuff? I thought you did a computer search and tracked him down?"

"I did the computer search, didn't find a death certificate on file for him, but I also couldn't find a recent address. So I tried Lisa Franklin Kane. And I found her. Simple as anything. She's living in a little town in Florida . . ." He opened the file folder and paged through his scribbled notes. "Palatka, Florida. I think it's somewhere in the middle of the state."

"And she talked to you?" I found that hard to believe. "Willingly?" That didn't exactly jibe with my father' description of Lisa Kane's hostile attitude.

"She might have misunderstood who I said I was," Austin said.

"You made up a big fat lie," I said accusingly.

"It's called a pretense. Your professional private investigators use them all the time to dig up dirt. Anyway, why not? It wasn't a lie that hurt anybody. I just told her I was an officer at a bank in Madison, and we had a safe deposit box made out to Darvis Kane, and there was twenty years' rent due on it, and I needed to know where he was to send him the contents."

"For real? What did she say?"

Austin winced. "Lord, God. The woman cusses like a trooper. She said her deadbeat rat bastard EX-husband had run off with another woman years ago, left her high and dry with two little girls to support, and by rights, anything in that box should go to her. I explained that her name wasn't listed on the rental agreement for the box, and if she had a claim on it, she'd have to take it through the courts. That's when she told me about the divorce and the back child support. She claims he still owes her thousands more, too, by the way."

"Does she have any idea where he is now?"

He shook his head regretfully. "None. Lisa Kane seems to think he's hiding out, not just from her, but from the law."

"Why? What's she think he's done?"

"She just said he was a crook. 'Once a crook, always a crook,' were her exact words. Along with a lot of other words I won't repeat in a family setting." He looked around guiltily at the little kids at the next table, who were busy pelting each other with paper napkin spitballs, and not paying the least bit of attention to us.

"What?" I leaned in closer to get the scoop.

"She said she'd do anything if I helped her track down Darvis Kane so she could get hold of the money in the safe deposit box," he whispered. "And I do mean anything." He blushed furiously.

"Austin! What did you say?"

"What do you think I said? I told her I was an officer of a bank, and her coarse language was offensive, and then I asked her if maybe her daughters had heard from their dear departed daddy."

"Good idea," I said. "I'd forgotten about the kids. Whitney and Courtney. They were a couple years older than me, so they'd be grown now, of course. What did she say to that?"

"She said on second thought, she didn't want to fuck me. She suggested I go fuck myself. And then she hung up."

I sighed and sat back in the booth. "Another dead end. Maybe this wasn't such a good idea after all. It was all so long ago. And nobody wants to talk about any of it."

"Hush!" Austin said. "It's not a dead end. You just gave me Darvis Kane's kids' names. I can try and track them down, same way I did their mother. It's worth a try. Anyway, what did you find out?"

"Next to nothing," I said. "Chrys Graham says she knew Jeanine was up to something in the months before she left town, because she asked to be paid in cash, instead of in trade, or with a check. And she as much as said my mother was hanging out with a 'wild crowd,' but she wouldn't name any names. Just said I should talk to mama's cousin Sonya."

"The one who moved to North Carolina?" Austin asked.

"Kannapolis," I said.

Austin slapped the tabletop in triumph. "See? That's not a dead end either. All we have to do is check in Kannapolis, North Carolina, for a Sonya . . . what did you say her last name was?"

"Wyrick," I said. I took some money out of my billfold and put it on the table. I felt drained, defeated. The whole experience reminded me of chasing rainbows as a child. The closer I got to finding out anything about my mother, the more distant the truth seemed to be.

"Where are you going?" Austin demanded. "I thought we were going to do some computer research back at my place."

"No," I said. "I'm done with research. I'm going for a drive. A Sunday drive."

"Today is Saturday," he pointed out.

"So I'll get an early start."

39

I stopped at the Minit Mart on the way out of town, ran in and bought a four-pack of Jack Daniel's hard lemonade. As I was pulling out of the parking lot, it occurred to me that this was the same place where I'd had my last sighting of Paige Plummer. The same place Will had demonstrated his kissing prowess. I opened one of the lemonade bottles and took a long swig. Not bad for screwtop. I thought about that kiss. That wasn't bad either.

At first I didn't have a plan. How unlike me. All my life I'd been a prodigious planner. I'd sketched and schemed and plotted and planned my life down to the last imported Italian silk tassel on the shimmery organza tablecloths at my wedding reception.

The tablecloths were in a box in Daddy's garage. I'd never even unpacked them. And now it was Saturday night, and I had no plans, nothing to do, and nobody to do it with. Anywhere would work, as long as it was away from here, with trees and a view and nobody around.

The lake, I thought. I'll go out to Lake Oconee and watch the sunset.

Lake Oconee isn't one of those lakes that have been around forever. In fact, I'd been just a little girl back in the late seventies, when Georgia Power created the lake by damming up the Oconee and Apalachee Rivers and a bunch of other smaller, local creeks. The power company bought up millions of dollars' worth of farm and timberland and created a 19,000-acre hydroelectric lake.

Our part of middle Georgia was changed forever after Lake Oconee was built. People who'd farmed their whole lives suddenly had a little bit of money, but no land to farm on anymore. Of course, the lake brought businesses, and jobs. People said the new lake had some of the best bass and crappie fishing in the state, because of all the old fallen trees at the bottom of the lake. Later developers moved in and built subdivisions, marinas, golf clubs, and fancy resorts. Only a few years ago the Ritz-Carlton opened a resort and spa on the lake—right on the same land that had once been a hunting lodge owned by the heir to a North Carolina tobacco fortune.

As recently as a month ago, on a Saturday night like this, I'd have been out at the Jernigans' house at Cuscawilla, one of the fancy golf resorts that ringed the lake. We probably would have had dinner at the clubhouse, then maybe taken a sunset "cocktail cruise" on A.J.'s daddy's pontoon boat.

The Jernigans actually owned two houses out at the lake. The "cottage" was a brand-new four-thousand-square-foot, three-level mini mansion, complete with a landscaped lawn that sloped down to a seawall and a double-decker boathouse.

But the original family lake place was at the end of an unmarked gravel road. Back in the seventies Chub Jernigan had sold off a hefty chunk of played-out cotton fields to Georgia Power when they'd mapped out the lake, but he'd retained some of the new lakefront lots and built a humble little tin-roofed fishing cabin on one of them.

Not even three miles away from the cottage, the "shack," as the family called it, had a screened porch instead of air conditioning, one bathroom, and a wooden dock that was on its last legs. It had been the place A.J.'s daddy, Big Drew, took the boys on camping and fishing trips, a family retreat back when roughing it was still the Jernigans' idea of fun.

A.J. had taken me out to the shack a half-dozen times after we'd first started dating, while the Cuscawilla cottage was still under construction. We'd cooked dinner in the fireplace, skinny-dipped in the lake, and made love on the lumpy Hide-A-Bed on the back porch, but I don't think A.J. or anybody else in the family had stepped foot in the place since the cottage had been completed.

Clouds of dust rose off the pockmarked gravel road as the Volvo bumped along through the old cotton fields that had been allowed to grow wild. A single brown horse grazed under the shade of an oak tree, and once a bright flash of blue and orange darted across the road—a bluebird. It had been another hot day, but the sun was getting lower in the sky now, and when I rolled the window down a little bit, I could smell the lake back behind a stand of trees that marked the entrance to the Jernigans' property.

I had to slam on the brakes hard as I rounded a curve in the road, and my open bottle of hard lemonade went flying out of the cup holder, splashing liquid all over the dashboard. Crap! A shiny metal cattle gate blocked the road. I frowned as I stared at it. When had the Jernigans decided that their derelict old shack warranted locking up?

I got out of the car and walked over to the gate to get a better look. A small sign was posted on the right gatepost. PRIVATE PROPERTY. NO TRESPASSING. POSITIVELY NO HUNTING.

There was a stout new padlock on the gate. I tugged at it, but it stayed locked.

This was beginning to piss me off. The Jernigans never used the shack anymore. Why should they suddenly start locking it up—and keeping me out? I was practically family. Or, I had been.

I fumed and paced back and forth in front of the gate. A casual impulse had brought me out here, but now, dammit, I wanted to take a dip in the lake, sit on the dock, drink my lemonade, and watch the sunset. I wanted to feel the sun on my back, to hear the birds calling in the treetops, to watch a fish chase a bug as it skittered over the surface of the water.

The gate and the sign, I decided, were the work of A.J.'s anal-retentive brother Kyle. Which made me even more determined to go through with my plan. I got in the Volvo and backed it up. A quarter mile up the Jernigans' drive, the road forked off to the right, toward the old Bascomb place. This drive was even more rutted and overgrown than the Jernigans'.

Vince Bascomb had been one of Drew Jernigan's partners in several business ventures, and at one time the two of them had owned all the land on this little cove of the lake. But Vince was in his late seventies now, and so crippled with arthritis that he rarely left his house in town. Vince and Lorraine Bascomb were divorced in the eighties, and Vince had remarried and divorced two more times that I knew of. I'd heard that wife number three had walked off with the remainder of Vince's family money five years ago. Lorraine had lived quietly on the edge of town until her death last year. The Bascomb children lived out of state, and hadn't been back to Madison since their mama's death.

The Bascomb drive had no fence, no gate, no padlock. It adjoined the Jernigans' property, but had no dock, because the Bascombs and Jernigans had gone in partners on the Jernigans' dock.

I allowed myself a smug smile as I pulled the Volvo up beside the Bascomb cabin and got out.

The cabin itself was sad. The tin roof had rusted through, and one corner of the porch seemed to have collapsed on itself. Kudzu vines clambered up the walls and through the broken-out windows. Weeds choked the little yard, and a four-foot-tall oak sapling had taken root in an overturned red rowboat.

As soon as my foot touched the ground I began to regret my unusual lack of planning. White slacks, silk blouse, cute little sandals—to hike through this weed patch? Wild blackberry brambles were already snagging the fabric around my ankles. What was I thinking? I almost turned around and got back in the car. But then I got a mental picture of Kyle Jernigan, that buttoned-down little prick, posting the no trespassing sign on the new fence across the way.

Hell yes, I would trespass. I only wished I had a shotgun and the actual will to shoot at something, just so that I could break all of Kyle's thou-shalt-nots. I opened the Volvo's trunk and reached for my gym bag. I hadn't actually been to the gym in at least six weeks, what with all the wedding preparations. The T-shirt was a little smelly, and the Lycra bike shorts wouldn't have been my first choice for lake attire, but I was really happy to see my Nike cross-trainers. I glanced around quickly to make sure the place was really as deserted as it seemed, before stripping down and changing into my gym clothes.

I tucked the cardboard lemonade carton under my arm and started to pick my way through the knee-high underbrush, toward the lakefront. I gave the fallen-down Bascomb cabin a wide berth. To me, there was something disturbing about the gaping doors and windows and the crumbling back porch where a rusted green glider still faced the water. A life had been lived out here. Somebody had rowed around the lake in that once jaunty red boat. I could imagine Bascombs sitting on that porch, a radio playing, a screen door slamming, and the rhythmic back-and-forth squeak of the metal glider. And then one day, they'd just left. A life abandoned, just like that. I wondered why. Why does someone walk away from one life, and into another?

It was a good question, I decided. Maybe someday, if I got the chance, I would pose that very same question to Jeanine Murry Murdock.

In the meantime I decided to concentrate on watching where I was walking. Snakes were a very real possibility out here. And those vines I was stomping through could just as easily be poison ivy as kudzu.

When I got to the water's edge I stopped and looked back at the Bascomb cabin. An involuntary shudder ran down my spine. I turned my back on it again, and picked my way through the underbrush toward what I knew was the edge of the Jernigans' property line.

My mood improved when I caught sight of the dock a hundred yards away. A few boards were missing, but at least it hadn't been allowed to fall completely apart. I caught a glimpse of the Jernigan shack through the trees, but I made a deliberate decision not to go any closer to it. I didn't want to look at that back porch, and I really didn't want to see that lumpy Hide-A-Bed. Although, come to think of it, Kyle had probably roped it off and posted it with a "No Trespassing, Absolutely No Fucking" sign.

The sun-blistered cedar planks of the dock buckled a little under my weight. I hesitated. Would the whole thing collapse? But then I moved forward. It hadn't been all that long since I'd been to the gym. And anyway, I hadn't really been able to eat much since the rehearsal dinner debacle. A lot of chocolate, yes, and a reasonable amount of wine, but very few actual meals.

Sunlight sparkled off the lake so brightly that I had to shade my eyes with my hand. It was at least fifteen degrees cooler out here than it had been in town. If I kept my back to the shore, all I could see was the green trees of the opposite side of the Jernigans' cove, blue skies, and the emerald waters of the lake itself. No one was in sight. No boats, no people.

Now I could feel the tension start to drain from my body as I reached the end of the dock. I put the lemonade carton down and did some stretches. I rolled my neck, then my left shoulder, then my right. I sat down on the dock and unscrewed the cap of a lemonade bottle.

My thoughts turned, inevitably, to my mother, and I felt a familiar, if unwelcome, sense of gloom settle over me. What, I wondered, if Austin was right? What if I really was incapable of having a lasting relationship, as long as I suppressed the unresolved issue of my own abandonment?

Dammit, Mama, I thought. Why couldn't you just get a divorce and stick around? Why couldn't you fix things up instead of walking out? I wondered again about the Bascomb place, and about lost causes and lost people. And then I shook it off. The gloom, the doom, and all the unanswered questions. So what if I never knew what had happened to my mother? Big effin' deal. Life is short, I thought. Get over yourself.

That's what I'll do, I promised myself. Let Austin play Nancy Drew if he wanted. Let him track down Darvis Kane and his ex-wife and his kids. If that led us to my mother, good enough. If not, so be it. I was nothing like that broken-down, haunted house at the Bascomb place.

I was a strong, resilient, capable woman with a great career and a promising future ahead of her. A. J. Jernigan was not the only man in Georgia.

Affirmation, I thought. What you need is a little affirmation.

I held the bottle up in a silent toast to myself. Here's to you, kid, I told myself. You are one lawless, trespassing, take-no-prisoners, spur-of-the-moment kind of babe.

I took a long drink of the lemonade and burped loudly. I giggled, liking the sound of it. I finished off the first bottle, then opened a second, finishing it just as quickly. I burped again, gaining momentum, hoping the sound of my lawless, spontaneous belch would echo and reverberate, and maybe, somehow, be heard at the Jernigan cottage three miles away at Cuscawilla. I gulped in a bunch of air, and burped it right back out again. Here's to you, Kyle Jernigan, I belched. And you, Big Drew. I belched again. And you, GiGi. But somehow it didn't seem enough to toast A.J. with a belch. Some other kind of gesture was needed. Something grander, yet trashier.

Half drunk with lemon-flavored malt liquor and the unaccustomed, yet heady feeling of spontaneity, I peeled off my T-shirt and shorts, and dressed only in my sparkling white Nike cross-trainers, I turned, and with a deliberate and dramatic flourish, bent down, touched my toes, and physically and metaphysically mooned my ex-fiance, Andrew Jackson Jernigan.

Talk about cathartic!

"That's for you, A.J." I hollered into the nothingness of the cove. I straightened up and took a bow. A slight breeze rippled across the cove. I was naked in the middle of nowhere. Well, almost naked. My skin prickled with the chill.

Without another thought, I sat down and unlaced my Nikes, and jumped into the lake. I let myself sink all the way to the muddy bottom before I powered back up to the water's surface. The lake was deliciously cool. I floated on my back and gazed up at the clouds, which had gone peachy and pink. I swam a few strokes and floated some more.

I threw my head back and shook the water out of my hair. When I opened my eyes, I was facing the dock. And Will Mahoney.

40

I took a deep breath of air and sank to the bottom of the lake. When I come up again, I promised myself, he'll be gone. I considered trying to swim away, but where? The Jernigan dock was the only one on the cove. And my clothes were still up on the dock. I counted to twenty-five, and when it felt like my lungs would explode, I let myself bob back to the surface. But I kept my eyes closed.

"You can't hold your breath any longer than that?" a voice asked.

I kept my eyes shut. "Go away."

"I can still see you, you know," Will said. "Even with your eyes closed, I can see you. That's how it works."

"Please go away." I said it very nicely.

"Tell me something," he said. "That thing you were doing out on the dock just now. Was that some kind of weird religious ritual?"

I opened one eye. He was sitting on the end of the dock, just a few feet away, dangling his toes in the water. I backpedaled away from him, wondering just how much he could see from there.

"I'll give you a hundred dollars if you'll go away right now and keep your mouth shut about what you just saw," I said.

"You can keep your money," Will said. "Nobody would believe what I just saw anyway."

"And you'll go away? Right now?" I opened the other eye.

He smiled. "Not just yet. I'm enjoying myself immensely. Great view out here."

"You're a pig," I said.

"Probably. But a happy pig. Beautiful evening, huh? It cools right down out here on the water."

It certainly did. My teeth were chattering and I was starting to shiver. And there were little fishies nibbling at my nether regions.

"Look. I'm really getting cold," I said. "At least turn around so I can get out and get dressed."

"Okay." He turned his back to me. I swam over to the dock, climbed up the ladder and toweled myself off with my T-shirt before hastily climbing back into my clothes. The Lycra shorts were a bitch to pull on when you were still half wet.

I was tying my shoelaces when he turned around again.

"How did you get in here, anyway?" I demanded. "The gate was locked. And there's a no trespassing sign."

He fished in the pockets of his shorts and brought out a key.

"Where'd you get that?"

"Kyle Jernigan," he said. "The family's thinking about selling the place. And I'm thinking about buying."

I felt the blood drain from my face. "Kyle? Tell me he's not out here too."

"Nah," Will said. "I came alone. I don't think your buddy Kyle likes nature. So how did you get in here? I'm assuming you no longer have membership privileges."

I was shivering badly now. My hair was soaking wet and my clothes were damp. "None of your business." I started down the dock. I just wanted to get in my car and get out of here.

"You walked over from the place next door, right?" Will asked, catching up with me. "The Bascomb place. I hear it's going on the market too."

I whirled around to face him. "Why would you be interested in a couple of falling-down old houses out here? Don't you have enough on your plate with Mulberry Hill and the bra plant?"

"I like it out here. It's nice and peaceful. Unspoiled. Anyway, if I don't buy it, somebody else will. The Jernigans and Bascombs have a total of sixteen lots on this cove. That's enough for a subdivision. With sidewalks and streetlights and all the trappings of town."

"And what would you do with it if you bought it?"

"Nothing. Maybe fix up the houses a little bit. Put up a boat-house. And the dock needs some work."

"That's all?"

"That's all," he said. "Anyway, why should you care what I do with my money?"

"I don't," I said. "But I do care about this cove. It's special. I wouldn't want to see it ruined."

"I won't ruin it," he said, his face serious now. "Hey, you really are shivering."

"I'll be okay once I get in the car," I said, heading back toward the Bascomb place.

"I've got the key to the cabin too," Will said. "Come on inside with me. I'll get you a towel. And there are probably dry clothes in the closets too."

"No," I said quickly. "I'll be fine."

"You afraid A.J.'s hiding out in there? Gonna jump out of a closet or something? There's nobody there, Keeley."

"I'm not afraid of running into A.J.," I snapped. But I really was cold and miserable. "I'll just grab a towel and take off. I've got stuff to do back in town."

I followed Will back toward the shack, but stopped when he got to the steps to the back porch. I was in no mood to confront the Hide-A-Bed.

"Let's go around front," I said, catching him by the elbow. "There's a cedar chest in the living room where GiGi used to keep clean towels and sheets."

He raised one eyebrow, but did as I suggested. The key fit in the lock, but the doorway was shrouded with a curtain of cobwebs and dead bugs, which I batted away. The door swung open, and I stepped inside before Will could, determined to show him that the Jernigans' house held no demons for me. At least not in this part of the house.

Nobody had been here in a long time. The living room air was stale, and there were more cobwebs and dead bugs. Sheets covered the furniture, and a fine film of dust covered the wooden floors.

"Not bad," Will said, walking around the living room, raising the shades to let in some light.

The cedar chest was where it had always been, in front of the sofa. I opened it and found a stack of faded but clean beach towels. I took the top one and started drying my hair with it.

Will knelt down on the hearth and stuck his head into the fireplace. "Does this thing work?"

"It did," I said. "We used to cook steaks in there. A.J.'s granddaddy Chub had the chimney built from granite quarried up in Tate. If you use the right kind of wood, that thing heats the whole room."

"Sounds like you used to spend a good bit of time out here," Will said, standing up and dusting his hands on the seat of his pants.

"Used to," I said, emphasizing the past tense.

"So what were you doing out on the dock?" Will asked. "Seriously."

"Just . . . thinking," I said. "This is a good place to get away to. To be alone. Not many people know where the cove is. No boats come in, because it's kind of shallow."

That was as far as I was going to go. Will Mahoney had obviously already seen me naked. I didn't feel the need to bare the rest of myself to him.

"I'm going now," I said, heading for the front door.

"Wait." He followed me out onto the front porch and locked the door behind us. Clouds had gathered overhead, and huge raindrops started to splatter around us.

"Come on," he said, pointing toward the yellow Cadillac, which was parked over by the toolshed. "I'll drive you back to your car."

We ran for the car, and by the time we'd gotten in, I was glad to have the beach towel wrapped around my shoulders.

Will stopped at the gate and got out to unlock it. I slid over to the driver's side and pulled the Caddy far enough forward for him to lock the gate behind us, and then he got in on the passenger side.

"The Bascombs' driveway is just up the road a little ways," I told him. "Are you really thinking about buying both places? Wait till you see it. I know you like to fix things up, but Vince Bascomb has really let his place go. It's pretty much a tear-down at this point."

When we got there, Will stared out the rain-streaked car window at the Bascomb cabin. "Wow," he said. "You weren't kidding. Bascomb's lawyer told me this was an 'as-is' deal, but he didn't mention what a wreck the place is."

"He probably didn't know," I said. "I don't think anybody has been back in here for a long time. Vince is pretty much house-bound now, and his kids live out of state and have no interest in moving back to Madison."

"What about his wife?" Will asked.

"Which one? He's had three. Lorraine, who's the mother of his children, is dead. The other two took off with what was left of Vince's money."

"I'd like to see the inside of the house," Will said. "I don't have a key, but from the look of things, I probably don't need one anyway. Want to take a look?"

"No," I said, shuddering.

"I thought you loved old houses."

"This place isn't all that old," I pointed out. "It was all farmland until Georgia Power flooded it. Probably built around the same time as the Jernigan shack."

"When was that?"

"Late seventies, early eighties."

"Looks like the roof is gone anyway," he said. "I'll come back and take a look after I get back to town. When the weather's better."

"You're leaving town? For how long?" I asked.

"Couple weeks," he said. "I've got some meetings in New York, and I need to see some people in South Carolina and Alabama. And I've got to go back to Sri Lanka week after next. It's actually a good thing I ran into you today. What's the schedule looking like for Mulberry Hill, now that the pump house is done?"

"I've got furniture ordered, but I can't do too much else while the workmen are in the house. By the way, how did dinner go last night?"

"It went," he said.

"That doesn't sound so good."

"It's just . . . she's pretty wrapped up in that law firm. Got a big real estate deal she's working on. She's a busy woman."

"Is she seeing somebody else?"

"We didn't get that far. I asked her to come over next weekend, but she said she has plans. Some big fund-raiser for the Humane Society. So I asked about the weekend after that, and she has plans for then, too. Her law firm is entertaining out-of-town clients."

"But she liked the house, right?"

"I guess. It's hard to tell with her." He tapped his fingers on the Caddy's dashboard. "I just wish we were farther along with the house. If she could see it, the way I do, the way it's going to be." He grabbed my arm. "You're going to make deadline, right?"

I sighed. "If your guys make their deadlines, I should be able to make mine. Christmas, right?"

"What? No! Thanksgiving. I told you Thanksgiving."

"You told me Christmas," I said, clenching my teeth. "And even that's a stretch."

"So stretch it," he said.

I pulled the Cadillac up as close as possible to my Volvo. "That's impossible."

"You'll do it," he said. "If you have any problems, need a check for anything while I'm gone, just call Nancy at the office. She can reach me anywhere."

I opened the Cadillac door and got out.

"Thanksgiving," he said, sliding back across the seat to the driver's side.

I slammed the door right in his face.

41

Gloria glanced over at me from her drawing board and laughed.

"What?" I asked, putting my colored pencil down.

"Your face," she said. "I wish I had a camera. You were actually scowling down at that sketch you've been working on all morning. What's wrong with it?"

I picked up another pencil and twirled it beween my fingertips. "I guess I'm frustrated. This is just so impossible. But Will wants it so badly, and I don't want to let him down."

She got up and walked over to my drawing board, looking over my shoulder at the sketch I'd been working on for the past hour. It was supposed to be the upstairs sitting room at Mulberry Hill. The room looked fine. I had the overstuffed sofas, the Aubusson carpet in soft greens and golds, the built-in bookshelves, and a huge antique Venetian mirror that set the tone for the whole room.

"What's so impossible? Gloria asked. "It's a wonderful room. Anybody would love it."

"Not just anybody," I corrected her. "Stephanie Scofield. She has to love it. She has to love it enough to want to give up her life in Atlanta and move right in."

"Isn't that Will's department?" Gloria asked. "Isn't he supposed to be wooing her?"

The old-fashioned word made me feel wistful. I wanted to be wooed. Maybe someday.

"He hasn't seen her in more than two weeks," I said. "He's miserable. He even went so far as to drive over to Atlanta last night to take her to dinner in Buckhead. On a Tuesday night, when he had to be back at the plant for an early morning meeting. And he hates Atlanta. The man is totally smitten."

Gloria patted my shoulder. "There's nothing you can do about that," she reminded me. "Your job is to just design the project and get it done. Period."

"He expects me to do more than that," I said. "The poor fool thinks I can make her fall in love with this house, and then him."

"Well, you can't." Gloria went over to the coffeepot and poured herself a mug. The smell of fresh-ground French roast filled the studio. She held up the pot toward me. "Want some?"

"It smells divine," I said, but I shook my head no. "I wish I could make Stephanie really see the house. Experience it with all her senses. You know, like they tell you in marketing classes. You can't sell the steak without the sizzle . . ."

"Maybe you should go over to the Wal-Mart and buy some of those strawberry-scented crayons they sell for the kids," Gloria said, laughing.

"No strawberries," I said, but that gave me an idea. I picked up my pencil again and started sketching. I put a beautiful petite blond in a flowing gold robe seated at a vanity in front of the Venetian mirror. Her back was to the room, but it would be clear who she was. Perched on an ottoman in between the sofas I drew a little brown and black dog. I tilted my head and considered, erased, and redrew. Yes. Now the dog was unquestionably a dachshund. A miniature dachshund.

I signed the corner of the sketch with a flourish. Done! I took it over to the photocopier and made two more copies. The original I put in the folder I'd send over to the Loving Cup plant for approval later in the day. I put one of the copies in our office file. The third copy I rolled tightly. I found a piece of gold silk moiré ribbon and tied it with a neat little bow. I slid the sketch into a mailing tube and headed out the door.

"Where are you going?" Gloria asked. "And why so happy?"

"I'm going to the post office to overnight the steak and the sizzle to Stephanie Scofield," I told her.

It wasn't even noon yet, but the day was already a scorcher. I could feel the heat of the concrete sidewalks through the thin soles of my shoes. I dodged a couple cars and jaywalked across Washington Street, then cut around the old courthouse to get to the post office. There was only one clerk on duty, and four people in line ahead of me, but the arctic blast of the air conditioning felt heavenly. I bought some more stamps, choosing the Audrey Hepburn ones, and I was walking out the front door when I bumped smack into GiGi Jernigan.

Crap! Why hadn't I just picked up the phone and called UPS to pick up the sketches for Stephanie? Why had I dawdled over the stamps? I should have just taken the damn flag stamps like everybody else. And why hadn't I worn my dark sunglasses and a wig that morning?

"Keeley!" GiGi exclaimed, seizing me by both wrists. She looked immaculate, as always, her pale blond hair freshly colored and coiffed, her hot pink linen pantsuit miraculously unwrinkled, her Easy Spirit walking shoes unscuffed by life.

"Uh, hi, GiGi," I said. "How are you?"

"Devastated," she said. "Simply devastated. I may never get over this whole awful thing."

She was devastated? Wasn't I the one who had been cheated on by her older son? Wasn't I the one who'd spent weeks repacking and sending gifts back to Jernigan family and friends? Wasn't my father the one who was out untold thousands of dollars for a wedding dress and sit-down reception with open bar for four hundred people? This was so like GiGi. My life had gone to shit, but she was the one doing all the suffering.

What do you say to something like that?

I had no idea. "I'm sorry," was the best I could come up with on such short notice.

"I've tried and tried to talk to you," GiGi went on. "But you never return my calls. And I've called for weeks. Didn't you get my messages? Or the notes?"

In fact, I'd been dodging GiGi's calls, and I'd tossed the handwritten notes she'd sent, unread, in the trash. And up until now, I'd managed to avoid seeing her, or any other members of her immediate family, through a combination of luck and planning. I never walked past Madison Mutual anymore. I took detours so I didn't have to go near The Oaks, and I'd steered clear of the local shops or restaurants I knew GiGi haunted. The trip out to the shack had been my one foray into Jernigan country, and look how that had ended up. I'd had a case of the sniffles for three days after my swim in the lake.

"I've been pretty busy," I said, wishing she would let go of my arms. "In fact, I'm on deadline on a big project right now."

Tears welled up in her large blue-green eyes. They were A.J.'s eyes, down to the thick black lashes. "Too busy for me? Keeley, you've been like a daughter to me. I thought . . . I thought, since your own mother hasn't been around . . . I remember the first time A.J. brought you home for dinner. You were wearing the prettiest flowered dress. So suitable. Keeley, my son brought home dozens of girls over the years. Beautiful girls, from fine families. But that night, when we were in bed, I turned to Drew, and I said, 'She is the one. She is the one I want to see sitting in my parlor, opening presents on Christmas morning with the rest of the family.' I said, 'Drew, tomorrow, first thing, you open up the safe deposit box. Bring home the blue velvet box. The one with Grandmother Jernigan's pearls in it. For our Keeley. She is the one who will bear our grandchildren.'"

"Grandchildren?" I yelped. She had probably picked out their gender and names too. If it hadn't been for that one little hiccup of A.J.'s I might even be incubating little Andrew Jackson III right this minute.

"GiGi," I started. But she cut me off again.

"Maybe I was fooling myself, to think we had a special bond."

I had thought our special bond was that she had plenty of money and liked to spend it on redecorating her houses. And yes, I'd been fond of GiGi. But there had never, ever, been a time when I'd thought of her as anything more than A.J.'s mother. I had a mother, thank you.

"GiGi, I'm not mad at you," I started again.

"Well, why would you be?" She looked startled at the very notion. "This has all been a horrible, unbelievable misunderstanding. But as I told Drew, sometimes bad things happen for a reason. Now that things have settled down, we can look ahead. Sort things out." She squeezed my hand. "Have a time for healing. Don't you agree?"

"Healing what? You don't seriously think I would ever take A.J. back—do you?"

She dropped my wrists and took a step backward. "Keeley, you need to look deep within yourself and think about things. A.J. has apologized to you. He told me so himself. The least you can do is meet him halfway. The boy has been half crazed with grief. It's time, Keeley."

Despite the sun beating down on my head, I suddenly felt icy cold. I had to laugh at the complete absurdity of this scene. This was downtown Madison. The middle of the day. People were peeking out of shop windows at the two of us. Two old ladies were hiding on the other side of the World War I doughboy monument, waiting to see what happened next, to see if that crazy Keeley Murdock was going to throw another hissy fit like the one they'd all heard about.

I didn't intend to give them the satisfaction. But I also didn't intend to let GiGi go on deluding herself about the possibility of my joining the family at The Oaks on Christmas morning, or of wearing Grandmother Jernigan's pearls, or of breeding yet another generation of selfish, self-absorbed, two-timing, double-dealing brats with big blue-green eyes.

"GiGi," I said. "Just so there are no further misunderstandings, let me fill you in on all the sordid details of the breakup between your son and me. I saw him, your son, my fiance, with my own eyes, that night at our rehearsal dinner. In the boardroom at the country club. He had his pants down around his ankles. My former best friend and maid of honor, Paige Plummer, was with him. Her dress was hiked up around her waist. Her panties were off, and the two of them were going at it like a pair of barnyard animals."

"OH!" She held her hand up to her cheek as though she'd just been slapped. "How dare you! I don't believe it. A.J. would never." She scuttled backward. She couldn't get away from me fast enough now. "How dare you spread such filth about my son?"

Suddenly GiGi wasn't as crazy to have me in the family anymore. She was halfway down the block. "Liar!" she screamed. "Liar, liar, liar!"

The old ladies behind the doughboy monument froze, goggle-eyed with a mixture of horror and amazement. What the hell? I decided to really give them their money's worth.

"It's all true," I hollered after GiGi. "Sad but true. And if I were you, I'd have the backseat of that Escalade of yours steam-cleaned next time you go through the JiffyWash."

42

When I got back to the studio, I went directly to the kitchen. I put my head under the faucet and let cold water pour over my hair. I squeezed it out, pinned it up off my neck, and went back to my drawing board, where I drew sketches of horrible, big-eyed babies wearing nothing but diapers and sensible shoes. They were scary even to me.

I'd been working for over an hour before Gloria said anything.

"Anything going on at the post office today?"

"You heard?"

She nodded. "Before you got back here. Arlene Gillman got it from Mae Finley, who, I'm guessing, got it from her sister, who works at the post office."

I put my head down and banged it a couple times on the drawing board. "I'm going to have to leave town," I said. "Maybe move to Michigan. Milwaukee, I'm thinking. Someplace cold, yet in need of good design services. Preferably where nobody knows me."

"Keeley, sweetie, Milwaukee is not actually in Michigan. It's in another of those M states I think. Anyway, none of this is your fault," Gloria said soothingly. "GiGi should have left you alone. She was in the wrong here, not you."

"Then why am I the one who's the talk of the town—yet again?" I asked. "Did Arlene tell you that GiGi actually expects me to take A.J. back? She thinks this whole thing is just an unfortunate misunderstanding!"

Gloria laughed. "I heard you told her in colorful detail just how you found A.J. and Paige. I believe the phrase 'going at it like a couple of barnyard animals' came into play? Is that accurate?"

"I was so mad I'm not sure exactly what I said, but that's probably a close approximation. But you know the amazing thing? She still doesn't believe any of it. GiGi flat-out called me a liar! The woman adds new dimensions to denial."

My aunt cocked her head and gave me a serious look. "The thing is, all the Jernigan men in this town have always gotten away with bloody murder. And do you know why that is?" She didn't wait for me to answer. "It's because they could. They run around and cheat and lie all week long, then stand up in church on Sunday in the front pew and sing louder 'n anybody—because everybody looks the other way. GiGi knows for damn tootin' sure that A.J. cheated on you. Just like she knows Drew cheated on her, and old Chub cheated on his wife. They all knew. They had to. But none of 'em ever said anything, 'cause they didn't want to cause a stink."

I closed my eyes. I could feel a tension headache coming on.

"But why? Why would GiGi want to live like that? I never knew A.J.'s grandmother, but I do know GiGi. She's an attractive woman, and no matter how she acts sometimes, I know for a fact that she's not stupid."

Gloria smiled, but it wasn't her usual, angelic smile. Her lips twisted down at one corner. "Family tradition. GiGi lives a nice life over there at The Oaks. And out at Cuscawilla, and wherever else she chooses. Drew knows she knows. And she makes him pay. And the sad thing is, for all their games, I think they probably do love each other in their own sick way."

I put my hand up to the back of my neck and rubbed the base of it. For a second I pictured Grandmother Jernigan's pearls wrapped there, choking me, tying me to a long line of other defeated women.

Gloria misses nothing. She got up, came over, and massaged my neck right where the muscles were all knotted up. "Anyway, it's over and done with. And I don't care what anybody says, you're much too young for pearls." She brightened then.

"I forgot! Speaking of ugly gossip, guess what else Mae Finley said when she called?"

"Don't know. Tell."

"Madison's official slut population just dropped by two."

"Huh?"

"Paige and Lorna! Mae saw them loading stuff into a moving van this morning. And there's a sold sign in front of their house."

"You're kidding," I said, feeling my spirits lift a little. "Where'd they go? What happened?"

"I heard they're moving to Marietta. Lorna's been on disability since June, with emphysema. And now Paige lost her job at the ad agency," Gloria said, her eyes sparkling. "A little bird told me they let her go because Madison Mutual took their account to another agency."

"No!" I had to laugh despite my wretched mood.

"The same little bird told me that GiGi let it be known to Drew that she didn't want to see that little blond hussy anywhere near her precious son. Didn't want Paige getting any ideas that once you were out of the picture she could just slide right into the picture."

"Poor Paige," I said. "I guess she won't be spending Christmas morning at The Oaks after all."

43

It had been nearly a month since I'd seen my biggest client, Will Mahoney. During that time, at the beginning of every week, Nancy Rockmore would call and give me his itinerary and usually a phone number or address where I could overnight sketches or have a conference call with him. For weeks I'd been making room sketches, all prominently featuring Stephanie Scofield and Erwin. I'd also attached fabric samples and photographs of furniture, light fixtures, rugs, and paintings I'd bought or put on hold.

I'd already spent over one hundred and fifty thousand dollars of his money, and Will hadn't seen a single actual thing I'd bought. I was beginning to get nervous about the heavy outlay of cash.

And Miss Nancy, who cut all the checks, was beginning to get downright grouchy about seeing all that money going out the door to what she called Will's own personal Taj Mahoney.

On the first Monday in July I dropped by the Loving Cup plant to pick up a check for a pair of cast-iron urns I'd bought for the front porch.

"Two thousand dollars," she said, with an aggrieved air, as she typed out the check. "Are them things made out of solid gold?"

"They're nineteenth-century jardinières," I said, feeling guilty. "From a sugar plantation in Barbados. And that includes the packing and shipping from the dealer, who is in Mississippi."

"For that kind of money they oughtta hand carry 'em on the back of a water buffalo," she said. "And speaking of which, the boss is gettin' in today from some heathen foreign place. He wants you to meet him out at the castle at four. Wants to take a walk-through."

It was already nearly two. Damn. I'd have to run out to the house right now to make sure the site was picked up and looking spiffy. The construction crew had been working overtime to get the addition done, and cleaning up after themselves had not been a priority. All the walls were up, the wiring and plumbing stubbed in, and the floors laid. But the finish work seemed to be taking forever.

Will had insisted that the walls in the addition be plaster—not sheetrock—to match the original portion of the house. It had taken me weeks to track down somebody who still did old-time plaster and lathe construction. His name was James Moody, and he was an artist. He was also seventy-two-years old, and on wet days, which we'd had plenty of, the arthritis in his hands was so bad he had to sit on an upended bucket and give detailed instruction to his apprentice—an eighteen-year-old Mexican youth who spoke only rudimentary English.

Miss Nancy banged away at the keys to her computer terminal without looking up at me now.

"How's it going around here?" I asked. There didn't seem to be a lot of activity at the plant. The parking lot was nearly empty.

She pursed her lips. "It ain't goin'," she said flatly. "The boss don't tell me much. But I know he came back from that last trip to New York in a terrible mood. The money men are telling him we can't make bras in this country anymore. Not even the fancy under-wire job he wants to manufacture here. They say the labor costs are too high down here."

She lowered her voice. "That's what all these goddamn foreign trips are about. He thinks I don't know, but hell, I'm the one makes all the travel arrangements, sets up all the meetings for him. There's a plant in Nicaragua he's looking at, and another in Mexico. He had the girls in the sample room make up a set of samples to take down there to them, see if they can produce the kind of quality he wants."

I held my breath for a minute. No wonder she resented Will's house so much. The way she saw it, every dime he spent out at Mulberry Hill was a dime taken away from getting Loving Cup up and running again.

"But, even if he did that, he'd still keep the company here, right? I mean, there would still be jobs here in Madison. Right? Like the packaging and shipping and ordering, that kind of stuff?"

"If by company you mean me and a handful of other people, yeah," Miss Nancy said. "The stitchers in the sample room would probably keep their jobs. But there's only half a dozen of them. Used to be, we had two hundred machine operators back out there on the floor," she said, her voice wistful. "Not to mention the cutters and pattern makers and all the other production folks. Most of them lost their jobs in the last buyout. But yeah, some of the marketing and accounting and computer types would have jobs. The college kids. The yuppies, they'd get to keep their SUVs and Rolex watches."

I didn't know what to say to her. Suddenly I felt a little like Marie Antoinette, gilding the lily at Versailles, while the French peasants starved. It wasn't the same; intellectually I knew there was no comparison. But I still wished I hadn't already gotten the okay to spend two thousand dollars for a pair of overpriced flowerpots.

"How's it going with the boss and his little girlfriend?" Miss Nancy asked, trying to sound casual.

"Stephanie? How'd you know about her?" I asked. Will didn't seem like the kind to share his private love life with people in the office, not even his assistant.

She made a sour face. "I send a dozen roses to a Stephanie Scofield at some fancy law firm in Buckhead every week," Nancy said. "It don't take a goddamn rocket scientist to figure out he's hot for her. So how's it going? What's she like?"

"You probably know as much as I do. She's very pretty. The athletic type. She seems interested in Will."

"Interested in the castle, that's for sure," Nancy said.

"How's that?" I asked, surprised.

"The boss had me make a set of keys and send 'em over to her," Nancy said. "For the castle and the little house. So she could check up on things while he's been gone."

This was big news to me. I'd talked to my client several times, and he hadn't said a word about Stephanie Scofield "checking up" on our progress. And I hadn't run into her out on the job site either.

Nancy was watching me closely. "That's good," I said. "I've got other projects to worry about. It's good to have another pair of eyes watching things. I'm sure Will appreciates her interest."

"Suuuuree," Nancy said. She went back to her typing, and I went home to change into jeans and sneakers before heading off to Mulberry Hill.

As usual, when I got out to the job site I marveled at the progress the workers had made in just six weeks, and at Will Mahoney's ability to prod, bribe, bully, and beseech his crew to buy into his vision of what the house could be.

He'd been adamant that the façade of the house be the first thing completed. All the masonry, trim carpentry, stripping, painting, construction of the side porches, and reinforcement of the columns, as well as the reinstallation of the windows and the "new" salvaged door—he had wanted it all in place, he said, so that everybody involved in the project could see what the finished project would look like.

And what it looked like was magnificent. As I drove down past the meadows, with newly painted white rail fences setting off the fields of wildflowers and grains, the sudden surprise of the emerald green lawn and the formal boxwood plantings made my heart leap. The old house gleamed snowy white against all that green. I couldn't wait to drag those jardinières out onto the porch and fill them with the fluffiest ferns in Morgan County.

As I followed the drive around to the back of the house my smile dimmed. Mulberry Hill was like a Hollywood stage set. Beautiful and bucolic from the front, but once you drove around to the backlot, it all started to seem like smoke and mirrors.

Pickup trucks and vans were parked all over the place. The sod that had been planted at the beginning of May was ruined, and the backyard was a sea of rutted red mud. A cement mixer churned on the patio of the pump house, and piles of lumber and bricks were strewn about in no discernible plan or pattern. And the trash! There were mounds of it everywhere. Fast food wrappers, scraps of wood, insulation and rebar, along with the discarded packing cases for the custom windows and the cardboard cartons for all the appliances had been tossed at random.

I parked the Volvo and hurried over to the back porch, where Will's foreman, Adam, was watching a worker nail weather stripping around the French doors. The porch floorboards were coated in mud, and my heart sank when I saw the muddy footprints leading into the new breakfast room.

"Adam!" I said breathlessly. "This place is a disaster. You've got to do something."

Adam was a muscle-bound black man in his early thirties. I doubt that he'd ever had to deal with an interior designer bossing him around on a construction site before. But Will had told him, in my presence, that I would be the oversight committee in his absence. We'd come to a tenuously workable arrangement. I didn't talk directly to any of his workers. If I had a problem with anything, I was to bring it up with him, in private. He didn't want his guys to think he took orders from some chick who drove a Volvo and wore high-heeled sandals on a construction site.

Now he tossed the cigarette he'd been smoking to the ground and regarded me cautiously. "What's up, Keeley?"

"This mess," I said, gesturing around at all the trash. "We've got to get it all cleaned up."

"It's a job site," he said, frowning.

"But Will's coming out for a walk-through at four," I said. "And I don't want him to overlook the incredible progress you've made because of all this trash."

This was better. Positive reinforcement, that was the ticket. "The front of the house looks so fabulous, and then you drive around here, and it's, uh, not so fabulous. Don't you think we could have a quick cleanup? Maybe burn some of that scrap lumber and get the rest of the trash in the Dumpster, instead of strewn all around? And could we park the trucks away from the house? The backyard's just a sea of mud. And it's getting tracked into the house. I don't want that beautiful new tile in the kitchen ruined."

He nodded reluctantly. "Norman's been bitchin' at me about the tile. I got it covered up, but he says the paper's torn near the threshold. He's talking about having to replace some of the tiles there."

Adam put his fingers to his mouth and whistled a blast so sharp, I thought it would burst my eardrums.

Instantly the hammering and sawing stopped. Workers drifted out to stand around us in a circle.

"Listen up," Adam shouted. "Mr. Mahoney's coming out here for a walk-through at four. I want all you assholes to get those trucks moved over off the sodded area. From now on, you park on the driveway in front, and walk around to the back. And stay off the friggin' grass. Soon as the trucks are moved, get busy cleaning up all the trash. You can burn the wood and paper scraps in the barrel in the back of the lot. Everything else gets loaded in the Dumpster. As soon as that's done, go through the house, pick up any trash in there. I want it looking sharp. Understand?"

"Got it," one of the men said. They started to wander off.

"Hustle, dammit," Adam hollered.

"Thank you," I told him, giving him a smile.

"Okay," he grunted. "But hey, you might wanta take a look around inside. See if it's like you want it."

The inside of the house was definitely NOT how I wanted it. There was mud and trash everywhere. I found a worn-out, dirt-crusted broom in the makeshift toolshed that had been assembled in the laundry room, and got busy.

I started at the front of the house and worked my way back, using a shovel as a dustpan, and an empty grout bucket as a trash can. Despite the debris, I had to admit that the house was shaping up. All the moldings in the original part of the house had been stripped and refinished, and Mr. Moody had wrought miracles with the plaster ceiling medallions in the parlors and the dining room. The chimneys had all been repointed and the fireboxes relined, and the marble I'd had shipped in for the hearths was in a shed out back, waiting to be installed.

On an impulse, I put down my broom and ran upstairs to check the progress there.

The landing was being used as a storage area. Huge cartons lined the walls, but the sight of them was a relief. I'd special ordered a reproduction claw-foot whirlpool bathtub for the master bath from Waterworks. It had been on back order since the beginning of summer, and I'd spent hours on the phone trying to make sure that I got the first one to come off the factory floor. The tub was here. So were the tinted green glass tiles for the shower surround. A huge package wrapped in moving pads was leaning against the far wall. I lifted the corner of the quilt and saw that it was the white marble slab I'd chosen for the vanity top.

Through the far wall, I could see Mr. Moody, laboriously slathering mud to the new lathe he'd nailed up for the walls of the master suite.

Quickly I gathered up an armload of trash littering the floors. I was on my way back downstairs to dump it when I heard a horn honking outside. I glanced at my watch.

It was five after four. I put the broom back in the laundry room and rinsed my hands in the laundry tub. It was showtime.

I was almost to the back door when I heard a car door slam. And then another door slammed. And then came a series of sharp, staccato barks.

"Erwin, no," a woman's voice wailed. "Wait for Mommy!"

44

"Will! Stephanie!" My voice was registering just the *eensiest* bit on the shrill side. I felt heavy breathing on my ankle. Erwin was looking up at me, his big liquid brown eyes saying . . . what? Maybe "I need to urinate"?

Will was wearing wrinkled khakis, a washed-out-looking golf shirt, and huge bags under his eyes. Stephanie looked vastly fresher, perkier, and more in control, dressed in what was probably her idea of pastoral: i.e., denim capri pants, a lighter denim crop top, and blue cork-soled wedgie sandals. There was that damn toe ring again. She clung to Will's arm like a sailor to a life raft.

"Hey, Keeley," Will said, giving me an awkward hug with his free arm. "The place looks great."

My mood lifted, instantly. "You really like it?"

"It's fabulous," Stephanie said. She broke away from Will and planted a big, wet kiss on Adam's cheek.

He blushed, but didn't seem displeased.

"Will," Stephanie said, "Adam has been so wonderful. Every Friday, whenever I've come out, he stops what he's doing and shows me all around. He even let me pick the paint color for the new shutters!"

I almost bit my tongue in half. New paint color? I'd spent hours and hours going over the fan deck, looking for the exact right color for the shutters for Mulberry Hill. In the end I'd driven down to Monticello, Georgia, to pick up a paint chip from an 1840s Greek Revival house museum. I'd taken the chip to my Benjamin Moore dealer and had it spectroscopically analyzed, and the paint color custom mixed. It wasn't blue, it wasn't green, it wasn't black. It was exactly what the house cried out for.

"Mochachino!" Stephanie was saying. She beamed over at Will.

"That's the name of the paint color I chose for the shutters. I just took my Starbucks cup to the paint store and matched it to what they had. Can you believe it? It's the yummiest color ever."

I was staring daggers at Adam. He looked the other way. At Erwin, who was relieving himself on one of the two-thousand-dollar jardinières.

"Let's go inside," I said to Will. "I guess you must be tired. Exactly where was it you flew in from today?"

"Mexico," Stephanie said. She held out her wrist and jangled three thick silver and turquoise bracelets. "Isn't he the most thoughtful man you've ever met? He sends me a present every week. Don't you love a man who understands the importance of presents?"

"Yes," I said. "Presents are lovely."

Will yawned. "I could sleep for a week."

The walk through the house wasn't what I had hoped for. Will tried to be enthusiastic. He admired the plaster medallions in the front rooms, and showed real interest in the vintage fireplace surrounds I'd bought from my favorite architectural salvage yard in Jackson, Mississippi. But it was clear he was really sleepwalking.

He shook hands with Mr. Moody and ran his hands over the still damp plaster in the new breakfast room, but just nodded at the leaded glass doors on the kitchen cabinets the carpenters were installing in the kitchen.

Stephanie, however, was deeply concerned with the appliances. I'd found a fully restored 1940s six-burner Chambers gas range in an antique appliance shop in Clayton, Georgia. Its porcelain was milky white, all the chrome was polished, it had a clock, a built-in soup kettle, and a shelf for condiments. I'd designed the rest of the kitchen around the range.

She thumped the porcelain with her thumb and forefinger. "Does this thing work?"

"Like a charm," I said proudly.

"Couldn't you get a nice Viking?" she asked. "One of those big stainless steel restaurant stoves? My girlfriend who's married to the dermatologist has one with warming ovens and a rotisserie and a grill. It's fabulous."

"Vikings are nice," I agreed "But we were going for a period look in here. And anyway, the Chambers has a warming oven too. And there'll be a fireplace with a gas grill right outside on the new patio when it's finished, so we didn't think we'd need two grills."

"Hmm," was all she said.

What would you need a grill for? I wondered. *Tofu? Chilean sea bass?*

"I can't wait for you to see the upstairs," I told Will. "The guys are right on schedule. I think it's going to be wonderful."

On the upstairs landing I pointed to the stacks of crates and boxes. "Here's the tile," I said, opening one of the cartons and showing Will what we'd planned for the two upstairs guest baths.

"Looks fine," he said. "Just like the photos you sent me."

It was clear he was too fatigued to care about tile just then, but Stephanie was deeply engaged in the whole shebang.

She kicked at the carton containing the whirlpool bathtub. I would have given a kidney to own that bathtub. It wasn't just the Cadillac of bathtubs, it was the Rolls-Royce. "What about the BTUs?" she asked, looking at the label and the drawing of the tub on the carton. "How much horsepower from the jets? And why does it have to be so plain? Why can't it have some brass, or gold plating?"

"It's an exact reproduction of a tub that would have been in the house by the 1920s," I explained. "But with the most modern plumbing. And the nickel-plated faucets and handles are historically accurate for that era too. Brass just wouldn't work with everything else going on in the bathroom."

"It reminds me of my high school locker room," she said. Now she was looking around at all the cartons of fixtures. "What about the bidet?" she asked. "Surely, in a house like this, we'll have a bidet?"

I glanced over at Will for guidance. He yawned again and gave me a pleading look. "Can we fit a bidet in the master bath?"

I felt a nerve in my jaw twitch. "If we cut down on the size of the shower enclosure. Which will mean reconfiguring the whole layout."

He waved his hand in surrender. "You can do that, right Keeley? Call up and order a bidet?"

"If that's what you want."

And while we're at it, why don't we just order you a new spine? I thought.

Will nodded and I added "Find bidet" to the punch-out list on my clipboard.

I held my breath when we got to the master bedroom. The architect and I had worked hard to design a seamless transition from the original part of the house to the new bedroom wing.

At the entrance to the new wing we'd placed a pair of columns we'd had made to match the front porch columns, but on a smaller scale. Between them, a pair of massive antique double doors opened into the sitting area of the bedroom.

At least the columns and doors were a hit with Stephanie.

"Oh," she exclaimed, clutching Adam's arm. "These weren't up last week. I just love them. Where on earth did you find columns like this?"

Adam had the grace to look sheepish. "Keeley and the architect designed them, and had them made in Alabama. Keeley found the doors, right?"

"At Back Road Antique Salvage," I said. "All the old doors and hardware came from them. And the fireplace surrounds and the urns for the front porch."

"What color are we going to paint the doors?" Stephanie asked, looking at Will.

We? I wanted to scream. *We aren't painting the doors.*

"Actually," I said, my voice calmer than I felt, "these doors have never been painted. They have the original patina." I ran my fingertips again over the satiny old wood, which had a hand-rubbed beeswax finish.

"I know," she said excitedly. "Mochachino! To match the shutters. Wouldn't that be perfect?"

Over my dead, lifeless body will you make these doors look like an advertisement for Starbucks, I thought.

Will rubbed his eyes. "I kinda like the look of the old wood," he said gently. "Let's leave them like they are. For now anyway."

Oh good, you grew some testicles, I thought.

Inside the bedroom, Will went immediately to the wall of windows overlooking the back garden. He stepped off a few paces away from it, and I knew what he was doing. Envisioning the view from bed every morning.

"Perfect," he said quietly.

I felt as though he'd handed me a sack of diamonds and rubies. The architect's drawings had specified windows, but he'd drawn in oversized stock windows and a Palladian demilune that looked more Italian than Greek Revival. I thought it was his only false move in an otherwise brilliant plan.

Instead, I'd gone to the talented carpenter Will had hired to do the rest of the trimwork on the house. He and I had measured and sketched all the original windows and come up with a new plan, incorporating two sets of tall, narrow fixed windows along the same scale as the front door sidelights, a pair of French doors to match the French doors in the dining room, and a slightly overscaled fanlight to top everything. The carpenter had built the windows on site, incorporating the wavy antique glass I'd scrounged from discarded windows the workers had found down in the root cellar.

It had been the architect's idea to add the hanging balcony that was a larger version of the front porch balcony.

Stephanie opened the French doors and looked out. The painter's scaffolding still surrounded the balcony. "Is it safe to walk on?" she asked, turning around.

"Just finished it yesterday," Adam said proudly. "It's solid as a rock."

Stephanie stepped out onto the balcony. "Oh," was all she said. It was all she needed to say. Will joined her, and the two of them stood gazing out over the fields. He slipped an arm around Stephanie's waist, and she sweetly rested her head on his shoulder. We heard the clip-clip of toenails on the wooden floorboards, and a sharp bark as Erwin dashed out to join them. Will reached down and scooped up the little dog with his free hand. It was an exquisitely private moment.

In mute agreement, Adam and I left them there and went back downstairs.

You've done your job, I thought. *Maybe a little too well.*

45

In August Daddy had a surprise for me. Two surprises, as it turned out.

He called me Wednesday morning, the same as always, to remind me of our supper date.

"Got a new recipe I'm trying out," he said. "I know how you love my salmon loaf, but I thought it was time to branch out. Come hungry, y'hear?"

I hung up the phone and thought about things. Something was different with him. He sounded excited, keyed up. I'd been so busy lately, getting ready to go on a big buying trip for Mulberry Hill, I hadn't paid much attention to the one constant in my life. In fact, I'd missed our supper the previous week, because I'd had to drive to Atlanta to pick up some wallpaper for one of the guest bathrooms at Will's house.

"Gloria?"

"Hmm?" She had the checkbook out, matching invoices with billing statements, doing our monthly books, a chore she enjoyed about as much as a root canal.

"Have you noticed anything different about Daddy lately?"

She looked up and gave it some thought. "Like what?"

"I don't know. He called to remind me about supper tonight, and he said he's got a new recipe."

"No more salmon loaf? Your prayers are answered."

"It's more than that. He sounded funny."

"Well, I noticed he's combing his hair a little different. And come to think of it, I've passed him twice this week on my way to work, and he was out jogging."

"Jogging? My daddy? Wade Murdock—jogging? I didn't even know he owned a pair of sneakers."

"I know," she said. "What's up with him, do you think?"

"Guess I'll find out tonight." I went back to my own work without giving it another thought.

At seven o'clock that night, when I pulled into the carport at Daddy's house, there was another car parked in my usual spot. Nothing too unusual about that. Daddy brought home loaners from the lot all the time. But his Tahoe was parked there too, and the second car was a red Hyundai, and I knew he'd never buy or sell a Hyundai.

The smell of garlic wafted from the house. This, I told myself, was my father's big surprise. He'd probably figured out how to make spaghetti and garlic bread.

I let myself in the front door with my key and walked to the back of the house, toward the kitchen. Daddy's back was turned to me, and he stood at the stove, with a dish towel wrapped around his waist. He had a long wooden spoon, and he was stirring something in a fying pan on the front burner. He wasn't alone in the kitchen. A petite woman, with a long dark braid that hung to her slim waist, was standing next to him, at the counter, chopping onions.

"Hello?" I called out, wondering if I'd somehow wandered into the wrong house.

"Keeley," Daddy said, putting down the spoon.

"Daddy?"

The woman turned toward me, offering a shy smile. She was Asian, and she wore wire-rimmed glasses and a pale green jogging suit. On closer inspection, I could see a streak of gray ran through her dark hair. Her face was unlined, and the only makeup she wore was a bit of pink lipstick.

Daddy put an arm around her shoulder. I thought I might faint.

"Shug," he said, "this is my friend, Serena. Serena, this is my girl, Keeley."

Serena put out her hand, noticed she was still holding the knife, and laughed before putting it down and wiping her hands on a dish towel.

"Keeley," she said, in a distinct Southern accent. "It's so good to meet you. I hope you don't mind my barging in on your family dinner, but your father insisted it would be all right."

"Oh, I don't mind at all," I said. "It's nice to have company."

Who the hell are you and what are you doing in my mother's kitchen?

"This is actually Serena's recipe we're having tonight," Daddy said proudly. "She's teaching me how to make it. Shrimp Creole."

I'd assumed they were making some sort of chop suey or stir-fry. Something Asian.

"Shrimp Creole?" I said dumbly.

"I grew up in Baton Rouge," Serena said. "This is an old family recipe. Although it isn't exactly like we make it at home, because your father's pantry is sort of limited."

"We're gonna send off for the stuff she needs," Daddy said. "You know, Tony Chachere's hot sauce, all that Cajun-Creole stuff. Serena's a great cook."

She gave him an affectionate peck on the cheek. "He's been eating his own cooking for so long, he doesn't know the difference between adequate and great. I told him, even Cheerios taste good as long as somebody else pours the milk."

Cheerios? Had she been staying over to fix his breakfast too?

Just then the rice started to boil over. I grabbed a potholder and moved the saucepan, and turned down the burner. Daddy went back to his roux, and Serena very competently managed to coach us both through a very strange dinner.

We were seated at the dining room table, eating off the good china, which I don't think had been out of the glass-front china cabinet for at least five years. Daddy was in his usual chair at the head of the table, and Serena sat beside him. How, I wondered, did she know to leave the chair at the foot of the table empty?

"You're wondering how we met, and what I'm doing here, I bet," Serena said, as she served up the tossed salad. "I told Wade he should have let you know we were seeing each other, but you know how men are."

Daddy blushed. "Serena is the branch bank manager in Green-ville," he said. "I had to run over there and do some business a month ago, and that's how we met."

"He came back twice in the same week, for no good reason," Serena said, laughing. "I knew he was interested, but he didn't have the nerve to ask me out."

"I was working my way up to it," Daddy protested.

"Maybe in a year he would have asked," Serena said. "So I asked him out. To lunch. Very proper. I think lunch makes a good first date, don't you?" she asked, turning for my opinion. "No obliga-tions, no awkward moments at the front door. Just lunch."

"Uh, yes," I managed to say. "So you've been seeing each other for a month?"

Where the hell have I been? My father is dating and I had no clue?

"It seems like longer," Daddy said. He must have noticed the odd look on my face. "I meant to tell you, shug, I really did. But you've been busy, and I was gonna tell you last week, actually, but you had to cancel, and then we had our dance lessons this past weekend, and a social Saturday night."

I looked from my father to Serena. They both acted like this was perfectly normal. But there was nothing normal about it. "Dance lessons?"

"Ballroom," Serena said. "It was Wade's idea. My bank has a com-panywide Christmas party in December, at the Marriott in Atlanta, and they have an orchestra and everything. I was telling him I never learned how to properly waltz, and the next thing I knew, he'd signed us up for ballroom dancing lessons."

"At the Y," Daddy said. "We're having a ball. You should come learn too."

Are you out of your freaking mind? You can't go dancing with this woman. You're a married man. And anyway, who am I going to dance with?

Somehow I managed to make it through the salad and the shrimp

Creole, which, I have to admit, was the best I'd ever tasted, and even through dessert, which was a crème brulée. When Serena went into the kitchen to brew what she said was the best chickory coffee outside the Café du Monde, I could stand it no longer.

"Daddy," I whispered. "Do you know what you're doing?"

He nodded. "Having the time of my life. She's wonderful, isn't she? Best thing that's ever happened to me."

"What about me?" I snapped. "I thought I was the most wonderful thing to ever happen to you? And what about Mama? Remember her? Jeanine Murry Murdock, your wife, the one you never bothered to divorce? You're still a married man, Daddy."

"You know what I mean," Daddy said calmly. "Serena's the best thing to happen to me in a real long time. I guess maybe she was right, though. I should have told you sooner, let you get used to the idea."

"I will never get used to this idea," I said coldly.

Daddy sighed. "I did not expect this from you, Keeley Rae. Your mama ran off from us more than twenty years ago. I spent all those years pining and wondering what I'd done wrong. I tried to find her, tried to find out what had happened, but I hit a brick wall. Now, when you say you want to know the truth, I didn't stop you. I believe you need to do whatever needs doing, to set your mind at peace. And I think you should extend that courtesy to me. I've been a lonely man all these years. I didn't go out looking for somebody else. It just happened. I went to the bank, and that beautiful face looked up at me and smiled, and I was gone."

"You're telling me that you're in love? Daddy, you haven't dated in over thirty years. How do you know you're not just . . . just . . ."

"Horny?"

I stared at him in horror.

"You haven't . . ."

"That's none of your business, young lady," he said sternly. "When you passed the age of twenty-one, I figured you were at the age of consent. When you spent the night out, I didn't ask a lot of questions. I trusted you to know right from wrong. And when you got engaged to A.J., even though I didn't care for the young man, I figured, she's free, white, and of age. Now, I'm more than twice that, so all you need to know is that I have found a wonderful companion. I enjoy her company and she enjoys mine, and we intend to spend a lot more time together."

I was near tears now. "But you're not thinking of getting . . . married, right? I mean, you can't. You're still legally married to Mama."

Serena came in then, with the coffee tray. She saw me crying, and the look on Daddy's face. She set the tray down on the table, gave Daddy's shoulder a sympathetic squeeze, and went back to the kitchen without a word.

Daddy handed me a mug of coffee and took one for himself. He dumped in two teaspoons of sugar and an inch of cream. He stirred the coffee for a long time.

"I wasn't going to tell you this, until I had some real news. But since you can't seem to let it go, I will tell you. I've hired another private detective. He's a real pro, somebody from Atlanta. One way or another, I'm going to find out the truth. You were right about one thing, Keeley. It's time."

46

Thursday morning Austin and I picked up an eighteen-foot panel truck at the Ryder rental place outside of town. I drove and he talked.

"Listen, there's a place I want to go to tonight in Savannah. You'll probably want to stay in after this long drive, but don't worry a thing about me. I know my way around."

"I'll bet," I said. We both knew he was dying to hit all the gay clubs he'd read about on some Internet chat site. "Anyway, there's an auction I want to go to at six. Just make sure you're around to help me load up tomorrow morning," I said. "I want to get an early start for New Orleans."

We'd spent weeks mapping out this buying trip. I'd intended to take Gloria with me, but at the last minute there was a snag on her kitchen project. She'd insisted I couldn't go alone, and had drafted Austin to accompany me. It hadn't taken much arm twisting to persuade him. Late August was his dead time, and as soon as he'd heard that the itinerary included Savannah and New Orleans, he'd put up the ON VACATION sign on the door at Fleur and started to pack.

Our first stop was in Atlanta. I'd spotted a massive German chip-carved oak sideboard in the Ainsworth-Noah showroom at ADAC on my last trip over there. At twenty-eight thousand dollars, it was a major purchase. But I'd taken a digital photo of the sideboard and e-mailed it to Will Mahoney, who agreed that it was the perfect piece for the breakfast room. We picked up a pair of faux stag-horn sconces in the same showroom, to go in Will's study, which I was decorating with a subdued hunting lodge feel, and a set of six beautifully framed and matted nineteenth-century watercolor studies of brook trout.

We made Macon before noon. Once we were on I-16, headed east toward the coast, I ran out of aimless chit-chat.

Austin began toying with the radio, trying to find a station we could both agree on. He hates country, I hate eighties disco, we both hate rap.

"So," he said, after finally giving up and turning the radio off. "What's new with the Murdock family? How was dinner the other night?"

He was trying to act all innocent, but I knew he'd heard the talk around town.

"Dinner was great," I said. "Daddy has a new dish."

"I heard," he said eagerly. "Chinese, right? What did you think? Did you like her? Is she way younger; do you think she's after his money?"

I kept my eyes on the road. "I was talking about his new recipe. He fixed shrimp Creole."

"Oh." He let it hang there, echoing in the half-empty truck.

"And I met his lady friend. She's all right. Not all that young. I'd guess early fifties. She's Asian American, but I didn't ask if she was Chinese. Grew up in Baton Rouge."

"Well? Is she a gold-digger? That's what I heard. That she works at the bank, so she knows exactly what your dad is worth."

The kudzu telegraph strikes again. It hadn't occurred to me that Serena might be after my father's money. In fact, I hadn't questioned her motives for seeing my father at all. I'd only questioned his motives in seeing her.

"She works at a bank in Greenville," I told Austin. "I don't think it has anything to do with Daddy's bank. He acts like he's crazy about her. And I think the feeling is mutual."

"Do you think they've done the deed?"

"Austin! Don't be disgusting."

"So they have. How does that make you feel? I mean, you've been the only woman in his life all these years. Daddy's girl, all that. Is that an Oedipal complex or an Electra complex?"

"Neither," I cried. "I'm fine with him seeing Serena. It's great. Anyway, his sex life is none of my business."

"I knew it!" Austin said, snickering. "Good old Wade. Good for him. Do you think she knows any of those, like, kinky geisha girl tricks? Sort of that whole Kama Sutra thing?"

"This is my father we're talking about here. Now you stop it right now or I'm putting you out of this truck, you perv."

"I'm just sayin'," he said airily. "You don't have to freak out on me. He may be your daddy, but he's only human. The guy has needs, for God's sake. I mean, how long has your mama been gone?"

"Since 1979," I snapped. "And he has no business having needs. Last I heard, he was still officially married."

"As far as we know," Austin said gently. "We've only checked the Southern states. And sweetie, there's always the possibility that Jeanine is dead. You know that, right?"

"You said there was no death certificate," I said.

"That we can find. But don't you think if she were alive, you'd have heard something after all these years? I mean, you said yourself, she ran off. She never got in contact with you. Don't you think it's probably over between your parents? For all you know, she went off and married Darvis Kane and had a passel of kids."

"That is not possible," I said flatly. "And I don't want to talk about this anymore."

"Suit yourself," he said. He leaned up against the passenger side door and promptly fell fast asleep. Austin didn't open his eyes again until we pulled up to the curb beside the DeSoto Hilton in Savannah.

"Here already?" he asked, craning his neck around. "Why didn't you wake me up? I could have driven for a while."

"You were sawing logs," I said. "Anyway, I was enjoying the quiet."

He stuck his tongue out at me. I checked us into the hotel. When we got up to the room, I felt like crying. I'd asked for a double. They'd given us a single king-sized bed.

"Crap," I said, sinking down onto the quilted coverlet. "Don't unpack."

I picked up the phone and called down to the front desk. They were apologetic, but resolute. The hotel was full; there were no other rooms available.

"Oh, who cares?" Austin said, taking his shaving kit out of his overnight bag. "We'll just sleep in the same bed. It's only for a few hours. And it's not like I'm going to violate you or anything."

I gave him a dark look. "You snore. And I've gotten used to sleeping alone."

"Pity," he said, ducking into the bathroom just before I threw my shoe at him.

When he came out of the bathroom, he was dressed to kill. Sharply pressed white canvas pants, a striped dress shirt, no socks, immaculate Docksiders. He smelled like expensive aftershave. He was tall and tan and young and lovely. The boy from Ipanema.

"You're gorgeous," I said glumly.

"You think?" he asked, twirling around so I could get the full effect. "They go for the preppie look down here."

"You'll be fighting the guys off with a baseball bat," I said.

He sat down on the bed beside me and put his arm around my shoulder. "I could go to dinner with you if you want. The clubs don't really start hopping until after ten, from what I hear. What do you say? I'll buy."

I kissed his forehead. "No thanks. I want to get over to the auction house before it starts, to take a good look at some of the pieces I saw online. I'll just grab a sandwich at the snack bar there. Take yourself over to 1790. It's the restaurant attached to an inn over on President Street. Sit at the bar for a little while, order a martini. You'll have a dinner date in ten minutes flat. Possibly even a marriage proposal."

"Well . . ." He hesitated.

"Go."

Pierce's Auctions and Antiques was headquartered in a dilapidated one-story concrete-block building in a seedy-looking industrial area on the west side of Savannah. I knew I'd found the right address when I saw all the pickups, U-Hauls, and trailers parked in the parking lot outside.

I gave a woman at the door my name, address, tax number, and other business information, and she gave me a numbered cardboard paddle. "We start in fifteen minutes," she said, pausing to flick the ash from her cigarette onto the concrete floor.

"Ten percent buyer's reserve. We don't hold nothin' for nobody. It's all cash and carry here."

I joined the crowds milling around at the front of the building. It was an interesting crowd. Good ol' boys with baseball caps and greasy fingernails mingled with well-dressed middle-aged dealers and a sprinkling of kids, who chased one aother around the room, throwing potato chips at one another.

The piece I was most interested in had drawn the attention of at least five other buyers. It was an early nineteenth-century walnut chest-on-chest. The catalog said it had come from an estate in Charleston, but then auction catalogs are never exactly the gospel truth. It had original brasses, nice hand-cut dovetailing on the drawers. The bracket feet looked right. It would be a wonderful addition to the master bedroom, or even the guest bedroom if I found something nicer down the road.

After I'd satisfied myself that it was the real thing, I looked around at the rest of the night's offering. Like the crowd, the merchandise was an eclectic mix. There were nine or ten really good pieces of furniture, some decent Oriental rugs, some nice original oil paintings, a good deal of silver and crystal, and several lots of blue and white export porcelains, which I marked down on my catalog. Mixed in with the good stuff were several hundred pairs of bootleg designer sunglasses and Gucci handbags, a pallet of power tools, and several huge cartons of knitting yarn.

A buzzer sounded, and the auctioneer took up his place in front of the microphone on the raised desk at the front of the room.

He was fast, I'll give him that. Within an hour he'd disposed of the sunglasses and handbags, half the power tools, and several of the rugs.

The prices were amazingly good. Almost without thinking, I bid on and won three large, somewhat threadbare Oriental rugs, for two hundred dollars apiece. I'd seen similar rugs earlier in the day at the Markanian showroom at ADAC, and none of them had prices under three thousand dollars. I looked around for someone to high-five, but settled for a self-satisfied smirk to myself.

But I didn't even have time to gloat over my bargain. The lots of blue and white came up for bid, and although the first couple lots went high—they were large Sheffield English platters—people lost interest rapidly. Within fifteen minutes I'd bought two box lots of platters, and plates, another of mismatched jugs, tureens, and urns, for a total of three hundred and fifty dollars.

I skipped to the front of the room to gather up the porcelain, then sat back down to examine my loot. The platters and plates were English, with good hallmarks on the back. There were some Wedgwood and some Staffordshire, and the best, which was a large Coalport meat platter. Altogether there were five platters and three smaller plates. The jugs had wonderful dark colors, but chips on the lip and some crazing on the glaze. The Worcester tureen was my favorite piece. More the size of a footbath, it came with an underplate—but a lid that had been cracked and clumsily damaged.

The nicest pieces of blue and white I could use at Mulberry Hill. I didn't know or care where the rest of the stuff would go; the prices were so good I might even save them for myself.

The auctioneer had saved the best pieces of furniture for last. I drooled as a pine Welsh dresser sold for three thousand dollars, and a gorgeous set of Georgian dining room chairs brought eight thousand dollars, but I resignedly kept my bid paddle in my lap.

Finally the moment I'd been waiting for arrived. I'd marked and starred item 328 on my auction catalog—the chest-on-chest—and I felt the familiar pounding in my chest as the auctioneer worked his way through the dross to the gold. Ten thousand, I told myself. If I could get the chest for ten thousand, the rest of the bedroom would fall into place around it.

As always, I remembered Aunt Gloria's formula for a beautiful room. "Wooden floors covered with Oriental carpets, for richness and texture. One true antique that gives the room elegance and a sense of place. And a beautiful painting or piece of art, that speaks to you, every time you enter the room."

The chest-on-chest would hold up one corner of Gloria's design triangle.

"Now folks, here's a humdinger," the auctioneer said, hunched over the microphone, his eyes constantly scanning the room. "Nineteenth-century walnut chest-on-chest, straight out of the Catabogue Plantation over there in Charleston. You won't see nothin' like this outside a museum. Whaddya say now? Who'll give me sixty?"

"Dollars?" hollered somebody in the back. "I'll give ya sixty dollars."

"Folks, there's a penalty for pulling the auctioneer's leg," he said. "I'm talkin' sixty thousand American greenbacks, and that's a bargain for a piece like this. Who'll give me sixty thousand?"

Everybody around me was craning their necks to see if anybody would bite. But they were obviously all pros who were steeped in auction wisdom—never be the opening bidder.

The auctioneer shook his head. "All right, cheapskates. Who'll give me fifty-five? Gimme fifty-five and walk out of here with the buy of the night."

No deal.

"Fifty?" he was incredulous. "Folks, I'd be giving it away at fifty thousand."

The room was very quiet. The buyers who'd huddled around the piece earlier were all watching one another to see who would be the first to give in.

The auctioneer blew into the microphone. He made an elaborate show of cupping his hand to his ear, in case the opening bid was a whisper. Finally, with an exaggerated shrug and the wounded air of a man who'd seen his firstborn child passed over for kickball, he started his patter.

"Allrightthen, gimme forty-five? No? Forty? Gimme thirty-five. No? Thirty? You're killing me folks. I'm dying up here. Say twenny-five. Twenny-five, twenny-five. No? Then twenty. Twenty, twenty, twenty? No? Somebody call the doctor! This place is a morgue. All right. Fifteen. Somebody gimme fifteen for this gorgeous piece right out of the plantation house. I'm not kiddin' it could be in a New York showroom for sixty thousand dollars tomorrow. Those Yankees would snap it up like that."

Silence.

The auctioneer took a handkerchief out of his pocket and mopped his brow with it. "Allrightthen. We'll do it your way. Gimme an opening bid. I mean it. We got a lot of stuff to move tonight. Gimme something to work with here."

"A thousand," called a thirty-ish man dressed in khaki shorts with a ballcap pulled low over his forehead. He held up his paddle so the auctioneer could see he meant business.

The auctioneer shook his head and muttered something inaudible. "I got a thousand. I don't want it, but I got a thousand."

Now the bidding picked up in a hurry.

A plump woman with huge horn-rimmed glasses sitting at the end of my aisle waved her paddle. "Eleven."

Someone at the very back of the room, who I couldn't see, must have waded in too.

"Twelve," the auctioneer called. And the room was suddenly alive with numbered paddles being thrust into the air.

"Now fifteen. Make it two. I got two. Make it twenty-five. I got twenty-five up front. Now three? I got three. Make it four. Five? That's better."

I looked down at the numbered paddle in my hand. Five thousand was less than half of what I'd planned to pay. The chest was the real thing. It was a bargain. But it was still five thousand dollars. And I had so many other pieces to buy for the house. I'd been spending money like a drunken sailor—twenty-eight thousand on that one piece in Atlanta alone, what was one more check? Certainly Will hadn't given me any kind of a budget.

But I kept thinking of having to hand over the invoices for this trip to Nancy Rockmore, back at the Loving Cup offices. I could even hear her voice, "Twenty-eight thousand for a sideboard? Five thousand dollars for a goddamn chest of drawers? Is this stuff made of gold?"

My hand stayed in my lap.

The auctioneer kept up his patter. "Fifty-five. Now six. I got six thousand. Now seven. Now eight. Now nine." Most of the bidders had dropped out after five thousand. There were only three left. Ballcap, the lady in the horn-rimmed glasses, and the bidder in the back who I couldn't see.

"Ten," the auctioneer said. He nodded to my right. "Eleven." Now to the doorway, "Twelve." The bidder in the back dropped out. It was a two-way race.

"Thirteen. Now fourteen." The auctioneer looked askance at ballcap. "Fifteen?"

Ballcap shook his had sadly and let his paddle drop to his side.

"Fifteen?" the auctioneer called. "Fifteen? Fifteen? All done. Sold! to the luckiest lady in Savannah." He paused. She held up her paddle so the clerk who sat beside him could register her number. "Fifteen thousand dollars to number 213."

There was a quick round of quiet applause. The woman in the horn-rims marked her catalog and looked up again, waiting for the next item to come up to bid.

I stood up and got my pocketbook. It was no use my staying here any longer. I felt like a kid who'd finally had too much candy. Everything here was too rich. It made my stomach hurt.

47

At six A.M. I heard the click of the key card in the lock and looked up from tying my sneakers. Austin stood in the doorway with his own shoes in his hands, and on his face, an alluring combination of glee and guilt.

"Nice night?" I asked.

"What are you doing?" he asked, letting the shoes drop to the floor. "We can't leave yet. I know you said early, but not *this* early."

"Relax," I said. "Get some sleep. I've got some shopping to do, so we probably won't get out of here until at least noon."

He dropped down on the bed beside me, and buried his head in the pillows. "Thank *Gawd*. I should know better than to drink gin in this climate."

"I take it you made some nice new friends?" I asked.

"Nice and naughty." His voice was muffled under all those pillows. "I could never live down here. I would be dead in six months. Partied completely to death."

I stood up and did some stretches. "Noon," I warned. "You've got six hours to make a complete and total recovery before we blow town."

I had the elevator all to myself. And the lobby of the DeSoto was nearly empty too. It was still near dark outside the hotel. As I walked through Chippewa Square, past a homeless man dozing on a bench near the statue of General Oglethorpe, I headed north down Drayton Street. I had no plan. Just to get a walk in before Savannah's ungodly heat and humidity blanketed the town. And maybe a little window shopping.

As I walked, I thought about Mulberry Hill. I had made a good start on decorating it, but there was something missing.

The sketches looked great, I knew. But when I totaled up all the pieces I had bought or ordered, nothing seemed to come together. It dawned on me that I was designing by rote, buying things because of a pedigree or name recognition. Stephanie would know a Brunswig & Fils fabric. Stephanie could appreciate the glamour of an Empire mahogany sideboard or a gilt Regency mirror and a custom-colored Stark carpet. But as I arranged the rooms in my mind's eye, it all seemed forced, and cold—stuffy and pompous and decidedly unimaginative.

How could this be? For the first time ever, I had a project with a virtually unlimited budget. And a killer deadline, it was true. But I'd had a killer deadline for the pump house and I'd had a field day decorating it on a virtual shoestring.

Gloria's rules echoed in my head. Good rugs. Good art. One good antique. I'd blown the opportunity to buy a museum-quality chest the night before. But why did good have to equal expensive?

I certainly had some good—and cheap—rugs. I'd planned on buying an expensive Aubusson for the dining room, and something equally grand for the twin parlors. But the jewellike reds and blues of the rugs I'd bought last night could work in the ground-floor rooms at Mulberry Hill. And the blue and white porcelains—even the slightly chipped and damaged pieces—would bring that imperfect English country house look to rooms that wanted to be warm and lived-in.

As I walked, I watched the downtown Savannah skyline—shabby, yet intimate—come alive with daylight. If I tilted my head at just the right angle, I could see a row of church spires poking above moss-draped oak trees. Slowly, a new plan came together. I would make a home that would make Stephanie fall in love—if not with Will, with it. But I could only do this well if I pleased myself, by pleasing Will. I would not throw money at this project. Instead, I'd invest my own well-trained eye and imagination.

I turned to the right, toward the next square. The historic district was dotted with elegant antiques shops, most of which I'd shopped in before. I paused in front of an old favorite, Josephine's, on Jones Street, which took up the basement and parlor floors of a red brick 1840s townhouse. In the basement window a woman was busily rearranging her merchandise. She'd stacked paintings, a grandfather clock, and a damask-upholstered Queen Anne wing chair to the side of the window and was pushing a new piece to the center of attraction. The woman had black horn-rimmed glasses. The new piece was the walnut chest-on-chest she'd purchased the night before. She turned and recognized me. A moment later the door to the shop opened and she popped her head out.

"You can still buy it," she called to me. "It's the best one I've ever seen, and I've seen a lot."

"It's wonderful," I agreed. "But too rich for me. What are you asking for it, can I ask?"

She smiled broadly. "Thirty thousand. A steal, don't you think?"

At York Street, on Wright Square, I stopped to look in the window of an antiques shop I'd never seen before. It was called @Home, and the vignette arranged there made me smile. A large pine demilune console table had heavily carved bowed legs and just traces of peeling palest blue paint. A black tole planter filled with lemons was placed askew on the table, with a casually thrown crocheted-lace cloth draping to the floor. I loved the artlessness of the vignette, but the table was clearly the star of the show. Its scale was cartoonish and its condition was imperfect, but it spoke to me. It would be the perfect centerpiece for the entry hall at Mulberry Hill. I put my face to the glass to peer in, hoping to catch sight of a price tag, but I couldn't see one.

I glanced at my watch. It wasn't even seven yet, and the stenciled sign on the shop's door said it didn't open until ten.

So I marched on. Around the squares, with a stop at the Amoco gas station on Drayton, for a surprisingly good banana nut muffin and a bottle of cold water and a copy of the local newspaper. Still only eight o'clock. I found a bench in another quiet square off Charlton Street, near the Cathedral of St. John the Baptist. I'd never seen Troupe Square before, but liked it instantly for the cool swath of green grass and the antique iron armillary in the center, instead of the more usual statue.

I sipped my water and nibbled at my muffin, shooing away the scavenging pigeons who flew too close. I killed time by browsing through the newspaper, saving the best—the classified ads—for last. I'd hoped for an estate sale to occupy my time until the shop on York Street opened, but the few sales advertised for that morning were garage sales in the far suburbs of Savannah that I was unfamiliar with.

At nine I trudged through the scorching heat back to the Hilton. When I opened the door to the room, Austin was splayed out on the bed, facedown, still fully clothed. I let the door close loudly. He didn't move.

I showered, changed, and packed my overnight bag. Finally I sat down on the edge of the bed and put my lips to Austin's ears.

"Wake up, loverboy," I whispered. "We've got work to do."

He groaned and put another pillow over his head. "Leave me here. I'll take the bus back to Madison."

"Not on your life," I said, shaking him now. "Come on. I found a great piece at a shop here, and I want to go buy it before somebody else beats me to the punch."

Austin moaned and groaned, but with a combination of threats and pleading, he finally got moving. While he showered, I went downstairs, paid the bill, and got him a cup of coffee.

We pulled the truck up to the shop on York just as a young woman was unlocking the shop.

I jumped out and met her at the door. "The table in the window," I said, momentarily throwing caution to the wind. Never appear anxious was the antiques buyer's rule. To hell with that. I wanted that table.

She jumped, startled, I guess, by my intensity so early in the morning. She had short dark hair, wore a tank top that bared an impressive tattoo on her left forearm, cutoff green fatigues, and black high-top Converse sneakers.

"It's an awesome piece, don't you think?" the girl asked, opening the door. A small gray kitten streaked past me as I stepped inside.

"Biedermeier," the girl cooed, scooping the kitten up in her arms. "Were you out all night, you bad tomcat?"

I looked out the window at the van, with Austin slumped down in the passenger seat. "There's a lot of that in Savannah, it seems."

She let the cat down and nodded sagely. "It's the humidity. People forget themelves."

"About the table," I began.

The girl moved around the shop, snapping on the lights. "It's six hundred," she said firmly. "We just picked it up this past week, so I really can't cut the price so soon."

I reached for my checkbook. "Perfect."

48

Austin helped me wrap the console table in a mover's quilt and stow it in the back of the van, along with the rugs and the boxes of dishes. "Good night last night?" he asked, stepping back from the van to fan himself with his baseball cap.

"Sort of," I said. "Great prices on the rug and porcelains, but on the one piece I really liked, the bidding got too steep and I dropped out. But I did have an epiphany."

He walked over to the driver's side of the van. "My turn to drive," he said.

I raised an eyebrow. "Are you awake enough for that?"

"No, but with two more cups of coffee I will be."

I was happy to turn the driving over to him. Headed out of town, he kept his eyes on the road. "What kind of an epiphany?"

"Hmm? Oh. Well, I just felt really guilty spending so much money on Mulberry Hill, when Loving Cup is teetering on the brink of closing down."

"Isn't that Will's problem?"

"It is. But it feels so decadent, blowing, like, ten thousand dollars on a single chest of drawers."

"You spent that?" Even he looked alarmed.

"No, but I easily could have, last night. But I didn't. And I decided I'm really better—more creative—when I'm scrimping and scrounging. Does that make any sense to you?"

He nodded. "Sure. It's like, when I have masses of gorgeous flowers, how hard is that to pull off a look? Anybody could do it. But give me an unusual container, some gravepines, pokeberries, dried hydrangeas, stuff you could pick out of anybody's yard, that's when it's fun. That's when I know that I'm fabulous at what I do."

"So I'm not crazy?"

"Only in the sense that you could make a lot more money by spending a lot more of Will's money. And it's not like he doesn't want you to do that."

"I know. But I just can't. That table I bought, back there in Savannah? That's the most fun I've had this whole trip. And now I can't wait to get back to the drawing table, to sketch out how I want the entry hall mural painted around it, and to find just the right mirror—nothing too frou-frou, and wall sconces . . ."

"I get you," Austin said. "I take it that means we're bargain hunting from now on?"

"You got it," I said. "We might even skip New Orleans. I was thinking about a Mallard or Belter tester bed for the master bedroom. It's what Stephanie would expect. And I could probably find one at one of those antiques shops on Magazine Street. They have divine stuff, but the prices are just so unreal."

"Skip New Orleans?" Austin looked crushed. "But you promised."

"All right, but only one night. I don't think you can survive that much more clubbing."

He breathed a heavy sigh of relief. "I promise I'll be good until then," he said. "I'm saving myself for New Orleans."

He gave my knee a proprietary pat. "Why don't you catch a nap? I'll wake you up when we hit Birmingham."

"No nap," I said, yawning. "I want to read . . ."

When I woke up again, we were at a rundown Shell oil station in what looked like the middle of nowhere. Austin was standing beside the van, pumping gas and looking down at a road map.

"What time is it?" I asked.

"After three."

I got out of the van, went inside the gas station to use the bathroom, and when I got back, he was just folding the top to his cell phone.

"Where exactly are we?" I asked, yawning again. "Birmingham?"

"Not quite," he said.

"Define not quite."

"We're in Alabama, but not Birmingham. Not yet. We're taking a little detour. This is Wedowee."

I blinked. "Why does that name ring a bell?"

"Because Wedowee, Alabama, is the hometown of Darvis Kane."

There was a Coke machine outside the cashier's office. I walked over and got myself a Diet Coke and got back inside the van.

Austin got behind the wheel and started the engine. He was waiting for me to say something. I was waiting for him to say something. Finally he gave in.

"Darvis Kane has a sister who still lives in Wedowee. Her name is Delores Akers. She's a good bit older than he is. I thought she might have some idea of where we can find her brother. That was her daughter I was just talking to on the phone. She said her mother is still napping, but if we come by in fifteen minutes, maybe she'll see us."

"And tell us what?"

"I don't know," Austin said calmly. "I've only spoken to the daughter. Her name is Bella. And she's not exactly a Chatty Cathy. Claims she's never met her uncle. But Wedowee is not that far out of the way. I thought it was worth a little detour."

"All right. We've come this far, we might as well see what happens."

Austin looked disappointed. "Aren't you going to ask me how I tracked her down? It took two weeks, you know."

"No," I said, looking out the window.

We drove around greater Wedowee for the next fifteen minutes. Not a lot to see.

Eventually, following a set of directions he'd scribbled on a paper napkin, we drove through a run-down section of town until we came to a cluster of concrete-block duplexes painted a drab yellow. A half-dozen dilapidated cars and trucks were scattered around the pockmarked concrete strip that ran in front of the units, and at the end unit, the front door was open, and an old lady in a pair of bright green shorts and a Braves T-shirt was vigorously sweeping dirt right out onto the front porch.

As we approached, she kept on sweeping. Clouds of dust rose up around us. We stopped at the edge of the little concrete porch. "Mrs. Akers?" Austin called. The old lady appeared not to have heard us. The sweeping got more furious. I had to stand back and cover my mouth to keep from inhaling it.

Another woman came out onto the porch. She looked only a shade younger, and wore a Braves baseball cap and blue jeans and a Bill Elliott NASCAR T-shirt. She grabbed the old lady's arm and cupped one hand to her ear. "Mama! Cut it out now. We got company."

The old woman looked up at us. Her face was pale as milk, and her short white hair stuck straight up in the air, like so many strands of white coat hanger wire.

"Who're you?"

"Austin LeFleur," Austin said, stepping right up and reaching out to shake the old lady's hand. "And this is my friend Keeley Murdock."

"I don't know nobody named Austin," the old lady said plaintively, hanging on to her broom with both hands. "Nor Keeley neither."

"They're strangers," her daughter informed her. "Come over here from Madison, Georgia. Want to ask you about your brother Darvis."

The old lady squinted at us speculatively. "What about Darvis? What you want with him?"

"Well," Austin hesitated. Clearly, Nancy Drew had never had to interrogate anybody as uncooperative as Delores Akers. He coughed and began again. "Could we maybe go inside and talk?"

"What for?" Delores asked.

"Mama!" her daughter scolded. "Be nice. They come a long way today."

"I don't know them and they don't know me," the old lady muttered. But she allowed her daughter to lead her back inside the dimly lit house. Bella Akers instructed us to be seated on a green metal glider. She helped her mother into a wooden rocking chair and sat in the only other piece of furniture in the otherwise bare room, a ladderback chair. An air-conditioning unit poking through the front window of the house churned mightily to little effect.

"Y'all want a Pepsi?" Bella asked.

"I'll take one," Delores said, but Austin and I politely refused.

While Bella went into another room, Delores studied us closely as she rocked.

"My little brother Darvis lived over there in Georgie one time," she stated. "Had a good house with wall-to-wall carpet."

"He worked for my father," I said. "At my father's car lot. In Madison. But that was twenty-five years ago."

"I 'spect," Delores said, rocking away. Bella walked back into the room and handed her mother a can of Pepsi with a straw poking out of it. The old lady sucked greedily and rocked some more.

Austin gave me a subtle nod.

"The reason I'm interested in finding out about your brother—" I started. But then I stopped. Why was I looking for Darvis Kane?

Another nod from Austin. But I just sat there, hopelessly tongue-tied.

"Your brother Darvis was apparently having an, um, relationship with Keeley's mother, back there when he lived in Madison," Austin said, stepping in. I shot him a grateful look.

"Keeley's mother's name was Jeanine Murry Murdock. She disappeared in 1979. And we think maybe she left town with Darvis Kane."

"Disappeared?" Bella asked, looking from me to Austin. "You mean, like, vanished? Like kidnapped or something?"

"Well, no, we don't think Jeanine left against her will," Austin said. "We think they just ran off somewhere. Together."

"Sounds like Darvis to me," Delores said, looking up from her Pepsi. "He always did like the ladies. Especially ones that was married to somebody else."

"Did you ever meet my mother?" I asked, leaning forward eagerly. "Did they come here?"

"Here? Why'd they come here?" Delores asked.

"We think they went to Alabama, after they left Madison," Austin explained. "They were driving Jeanine's car. A red Malibu. And we know the car was sold in Birmingham, not long afterward. But that's all we know."

Delores went back to sucking on her Pepsi and rocking.

"Mama?" Bella said, leaning forward and putting her foot out to stop the rocking. "Tell them what you know about Darvis. Did he ever bring a lady around here? Back in 1979?"

Delores's pale lips formed a pout. "He brung a lady he *said* was his wife. Had a couple young'uns with 'em too. But that was a long time ago."

"Lisa?" I cut in. "Darvis was married to a woman named Lisa. And they had children."

"I got cousins?" Bella asked, startled. She kicked at her mother's shin. "You never told me I had no cousins."

"Ow, dammit," Delores hollered.

"Darvis was married to a woman named Lisa Franklin. She divorced him after he abandoned her and their children," Austin said. "Lisa lives down in Palatka, Florida. And your cousins, Courtney and Whitney, live in that area too," he said, looking at Bella.

"Courtney and Whitney," Bella said, rolling the names around on her tongue. "They sound nice." She gave her mother another kick. "That's for not tellin' me."

The old lady howled and started rocking rapidly back and forth.

"When exactly was the last time you heard from Darvis?" Austin asked.

Bella poised her foot just above her mother's shin again. "Tell 'em right now, Mama. Or I'll kick you clear to the next county."

Delores scooted her chair backward, away from her daughter. But she stopped rocking. After a minute she said, in a low voice, "I knew he was doin' wrong. Darvis was always doin' wrong. But he was my mama's baby, and he never had a hand laid on him. Spoilt rotten, that was Darvis."

"What was he doing wrong the last time you saw him?" I asked gently.

"Driving that fancy car you talked about," she said defiantly. "Big old shiny red Malibu. He come driving up here out of the blue one day. Wanted me to follow him over to Birmingham in my car, so he could sell that one. Said he'd give me five dollars gas money if I'd do it. So I did."

"What about my mother?" I whispered. "Was my mother with him?"

She shook her head vehemently. "He didn't have no lady with him that time. It was just him. And he was in a big hurry too."

"Did he say why?" Austin asked.

"I didn't ask," Delores said. "He wouldn't have told me the truth, noways. We rode over there to Birmingham, and a fella in that car lot gave Darvis a wad of cash money. After that he had me to take him to the Trailways bus station, back over in Anniston. He give me my money, and I left him off."

"Did you see where he went? Did he buy a bus ticket?" I asked.

"No ma'am," she said emphatically. "Wasn't none of my business. I come on back home after that. And I never did see my baby brother again." She closed her eyes and started rocking.

Bella followed us outside to our car. "How about you?" I asked. "Do you know anything about your uncle's whereabouts?"

"No ma'am," she said somberly. Up close like this, she didn't look as old as she had initially. Maybe in her early forties. Her face had a wistful expression. "I didn't even know I had cousins. Whitney and Courtney. Down there in Florida. You reckon they'd take me to Disney World?"

49

"**I'll drive,**" I told Austin. I needed to be in charge for a while. It was a little tricky, finding our way back to the Interstate, and it was good to concentrate on alternate routes and road signs instead of the even trickier matter of my mother's whereabouts.

Austin drummed his fingertips on the van's dashboard. "Well," he said finally. "What do you think?"

"I think it's tragic that a woman in her forties has never been to Disney World," I said, staring straight ahead.

"No, I mean about Darvis Kane. He didn't have your mother with him when he sold her car. What can that mean?"

"Lots of things. Maybe she was meeting up with him someplace in Anniston. The old lady said she didn't hang around to see if he got on a bus. Or maybe he arranged to meet her someplace else. Or . . ." I let my voice trail off, not wanting to speak about the possibilities that were whirling around in my own mind.

"Maybe Jeanine didn't know he took her car. Maybe he left her back in Madison. Maybe she really didn't run off with Darvis Kane," said Austin, ever helpful.

I pushed a strand of sweaty hair off my forehead. "That still leaves us with more questions than answers. Again. We still don't know where my mother is, and we don't know where Darvis is."

Austin reached over and massaged my taut shoulder muscles. "Is this upsetting you?"

"No. Sort of. I don't know. Maybe we should just let Daddy's private detective sort it out."

He clamped his hand down on my arm. "Private detective?"

I nodded. "Now that he's started dating, Daddy has decided maybe he does need to have some answers about Mama. He told me

Wednesday night that he's hired another detective. Somebody from Atlanta. A real pro this time, he claims."

"Keeley!" Austin said, looking peeved. "I can't believe you're just now telling me this. Who is it? Has the guy found anything out yet? Maybe we should get together and exchange information."

I laughed. "Daddy didn't tell me his name. Not that it matters, because we don't have any real information, Austin. I think we really have hit a dead end this time."

"What?" he screeched. "How can you talk like that? This isn't a dead end. We just uncovered a really important fact. Darvis Kane was alone when he sold your mama's car. And he probably took a bus from Anniston to wherever he was meeting your mother. All we have to do now is get the bus company to check their records and tell us where he went."

I hated to rain on Austin's parade, I really did. But it wasn't fair to let him keep up with the fantasy that he was going to track down my mother after all these years, and everything would be peachy-keen. And it wasn't fair to me either, to let that fantasy take root in my mind.

"What records?" I asked. "Twenty-five years ago, they didn't have computers. Anyway, it was a bus station, not an airport. Have you ever actually ridden on a Greyhound bus? They don't take down your name and address and Social Security number. You give them some cash, they give you a ticket, you get on the bus next to some stinky guy with a mullet hairdo wearing a Walkman."

"It's still an important piece of information," Austin said sulkily.

I patted his knee. "You're right. It is. When we get back home, I'll tell Daddy to pass it along to his private detective. It could be the key that unlocks this whole mystery."

"Now you're patronizing me," Austin said. "I can't stand when people do that."

"Okay," I said. "Let's talk about something else. Like where do you want to stay tonight? It's at least seven hours to New Orleans.

Should we find a motel, maybe in Mobile or Biloxi, or keep going to the Big Easy?"

"Either way, I miss Friday night in New Orleans."

"It's always Friday night in New Orleans," I pointed out. "Okay. I don't know about you, but I'd kill for a shower right about now. Let's just take I-65 down to Mobile and spend the night there. We can have a nice dinner and get an early start to Biloxi in the morning. I wouldn't mind touring an old antebellum plantation house either, if there's one on the way to New Orleans. For research purposes. I'm not doing an exact historic reproduction at Mulberry Hill, but it always helps me to see the real thing."

"It's your party," Austin said. "I'm just along to do the heavy lifting."

"Not true. You get to do some of the driving too. And I need your design sensibility. You're a man of many talents, Austin."

"I'm an excellent detective too," he said. "Despite what you think, we are making progress on finding out what happened to your mother. We've eliminated a lot of possibilities, and now there are just a few people left who we absolutely have to talk to."

"Who?"

"That cousin of yours up in Kannapolis, mainly," he said.

"Sonya Wyrick," I said.

He nodded. "I found her. She's still right there in Kannapolis."

I stared at him. "Have you talked to her?"

"Sort of. A woman answered the phone at the house I called, but she hung up before I could even tell her what I wanted. I think she thought I was trying to sell her something."

"She probably won't talk to me either," I said.

"Why are you being like this?" Austin asked, exasperated. "You're such a defeatist!"

"Talking to people about Mama, it's just really hard. I mean, it's not like I'm dredging up happy memories, for them or for me. This was a scandal, and even though it all happened a long time ago, it seems like just about everybody in Madison would just as soon forget the name Jeanine Murdock."

"But you wouldn't," Austin said gently. "And neither would your daddy. And if you won't find out for yourself, find out for him. Don't you think it's about time these old secrets get aired out?"

"I guess," I said. "But I don't have a good feeling about this. There has to be a reason it's been a secret all these years. And I just don't think this is going to have a happy ending. That's why I'm so reluctant to keep going. Somebody is going to get hurt."

"Somebody already has been hurt," Austin said. "You and your daddy. Probably a bunch of people you don't even know have been hurt by your mother's disappearance too. It can't get any worse, can it?"

I'd been thinking about that too. All the awful possibilities. But in the end Austin was right. Daddy and I needed to know. Now. So we could get on with our lives, with or without Jeanine.

"All right," I said finally. "I guess I wouldn't mind seeing Sonya again. I know so little about Mama's family, maybe she can fill in some gaps."

"That's my girl," Austin said, beaming. "I'll even go with you. And after we've caught up with cousin Sonya, we can go on up the road a little bit and hit the High Point furniture outlets. They have the most fabulous website. I've already checked it out. We can head up there, right after we're done in New Orleans. I mean, we already have the truck, and I've got the week off to play. And best of all, we can do our little research and still write the whole trip off on Will's dime."

"You've been plotting against me," I said.

"Somebody has to."

50

We found a motel just off the Interstate in Mobile, and this time we got one room—with two queen-sized beds. I hit the showers while Austin went to forage for food. I was sitting on my bed toweling off my hair when he came in holding aloft two large paper sacks.

"That smells divine," I said. "What is it?"

He smiled. "Cheeseburger in Paradise." From one sack he unloaded two quart-sized Styrofoam cups. "Sweet tea." I put mine on the nightstand. From the other came two foil-wrapped packages.

I unwrapped my sandwich. Cheese and bacon and what looked like a half-pound slab of ground beef slopped over the sides of a huge bun. "It's got lettuce and tomato too," Austin said. "So it hits all your basic food groups."

Delicious. And there were fries too. We sat on our beds and ate like a couple of pigs, and then Austin took a shower, and we watched HGTV in our pajamas until I heard the sound of gentle snoring coming from the other bed. So this was what my life was like.

I was sacked out in a cheap motel in Mobile, Alabama, on Friday night, eating junk food and watching cable TV in bed—with a gay man. All right. I decided that was fine with me. Austin was fun. He liked the things I liked, he could move heavy furniture, and as a bonus, there was very little probability that he would end up screwing my best friend in the boardroom of my father's country club.

In the morning Austin declared that we would have only a "petite de jeuner" as he put it—which meant a Diet Coke for me and black coffee for him. "But I'm hungry now," I said.

"Wait!" he said, trying to sound mystic. "And you will be rewarded."

After breakfast we went looking for antiques stores. And then it occurred to me that it was Saturday. So we hit the flea market out on Schillinger Road.

"Let's split up," I told Austin. "You take one end, I'll take the other. If you see anything good, call me on my cell phone."

"Exactly what are we looking for?" he asked.

"We still need dining room furniture, sofas for the twin parlors, bedroom furniture, and stuff for the breakfast room," I said. "Paintings, prints, all that kind of stuff. And remember, keep it cheap. Gorgeous, but cheap."

"Like me," Austin said, giving me a wink and heading toward a distant row of dealers.

It was hot and the going was slow. I waded through a lot of ratchet sets and garage sale rejects, but finally managed to strike gold when I caught a dealer unloading the truck he'd backed up to his space. He had it in his arms, and I was happy to lighten his burden. It was a perfectly swell wicker porch swing. Probably 1920s, Bar Harbor style. In mint condition, and best of all, it had never been painted. I could already see it hanging on the veranda outside the breakfast room at Mulberry Hill.

"How much?" I asked, trying not to admire my find. He tilted the bill of his baseball cap to take my measure. I was dressed in khaki shorts and a red tank top, with the twill fishing vest I always wear to flea markets—the pockets are great to stow money, car keys, checkbooks, and my notebook. My hair was twisted into a ponytail poked through the back of my own baseball cap. No makeup. No jewelry.

"Five hundred," he said. I started to walk away. "Hey," he called. "I was just kiddin'." I walked back and stood there, not saying a word. "This is from a house down at Bay St. Louis," he said. "I can't hardly find these anymore."

"It's lovely," I said. "What's your friendliest price?"

"Friendly?"

"Dealer price," I said. "I'm on a pretty tight budget. What can you do for me?"

He shook his head, wounded. "Two-fifty."

I started to walk away again, praying he would call me back. I got all the way over to the next booth, where I pretended to be fascinated with the ugliest 1960s pole lamp I had ever seen. When I looked up, he was standing there.

"I know you?" he asked.

"Don't think so," I said. "I'm from Georgia."

"Good," he said. "'Cuz if it gets out around here I'm selling for these prices, I'll be out of business in a month. Hundred fifty, and that's it. I got more than that in it."

I knew he probably only had about seventy-five dollars in it, but that was okay. The swing was a Stephanie piece. I could already see her curled up in it, with Will's arm around her, and Erwin in her lap, barking at an errant squirrel.

I paid the dealer and promised to come back for the swing. I moved down the rows of booths quickly, letting my gaze bounce back and forth with no particular thing in mind.

At the end of the same row where I'd found the swing, I hit pay dirt again. The dealer had it covered with stacks and stacks of mismatched Franciscan china, but I could tell just from the chunky one-column leg profile that it was what I needed. A mahogany Empire dining room table.

I circled it warily, moving the china about to get a good look at the tabletop. There were some scratches and gouges, but that could be fixed by my refinisher. I looked around the booth until I found what else I needed—the leaves. There were three more leaves in all, which I estimated meant the table could seat eighteen. This table could be just the thing. If I waited until I got to New Orleans, I might find a slightly better one at one of the shops on Magazine Street. For over five thousand dollars.

I found the dealer sitting in a lawn chair, reading the Sunday *Mobile Register*.

"The table," I started. "I don't see a price."

"Four hundred," she said, not bothering to look up. "Don't ask me where it come from, and don't expect me to clear it off or help you load. It's four hundred. Cash. No checks."

I reached into my vest pocket and started peeling off twenties. She held her hand up, I gave them to her. "Are there any chairs to go with it?" I asked.

"No," she said, still fascinated with the newspaper. "And I'm leaving at two. If you're not here by then, tough."

Always a pleasure doing business with a people person, I thought.

I wandered around enjoying my bargain buzz for a while, and was contemplating food when my cell phone rang.

"It's me," Austin said breathlessly. "I might have found something."

He gave me directions, and five minutes later we were standing in front of a table stacked with pictures—oil paintings, watercolors, and a large stack of pen and ink architectural drawings.

With a flourish he pulled out a spectacular portrait. It was an oil painting, probably five feet wide, of a pensive-looking pair of children, dressed in nineteenth-century finery. The little girl cradled a kitten in her lap, the little boy held what looked like a top. It had a magnificent carved gilt frame, a tiny tear in the lower left corner, and a signature in the lower right corner. I whipped out my magnifying glass for a better look. Jacques Amans. I was fairly sure he was a listed artist, but it wouldn't matter. The painting was perfect for the dining room.

"How much?" I whispered.

"No prices on anything," he whispered back.

The dealer was standing at another table, extolling the virtues of a bad twentieth-century English watercolor to a couple who were dressed for brunch at the country club.

He wore a T-shirt stretched tight over a not-so-tight belly, and the writing on the back said "I Buy Art!"

"Excuse me," I said, tapping him on the shoulder.

He turned and gave me a sharp look. I was a pro, I could take it. "The portrait of the children. It's really charming. How much?"

"The Jacques Amans?" he asked.

Uh-oh. So it was a listed artist.

"It has some slight damage," I said. "A tear in the canvas."

"A minor repair," he said. "Cost you a hundred bucks to have it restored."

It would cost a lot more than that, and we both knew it.

"And some chips in the gilt," I added.

"It's the original frame," he said, glaring at me. "An Amans went up at auction at the St. Charles Gallery in New Orleans this spring and brought six thousand dollars."

"But this is a flea market in Mobile. Your painting has a tear and the gilt is chipped, and it's Saturday afternoon," I said sweetly. "And I'm a dealer."

He shrugged. "Say twelve hundred."

"Say nine hundred."

He looked around his booth. It was still stacked high with merchandise, and it was, as I'd already pointed out, only a few hours away to quitting time. And I did look pretty fetching in that fishing vest and baseball cap.

"Gimme a break," he said.

I took out my checkbook and held my pen poised above it. "You'll take an out-of-town check with ID, right?"

I fairly danced away from the booth, but waited until we'd gone a prudent distance away to set my painting down carefully and give Austin a huge hug and a big wet kiss.

"You're a genius," I told him. "I'd just finished buying the dining room table. It's heavy mahogany, Empire, will seat eighteen. For only four hundred bucks. And now this painting! It's worth at least four times what we paid for it, maybe more. Austin, it's absolutely the right thing for that room."

"I know," he said simply. "I'm gay, remember?"

We decided we'd had enough triumphs for the day and went back around to collect our prizes. I paid a porter to help us load the table, and by noon we were cruising the streets of Mobile, looking for the promised perfect lunch.

"What's the place called?" I asked, craning my neck for any sign of a restaurant.

"I don't want to tell you until I see it," he said. "It'll spoil the surprise."

I slowed the van to a creep, and when I saw the sign I knew I'd found what we were looking for. "The Tiny Dinee?" I yelped. "For real?"

"Who's your daddy?" he replied.

We found a table wedged into a corner. The place was full of locals who were concentrating very seriously on their food.

When the waitress got to our table to take our orders, I had to focus on the menu to keep from looking up at Austin and laughing out loud. She had the biggest hair I'd ever seen—and I'd been raised in Georgia.

But the food was no joking matter. Since Austin had the meat loaf, I had the meat loaf. Why go out on a limb? There were perfectly ripe sliced tomatoes and macaroni and cheese and pole beans.

I pushed away from the table and declared my intention to go out to the truck and take a two-hour nap in the back.

"No," Austin said urgently. "Pie. That's why we're here. You have to have the pie."

Who was I to question this man? We had coconut custard pie, with meringue as high as the waitress's hair.

And then I went out to the van and had a nap. But only for an hour. We were obviously on a roll. And our work was far from done. New Orleans was just down the road.

51

"A flea market in Metairie, when I could be wandering the streets of the French Quarter? No, *chère*, no way."

Austin had mysteriously picked up a Cajun accent just as we hit the bridge over Lake Pontchartrain. The accent only got thicker as we treated ourselves to beignets and café au lait at the Morning Call in a nondescript shopping center near our motel in Metairie.

"Me, I cannot do another flea market," he said, as he sipped his coffee and watched the waiters wielding their long-spouted pitchers of hot milk. I sighed and bit into yet another beignet. My face and shirt were covered in powdered sugar, but everybody in the place was also covered with powdered sugar. I wondered if white lung was an occupational hazard for the Morning Call's waiters.

I tried flattery. "You're so good at this. Look at that painting you found back in Mobile." I tried whining. "It's no fun without you." I tried idle threats. "If you don't come with me, I'm never speaking to you again."

But Austin would not be moved. In the end, I dropped him back at the motel, with cab money to go into the city.

I had heard about the flea market on Veteran's Highway in Metairie, but never experienced it for myself. And since I'd hit it so big in Mobile, I decided to try my luck again in the New Orleans suburbs.

Judging by appearances, the Metairie market didn't look promising. The first wave of booths I scouted was depressing. It looked to me as though the dealers had picked up their merchandise from the garage sale rejects offered by the Mobile dealers. After an hour of traipsing up and down the aisles, I was tempted to turn around and follow Austin into New Orleans.

But as I soldiered on, things began to look brighter. At a booth full of nightmarish seventies and eighties lamps and light fixtures I found a pair of bronze and crystal French wall sconces, probably from just after the turn of the century. The paper tag fluttering in the breeze was written in ink so faded I couldn't read it.

"Those are nice, aren't they?" I turned to find a slender man with a Fu Manchu mustache and close-cropped graying hair peering over my shoulder. He looked to be in his mid-fifties. He wore a loud Hawaiian shirt and a tiny diamond stud in his left ear.

"Are you the dealer?"

"That's me," he said. "These were candleholders when I bought them, so I did the wiring myself."

"French?" I asked.

He laughed. "I got them out of the estate of a couple of old queens over in St. Francisville. They had stuff from all over, but yeah, I thought they looked French."

"I like these a lot," I said. "But I'm an interior designer and I'm doing a restoration of an antebellum plantation house in Georgia. I still need a lot of other stuff yet, so my budget is stretched kind of tight."

"How tight?"

"Tight," I said, giving him my winning smile, which I had a feeling was wasted on him, since he was definitely playing for the other team.

"Why don't you look around and see if you can find anything else, and I'll make you a better deal," he suggested.

"No offense, but the rest of the stuff here just won't fit into my plan."

"Oh," he said, nonchalantly, "I didn't mean just in here. No, this stuff won't do for you. This stuff is for my boys who are into that whole *That '70s Show* look. You wouldn't believe the crap those boys like. Lava lamps! I can't keep 'em in stock. No, what I meant was, the next three spaces in this row are all mine. And I've got a warehouse too. I take it you're going for the whole Grand Tour look? English, French, like that?"

I nodded. "I wouldn't mind having some good American pieces too. The owner's girlfriend is very brand conscious. If I could find, like, a Belter piece, something like that, she'd probably wet her pants."

"If *I* could find a Belter piece I'd wet *my* pants," he drawled. "But I've got things that are just as nice, over in the warehouse. I don't like to bring them out here, because you never can tell about the weather. Tell you what. Look around here, figure out what works for you, and we'll talk. And if you can wait until my helper shows up, in an hour or so, I can run you over to the warehouse, if you like."

"Really?" I said, feeling my mood lift. "That would be awesome." I stuck out my hand. "I'm Keeley Murdock."

"Nice to meet you, Keeley," he said, shaking my hand. "I'm Robert. Now run along and shop."

For the next hour I poked around in Robert's adjoining booths, where the merchandise was, as he promised, more my style.

Artful merchandising was not Robert's strong suit. Everything had been thrown out haphazardly on tables or stacked, still wrapped in old newspaper, in crumbling cardboard boxes. Still, with prodigious digging and sleuthing, I found a series of six nice architectural drawings in cheap frames, which I thought would appeal to the engineer in Will, a heavily battered mahogany Empire card table that would need extensive refinishing, a pair of heavy Georgian sterling silver candlesticks, and a box of hand-etched crystal wineglasses, which, though unmarked, looked English.

I dutifully stacked everything in a pile under a table at the back of Robert's booth. His helper, who turned out to be a delicate blond woman wearing a black leather bustier and cutoffs, turned up at the appointed time, and Robert and I hopped into my van.

The warehouse, it turned out, was a closed-up barbecue restaurant only a block away from my motel. The plate-glass windows were caked with grime, and a rusted-out Buick stood on rotted tires near the front door.

"Scary, huh?" Robert said, seeing the skeptical look on my face as I parked the van. "The police presence around here isn't the greatest. I keep it this way on purpose. Wouldn't want anybody to think there's anything in here worth breaking in for."

He unlocked the door, stepped inside, and flipped a light switch.

"Wow," I said, following him inside. The place was packed with antiques, floor-to-ceiling. Rows of chandeliers hung from pipes running the length of the old restaurant. Dozens and dozens of chairs hung from hooks on the walls, and tables and breakfronts and dressers and sofas were stacked cheek-to-jowl along the walls, with more cardboard boxes stacked on every available surface.

Robert busied himself locking the door behind us, and for a fleeting moment I wondered if I'd gotten myself abducted by some insane slasher rapist. Nah, I decided. Nobody with taste this great could possibly be a criminal.

"Let me show you some things," Robert said. He shoved an overstuffed 1940s armchair out of the way, and we threaded our way to the back of the restaurant. A pair of ornate rosewood rococo revival sofas were stacked high with plastic milk cartons full of old copies of *Antiques* magazines.

"Ta-da!" he exclaimed. "Now, they're certainly not Belter or Mallard. They're not marked at all, and believe me I looked. They look like twins, but if you look closer, you'll see slight differences."

I moved the boxes to the floor and edged between the sofas to get a better look. The old green velvet upholstery on both was in shreds, and bits of horsehair stuffing sprung up through the holes. The rosewood carvings were intact, although caked with layers of blackened varnish. I could already picture them in one of the parlors, refinished, upholstered in a wonderful silk damask.

"How much?"

Robert smiled. "One price for all. Come on, I've got some other stuff to show you."

The other stuff included an elaborately carved six-foot-tall mahogany bookshelf with leaded glass doors, a pair of oversized Queen Anne–style armchairs, two Oriental runners, an Empire daybed, and the prize of the day, an immense marble-topped three-tiered sideboard.

"Now, this," Robert said dramatically, patting the cracked marble top, "is by Prudent Francis Mallard, whom you know. Very famous French cabinetmaker. La-di-damn-dah, right?"

"Oh yes," I assured him. I knelt to the floor and opened the cupboard doors. Inside were stacks of fine old Limoges dishes. "Does it come with the china?" I asked.

Robert knelt down beside me and took a look. "I'd forgotten that stuff was in there," he said. "Yeah, if you want it, I can throw it in. There's probably, I don't remember exactly, maybe ten, eleven place settings? And some assorted serving pieces."

"Is there a story behind this?" I asked him, wincing as I stood up. My back ached from all the walking and stooping and driving of the past several days.

"There's a story behind all of it," he said. "So, do we have a deal?"

"Depends on the price," I said. "But yeah, I think we probably have a deal. I feel like I've hit the mother lode."

"You have," he said.

I followed him back to the front of the restaurant. He sat down on a rickety pressed oak armchair and I perched on the edge of a chintz sofa from the 1980s while he tallied up my shopping list on a piece of cardboard he ripped from a box of silver-plated trays and bowls.

"Let's see," he said, mumbling to himself. "Umm. Looks like fifteen thousand dollars? That sound right to you?"

It sounded like he'd lost his mind. We both knew the Mallard sideboard alone was worth much, much more than that.

"That sounds fine," I said, and then, deciding to push my luck, asked, "does that include the stuff from the flea market?"

He laughed. "I love a woman with balls. Sure, you can have the stuff from the flea market too."

I cocked my head and looked at him carefully. He wore a gold pinkie ring on his left hand, with a sizable diamond in it, and the diamond stud earring was at least half a carat. Robert did not look hard-up. He also did not look like an amateur at the antiques business.

"Can I ask you something?"

"Sure," he said, getting up and dusting the seat of his pants. "Ask away."

"How come you're making me such a great deal on all this stuff? That Mallard. I mean, that's quite a nice piece. Seriously, seriously underpriced. And the rest of the things I'm taking, well, all of it would bring big money at a shop on Magazine Street."

"I know," Robert said. "Most of this stuff came out of a shop on Magazine."

"Whose?"

"Mine," he said. He gestured toward the door. "We'll have to recruit some help to load you. It took three fellas just to get that sideboard in here. And none of them included me."

My cell phone rang as I was unlocking the van.

"Keeley?" It was Austin. He didn't sound too happy. I could hear the faint sounds of music and laughter in the background. "Having fun?" I asked.

"Not so much," he said. "I've been robbed."

"No! Are you hurt?"

"I'm fine. Just out three hundred dollars and my pride," he said. "I don't even have cab fare. Do you think you could come get me?"

"I'm on my way," I promised. "But where?"

He gave me directions to a bar called Shadrack's, on Decatur Street, across the street from Jackson Square.

I hung up and told Robert what had happened. "Shadrack's?" Robert looked surprised. "Is your friend gay?"

"Yeah. Why?"

He shook his head. "Shadrack's is a cesspool. It's a wonder he didn't get hurt in there. How well do you know New Orleans?"

"Not that well. The French Quarter I don't really know at all."

"I'd better go with you then," Robert said, settling back in his seat.

When we got to Decatur Street, Austin was standing on the corner, leaning up against one of the famous French Quarter street signs, looking like he'd lost his last friend. I pulled up to the curb and tooted the horn.

Robert slid nimbly into the back of the van and Austin hopped into the front seat.

"Thank God," Austin said. He made a production of locking the door. "Let's get out of here. I hope I never see New Orleans again."

Robert laughed, and Austin turned around to see where the sound was coming from. "Don't be so hard on us," Robert said. "New Orleans isn't all bad. You just happened to pick the worst pickup bar in the Quarter is all. I've never understood how those people keep their liquor license, with all the tourists who get victimized in there."

Austin raised one eyebrow and tried to look haughty. "I was *not* trying to get picked up. I just wanted a drink. And who, may I ask, are you? And how do you know so much about a place like that?"

Now I was laughing. "Austin, this is Robert. He's an antiques dealer I met at the flea market in Metairie. And he's the only reason I didn't get lost coming to get you, so don't be getting all pissy with the man."

"You'd be pissy too, if you just had all your fun money lifted," Austin muttered. "I was just standing at the bar, minding my own business, and these two *boys* were standing beside me, and the next thing I know, they're screaming and pulling each other's hair. It was an absolute melee! But it was over in a couple minutes. The bartender told them to leave. And then, when I went to pay for my drink, my wallet was gone. Did you ever?"

"Oldest game around," Robert said. "The bartender was probably in on it. When you told him your wallet was gone, he didn't make a stink about paying for your drink, did he?"

"No," Austin said. "He even bought me another one. Hey! . . ."

"Never mind," I said. "I'll reimburse you for what you lost. I just saved so much money shopping with Robert that I'm feeling very, very generous. Why don't we go get some dinner?" I asked, looking around at Robert to let him know he was included.

"I'm not hungry," Austin said peevishly.

"Well I am, and I'm driving," I said. "And I'm not leaving New Orleans until I get some seafood. Where to, Robert?"

"Back to Metairie," Robert said. "The best seafood in New Orleans isn't even in New Orleans. It's right back in Metairie. Ever hear of a place called Drago's?"

"Sounds like a dive," Austin said. I punched him in the arm, and we drove back to Metairie to what was, as Robert promised, the best seafood I'd ever had.

"Oysters are what you come here for," Robert told us, between bites of shrimp Arnaud and deviled crab. "Drago supplies oysters to some of the best restaurants in New Orleans. Call me old-fashioned, but I won't be ordering them again until the weather cools off."

Austin sipped his wine and nibbled on a piece of French bread. I couldn't understand why he was being so rude to our host. Robert was witty, attractive, and obviously well-off—in short, a great catch.

"I'll definitely be back on my next buying trip," I said. "But I think you owe me a story. Remember? Right before Austin called? You were saying something about having a shop on Magazine."

"Had," Robert said. "No more. I closed it down two years ago. Now I just sell out at the flea market, or by word of mouth. It keeps me off the streets, for now. Eventually I'll sell down the rest of the inventory, and when I do, I'll be out of the business once and for all."

"Why?" I blurted.

"It's just not fun anymore. We had the shop for fifteen years, traveled all over, met lots of nice people, and a few not-so-nice people, and now that's in the past."

"We?" Austin leaned forward.

"My partner and I. Actually, my former partner," Robert said.

"AIDS?" Austin said, sounding sympathetic.

"I wish," Robert said, laughing. "No, he left me for someone younger, cuter, richer. You know how it goes. It's not really a very interesting or original story."

"What will you do when the antiques are gone?" I asked, kicking Austin under the table.

"Who knows? Maybe I'll retire for real this time."

"What did you retire from last time?" I asked.

"I was a dentist," Robert said. "Can you believe that? Seems like a lifetime ago. But I retired at forty. My mother was already dead or it would have killed her."

"Austin is a floral designer," I volunteered. "Amazingly talented. He's going to do all the flowers for this plantation house I'm decorating. And he owns his own business."

I felt a sharp pain in my left shin. Austin looked away.

52

Austin and I were still arguing as we drove back across Lake Pon-chartrain the next morning. "I do not need to be fixed up," he said, sipping from the go-cup of coffee we'd picked up at the Morning Call. "And certainly not by a woman whose own judgment in men, is, I regret to say, deeply flawed."

"Deeply flawed." I pondered the phrase as I threaded the van through the early morning traffic. "And what, exactly, is that sup-posed to mean?"

He reached across and dusted the powdered sugar from my face and shirtfront. "Just what it sounds like. You picked A. J. Jernigan, right?"

"I suppose."

He tsk-tsked. I had never heard anybody younger than seventy tsk-tsk before, but Austin did it very believeably. "Strike one," he said. "And now when there is a perfectly *adorable* man right there, ripe for the picking, you completely ignore him. Worse, you con-spire to marry him off to some trashy little money-grubber who thinks *mochachino* is a color. Strike two."

"I assume you refer to my client Will Mahoney?"

"I do."

"First of all, I do not find men with red hair and freckles adorable. You may, but I do not. And secondly, the man is totally ga-ga over that trashy little money-grubber. And he has hired me to see that she reciprocates that affection," I said. "And may I remind you that he is paying me quite nicely for my efforts?"

"Pish-posh," Austin said.

I did a double-take. "Pish-posh? What kind of a word is that?"

"It's a word," he said airily, gazing out the window. "My granny said it all the time. Anyway, don't try to change the subject. Two strikes against you already. And then you have the massively stupid idea that I should be paired up with the first aging drama queen you meet up with in New Orleans. Strike three. You're as out as I am. Really, Keeley Rae, do I look that desperate?"

"Listen," I said hotly. "Robert would be perfect for you. He's smart and funny. He's educated. He's been all over the world. He likes a lot of the same things as you. How can you not be interested?"

"I'm just not," Austin said. "And now the subject is officially closed."

"Right," I said under my breath. "Because you say so."

"Listen, little missy," Austin said. "Don't make me come over there. I'll turn this car right around and we'll all go home. Is that what you want?"

What I wanted to do was turn the van back toward Madison. But Austin was emphatic. We had the van, we had the time, and he was dying to hear what my long-lost cousin Sonya had to say about my mama.

We took turns driving, spent the night at a hotel in Charlotte, and the next morning I found myself dreading every mile that brought us closer to Kannapolis.

"Have you even talked to Sonya?" I asked Austin. "Does she know I'm coming to see her?"

"She knows," he said airily. "Take the next exit, turn left, then right. We're meeting her at a Waffle House."

"Why?"

"That's what she wanted. I didn't ask why."

It was midmorning, but the Waffle House parking lot was still full.

As we walked to the restaurant entrance, Austin kept his hand on the small of my back, exerting just the slightest pressure to keep me moving forward.

"Mornin'!" called a waitress who was wiping a tabletop near the door. "Mornin'!" called the skinny kid who was ringing up a check at the cash register. All the seats at the counter were full. I looked from one side of the room to the other, wondering if I would recognize Sonya after all these years.

In a booth at the far left corner of the room, an older woman with bouffant gray hair and dark sunglasses was sitting alone, a coffee cup in one hand, a lit cigarette in the other. She looked up, took off her sunglasses to get a better look, and then gave us a tentative wave. "Keeley?" she mouthed the word. I nodded, and Austin gave me a little shove in her direction.

"Sonya?" I said, standing over her at the booth. Even with the sunglasses off, I did not recognize my cousin. How could this blowsy woman, her eyes sunken into fleshy folds of pale skin, and the only makeup a slash of carelessly applied pink lipstick, be the skinny little blond home-wrecker who'd cut such a swathe through Madison? She would be in her late fifties, I thought, but she looked at least seventy. A hard seventy.

"Keeley Rae," she wheezed. "I woulda known you anywhere. You are your mama made over. Excuse me for not gettin' up, honey, but my legs are giving me a lot of trouble these days."

I bent over and gave her a peck on the cheek, which was surprisingly smooth and wrinkle-free. "Don't get up," I said, and slid into the booth opposite her. I gestured toward Austin, who stood a discreet distance away. "This is Austin, my friend who tracked you down. Do you mind if he joins us?"

"Come ahead on," Sonya said, giving him a curious look.

While the waitress poured us coffee and took our orders, Sonya filled us in on the gaps in her life. My cousins were grown up with children of their own. "Kimmy, that's my oldest granddaughter, she's expectin' her first child in a couple months," Sonya said. "I can't hardly believe I'm a grandma, let alone soon to be a great-grandma." She shot another look at Austin, and then at me. "How 'bout you, honey? I don't see a wedding ring on your hand."

"No," I said quickly. "I was engaged, but called it off. Austin is a friend and business associate. I'm in business with my Aunt Gloria, you know. An interior designer."

"Gloria," Sonya said. "How is she? And your daddy? Is he doin' okay? All of y'all still living in Madison, is that right?"

"Gloria's fine," I said. "She helped Daddy raise me, you know, after Mama left. And Daddy's the same as ever. Still running the car lot. He plays a lot of golf with his buddies and that keeps him busy. And the thing is, he's just finally started dating again."

"Is that right?" Sonya said warily. "Good for him."

"That's sort of why I'm here," I said, taking a sip of coffee. "Daddy never really did get over Mama's leaving like she did. He even hired a private detective, just so we could have some answers, but we never did find out where she went. Technically, Mama and Daddy are still married. He feels funny about that, dating now, when she could still be alive."

"Hmm," Sonya said. She held up her coffee cup, and the waitress came back over to refill it.

"The thing is," I said, putting my own coffee cup down, "It's not just Daddy who needs to know. I need to know too. It's been almost twenty-five years. I want to know why. I want to know where she went, and what happened that she never called, never wrote, never came back to see us."

"I see. And why do you think I can help you with that?"

"You were her best friend," I said. "Her only close relative in town. I asked around a little bit. People said you two sort of ran around together."

"Ran around?" She raised one graying eyebrow.

"I know about Darvis Kane," I said defiantly. "I know Mama was seeing him. They left town together. He left his wife and kids; Mama left us. Lisa Kane was lucky. She managed to track Darvis down and get a divorce. At least she has some answers to her questions."

"Darvis Kane," Sonya said, rolling the words on the tip of her tongue. She lit another cigarette. "I told Jeanine he was no good for her. Of course, why would she listen to me? I didn't have a great track record of my own. And your daddy knew it too. He knew I was bad news back then."

She closed her eyes, inhaled deeply, and let a thin plume of smoke waft toward the restaurant's ceiling. "There's something I want you to know right now, Keeley Murdock."

I clenched my hands in my lap. "Yes?"

"I am a saved woman," Sonya said. "Born again in the blood of Jesus, as of eight P.M. on July 11, 1986. I took all my troubles to the Lord that night, right here in Kannapolis, North Carolina. And I was born again." Her red-rimmed eyes bored into mine. "I will not claim to be perfect. No ma'am. Not Sonya Wyrick. Not perfect, but I am forgiven. Can you say as much?"

"Not perfect," I agreed. "I don't know about the forgiven part. Not yet."

She reached over and clutched at my hand. "That will come, honey. Just let the Lord into your heart. If he came into mine, he can come into yours."

I bit my lip. This was not going as I'd planned.

Austin must have sensed how close I was to losing it.

"Miz Wyrick," he said now, slipping his arm around my shoulders, "Keeley is at a place where she wants to forgive her mama. She's been bitter all these years, but now she's an adult, and she understands that everything isn't always black and white. But she needs some answers."

"Look in the Bible," Sonya said. "All the answers you need are written right down in there. Start with Revelations."

"We thought maybe we could start with the winter of 1979," Austin said smoothly. "Back when you and Jeanine Murdock were so close. When she was seeing Darvis Kane on the sly and you weren't exactly an angel."

Sonya gave that some thought. She nodded slowly. "I was a wild one back then, and I won't deny that. I knew Jeanine was carrying on, but I didn't know who he was, not at first. I sure didn't know the boy worked for Wade. The thing was, I had a boyfriend of my own at the time." She smiled ruefully. "You wouldn't know it to see me now, but back in those days, I was something. I always had a boyfriend. Married, usually." She grimaced.

"A lady Mama worked for in Madison, at the dress shop, she sorta hinted that there were quite a few people back then who were running around on the sly," I said. "She wouldn't name any names. She just said they were 'prominent' citizens, and all of y'all were slipping around cheating on husbands and wives."

"That's true enough," Sonya said. "If I told you the names, you wouldn't believe it anyway. My boyfriend at the time, now, he was from an old Madison family. So we had to be careful. He had a wife and children and a reputation to protect." She laughed bitterly. "Never mind about my reputation, right? Anyway, he had a little hunting cabin, out there at Ridgeland Creek, and that's where we had our 'dates,' if you can call them that. Later on I found out that there were quite a few couples having 'dates' out there."

"Mama?"

She nodded. "I let it slip that I had the key to my friend's cabin, and she pestered and pestered, until I let her have it for a weekend, when I knew he and his family were down at the beach. I feel right ashamed of that, Keeley. I was older than your mama, and I didn't set no kind of example for her."

"Did she talk about Darvis to you? Did she love him?" I asked, clenching and unclenching my fists.

"Remember now, I didn't know who he was for a while. I only found out one day by accident, when me and Vince went out there to the cabin on the spur of the moment one afternoon, and here comes Jeanine and this man in that red car of hers, flying down the driveway."

"Vince?"

Sonya pressed her lips together and looked out the window.

"Vince Bascomb? He was your boyfriend?"

Tears glittered in her eyes. She nodded and wiped at them with a paper napkin.

"I am so ashamed of that," she said, still looking out the window. "To this day, that is a shame that haunts me. I knew Lorraine Bascomb. She was a nice lady, and I liked her. But I didn't have no problem taking up with her husband. None at all."

Austin was looking perplexed. "Why do I know that name?"

"Vince Bascomb is one of Drew Jernigan's oldest buddies," I explained. "They were partners in lots of business deals. And they had lake houses right next to each other on one of the coves out at Lake Oconee. I was just out there not long ago."

"Drew Jernigan," Sonya spat the words. "He was another one that liked to slip around on the sly."

"Runs in the family," I said.

She tapped some ash into the saucer of her coffee cup. "Only thing was, he didn't even bother to try to hide it from his wife. He used to claim he and GiGi had what they called an 'open marriage.'"

"He told you that? Did he know you were seeing Vince?"

She blushed. "There were a whole group of us, used to go out to that cabin that last winter. Me and Vince, Drew and his date, and some other people too. It was cold and rainy a lot that year. Vince had fixed up a little kerosene heater inside, and we had us campfires outside. We'd drink and carry on. It was our hideout, you know? That's what we called it, the hideout. And we were the outlaws."

"Were Mama and Darvis ever there with you?"

She shook her head. "Not with me personally. I don't know about the others. I know your mama loved going out there. She thought it was exciting, you know? Having secrets from everybody? She didn't dare call Darvis, at home or at the car lot. And he sure couldn't call her. They used to leave notes for each other, setting up their rendezvous. That's what Jeanine called it, 'our rendezvous.'" Her lips twisted. "Fancy name for rutting in a drafty old trailer 'cuz the man is too cheap to rent a motel room."

I got a sudden mental picture, and my stomach twisted.

"I'm sorry, honey," Sonya said. "I keep forgetting she was your mama."

I shook my head in a vain attempt to dislodge that vision. "Did Jeanine talk to you about divorcing my father?"

"No," she said emphatically. "Not to me, and like you said, I was her best friend. She was just young, honey. I think she got caught up in the excitement and the intrigue. You know, of being part of something forbidden."

"She didn't tell you she was leaving?"

Sonya twisted her paper napkin into a tight corkscrew. "That was when, February, March? I was just as surprised about it as everybody else when your daddy called to ask if I knew where she'd gone. See, Vince and Lorraine had had a big fight. She found out he was catting around on her. I didn't dare go near him. I couldn't call. And we stopped seeing each other not too long after that."

"Can you remember when the last time was that you saw Jeanine?" Austin asked. "Did you ever see her after Darvis Kane left town?"

"I always thought they left together," Sonya said.

"We did too," Austin said. "But we talked to his sister, over in Alabama. She says Darvis came to Wedowee, driving Jeanine's car, but without Jeanine. He sold the car in Birmingham, and she dropped him at a bus station, and that's the last time anybody saw him after he left Madison."

"The car? That red Malibu of hers?"

"It was a birthday present from Daddy," I said.

"She loved that car," Sonya said. "First new one she'd ever owned. That was her baby.

"And you, of course," she added quickly, squeezing my hand again. "I just have a really hard time believing she walked away from her little girl, and never came back."

"Well, she did," I said flatly. "So maybe you'll understand why I'm having some trouble with forgiveness right now."

Sonya lit another cigarette, and the queasiness in my stomach intensified.

"Honey," she said, looking away, "I have told you all I know. My advice to you is to look to the Lord for guidance on this thing."

I nudged Austin, and he slid out of the booth. I did the same. I put some money on the table.

"Anybody else you can think of, besides the Lord?" I asked, just a little on the flippant side.

She inhaled and exhaled and looked out the window again. "How 'bout old Lorna Plummer? She still hanging around in Madison?"

Now Austin was nudging me. "She just moved," I said. "What would Lorna know about any of this?"

"Ask her," Sonya said. "She was Drew Jernigan's honey, at the time. Maybe she knows something."

53

Will had decided that the first big official event at Mulberry Hill would be a company picnic for Loving Cup Intimates.

"The house isn't done," I protested.

"We'll have it outside," he declared. "We'll rent some tents and tables and chairs. We can set up in the meadow. It'll be a barbecue. A caterer will bring in the chopped pork and buns and drinks, and all that. And the employees will all be asked to bring a side dish. You know, make it a real old-fashioned supper on the grounds kind of thing. We'll have pony rides for the kids, and sack races, set up a volleyball net, all that kind of thing."

"When were you planning this event?" I asked, feeling a caution alarm ringing in the back of my head. "Next spring?"

"Labor Day," he said.

"That's next weekend. It can't be done."

"It's already set up," Will said. "Miss Nancy took care of everything, once she quit bitching and complaining about all the extra work it was causing her."

The door to the reception area opened, and Miss Nancy herself stood there, leaning on her cane.

"He tell you what he's cooking up for Labor Day?" Miss Nancy asked me.

"Just now," I said.

She glared at her boss. "I tried my best to talk him out of it, but you know how he is once he gets an idea in his head. How do you think that's gonna make all those folks feel? Here they are, fixing to lose their jobs for good and probably end up on welfare, and he's rubbing it in their noses that he's got the biggest, fanciest house in the county."

"Not yet, he doesn't," I said, looking down at the folder of invoices from my buying trip. Construction was moving along well, and we were on schedule, but there was still a lot to be done before the house was livable.

"I wish you'd tell him this picnic deal is a terrible idea," she said. "He don't listen to a goddamn thing I tell him."

"Will," I said, turning back around to face my client. "She's right. I know your heart is in the right place, but really, this picnic thing is not a good idea. If you want to do something nice for your employees, give them a little cash bonus or something."

"We're having a picnic," Will said. "It'll be grand. And you'll be there too." He gave Nancy a curt nod. "And don't you have some work to do out there?"

She let the door slam.

"Why should I be at your company picnic?" I asked. "I work for you, not Loving Cup."

He smiled sweetly. "Because I asked you. Because I need you to make sure the house is looking good, so people can take tours through it, see how it's coming along. And because, dammit, you make things look nice. I want this picnic to be nice."

"Nice?"

"You know. Flowers, tablecloths, that kind of thing. You can do that, can't you? Get your friend Austin to make up some bouquets. And flowers for the house. Even the rooms that aren't done. Steph says flowers make even a pigsty look nice."

"And will Steph be there too?" I asked.

"Of course," he said, surprised that I would doubt it. "It's a big day for me. And the company. She wants to be there."

"At a barbecue? Does she realize pork is involved?"

"Don't be such a bitch," Will said. "There will be lots of different kinds of food. Not just pork. So. You'll do it, right? You'll be on the clock, of course. Bring your Aunt Gloria too. Hell, bring a date if you like." He gave me a searching look. "You have started dating again, right?"

"A little," I lied.

"Who is he?"

"Nobody you know."

"But he's not an ash-hole, is he?"

I got up to leave. "What time is this clambake?"

"Two o'clock, on Labor Day," Will said. "And hey, Keeley. Steph loves the new furniture. But she wants to talk to you about something. Get with her, will you? Nancy will give you her phone number."

I made a very determined effort not to grind my teeth. And then I went back to the office to start making plans for a "nice" company picnic.

54

I was upstairs in my apartment, finishing up the covered dish I was taking to Will's company picnic when I heard the doorbell ring downstairs in the studio.

"Crap." I was running late as it was, and the grits for my grits and greens casserole were too runny. I threw another handful of grits in the pot and stirred furiously.

"Hello?" a voice called. "Anybody here?"

I froze. Put down the wooden spoon. Turned off the burner and sat down on the sofa, hoping my unwelcome visitor would give up and leave. I sat, immobile while he moved around downstairs.

"Keeley?" Now he was at the bottom of the stairs. "Come on, Keeley," he called again. "I know you're up there. I saw your car outside. You can't hide from me forever. It's too small a town."

He had that right. And dammit, why should I have to hide from A.J. Jernigan? This was my home, and I hadn't done anything wrong.

I checked on the grits and gave them a final stir. The collard greens had been simmering all morning, with a smoked ham hock, some chopped-up onion, and some red pepper flakes. I poured the greens into the colander in the sink and let them drain.

A.J. was halfway up the stairs looking up, sniffing like a bird dog on point.

"Are you cooking collard greens?" he asked.

"Yes," I said. "What do you want?"

He started up toward me, giving me that grin of his. "A mess of those greens would be nice," he said. "I didn't know you ever cooked stuff like that."

"It's an old family recipe," I said stiffly. Which was a lie. I'd clipped it out of *Southern Living* magazine a few years ago, and doctored it up to suit myself. "And you still haven't told me what you're doing here."

"Can I come up and talk to you?" he asked. He was at the top of the landing.

"No. I'm going to a picnic and I'm already late," I said.

"Just for a minute," A.J. wheedled. "Please. It's about Mama."

"What now?"

He took that as a yes and followed me into my galley kitchen. "Got a beer?" he asked. "It's already scorching out there. I'll be glad to see this summer end." Before I could stop him, he had the refrigerator door open and his head stuck inside it.

I shoved him aside and shut the fridge door, but he'd already helped himself to a Michelob Light.

"What's the deal with GiGi?" I asked, busying myself with the casserole. There wasn't that much left to do. I'd already cooked the grits with chicken broth and half and half, and they'd finally thickened up. I took a paper towel and squeezed the rest of the moisture out of the collards, then dumped them into the pot of grits. To this, I added a big handful of parmesan cheese and a healthy dollop of pepper vinegar. I stirred while A.J. talked, glad to have something to do.

"I heard about her stopping you outside the post office the other day," he said. "Hell, I guess the whole town heard."

"Oh that," I said cautiously, stirring while it was no longer necessary. "That was weeks ago. I'd forgotten all about it." Another lie.

"Well, I haven't." He shoved one hand in the front pocket of his jeans and sipped his beer. He looked good. Thinner maybe, and he needed a shave, but he was deeply tanned, and his blue-green eyes glowed with whatever drama he was into. He'd probably been spending a lot of time out at the lake, I told myself, just to be cruel.

"Look," A.J. said. "I had a long talk with Mama. And I admitted to her exactly what happened that night at the country club. She didn't wanna hear it, and she sure didn't want to believe it, but I set her down and told it to her straight. And I told her you had every right to react like you did."

"How noble of you," I said. I picked up the pot of grits and tipped it carefully into the greased Pyrex casserole waiting on the kitchen counter. I smoothed the top with the back of my wooden spoon, then dusted more parmesan on top. Over all of that I sprinkled bacon bits.

Before I could slide the casserole into the heated oven, A.J. picked up the spoon I'd just used and dipped it into the grits and greens. He smacked his lips. "Day-yum, woman. That is awesome. Whose picnic are you going to? Anybody I know?"

I put the casserole in the oven. "It's a client. Will Mahoney."

"Oh. Him. Mr. Loving Cup. How's that house of his coming along? I heard you were doing it up big-time."

"It's right on schedule," I said. I crossed my arms over my chest and leaned back against the counter. "What's this visit really about, A.J.? You want me to pat you on the back for coming clean with your mama?"

He took another sip of beer and set it on the counter. I wished this conversation wasn't happening. I really wished it wasn't taking place in my tiny, steamy kitchen, where we were standing only a couple feet apart.

"I want you to know that I am not my daddy. I am not like him. Not that way. That night with Paige, it was a one-time deal. I'd do anything if I could take it back. Because that's not who I am, Keeley. It's not."

"What's that supposed to mean?" I had an idea, but I wanted to hear him say it.

He blushed. "Yeah, I know about Daddy's other women. I've known for a long time. Since I was like, fourteen."

"He told you he cheated on your mama?"

"No. It was Kyle. It was during my first year at boarding school. He called me one night, bawling like a baby. He'd skipped school and gone out to the shack with some buddies. Caught Daddy red-handed with some little tramp. I don't guess it was the first time or the last time he had his girlfriends out there. I think that's why Mama got so she wouldn't step foot in the place. I don't know how she knows, but she does."

"I'm sorry, A. J," I said. And I meant it. He'd always had a love-hate relationship with his father, but I'd always thought it was because they all worked together at the bank. I'd never realized before how twisted the dynamics of his family were.

He took another sip of beer. "I'm not asking you to take me back right now. I know it'll take time for you to ever trust me again. But here's the thing, Keeley. We both have screwed-up families. I never judged you by what your mama did. All I'm asking is, don't judge me by my daddy and what he's done. I screwed up, but that's not me. That's not who I want to be."

I reached out and helped myself to a sip of his beer. "Who do you want to be, A.J.?"

He took the beer from me and held my hand. He turned it over and kissed the palm. "I want to be the man who deserves you. Deserves your love. And your trust. That's all."

The oven timer buzzed and I jumped. I glanced at the kitchen clock. "God," I said. "It's close to one. I've still got to get out to Mulberry Hill and make sure all the tables and chairs are set up, and Austin's flowers have been delivered. And I've got to put the plastic runners down in the house. We just had the floors refinished, and I don't want them getting scratched up."

A.J. frowned. "Will you think about what I just said?"

"I can't talk about this now," I said helplessly. "I'm late."

"Let me go with you," A.J. pleaded. He reached in the drawer, got out some potholders, and took the casserole out of the oven and switched it off.

"No," I said quickly. "I'm working."

"I can help you," he said. "Come on, Keeley. It won't be a date.

Just a friend helping a friend. It's Labor Day, I've got nothing to do. I haven't had anything to do all summer," he said bitterly.

"What about Paige?"

He busied himself putting foil over the casserole. "Nothing about Paige. She's moved, you know. Lost her job."

"So I heard. I also heard it was GiGi who ran her out of town."

"That's news to me," he said. "I haven't seen Paige. I don't intend to see her." He looked up. "Please?"

"I've got to go," I said, snatching up my tote bag.

He picked up the casserole. "I'll drive. Okay?"

"Go away," I said faintly. "I do not want this to happen."

But it already was happening.

Somebody had pinned red, white, and blue bunting to the entry gates at Mulberry Hill. A large banner read WELCOME LOVING CUP ASSOCIATES. Red, white, and blue balloons bobbed in the light breeze.

"Not too shabby," A.J. said as he drove through the wrought-iron gates. "You design all this?"

"Not the gates," I said. "That was Will's design."

A.J. looked impressed. He made all the appropriate noises as we approached the meadow, whistling when he got the first glimpse of the now gleaming façade of the old Greek Revival mansion.

"Day-yum. The guy must have dropped a bundle on all of this, huh?"

"He likes things done right," I said. I noticed with gratitude that the rented funeral home tents had been erected in the meadow, and one of the construction workers was busy unfolding the tables and chairs. A makeshift plywood bandstand had been erected, and a group of musicians with fiddles and banjos were setting up instruments. A haze of smoke floated over the meadow, and the sweet smell of roasting pig wafted through the boxwood hedge. The Fleur van was parked at the edge of the meadow, and Austin himself was ferrying cardboard boxes of centerpieces over to the dining tent.

"Oh good," I murmured. "We've got food and flowers. And a bluegrass band, I guess."

A pickup truck towing a horse trailer came bouncing up the road right behind us. "And ponies. So I guess we're set."

I directed A.J. around to the back of the house, where more than a dozen cars and trucks, including the yellow Caddy, were already parked.

Miss Nancy stood in the open back door of the kitchen, leaning on her cane, watching me unpack the sacks containing the linen tablecloths and other last-minute party supplies. A tiny brown dog came zipping out the door, yapping and barking and hurling itself against my ankles. "Hey Erwin," I said, trying not to trip. "Hey, Miss Nancy," I called to her.

She glared back at me. "Somebody better get that goddamn dog outta here. And its owner too."

55

The kitchen was full of people. The caterers were bustling about, filling jugs with iced tea and lemonade, chopping the roasted pork and loading it into large foil warming dishes, and Austin's helper had commandeered the big soapstone farmhouse sink to fill her flower vases.

Will stood in the middle of it all, issuing directives that everybody seemed to be ignoring, while Stephanie fluttered around being . . . Stephanie. Erwin barked and jumped and ran in circles until it looked like he had worn his short brown legs down to a nub.

A.J. came in and set the casserole on the big marble-topped island that had just been installed earlier in the week

"Help me get those runners laid down before people start tracking in clay on the new floors, will you?" I asked A.J.

"Keeley," Will said, staring right at A.J. "Introduce me to your date."

I felt my face heat up. "This is my friend A.J.," I said deliberately. "But I think you two have already met."

A.J. held out his hand to shake, but Will acted like he hadn't seen it. "Oh yeah, maybe we have met."

"Well, we haven't met," Stephanie said, twining one arm around Will's waist and extending her own hand to shake A.J.'s. "I'm Stephanie Scofield. It's so nice to see Keeley in a social setting for once." She leaned forward and gave A.J. a confidential wink. "You've got to see what you can do to get this girl to slow down and smell the roses. Up until now, the only man I've seen her with is that perfectly sweet florist friend of hers. If you know what I mean."

Just at that minute, Austin bustled into the kitchen, holding out a glass canning jar full of wilted daisies and zinnias. "Keeley!" he exclaimed. "You've got to help me salvage this thing. The water must have spilled out of it in the van on the way over, and I didn't bring any spares." He stopped talking when he caught sight of A.J.

"Oh," he said, dramatically, looking A.J. up and down. "How are you, Andrew?"

Nobody in Madison ever called A.J. Andrew. But A.J. was being a sport. "I'm fine, Austin," he said. "Hope you're the same."

It got very quiet in the kitchen as everybody gauged everybody else's reaction to the fact that I'd brought my ex-fiance to the party.

"Yumm!" Stephanie said, in an exuberant attempt to break the stalemate. She poked the tip of her pinkie nail into the top of my casserole. "What is this divine creation you've brought, Keeley?"

"Grits and greens," A.J. said proudly. "It's from an old family recipe."

"Whose family?" Will drawled.

"Mine," I said firmly, as Stephanie poised a spoon over the casserole. "It's got collard greens and grits . . . and ham hocks and smoked jowl and bacon bits."

Stephanie dropped the spoon to the counter with a clatter.

"And parmesan cheese and half and half and chicken stock," I added. "What did you bring, Steph?"

Will dropped a fond kiss on the top of Stephanie's head. "She brought something all the way from Atlanta," he said, pointing to an elegant silver chafing dish on the marble countertop.

"Stop bragging, Will!" she protested. "Really, it's nothing special. Just some couscous with roasted red peppers and shallots," Stephanie said modestly.

I found a pair of scissors and started attacking the stems of Austin's wilted flowers. "I'll fix these," I told him, "if you'll help A.J. get those runners in place."

"Sure," Austin said.

"Okay," Will said, looking around at the controlled confusion.

"I'll get out of your hair and see what's happening outside. Coming, Steph?"

"Absolutely," she said, following him out the back door. "Come on, Erwin," she called, "Mommy wants to show you the ponies." The dachshund dashed out the back door.

I was trimming the ends of the daisies and zinnias and poking them back into their container when Miss Nancy sidled up beside me. "Speaking of show and tell," she said in a loud stage whisper, "lookit what I just found in the trash over here." She held it out. It was a plastic carry-out container from Eatzi's, the poshest deli and takeout food shop in Buckhead.

We both laughed. "Well, she wasn't lying about that. She did bring it all the way from Atlanta."

Nancy shook her head. "That must be one fancy piece of tail."

"Miss Nancy!" I said, pretending to be shocked.

"He's shopping for diamonds, did you know that?" she asked, her expression grim.

"An engagement ring?"

"No," she admitted. "Earrings. But you just wait. She'll have a diamond ring on that third finger of her left hand any day now. And he'll have a matching one. Right through his nose."

When I was satisfied that everything was in place in the house, I walked outside to take my casserole to the food tent. The grounds were filling up rapidly. By three o'clock I estimated that there were at least a couple hundred people milling around the old plantation house.

It was funny to see all these people who associated themselves with Loving Cup. In all the months I'd been back and forth to the bra plant, I'd only ever seen a handful of people, mostly office workers or maintenance men. But the people crowded around the tables, laughing and gossiping, oohing and aahing over the house, and filling their plates from the endless rows of food, seemed like a huge family—and the majority of them were women. These were the stitchers, I realized, whose machines had been mostly idle for so long. Many of them knew and greeted me. "Your daddy sold me my first car when I was sixteen," gushed one woman. "Wish I still had that thing. Old as I am, it'd be a by-God antique." I was surprised too by how many of the workers were Hispanic.

I'd gone back into the house to show it off to Dianne Yost, who ran the local public relations firm Will had hired, when Stephanie joined up with the tour.

They were examining the pencil sketches taped to the foyer walls. "The muralist has been taking photos of local scenes for weeks," I explained. "And these," I said, pointing to the smears of gray, blue-green, turquoise, and gold paint on another sheet taped beside it, "are the colors he's using."

"It's all the same colors," Stephanie said, wrinkling her nose. "How is that going to look?"

"It's a technique called grisaille," I explained. "It's supposed to be tone on tone. And when we put the console table I bought in New Orleans here, and this big, gilt Empire mirror above it, it'll really set a beautiful, peaceful tone for the rest of the house. Don't you think?"

Dianne nodded enthusiastically. "Let me know when it's completed, and I'll send somebody over to photograph it," she said. "I think maybe we could place something in *Veranda* magazine. And of course we'd buy an ad for Loving Cup, to get a double hit."

"It's going to be wonderful," Stephanie said, as we walked through the rest of the rooms. "And I've loved those adorable sketches you send every week." She twinkled at Dianne, "Keeley does the sweetest sketches. Every room, all the furniture, the pictures, everything. And I'm in them all! In the bedroom, at the dressing table, in the dining room, pouring wine. And my little dog, Erwin, he gets star billing too. How precious is that?"

"Very," Dianne murmured. She was jotting down notes to herself and taking digital photos as we walked and talked. When she excused herself to find her children and see that they'd eaten, Stephanie followed me back out to the kitchen.

"Has the bidet been delivered yet?" she asked. "I didn't see it up-stairs."

"No, it's still on back order," I said. "But I'm sure it'll be here by deadline."

"Deadline." She sighed. "Will has been dropping hints like crazy about that deadline. I swear, he has swept me totally off my feet. And I'm putty in his hands. I've never met a man with his energy. And de-termination. I'll be so glad when he gets this overseas thing taken care of. Then we'll really be able to sit back and enjoy all this. I think we'll be spending a lot of weekends out here, thanks to you, Keeley. It'll be the ideal place to entertain my business clients. And Will's, too."

"Weekends?" I said.

"And some holidays," she added. "I know it's a little early, and don't you dare tell Will, but I've got my eye on a house over on Tuxedo Road in Buckhead. And I wouldn't dream of hiring anybody but you to decorate it. Wait until you see it, Keeley. There's a swim-ming pool, and a guest house—that'll have to be completely gutted—and a tennis court . . . Oh, and I almost forgot. There are two vacant floors in my law firm's office tower. I've talked to our broker, and Will can have state-of-the-art high-speed Internet access. There's a nice reception area, and the executive suite is to die for, and of course, the best thing is, we're only fifteen minutes from the airport."

"But Loving Cup is here, in Madison," I protested. "He's not thinking of closing the plant. He wouldn't throw a picnic and then throw everybody out of work."

Stephanie went over to the back door and closed it, then poked her head into the dining room to make sure we were alone.

"I shouldn't tell you this and spoil Will's surprise, but I happen to know that he is planning a big announcement today. That's one of the things I love about him. He really talks to me about his business. Do you know how rare that is in a successful man? Will recognizes that I have a head on my shoulders—not just a pretty hairdo. That's what all these trips to Mexico and Sri Lanka have been about. He's lined up a maquiladora down in Mexico. And as soon as he has the financing nailed down, they'll start producing. The new line should be in stores by next spring."

I was too stunned to say anything at first. "But . . . the underwire—Will told me he'd figured a way it could be produced here in Madison. The thread could be woven in Alabama and the fabric made in South Carolina . . . and the plant here would be retooled . . ."

Stephanie made sympathetic clucking noises. "That was just Will being a cockeyed optimist. But the economics don't work. He can't compete with Maidenform and Vanity Fair and the others if he tries to keep production domestic. He feels awful about it. And the plant here won't completely close down. Not yet."

Somehow I made it out of the house and managed to extricate myself from Stephanie's clutches. I felt like I'd been hit up the side of the head with a two-by-four.

I walked around among all those smiling, happy workers, and I felt like a complete traitor. I'd helped Will build his little Xanadu, and now these people were all going to pay for it with their livelihoods. Well, at least it was for a good cause, I told myself. Stephanie seemed to be head over heels for Will. I'd done my job.

Out in the meadow there was a sack race in progress. As I got closer I saw that Will and A.J. and two Hispanic teenagers seemed to be leading the pack of ten contestants. The two adults were red-faced and gasping from their efforts, hopping furiously toward the finish line. Five yards away, A.J. managed to grab the lead, with Will hot on his heels, and the two kids closing in fast. I saw Will glance around, and then suddenly he seemed to lose his balance, sprawling to the ground and somehow taking A.J. down with him. The shorter of the two kids hopped past both of them, and the crowd cheered for the winner.

I was standing at the iced tea dispenser, handing out cups of ice when A.J. and Will came limping up. Will took the glass of iced tea I handed him, gulped it down, and then motioned for another. "A.J.?" I said, offering him a cup.

"Nah," A.J. gasped. "I think it's Miller Time for me." He headed off for the kegs on the far side of the tent.

Will gulped the rest of his tea and threw the cup in the trash. "You and Nancy did a great job organizing all this in such a short time," he said. He mopped at his glistening forehead with a handkerchief.

"Miss Nancy did all the hard work," I said. "I just showed up."

"And made it all work," Will said. "Don't sell yourself short. If you ever get tired of interior design, I wish you'd come to work for me. You've got a great eye for design, and you're detail-oriented. Of course," he added, picking at the strap of my bra that was sliding off my shoulder, "you don't know squat about bras, but I could teach you that."

I slapped his hand away. "The way I hear it, you're not exactly in a hiring mode these days. So if it's all the same to you, I think I'll keep the job I have."

"Huh?" Will said.

"Stephanie tells me you're going to make a big announcement today," I said. "On Labor Day, of all times. You certainly do have a flair for irony."

Will looked down at his watch. "I guess I'll take that as a compliment. And yeah, I guess it's about that time. I'll give everybody a little more time to eat, then I'll take the stage."

He gestured toward the food tent. "I've seen you bustling around all afternoon. Let's go over there and get a plate before all the good stuff gets gone. Nancy will have my hide if I don't have a slice of that fresh apple cake of hers."

"No thanks," I said. "I think I've lost my appetite."

"Suit yourself," he said, shrugging and heading toward the food.

I started looking around for A.J. He wasn't in the crowd of men milling around the beer keg, and he sure as hell wasn't taking a pony ride. After fifteen minutes of circling the meadow, I decided to look in the house. I checked all over the place and finally found him, coming out of the bathroom in the pump house.

"Hey," he said, looking a little embarrassed. "It's okay to use the bathroom in here, isn't it? I didn't want to mess up the fancy ones in the house."

"It's fine," I said. "I think I'm ready to leave now."

"Can I just look around in here?" he asked.

"Why not?" I said. "I'm sure Will would want you to. That's one of the reasons for this whole shindig. To show everybody how rich and successful and tasteful Will Mahoney is."

A.J. walked around the sleeping area, touching the walls and looking out the windows. He paused at the bed, with a puzzled look on his face.

"Have I seen this bed someplace before?"

"Yes."

He rubbed the fabric of the quilt. "I'd love to have a big old bed just like this someday."

"You almost did," I told him. "I bought it for us. After the wedding was called off, it was just sitting there in storage. It was way too big for my place, and Will needed furniture in a hurry for this place, so I sold it to him."

A.J. thumped the mattress. "There's a metaphor in all this, but I'm damned if I want to bring that up just now."

I walked out into the living area, and A.J. followed. He was really fascinated with the pump house. I think men love the solidity of brick and mortar and heavy beams. He walked back and forth, admiring the rock fireplace, and examining all the old framed art; the advertisements, drawings, and black and white photographs.

He tapped the glass on the photograph of the beauty queens. "That's your Aunt Gloria, right? My daddy always says she's one of the best-looking women he's ever met." A.J. laughed ruefully. "And considering the source, that's a high compliment."

"I'm sure."

He was still staring at the photograph. Now he looked from it to me, and then back at the photo again. "Is this . . . ?"

"Yeah," I said. "That's my mother."

"I think this is the first picture of her I've ever seen," he said. "Your daddy never had any around the house."

"No," I said. "It was pretty painful for him."

"She was a beauty," A.J. said. "Like her daughter."

"Thank you." I hesitated. "I met Mama's cousin Sonya a couple of days ago. She moved from Madison to North Carolina the first time the bra plant closed down. She says I'm Mama made over."

A.J. stood very close to me. His finger traced the outline of my eyes, then my nose, then my lips.

"No," he said. "There's a lot of your daddy in you. And probably some of her. But mostly you're just you. You're not a carbon copy of anybody else. You are uniquely one of a kind, Keeley Rae Murdock."

He bent down and touched his lips to my forehead with the gentlest, the lightest of kisses.

Outside I could hear the hum of voices, kids laughing and screaming. The bluegrass band segued out of "Rocky Top" to a dramatic fanfare, and then Will's voice came over the loudspeaker.

"Welcome everybody, to our Loving Cup company picnic," he boomed. "Now, if everybody will just take a seat, I have some news I want to share with all of you."

The band played another fanfare.

"Let's go," I told A.J. "I've got a headache."

56

"**Let me get you** some aspirin," A.J. said, looking concerned. "You've been running around in the heat all day; you probably have sunstroke or something."

I gave him a grateful smile. "Maybe some aspirin and a Diet Coke. Gloria says the caffeine helps a headache because it dilates the blood vessels in the head."

We were out on the highway, headed away from Mulberry Hill. My head really was throbbing. I felt sick and, worse, betrayed. I couldn't understand how Will Mahoney could be so cavalier about going back on all his promises to keep Loving Cup going.

"Since we're out this way," A.J. said cautiously, "we could just run over to Cuscawilla. Mama's got a whole pharmacy in the bathroom there. And she's still got cases of Diet Coke. She always kept it around because of you."

I smiled wanly and kneaded my forehead. "I guess that would be all right. Just for a little while. I've got to work tomorrow, you know."

"Just for a little while," A.J. promised. "I'll doctor you up and then take you right home."

But he didn't of course. We found the aspirin and the Diet Coke, and A.J. got me a damp washcloth and put it on my forehead. I only intended to lie on the sofa in the darkened den for a little while, until the headache went away, but when I woke up, it was after seven o'clock.

I was just sitting up when A.J. came in to check on me. "Feeling better?" he asked, sitting down beside me.

"Yeah," I said. "The headache's gone. Guess you better take me home. I didn't mean to fall asleep on you like that."

"It's okay," A.J. assured me. "I watched the Braves game on the television in Mama and Daddy's room. Braves are beating the tar out of the Mets, 6–0, bottom of the seventh."

"Hey," I said. "Where are your parents? Don't they usually spend Labor Day weekend out here with all your dad's golf cronies?"

"Nah," he said. "They're up in Highlands, with all my dad's golf cronies up there."

"Oh."

"You don't have to rush off in the heat of the day, do you?" A.J. asked. "Let's get some wine and sit outside on the patio. It's finally started to cool off, and there's a breeze coming in off the lake."

"That sounds nice," I agreed. I secretly dreaded going back to the apartment right now. I loved my little nest, but sometimes, on nights like this, the walls seemed to crowd in on me, and I started to wonder why I was still living in a cramped efficiency just upstairs from the store. I was thirty-two years old. By now, I always thought I'd have a home of my own. And a husband and a garden, and a porch swing . . . I got up and hurried out of the den.

The patio at the Jernigans' Cuscawilla house was something out of *House Beautiful*. I knew, because GiGi had found a picture in an old issue of the magazine, and insisted that I order that exact same set of Palacek wicker furniture, all sixteen pieces in that particular line, for the new patio. We'd even ordered the same fabric shown in the magazine. GiGi had balked, but I had managed to talk her into some pillows made of a coordinating fabric, and even some antique cast-iron urns that hadn't been pictured in the *HB* spread.

I slipped off my shoes and sat back on an oversized chaise longue and looked out on the lake. It wasn't quite dusk yet, and fireflies danced in the shrubbery at the water's edge. A party barge chugged by, strung with twinkling white lights, and a woman's silvery laugh floated across the water.

A.J. came out of the house with two goblets and a bottle of white wine stuck in a silver ice bucket. He poured me a glass and perched himself companionably on the edge of the chaise.

We sipped our wine and watched the sun dip across the horizon. Lights came on in the other houses across the lake, and we could hear faint strains of music.

"Been a funny summer, hasn't it?" A.J. mused, his arm slipping around my shoulder just as naturally as if it had never left.

"Very," I agreed.

"I'll be glad when it's over," he said. "Weather will start cooling off. And I'll be taking off."

"Really? You going on a trip?"

"Sort of." He grinned like a kid who'd found the toy in the Cracker Jack box. "I'm going up to Chicago for a few months. A college buddy of mine thinks I'd do great at mortgage brokering. He's going to train me, show me the ropes, then get me set up."

"For real? You're leaving Madison?"

"For a while. I think it's high time I got out from under my daddy's shadow. I've been kind of bored for a while now, and this seems like a good opportunity. If it goes well, I'll be back by spring, and set up my own office, right downtown."

"Wow," I said, squeezing his hand. "That's terrific, A.J. I'm so proud of you. And I think it'll do you good to get out of here for a while, kind of stretch your wings."

"Just for a while," A.J. said, stroking my hand with his thumb. "I've got a lot going on back here, you know."

"I've got a busy fall too," I said, trying to change the subject. I finished my glass of wine, and before I could resist, A.J. poured me another. "Will wants Mulberry Hill totally completed—and I mean right down to the last fish fork and salt cellar—by Thanksgiving."

"Can you do that?" A.J. asked. "I mean, usually a big job like that takes you guys months and months. Hell, it took six months for us to get new furniture and drapes for the conference room at the bank when GiGi decided we needed a redo."

"We'll be pushing it," I admitted, taking a sip of wine. "The thing is, I think Will wants everything ready because he's about to pop the question to Stephanie. And I know for sure that she's expecting a ring any day now."

"The boy works fast, I'll give him that," A.J. said admiringly. He nuzzled my neck. "It took me a whole year to get up the nerve to ask you. And it wasn't like we hadn't known each other our whole lives, practically."

I sat up, spilling a little wine. "We didn't know each other all that long, A.J. You were ahead of me in grade school, and then you went off to boarding school, and then Washington and Lee. I really didn't get to know you until after GiGi hired me to redecorate The Oaks."

"And it didn't take a month after that until you'd tricked me into going to bed with you, you sly little vixen," A.J. said, laughing.

I took another sip of wine and punched his arm, feeling warm and giddy and carefree for the first time in weeks. "Who tricked who? Anyway, you promised you'd take that secret to the grave. I am still mortified that I allowed you to seduce me like that."

"Aw, don't be mortified, Keeley," A.J. said, landing a kiss on my shoulder. "That's a memory I will always cherish, darlin'. You, up on that ladder in my bedroom . . ."

"And you looking right up my skirt," I giggled, brushing away the hand that had managed to find a resting place on top of my left breast.

"Hey," I said, standing up. "You know what I just realized? I bet the reason I had that headache is that I haven't eaten all day."

"No shit?" A.J. said. "That barbecue was amazing."

"I didn't eat a thing," I said.

"Come on," he said, standing up and tugging me by the hand. "Let's go see what GiGi's got out in the kitchen. We can raid the fridge. Just like that first time you stayed over."

"You promised not to mention that again," I reminded him.

"Not the sex, just the raiding," A.J. said.

I sat at the kitchen table while he unloaded the weirdest combination I'd ever seen: jalapeño stuffed olives, a slab of cold lasagna, and some green plums. But washed down with another bottle of Chardonnay, it tasted just fine.

When it was all gone, we went back outside and watched the show the stars were putting on. By now A.J. had squeezed himself in beside me on the chaise longue. "I'm still hungry," he said, after a while. "Let's go back inside and see if we can find some dessert."

He came out of the pantry with a huge smile on his face, and a cardboard box in his hand. "Brownie mix," he crowed. "Remember?"

"Oh no," I said, backing away from him. "Not again."

"Come on," A.J. said. "It'll be good." We got as far as putting the mix in a bowl and adding a couple of eggs and some vegetable oil, before the situation totally deteriorated. Fifteen minutes later we were back out on the patio, eating raw batter with a wooden spoon.

"Mmm," A.J. said, licking the last of the chocolate from my fingertips. "Remember the brownies we had that night?"

"No," I said.

"Liar." He kissed my neck, deliberately smearing chocolate on my blouse.

"Oh, here," he said, "Let me get rid of that."

I pushed him away, but he was as persistent as ever. I made a weak attempt to keep things under control, but I wasn't having much luck, and to tell the truth, maybe my heart wasn't in it.

"Come on, baby," he whispered, reaching around me to try to unhook my bra. "It's the last night of summer. The worst summer of my life. And it should have been the best. I think about being in Provence, with that ape Nick. God. I stayed drunk most of the time."

"At least you got to leave town," I told him. "I was stuck right here in Madison. Your daddy was so mad he tried to force us out of business. Paige's mom was threatening to sue me for slander, and my daddy got kicked out of the country club. Plus I was the laughingstock of the whole town."

"Shhh," he said, shutting me up with a long kiss. "That's all behind us now, don't you see?" He twisted his wrist so he could see his watch in the moonlight. "Look. It's almost midnight. I think we ought to celebrate. Right at midnight. Get a clean start."

"And how are we going to do that?" I asked warily.

He chuckled and fumbled for the buttons on my blouse. "Just like the good old days," he promised. "Before everything went to shit. Just you and me, and the moonlight. Remember when we used to sneak off to the shack?" He groaned. "I get wood just thinking about it."

"So I noticed," I told him, laughing and pushing him away.

"You know, Kyle finally talked Daddy and Vince Bascomb into putting his shack and ours on the market. Of course, Mama could not be happier, considering."

Memories of Vince Bascomb's forlorn cabin came flooding back to me now, and I shuddered involuntarily.

A.J. felt the shudder and pulled me closer.

"I was out at the Bascomb place last month," I said. "It's a complete wreck. Why has he waited so long to sell it?"

A.J. had worked his knee between mine, and his voice was muffled. "Damned if I know. Kyle has been after the two of them to sell for ages, but Vince wouldn't budge, and Daddy thought it would bring more money if they sold off all the lots as one parcel. So he just waited Vince out. To tell you the truth, I think the old guy is in pretty bad shape. He's broke, and he needs the money."

"Yeah, I heard he's pretty crippled up with arthritis," I said.

A.J. looked up and kissed me hungrily. Nothing ever satisfied his appetites.

"Not just the arthritis," he said after a while. He had my bra off, and his hands were tugging at the waistband of my shorts. "Now he's got a brain tumor. Inoperable, poor bastard."

Suddenly I had a mental image of Vince Bascomb, not as he must be now, ridden with arthritis and cancer, but as he was twenty-five years ago. The image was of him and Sonya Wyrick slipping off to that hunting camp in the woods. And of Drew Jernigan and Lorna Plummer. And yes, of my own mother and Darvis Kane.

I had deliberately pushed all these thoughts out of my mind minutes after we'd left that Waffle House in Kannapolis. But now the images came flooding back, unbidden. I felt my scalp prickle and goose bumps raise up on my arms.

"Come on, baby," A.J. was whispering. "I can't get this damn zipper of yours. Help a guy out, can you?"

I struggled upright so suddenly that I knocked A.J. off the chaise longue.

"What the hell?" he yelped. "What's wrong with you, Keeley?"

I buttoned my blouse hurriedly. "Oh God, A.J. I can't do this. I'm sorry. I don't mean to be a tease."

He groaned and ran his hand through his hair. "Where are you going? You're not going to just leave me like this, are you? I thought we were going to start over. I thought we had an understanding."

I stepped into my shoes and smoothed my clothes, and looked around for my purse. "More like a misunderstanding," I told him. "My fault this time, not yours." I dropped a kiss on his cheek and ran like hell out of there.

57

I dreaded returning to Loving Cup on Tuesday, but there was no getting around it. I needed decisions on the fabrics for the parlors, the dining room, and the upstairs sitting room, and I needed them fast, if I was going to get my workroom going on drapes and upholstery. I threw the samples and my presentation boards in the front seat of the Volvo and drove slowly out to the plant.

Somehow the fun and excitement of this project had quickly drained away, to reveal just another big, expensive job. I chided myself for getting so emotionally involved in the project. So what if Mulberry Hill wouldn't be Will's primary residence? If Stephanie had her way—and she *always* got her way—Glorious Interiors would soon have another assignment—a big splashy mansion in Buckhead. So what if I'd invested all this time and creative energy for a house that was just for show? If the check clears, my daddy would say, your job is done.

I'd expected to find the bra plant shrouded in doom after Will's big announcement of the previous day, but what I found was just the opposite. One of those big, portable electric flashing signs had been set up on the plant's front lawn. "Now Hiring Experienced Stitchers and Pattern Makers. Competitive Pay, Great Benefits. Apply Within."

Was this somebody's idea of a practical joke? I wondered. If it was, plenty of people had been taken in. Traffic streamed into and out of the parking lot, and an off-duty uniformed Morgan County sheriff's deputy directed me to park on the grass behind the plant because all the parking slots were full.

Inside the main building was just as busy. I had to pass through a security guard and pin on a plastic visitor's badge just to get through the front door—which was a first. As I walked down the hall toward Will's office I heard phones ringing, the steady clack of computer keyboards, and from the back of the building, where I knew the factory floor had been, I could swear I heard the hum of sewing machines.

Miss Nancy was on one phone line when I went into Will's office, and I could see all the lights on her phone console had blinking lights for calls holding. She looked up, mouthed "Just a minute," and went back to her call. I would have taken a seat, but all the chairs in the reception area—all three of them—were already taken. Will's visitors looked as out of place in that shabby office as a peacock in a henhouse. All three of the women were gorgeous in a vaguely exotic way. All three wore black—black leather, black denim, black spandex. They weren't all that young, maybe ranging in age from twenty to fifty, but they had that big-city look, tattoos, nose piercings, bizarre hair, and they all carried tote bags. They looked supremely bored.

Miss Nancy finally hung up the phone.

"Well, what do you think?" she asked. "Can you believe it? I knew that boy would turn things around for us, and he has."

"What's going on?" I asked. "What's with the sign out front, and the security guards and all these—-people? I thought Will was laying everybody off."

"Hell no!" she sputtered. "Where were you yesterday, under a rock? Didn't you hear the announcement?"

"I left early," I said. "I had a terrible headache. But Stephanie told me that Will had decided to set up production offshore. She said that was going to be the announcement. That he'd lined up one of those maquiladoras in Mexico to do the sewing."

"In her dreams." Miss Nancy snorted. "We're going back into production as soon as we finish hiring. The gals in the sample room have already started work."

I leaned over her desk and whispered "What's with the chicks in black over there? Is Loving Cup expanding into bondage wear too now?"

"Those are the new fitting models," Nancy whispered back. "Did you ever?"

"What happened to the old fitting models?"

"The old ones were all about a hundred-leven years old and had titties hangin' down to their knees," she said. "We sent off to New York for this bunch. Honey, we're going uptown all the way."

Her phone rang, she picked it up and put it down again. "He's ready for you," she said.

I pushed the door open to Will's office and went in. His desk was covered with bras, lace samples, sketches, and paperwork.

"Hey," he said curtly. "I can only give you like ten minutes. As you can see, I'm really swamped."

"Fine," I said. I took my own stack of fabric samples out and set them in front of him. "These are for the two settees in the parlor, the armchairs, and the drapes. Plus the fabric for the dining room drapes, and two of the upstairs guest rooms. I'll have a better idea of what to put in the family room once I've found some new sofas . . ."

But he wasn't really listening. "No," he said, putting one swatch aside. "No. I like this. Not this. Too shiny. Too busy. Too cheesy. Fine. This'll work. Okay."

He pushed the two stacks of fabrics, the rejects and the chosen ones, across the desk toward me. "Anything else?"

"I just need your approval for one more buying trip. It's too late to have sofas custom-made, but once the International Furniture Mart is over in High Point, I can run up there and pick up some really high-quality showroom samples."

"Fine," he said. "Do it."

"Okay." I got up to leave.

"Where'd you get off to yesterday?" he asked. "I went to look for you, after the announcement, but you'd vanished. Did you and your 'date' take off for a nooner?"

I felt the color rising in my cheeks. "I had a terrible headache. We went out to the lake, if you must know."

"Shacked up? I thought you hated that place," Will said.

"Not the shack. The big house, over at Cuscawilla."

"Of course," he said.

"Nothing happened."

"You don't have to make excuses to me," Will said. "I'm your client, not your father."

"I'm not making excuses for anything," I said curtly. "I'm an adult."

"Absolutely," Will said. "Anything else I need to look at?"

"That's it for now," I said. "Pretty busy here today. So, you're not closing the plant after all?"

"I was never going to close the plant," he said sharply. "Where'd you get that idea?"

"Stephanie told me yesterday, and all those overseas trips of yours . . ."

"She must have misunderstood," Will said, frowning. "The overseas thing didn't pan out. It was an all-or-nothing deal. It wasn't feasible to keep the plant here and do partial production over there as I'd hoped. So we're going another route."

"You can do that?"

"We can now," Will said. "We couldn't compete head-on with the big brands, Warnaco and Sara Lee and Vanity Fair. All their garments are made offshore. But what we can do is niche market. That's where the UnderLiar comes in."

"UnderLiar?"

"That's the name we came up with for the underwire bra you tried on. Nobody else has it. Nobody else knows how to make it. Except us. We'll make it here in Madison and sell it private label to Victoria's Secret. We have no marketing, sales, or distribution headaches, or expenses. We just make bras. Very, very good bras."

"But they'll be sold as Victoria's Secret UnderLiar. Does that mean the Loving Cup label is history?"

"Our people know who they are and what we do. And what they

care about most, as you pointed out to me some months ago, is having good jobs."

"Then it's good news," I said. "That's great." I scooped my samples up and headed for the door.

"Keeley."

I turned around.

"Stehanie really dislikes that mural thing in the foyer out at Mulberry Hill. She thinks it's going to look stupid."

"Stupid?" I yelped. "Kip Collins is the most sought-after decorative painter in the Southeast. His work has been published in all the big magazines. Maybe if I showed Stephanie some of the layouts, she'd see what I'm after."

"She hates it," Will said. "How 'bout, instead, some nice flowers? Can your guy do that? Or maybe just some nice flowered wallpaper. Maybe something with red in it? Stephanie really likes red."

Now I was seeing red. I was seething, steaming, smoking. I'd already commissioned the mural. I'd paid Kip a third of his fee in advance for the preliminary sketches, which Will had loved, and even booked Kip's time to come to Madison to paint. And that fabulous console table—the whole room had been planned around it.

"Red flowered wallpaper," I said out loud.

No effin' way, my subconscious screamed.

"I'll see what I can do." I had to get out of there before I exploded.

"Hey Keeley? About A.J. I know it's none of my business . . ."

I turned again, impatient now. "I thought you could only spare me ten minutes. I think probably you should concentrate on bras, don't you?"

"Oh yeah," he said sheepishly. "I gotta take a look at the fitting models the agency sent down from New York. They get paid a hundred bucks an hour, plus airfare and travel expenses, so every minute they spend sitting around here fully clothed, instead of having bras fitted, is costing me money."

"Poor you," I said.

58

A week later, when I went back to Loving Cup with the most recent set of sketches for Will and Stephanie, the place was at fever pitch. Miss Nancy had installed her own assistant in the outer office, and had given herself a bigger, grander office down the hall.

Will thumbed rapidly through the sketches. "Stephanie will call you about any changes," he said, obviously distracted.

I ground my teeth. Stephanie was no longer contenting herself with a long-distance role in the restoration process at Mulberry Hill. Every other day now, it seemed, when I arrived on the job site, her white Porsche Boxster was parked in front of the pump house, and I could hear the clip of Erwin's nails on the polished hardwood floors. She'd already cost us ten thousand dollars in last-minute change orders—demanding that the downstairs powder room wallpaper be ripped down and replaced with a limited edition hand-blocked paper that had to be special ordered from Italy—for two hundred dollars a roll, sending the Sub-Zero refrigerator back to the distributor because she'd seen a bigger, glass-fronted number in a decorator showhouse in Buckhead, and insisting that the Stark carpet in the den, which I'd had custom colored to match the exact shade of Erwin's coat—be changed, because, as she put it, "That disgusting color bears no resemblance to my angel. Erwin is fawn colored. That carpet is brown!"

"I've got another assignment for you," Will said, leaning back in his chair.

"What now?"

"Aw, this is a fun one," he said, laughing. "No change orders, I promise. We're gonna have a dove hunt out at Mulberry Hill, and I need you to help make the arrangements."

"Since when did you turn into the great white hunter?" I asked.

He reached in his top desk drawer and took out a glossy sporting goods catalog. Cabela's. I sighed. He was gone for good.

"I used to do some bird hunting growing up," he said. "Till my folks moved to the city, and we couldn't keep a dog anymore, and I didn't know anybody with land to hunt on. I've been thinking about taking it up again. Get me out of the office, out onto the land."

"You've got the land to hunt on now," I admitted. "I think my daddy used to go dove hunting out there, years ago. He knew somebody who had permission to go on the property."

"A big dove hunt used to be a yearly tradition back in the day," Will said. "Every year they'd have a big hunt breakfast the first day of dove hunting season. The Cardwells invited folks from all around. People really looked forward to it. I've been talking to the fellas at Ye Olde Colonial, and they think it would be a good community gesture if I started the hunt up again."

"Since when do you eat with the breakfast club guys at Ye Olde Colonial?" I demanded. "Aren't you kind of young for that group?"

"I've been stopping by for a while now," Will said. "Anyway, we can't have it the first day of hunting season. I'll be out of town. We'll do it October 20."

"I don't know anything about dove hunts," I said.

"Don't you worry about the hunt part," Will said. "I just want you to take care of the arrangements. Nancy's already hired the caterer. We'll have scrambled eggs and grits, sausages, bacon, fried apples, biscuits, all that kind of thing."

My stomach growled at the mention of all that food. "Sounds good."

"I need you to line up a tent, not as big as the one for the picnic. I think we'll only have maybe a couple dozen guys. And tables and chairs. And I want some hay bales scattered around, you know, nothing fancy, really, but folksy. Outdoorsy. It's gotta look good. I'm gonna invite some business associates. One of the executive

VPs from Victoria's Secret is a big quail hunter, and he's coming down."

"October 20," I said, making a note of it in my planner. "Folksy. Outdoorsy. I think I can handle that."

"Oh, uh, Keeley," Will said offhandedly. "Let's just keep this dove hunt on the Q.T. from Stephanie, okay? As far as she knows, I'm meeting with some out-of-town clients that day. The less said about it, the better."

"You want me to lie," I said. "To Stephanie." That would be a day brightener.

"Not lie, exactly," Will said. "Just not give her all the details. She's a city girl, you know, and she doesn't eat meat. She's so tender-hearted, such an animal lover, I just think the idea of a dove hunt would upset her unnecessarily."

"Right," I said. I wondered if he'd ever noticed Stephanie's predilection for pricey leather shoes and boots and suede jackets.

I put my finger to my lips. "Shhh. It'll be our little secret."

I was getting good at keeping secrets of my own.

The minute I'd driven away from Cuscawilla that night with A.J., I'd started regretting what had almost happened. For all his apologies and sweet words, I knew it was over between us. I'd had too much to drink, and when I sobered up I realized that my hormones had nearly led me back to bed with someone I no longer loved.

I knew I was over A.J., but what I didn't know was how to break the news to him, or even how to keep him at arm's length.

Now I was out at Mulberry Hill, checking on the delivery of Stephanie's beloved bidet. My cell phone rang and I flipped it open.

"It's me," A.J. purred. "I've been thinking about you all week, baby."

"I can't talk," I interrupted. "I'm in the middle of a business meeting."

" I think we've got some unfinished business of our own," he said.

Joey, my plumber, was circling the wooden crate the bidet had arrived in, scratching his head and puzzling over the thing.

"It's a bidet," I told Joey.

"What's that?" A.J. asked.

"A bidet," I told Joey, who was still awaiting enlightenment. "It's for feminine hygiene. You know, like in Europe, they have them?"

"I've been to Europe," A.J. said, annoyed. "Stop trying to change the subject. I want you. Right now. Naked . . ."

I felt my face go scarlet. "I'm talking to the plumber right now," I said urgently. "I'll have to call you back."

Half an hour later A.J. called again. Joey had uncrated the bidet and was trying to decipher the installation directions, which were in French.

"Here's what I want," A.J. continued. "You. Naked. Chocolate. Are you getting the drift here?"

"Excuse me, Joey," I said. "I think this is the, uh, lumberyard, about those studs I ordered for the shower enclosure." I took the phone and walked rapidly downstairs.

"I'm the stud you ordered, all right," A.J. growled.

"Stop this," I whispered. "I'm trying to work. I'm up to my eyeballs in plumbers and plasterers and electricians. Will is out of town for the next few days, and when he gets back, I've got to have the chandeliers hung and the master bath finished, and I've got a damn dove hunt to organize now. I cannot see you tonight."

"So Will's out of town?" A.J. said. "I've got an idea. What do you say I meet you out there at his place tonight. Say, eight? I'll stop and pick us up a nice bottle of wine, and some dinner. You can tell me about your bad old day and the mean old carpenters. And then we can take that fancy bed of ours out in the pump house for a test drive."

"Are you out of your mind?" I could feel my already elevated blood pressure spiking. "You are not coming anywhere near this place tonight. I am not meeting you, and we are definitely, positively, not getting anywhere near my client's personal bed."

"Your bed then," A.J. said.

"No."

"Mine."

"God, no." The thought of bumping into Drew and GiGi gave me the willies.

"Cuscawilla."

"No!"

"I'm running out of real estate here, darlin'. Hey, I know. The shack. Nobody goes out there anymore. It's got a gate and it's locked up tight. But I know where Kyle keeps the key."

"Yuck!" I said. "Look. I really have a killer day ahead of me. I can't see you tonight. I'll call you. I promise."

He hung up.

Fifteen minutes later I was back upstairs, trying to salvage some college French to help Joey with the bidet installation. The cell phone rang again. Joey gave me an annoyed look.

I took the phone out into the hallway.

"Phone sex," A.J. said. "I'll start. First, I unzip—" I closed the phone, turned it off and put it outside in the Volvo. Turning off A.J., I thought ruefully, would not be this easy.

Hours and hours later, Austin came over with Chinese takeout. We sat in my living room eating moo goo gai pan while we dissed about all the terrible design dilemmas on *Trading Spaces*. And I told him about A.J. I knew he would tell me I'd made a hideous mistake, but Austin was the only person I could talk to about A.J.

"Once you take up with that rascal again, where will it end?" Austin wanted to know.

"I don't know," I said truthfully. "The thing is, I know what he did to me was selfish and demeaning. And I know I'm pathetic and needy. I know it! But that night, after the picnic, at Cuscawilla, I was this close . . ."

Austin shook his head slowly. "Why?" was all he said.

"Something he said. In the pump house. He was looking at that old beauty queen photo. You know, the one with Mama. He'd never seen a picture of her before. And I told him what Sonya said. About how I was her, made over. And he stopped me cold. He said I'm *not* like her. I wouldn't do what she did, lie and cheat and run around. And I just loved him for that right then. Because he was right. I'm not like her. And then he said the thing that made me open my eyes. He said he isn't like his daddy. He's known for a long time about Drew's womanizing, and he's always resented him for it. And he asked me to give him another chance. So he can prove that's not who he is."

"Very touching," Austin said.

"You don't believe it?"

"No. But don't go by me, honey. I will never understand straight men as long as I live."

"So that's what did it. He basically talked his way into my heart."

"And your pants," Austin said. "But you didn't go all the way. Why not?"

"It didn't feel right. I wasn't . . . swept away? I can't really explain it. And then, somehow, A.J. got on the subject of the good old days, and how we used to go out to the shack and fool around . . ."

"You didn't!" Austin said.

I went right on. "And A.J. mentioned that Kyle has finally talked Drew and Vince Bascomb into selling those cabins and all their lake lots."

"Interesting," Austin said, nibbling on a bit of chicken. "Did you happen to tell him what Sonya told us about his father and all those other couples using Bascomb's camp as their little love nest?"

"No. But when A.J. mentioned Mr. Bascomb, I just got this sick feeling in the pit of my stomach. You know, I had this image of all of them sneaking around. Rutting, like Sonya said. It was just so lurid."

"A real passion killer," Austin said sympathetically. "Thank God you came to your senses."

"The other thing A.J. told me is this. Mr. Bascomb has an inoperable brain tumor. Austin, he's dying. A.J. says that's the only reason he agreed to sell. Because he's broke and he's dying."

I sighed. "I think I'd better go talk to him, while I still can."

59

Austin and I sat in my car outside Vince Bascomb's shabby brick ranch house on the edge of town. It was a beautiful Indian summer afternoon, the kind that made you want to rake leaves into a pile just to jump into them.

"This is so sad," I said, taking note of the peeling paint on the trim, the weed-infested yard, and a front door that seemed to be held together with duct tape.

"When I was a little girl, the Bascombs lived in that big Victorian house on Jefferson Street. It was called Birdsong," I told him, "and I think it had been in the Bascomb family for generations. Lorraine always drove a big Lincoln Town Car, and Vince bought a brand-new pickup from my daddy every other year. They used to have a lot of money."

"Not anymore, from the look of this place," Austin said, wrinkling his nose. He pointed out a battered brown eighties Honda Civic parked in the driveway. It was covered with pine needles and fallen leaves, and two of the tires were flat. "That ain't no Lincoln."

"Maybe he's too sick to talk," I said, starting to chicken out. "I should have called first. He doesn't know me. This is ghoulish."

"If he doesn't want to talk, he won't," Austin said firmly. He got out of the Volvo. "Coming?"

"All right."

The concrete porch of the house was caked in grime and more fallen leaves, and a black plastic trash bag sat beside the door, where it had seemingly been for months.

Austin rang the doorbell, and I took a deep breath. A minute passed, and then what seemed like five. "Let's go," I said, tugging at Austin's sleeve. "I can't do this."

"Somebody out there?" a thin voice called. "Is somebody there? Tanya, is that you?"

"Answer him," Austin whispered. "Or I will."

"Mr. Bascomb," I hollered, "It's not Tanya. My name is Keeley Murdock. You used to know my daddy, Wade Murdock. Can you come to the door, Mr. Bascomb?"

"Hell, no," he shouted. "I'm laid up on this sofa in here. You might as well come on in, since you're here."

The door pushed open without much resistance. When we stepped inside, we were hit with a blast of hot, urine-scented air. The room was dim, lit only by a low-wattage light bulb on a table lamp. A sofa was pushed against the wall, and I could just make out the shape of a man propped up there.

"Well?" he said. "Don't stand there with the door open. I'm not paying to heat the whole damn block."

As I stepped into the room, I could see him more clearly. He wore a red knit ski cap pulled down almost to his eyebrows and a gray sweatshirt. The rest of his body was swathed in a bright pink and blue crocheted afghan. The shocking thing was his size. The Vince Bascomb I remembered had been a big, stocky man. Now I doubt he weighed ninety pounds.

"Come on, come on," he said. "What is it you want? Did Tanya send you?"

"Who's Tanya?' Austin asked.

"Tanya's my so-called home health nurse," the old man said. He squinted up at us. "Who the hell are you?"

"I'm, uh, Austin LeFleur, Keeley's friend." Austin thrust a brightly wrapped yellow potted mum toward Bascomb. "We brought you some flowers. We heard you'd been ill."

"Ill? That's a good one," Bascomb said. "I'm dying. Those flowers will probably last longer than me."

Austin and I had been slowly inching toward him, until we were only a few feet from the orange-flowered sofa.

Bascomb reached out and knocked the shade from the table lamp and thrust the naked bulb toward me like a saber. I had to shade my eyes from the now-bright light.

"You're the Murdock girl?" he asked. I noticed for the first time that he wasn't wearing his dentures. His gums shone shiny pink, and combined with the knit cap and afghan, he reminded me of an overgrown infant.

"Yes sir," I said.

"I know your daddy," he said, satisfied that he'd figured out my pedigree. "Used to know your mama, too."

Austin nudged me. I was getting bruises on my side.

"Yes sir. That's kind of why I wanted to talk to you."

"What about?" he asked. "What have you heard?"

"Well . . ." I looked around the room. The orange shag rug was matted with dirt, a low coffee table in front of him was covered with medicine bottles, a tissue box, and a tattered stack of *Reader's Digest* magazines. On the far side of the room, a kerosene space heater glowed orange hot. Beside it were two chrome and plastic dinette chairs.

"Would it be all right if we sat down while we talked?"

"Can't stop you, can I?" he said querulously.

"Could I get you anything first?" I asked, remembering my manners. "A drink of water? Do you need your medicine?"

He yanked the neck of his sweatshirt down to expose a pale, shrunken chest. A blue patch was pasted above his left nipple, and a thin plastic tube ran to it. "My medicine's right here," he croaked. "For all the good it does me. You can sit if you want."

We dragged the chairs as far away from the kerosene heater as we could, which meant we were only inches from the sofa.

"About my mother," I started.

"Good-looking woman," Bascomb said, nodding. "You favor her some, but I expect you know that."

"How well did you know Jeanine Murdock?" Austin asked.

Bascomb leaned his head back against the sofa cushions with his eyes closed. At first I thought he'd drifted off to sleep.

"I suppose you know about my sorry marital history?" he asked, his eyes still closed.

"Yes sir. I knew Miss Lorraine, and I went to school with your daughter."

"Lorraine was a fine person," he said, opening his eyes now. "A real lady, unlike those other two tramps I was fool enough to marry. This cancer I have now, the suffering I'm going through? This is God punishing me for the way I treated the mother of my children."

"I'm sorry," I said quietly.

"Hell on earth," he said. "And I brought it all on myself."

"About Jeanine," I hinted.

He sighed and looked right at me. "If you know about my history, I assume you know about your mother's too. Is that about right?"

"I know she was having an affair with a man named Darvis Kane, who worked for my daddy at the car lot," I said. "I know she and Kane used to meet out at your hunting cabin to have sex." I bit my lip and decided not to pull any punches. "I went to see my mother's cousin Sonya Wyrick last month. I knew she was Mama's closest friend, and thought she might have some idea of where my mother went and where she's been all these years."

"Sonya Wyrick," Bascomb said, smiling slightly. "Is she still up there in South Carolina?"

"North Carolina," I corrected him. "She's still in Kannapolis."

"Sonya was the straw that broke the camel's back for Lorraine," he said. "There had been other women before her, but Sonya was more than Lorraine could bear. She found out about us, and there was hell to pay."

He sighed again. "Hell on earth. Hell to pay. Living hell. That about sums up my life after Lorraine threw me out." He licked his lips. "Does your father know you're poking around in this matter?"

"He does," I said.

"I traded with your daddy ever since he opened that lot," Bascomb said. "Good man. What does he think of all this?"

"He thinks it's about time we both got some answers to our questions," I said. "It's been almost twenty-five years."

"You might not like the anwers you get," Bascomb warned.

"We realize that. But Daddy has finally started dating. She's a nice person, and he feels guilty about seeing somebody without knowing . . . about Mama."

"Sonya was the one who gave Jeanine the key to the cabin," Bascomb said. "But I didn't have a problem with it, as long as she kept her mouth shut about what went on out there. I didn't know at first who her boyfriend was." He frowned. "Darvis Kane. Your father's employee. I thought that was in poor taste. But who was I to judge? It wasn't like we were holding Sunday school out there."

Bascomb reached out and fumbled around among the pill bottles until he found what he was looking for. A tube of Chap Stick, which he then smeared over his colorless lips.

"Other people were also involved out there," he said carefully. "People whose names I would prefer not to mention."

"I already know that Drew Jernigan took Lorna Plummer out there quite often," I said calmly.

"Sonya told you that?" He seemed surprised.

"Yes, sir. But I'd already heard about Drew's affairs."

"Drew is a Jernigan. He can't help himself. He was my best friend for forty years. My business partner some of that time. And unlike Lorraine, GiGi chose to turn a blind eye to her husband's extracurricular activities."

I winced. "It's called cheating. He's a cheat."

"In that respect, yes. But I've always found Drew Jernigan to be honorable in his business dealings with me."

"In other words, he only screws women," I said angrily.

Bascomb looked surprised at my sudden flash of emotion. "That's a vulgar way to put it."

"As far as we can tell," Austin said, inserting himself smoothly into the conversation, "Jeanine and Darvis left Madison in mid-February of 1979. A short time after that, Darvis apparently drove Jeanine's Malibu to Birmingham, Alabama, where he sold it. Right after that, he got on a Greyhound bus, and we haven't talked to anybody who's seen him since that time."

"Lisa Kane managed to track Darvis down sometime in the eighties, and get a divorce," I said. "But that still leaves Mama unaccounted for since the day she left Madison."

Bascomb rolled the tube of Chap Stick between sticklike fingertips. He looked up at me, dry-eyed.

"Your mother never left Madison."

60

"Your mother's dead," Vince Bascomb said. "So you can tell your daddy to get on with his life now. And you go ahead on with yours. Is that what you wanted to hear?"

I blinked and tried to catch my breath. Suddenly I could not breathe that foul air for another second. I made a mad dash for the front door.

I collapsed on the edge of the porch, gulping in great swallows of fresh air. A patch of gray clouds had moved in, obscuring the sun. One small golden leaf sifted down from a nearby tree and landed on top of my shoe. I picked it up and traced its jagged outline with the tip of my finger. It was a ginkgo leaf.

Indian summer had slipped away. Soon this yard and all the others in town would be blanketed with leaves. I thought back to another autumn day like this one.

Mama had helped me collect fallen leaves from our yard, only the very finest, blemish-free specimens. We'd had a ginkgo in our yard too. Back inside the house, she'd set up the ironing board. With a hot iron, we'd pressed the leaves between squares of waxed paper torn out of the blue and white box in the pantry. The smell reminded me of melted crayons.

When we were done, we'd mounted the pressed leaves on cardboard squares that came back from the laundry with my father's dress shirts. Mama had me carefully letter the name of each leaf on the cardboard. Red Maple. Pin Oak. Sycamore. Pecan. Ginkgo.

I'd loved the look of the leaves, which we pinned up on the kitchen walls. But I'd been a little mystified about the reason for the project.

"Why?" I'd asked, watching as the hot iron sealed the leaves inside the waxed paper. "Why do we do it this way?"

"So they'll last forever," she'd said, ruffling her hand through my hair. "Nature has a way of letting beauty disappear. If we left these leaves alone, they'd turn brown and crumble like dust. But we're going to trick nature so your leaves will always stay just as pretty tomorrow as they are today."

She had been right. The leaves' brilliant color had stayed locked inside their waxen coat for months, until we'd replaced them with construction paper Easter bunnies made from cotton balls and broomstraw.

I heard the front door open behind me. Austin sat down on the stoop beside me. He patted his perspiring face with a handkerchief. "Well, we won't have to have a steam facial this fall."

"No," I agreed.

"You all right?"

"Sort of."

"Want to go back in now? The old guy's getting pretty tuckered out. I don't think he's used to talking this much."

I nodded and followed Austin back inside.

"I'd like a glass of water," Bascomb said to me. "In the kitchen. And there should be a bottle of Scotch in the cabinet, under the sink. You could top it off with the Scotch. Three fingers should do."

"I'll get it," Austin said.

I sat back down in my chair. When Austin brought his drink, Bascomb took a sip, nodded, then put it down on the coffee table.

"How did my mother die?" I started, a flood of questions swirling around in my head. "Who killed her?"

He held up his hand. "There was no murder. It was an accident. Just a freak accident."

"Then why didn't you tell somebody?" I cried. "You son-of-a-bitch, you knew she was dead all these years?"

"Keeley," Austin took my hand and squeezed it. "Let the man talk."

Bascomb picked up the Scotch and downed half of it in one long gulp.

"It's all right," he said, smacking his lips. "She can't say anything to me that I haven't said myself."

"What happened?" I demanded. "How did she die?"

"I wasn't there, not right when it happened," he said. "Sonya called me, at two in the morning, hysterical. Lorraine had already kicked me out, and I was sleeping on the sofa in my office. I went right out there, but it was too late. She was dead. Past help, you understand?"

"No," I said stonily.

He reached for his drink and clasped it tightly between both hands.

"This is why she died," he said moodily, staring down into the amber liquid. "The booze." He looked up at me. "I quit after that. Didn't have another drop until after the doctor told me about the cancer. Now I figure, what the hell?"

"Just tell me what happened, okay?" I said.

"They'd all been out at the camp that night, drinking. Darvis Kane, your mother, Drew, and that Plummer woman."

"Lorna."

"Yes. According to Drew, your mother and Kane had been out there all afternoon, drinking and fussing and cussing. Kane had an ugly temper, and it got even uglier when he drank. At some point, Drew said, Kane hauled off and slapped Jeanine right across the face. That's when Drew sorta suggested that things were getting out of hand, and Kane might want to leave. And Kane did leave. He drove off in Jeanine's Malibu in a big hurry, stranding Jeanine out there in the middle of the woods like that. So she called Sonya and asked her to drive out there and bring her home."

Bascomb put his head back against the sofa cushions. "Twenty-five years. I didn't realize it had been that long ago. After it all happened, it seemed sort of like a dream. So that's what I treated it like, a dream that never happened."

"That dream of yours was more like a nightmare for my daddy and me," I said. "And it never would go away. What happened after Kane left? How did my mother die?"

"Kane came back to the cabin," Bascomb said. "But this time he had a gun. He was waving it around, threatening to kill Jeanine. He got off a couple of shots before Drew tackled him and tried to wrestle the gun away. Somehow, another shot was fired. And this time, Jeanine was hit."

He picked up the Scotch and drained the last sip from the glass.

"And that's when Sonya walked in. Jeanine was bleeding, and Lorna was screaming, and Kane, when he saw what had happened, bolted. He was gone before anybody could stop him."

"And my mother was dead."

"There was nothing anybody could do for her," Bascomb said. "They couldn't call the police. How would they explain the circumstances? The married president of the local bank, in some remote cabin in the woods with his mistress? Drew was about to run for reelection to the County Commission. A married woman shot through the chest? And blood all over the floor of my cabin. They panicked. They'd all been drinking, and they just panicked. By the time I got out there, it was over and done with. All we could do was clean up the mess and get our stories straight. So that's what we did."

"Where is she now?" I whispered. "What did they do with my mama's body?"

"I don't know," Bascomb said. "Drew never would tell me. It's out there somewhere. He and Lorna hid it somewhere, but they never would say exactly where. I never have known."

"You didn't know?" I screamed, standing up. I was in a rage. A blind rage. I stood over Bascomb with my fists clenched, and he cowered back against the sofa cushions.

I picked up a sofa cushion and whapped him on the head with it. The knit cap flew off, and his bald head shone softly in the lamplight. "Don't," he whimpered.

"You didn't want to know," I cried. "You didn't give a rat's ass. None of you did. You could have called the police, told them what happened. Told them it was an accident. A big deal like Drew Jernigan, he never would have gone to jail. They could have blamed it all on Darvis Kane. And at least we would have known. At least we could have buried her."

I had the cushion cocked and aimed again, but Austin wrenched it away from me. "Keeley," he shouted. "Keeley!"

There were two more sofa cushions, but the fight had gone out of me. I looked down on the shrunken, pathetic husk of a man who stared up at me now, waiting . . .

"I don't want you to die yet," I said. "Not until you and Jernigan and Lorna Plummer answer for what you did to my family."

I left the front door open and scuffed out through the carpet of softly fallen leaves.

61

It was Wednesday night. Salmon loaf night. After I dropped Austin off, I drove aimlessly around Madison, around and around the square, past the Charm Shop, then the drugstore, then the closed-up Piggly Wiggly, every place in town I could ever remember going with Mama. And then I drove out to the last place I'd seen her. Home.

I breathed a little sigh of relief when I saw that Serena's car was not parked in Daddy's driveway. I'd had some time to get used to the idea, and after some time spent with Serena, I'd concluded that she actually was a very nice person. Maybe not who I would have picked for him, but in real life, you seldom get to pick a parent's new partner. Anyway, tonight needed to be a night for just the two of us.

"Hey, shug," Daddy said, when I came in the back door. He was bustling around the kitchen, whistling along with a big band tune on the CD player I'd given him for Father's Day, and having a high old time. The room smelled like roasting meat and onions. It smelled familiar. It smelled like home.

He turned from the saucepan he was stirring and gave me a kiss on the cheek.

"What is it?" he asked. "You've been crying."

"A little," I admitted. "Can you put dinner on hold for a little while?"

He nodded. "Just let me turn off the potatoes. The chicken's already done. I'll leave it in the oven."

I went to the liquor cabinet and got out a bottle of bourbon and two glasses. I poured some in each glass, then added ice and water. Daddy was sitting at the kitchen table. I held my glass up to his and clinked it.

"To Mama," I said. "To her memory."

He looked up, surprised. "That's what this is about? You found out something?"

I sank down into my chair and took his hand in mine. "She's dead," I said softly. "She's been dead all these years. She never even left Madison."

He nodded. There were tears in his eyes. "I always had a feeling. Nothing I could put a finger on. Just a feeling. So. That's it, then. She's dead. What happened? How did you find out?"

I told him then, starting with our meeting with Sonya Wyrick and ending with Vince Bascomb. I left out a couple details, including the part where I'd hit a sick old man. That I wasn't particularly proud of.

"I want to bring her home now," Daddy said when I'd finished telling the story. "Give her a proper burial. And a headstone. In the family plot."

"Bascomb says he doesn't know where Drew Jernigan hid the body," I said. "But I intend to find out. I want him to pay for what he did to her. To us."

"Keeley Rae," Daddy said, shaking his head. "You've done enough now. More than I could have done. You leave this up to me now."

"But Daddy," I protested.

He put his finger across my lips. "Shhh. I mean it. I want to think about this now. Think about what it all means."

"Vince Bascomb is at death's door already," I said gloomily. "Eaten up with cancer, from the looks of him. And anyway, he claims he wasn't out there when it happened. But it should mean obstruction of justice, for Drew and Lorna, in the very least," I said hotly. "And even Sonya. Mama was her cousin. How could she cover up for those criminals? It should mean jailtime for all of them. And if the law gets involved again, maybe they can track down Darvis Kane. We know he was alive up until the mid-eighties. Maybe they could put his picture on that *America's Most Wanted* program on television, and then—"

"Shhh," Daddy repeated wearily. "Not tonight. Give me some

time." He got up from the table and went back to the stove. "Supper's almost ready." He opened the oven door so I could get a peek. "Coq au vin," he said proudly. "Serena's recipe."

"Smells wonderful," I said. But my stomach was in knots. I forced myself to eat a few bites of Daddy's chicken, which, amazingly, tasted as good as it smelled. We managed some conversation, but whenever the discussion came too close to Mama, Daddy firmly declared the subject closed. I couldn't understand it. This was the moment I'd been waiting for for years. We finally had some answers. But Vince Bascomb was right about one thing. It didn't make us happy. And later, as I washed up the dinner dishes, I realized that it didn't even make us any different.

My mother was gone. She'd been gone for almost twenty-five years. For a long time I'd expected her to come back again. When, exactly, I wondered, had I given up? And when had my father given up?

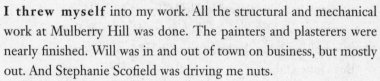

62

I threw myself into my work. All the structural and mechanical work at Mulberry Hill was done. The painters and plasterers were nearly finished. Will was in and out of town on business, but mostly out. And Stephanie Scofield was driving me nuts.

Her weekly visits had morphed into daily phone consults. "It's me!" she'd chirp gaily. "I woke up in the middle of the night, thinking about the towel bars in the downstairs powder room . . ."

I'd been thinking about braining her with one of the aforementioned towel bars.

Finally, the week before the dove hunt, I couldn't put it off any longer. I had one more buying trip to make for Mulberry Hill. The plan was for me to go up to High Point, North Carolina, to shop the after-market sample sales at all the big furniture showrooms. I'd pick up the last few pieces of furniture for the house, as well as shop for things for our other clients, and be back Friday, in time to supervise the preparations for Will's big dove hunt.

So far everything was fine. Miss Nancy had the food lined up, and Austin had been designing "rustic chic" flowers for weeks. Before I left, I got caller ID for the phones at the studio, and instructed Gloria to keep Stephanie the hell away from Mulberry Hill, at any cost.

"You keep on avoiding her, she's just going to come over here and be a pain in my ass," Gloria complained.

"She won't," I assured my aunt. "She knows Will's out of town, and I've told her I'm going up to High Point. At one point, God help me, she even talked about going with me. 'A shopping trip just for us girls!' is the way she put it. But she's got some big closing this week, and we've had to put it off."

"Pity," Gloria said. She pushed away the stack of fabric samples she'd been sorting through. "Are you going to see Sonya Wyrick when you're up there in North Carolina?"

I'd filled Gloria in on what I'd learned about Mama's death, and hoped she'd persuade Daddy to let me deal with Drew Jernigan and the others. But to my surprise, she'd sided with her brother. "Your daddy knows best this time, Keeley," Gloria had said.

"I want to see the look on her face when I tell Sonya I know Mama's dead, and that she had a hand in it," I told Gloria.

"But Wade said . . ."

"I know. And I promised him I'd let it alone. So I guess I will."

And I meant to keep my promise to my father. But when I reached the Kannapolis exit off I-85, I thought about turning off. Telling myself it was just a pit stop. I'd top off the rental van's gas tank, get a cold drink, and use the bathroom. But I wasn't really thirsty, and didn't need to pee. Without giving it another thought, I pulled into the Waffle House where we'd met with my cousin Sonya the previous month. I called information for her phone number, and reached her at home on my cell phone.

"Sonya? It's me, Keeley Murdock."

"Hey," she said, her voice cautious. "How are you?"

"I'm fine," I said, trying to sound finer than I actually was. "I was just passing through town on my way to High Point, and I wanted to get a bite to eat. I'm up here at the Waffle House, and I wondered if you'd join me for a cup of coffee."

"I'm kinda busy right now," she said. "The grandkids was here this weekend, and the house is all tore up, and I got prayer meeting tonight, and I'm giving the lesson."

"I've talked to Vince Bascomb," I cut in. "He told me Mama's dead. I know all about what happened that night. My daddy has hired a lawyer and is considering pressing legal charges against all of y'all."

"What!" she shrieked. "I wasn't even out there when it happened. If Vince Bascomb says I was, he's a goddamn liar."

Her churchiness had gone out the window with breathtaking suddenness.

"I'm at the Waffle House," I said, my voice steely. "See you in five minutes?"

"Ten," she said. "I got a cake in the oven."

I ordered coffee and rye toast, and amused myself by reading the song selections on the tabletop jukebox, all of which included something about Waffle House in the titles.

I was on my second cup when Sonya came lumbering into the restaurant. She glared at me as she eased herself into the booth. "You got no right to be calling me up and making accusations about something that happened twenty-five years ago," she said, right off the bat. "If it hadn't been for me, you still wouldn't know nothing about your mama. I done you a favor, and look how you treat me. My own flesh and blood, and you're threatening to call the cops on me? If your mama were alive today, she'd be ashamed of you."

"I doubt that very much," I said. "There's just one thing I want from you. I want to know where her body is."

She shrugged. "I don't know."

I leaned forward. "I don't believe you. You lied before. Vince Bascomb told me you were there. It was pitch dark. Nobody around. Drew Jernigan didn't hide that body by himself. I know you helped him."

"Vince Bascomb would rather tell a lie than eat when he's hungry," Sonya said. "He's a bad man. He's spent his whole life whoring and drinking and sinning. If you want the truth about your mama's death, you better ask somebody who knows the truth when she sees it."

"He's dying," I said abruptly. "He doesn't even weigh ninety pounds. He's got nothing to lose now. Why would he lie about any of this? Come on, Sonya. I know you were there. I know you know where her body is. You say you've got religion now. You say you're saved. Prove it. All my daddy wants now is to find Mama's body and give her a decent burial. If you're such a good Christian now, help us give her a Christian burial."

She drummed her stubby fingertips angrily on the laminate tabletop.

Finally she folded her hands in front of her. "She was dead when I got there. I don't care what Vince told you, she was already dead. Drew Jernigan and that fool Lorna Plummer were standing around like a couple of statues, and Darvis had already run off. Lorna wanted to leave Jeanine's body in the cabin and set it on fire, but Drew wasn't having none of that. He was afraid the fire would spread to his own place, or burn down the whole woods. He said he had a better idea. The well."

"What well?"

"There was an old drinking well out at Vince's hunting camp. It had gone dry years before; nobody ever used it. So that's what he did. He and Lorna drug her out of there, and put her down in that well, and chunked in a bunch of rocks and stuff to cover her up. As far as I know, that's right where she's at today. But I had nothing to do with it. I stayed back behind in the cabin, waiting for Vince. And when he got out there, we cleaned the place up. And that's all." She put her hand on her heart. "As God is my witness."

"Don't you dare bring God into this," I said angrily. "The last time I saw you, you were talking about forgiveness, and turning to God for the answers. When you had the answers all along." I took a deep breath. "I grew up thinking my mother had abandoned me. Thinking she was still alive, and didn't care enough about me to get in touch. You could have prevented that. You could have changed it with one phone call. But you and the others were more worried about saving your own sorry asses. So don't you dare talk to me about forgiveness. And don't you dare say you're flesh and blood to me. Or my mother."

Sonya blinked, and then burst into tears. Her chest heaved with sobs. Rivulets of mascara dripped down her cheeks. The people sitting at the counter turned around to stare, and then turned back to their waffles and eggs. I watched the show impassively, sipping my coffee, waiting for intermission.

Finally I'd had enough. I got the waitress to bring her a glass of cold water. I handed her a wad of paper napkins. She drank the water and blew her nose on the napkins, and managed to mop up some of the mascara on her face.

"I know you don't want to hear it," she whispered. "But I am sorry. I don't have a right to ask you to forgive me, and I won't. You know, I'm glad you came here today, and made me tell the truth. I been hiding from it a long time. You're right. I was just as much a part of it as they were. I been a coward. I been lying to myself, telling myself that because I'm a Christian, I'm forgiven. But you can't get forgiven until you take it all to Jesus. I took the rest of it to him years ago, the drinkin' and running around, the lying and hurtful things I done to my children and my friends. But that's the last thing I was holdin' on to. My one last, awful secret. And you made me face up to it. You helped me to lay that burden down. Now your daddy can call the law if he wants to. I'll stand up and tell the truth, and I won't care what happens on this earth. Because this is not my home."

She reached over and squeezed my hand so tightly, I thought I would scream with the pain.

"Thank you, Keeley Rae. For bringing me some peace. I thank you." She leaned across the table and planted a kiss on my cheek.

And I walked out.

I had to check myself in the sun visor mirror to see if I recognized myself. I'd gone into the Waffle House determined to confront Sonya and force her to tell me the truth. And I'd done that. I'd walked out of there with the one last missing piece to the puzzle. I knew now where my mother was. She was at the bottom of an abandoned well. And I was still no closer to feeling whole. Where was the closure you always hear people talking about? Where was the healing?

I thought about it the whole two hours between Kannapolis and High Point. And then I checked into my room at the motel next to the Atrium Furniture Mall. I was at ground zero for the furniture capital of the world. The twice yearly international market week had just closed, and now most of the showroom samples were on sale. The hell with closure, I told myself. The hell with healing. The hell with the Jernigans and the Plummers, and Stephanie Scofield and all of it. What I needed right now was some good old-fashioned retail therapy. But at wholesale prices.

Armed only with my checkbook and shopping list, I hit the streets. First I went over to Rose Furniture Company. The very sight of the building made me start feeling better. I'd done my research— one hundred eighty thousand square feet and more than six hundred different manufacturers.

I signed in and got myself assigned a salesman named Tim who was some kind of kin to the Rose family who'd opened the show- room in 1925. Six hours later I kicked my shoes off my swollen feet and fell onto the bed in my motel room.

The van was full to overflowing, and I'd paid for the rest of my finds to be shipped down to Madison the following week. For the den, I'd bought a pair of luscious leather club chairs, similar to the an- tique ones I'd put in the pump house, two overstuffed sofas, a heart- pine armoire for the entertainment center, and assorted side tables, along with a massive wrought-iron and glass-topped coffee table. I'd bought a pair of Ralph Lauren four-poster beds for one of the guest rooms, and, God help me, a Martha Stewart bed for another room. I bought a long oval table for the family dining room, and eight repro- duction Hitchcock chairs to go with it. After leaving Rose Furniture I'd gone to my favorite big antiques showroom, then hit Butler's Elec- tric for lighting fixtures, and finally back to the Atrium, to About Last Night, a linen showroom where I let myself go nuts buying the creamiest, most exquisite towels and bed linens I could find—aside from the monogrammed Pratesi sheets I'd already ordered for the master bedroom.

The next day, Thursday, I allowed myself one last binge. I started at the Boyles gallery, but by three o'clock I'd run out of steam. I was easing myself back into my room when my cell phone began ringing.

"Keeley?" Gloria was out of breath. "I think you better get back here in a hurry."

"Right now? I was going to take a hot bath and order some dinner from room service. I thought I'd head back first thing in the morning. You won't believe all the great stuff I've found."

"Now," Gloria said. "You better get back here right now. There's trouble out at Mulberry Hill."

63

"So far, so good," I told myself as I drove through the unlocked gates at Mulberry Hill late that evening. I'd driven straight through from High Point, arriving around ten P.M.

It wasn't until I approached the meadow area that I had an inkling about the disaster Gloria had hinted at over the phone. For the first time I noticed that the drive was suddenly lit by more than moonlight. Uplights sent eerie shadows through the leathery leaves of the huge old magnolias, and there were downlights mounted high in the tops of some of the pecans and oaks. As I got to the area where the driveway bisected the meadow, I had to pull off the drive.

It was lined with heavy machinery; a backhoe, bushhog, and other pieces of industrial yellow equipment whose names I didn't know. And right in the middle of the left side of the meadow, right where bales of hay and a tent should have been erected, there was now a gaping hole in the landscape.

A pond, I guess you'd call it. A huge pond had sprung up where none had been on Monday. The treetop lights glanced off the surface of the water, and now I could see that there was a fountain in the middle of the pond with a pair of creatures—seahorses? centaurs?— spurting water from their gaping mouths.

It was . . . amazing. It was spectacular. It was perfect—for Vegas. And it was, as Gloria had so aptly described, a disaster for Mulberry Hill.

I pulled the Volvo up beside the largest piece of equipment and hiked over to the pond. "Crap," I said, moaning. The meadow had been mowed—no, obliterated. In its place was a thick carpet of emerald green sod. I trudged on toward the pond, to get a better look. A pair of ornate wrought-iron benches had been thoughtfully arranged at the water's edge, and as I approached, I heard a loud honking, and flapping wings, and suddenly, some large black creature was rushing toward me, flapping its wings, and hissing and braying. It nipped at my ankles, and I turned tail and ran like hell for the safety of the Volvo, where I rolled up the windows, locked the doors, and proceeded to bang my head repeatedly on the dashboard.

When I woke up the next morning, I tried to convince myself that it had all been a bad dream. I'd been overtired. It had been dark. Maybe I'd taken the wrong turn off and ended up at another Greek Revival plantation house on the outskirts of Madison.

I drove straight out to the house, without even stopping for coffee. In the daylight the massive iron gates looked the same. The drive looked the same, and as I approached the meadow, I could see the same hulking yellow heavy machinery.

Only now the pieces were in motion, being loaded onto two long flatbed trailers. I pulled off the road, got out of the Volvo, and went over to the man driving the first of the trailers.

"What the hell are you doing?" I demanded.

"Loading up," he said. "Y'all only rented this stuff for three days."

"Y'all? Who is y'all? I certainly did not order any of this stuff. And I sure as hell didn't order anybody to dig any pond, or to knock down any trees out here."

"Hey. I just pick up and deliver." He picked up a clipboard with a sheet of yellow paper on it. "Mulberry Hill. This is it. Right?"

I nodded, but pointed at the signature at the bottom of the sheet. "Who signed for it? Who authorized the work?"

He picked up the clipboard and handed it to me, but the handwriting was an indecipherable scrawl.

"It's a mistake," I told him. "A horrible mistake. The owner didn't order any pond. He doesn't want a pond. He wants a field for dove hunting."

The driver laughed. "Dove, huh? He might want to change his mind about that. Once he gets some brush growing at the edge he might eventually attract some ducks, or something like that. But lady—no respectable dove is coming near that place now."

I glanced over at the meadow. Or the lawn, as it could more correctly be called now. In the daylight I could see that some sort of rose garden had been planted near the seating area.

And the fountain. The fountain was even more hideous in the light of day. It appeared to be a pair of unicorns, spouting water from their horns.

"Put it back," I said.

"Huh?"

"I want you to put it back. Fill in the pond. Scrape up that sod. And that fountain." I shuddered. "Take that godawful fountain back from wherever it came from."

He scratched his head and smiled. "You're pulling my leg—right?" And then he turned around and went back to loading up the heavy equipment.

I sighed heavily and drove on to the house. Adam, the project foreman, was out on the veranda, looking at a section of railing one of his painters had just primed.

"Hey, Keeley," he greeted me.

"Adam," I said sternly. "Did I tell you to have a pond dug out in the meadow?"

"No ma'am," he said.

"Does the landscape plan call for a pond?"

"Not that I know of."

"Did Will order a pond?"

He laughed. "Nah. What would he want with a pond?"

I closed my eyes and took a deep breath. "Then who in the hell had a pond dug and a hideous fountain, and grass and rose bushes installed out there? How can this have happened? We've got a couple dozen men coming over here tomorrow for a dove hunt. This cannot be happening."

He stuck his hands in his back pockets. "It was Miss Stephanie."

"Stephanie?"

He nodded, abashed. "I come out here Monday morning, and the earthmover was already there, doing its thing. The next thing I know, there's a backhoe, and a bushhog, ripping up all of Will's dove habitat. I tried calling him on his mobile phone to check on it, but I didn't get an answer. Pretty soon Miss Stephanie drove up. She was pretty excited about the whole thing, I can tell you. She said it was a surprise for the boss."

"She ordered a pond? And the fountain? And rose bushes? As a surprise?"

"And the swans. A pair of 'em. I never seen black swans before. I think they must be some kind of special item. If I was you, I'd stay clear of 'em. They're mean as a couple of snakes."

"Swans." I moaned. "Special-order swans."

"Mean-as-hell black swans," Adam volunteered. "Worse than Rottweilers, if you ask me."

As we were standing there, Nancy Rockmore came walking slowly toward us, leaning heavily on her canes and shaking her head. "I still can't believe it. The caterer called me yesterday and asked me if I wanted the tent beside the pond, and I said, 'Pond? What pond?' There ain't no pond at Mulberry Hill.' And he said, 'Check again.' That's when I called your aunt."

"We're screwed," I said. "Completely screwed."

"This is her," Miss Nancy said. "That goddamn Stephanie."

"It sure wasn't me," I said. "According to Adam, she planned it as a surprise for Will."

"Surprise my ass. Now what are we gonna do?" she demanded.

"I asked the heavy equipment guy if he could just fill it back up and rip up the sod. He laughed like crazy. And he kept on loading the stuff on the trailer."

"We can't have a dove hunt out in that meadow," Miss Nancy said. "It ain't even a meadow anymore. We'll just have to cancel, that's all." She grimaced. "The boss's been talking this thing up for weeks. He's got guys coming in from all over the country, including some of the big honchos from Victoria's Secret, coming in from New Jersey. We gotta think of something else."

We both leaned on the railing and looked out over the landscape. We'd been so close. And now this. I'd thrown myself into my work, hoping to forget all the crap going on in my personal life. And now I'd run up against another brick wall. I felt like crying.

I wanted my daddy. But that gave me an idea.

"I'll call Daddy," I told Miss Nancy. "He knows every hunter in three counties. Maybe we can lease a field or something. And we'll just have to call everybody on the invitation list and tell them the plan has changed a little bit."

"I'll head back to the plant," she said. "The invitation list is on my computer. We'll have to split it up, to get all the phone calls made in time. Call me there when you know something."

I sat out on the front porch of Mulberry Hill to make my phone calls. But I couldn't look at the pond. I turned my back to it and called Daddy at the car lot. He'd been invited to the dove hunt too, and he was clearly disappointed that it wasn't going to happen as planned.

"Damn," he said. "I been waiting for years to get invited out there for that hunt. I even bought a new shotgun for the occasion."

"Can you do it?" I asked. "Can you help me find another field to lease?"

"Pretty short notice," he said. "Most folks who have a field have already made arrangements to either hunt it themselves or lease it out. Lemme make some phone calls, shug."

An hour later he called back. "The news ain't good," he said. "Sorry, shug."

I was just getting ready to call Miss Nancy to deliver the bad news when I saw the yellow Caddy come rolling slowly down the driveway. I saw it stop at the edge of the meadow. I saw Will get out, run over to the edge of the pond, and look wildly around, as though he wanted to make sure he wasn't hallucinating. And then I saw one of the swans go on the attack, darting at him, beak open, ready for the kill. To his credit, Will was a lot braver than I'd been. He kicked at the thing, driving it back to the pond. And when the other swan came flapping over to rescue its mate, that's when Will made a run for the Caddy.

The Caddy sped the rest of the way down the driveway, around to the back of the house. I sighed and went inside to face the music.

"What the *fuck?*" Will's face was contorted with anger. "What the hell went on around here while I was gone? I'm away five days, and you manage to turn my dove field into a fucking golf course?"

"No," I started to say. "I mean, I didn't do it. I think it was a mis-understanding."

"You bet your fucking life there's been a misunderstanding," he shouted. We were standing in the library. The rugs were down, the bookshelves had been installed, and some of the furniture was in place. The only piece of furniture Will had chosen, a huge nineteenth-century planter's desk, sat in the middle of the room, and he stood with his hands clamped on the back of the leather chair behind the desk, glaring at me. This library was the closest thing in the house to being finished. Will's voice echoed throughout the empty house.

I walked over and closed the door to the library so that Adam and his workers wouldn't witness my humiliation.

"I can't believe this," Will said, lowering his voice. "I know you've had your own ideas about this project all along, but I can't believe you would deliberately sabotage the one thing I planned for myself."

"I didn't sabotage anything. I was as surprised as you were when I got here last night and I saw that pond."

"And where the hell were you?" he demanded. "You were sup-posed to be right here at Mulberry Hill, supervising this project. I'm paying you thousands and thousands of dollars, and you go running off on another project?"

"I wasn't running off on another project," I said, getting hot now. "I was making one last buying trip for this house. To High Point. So

I could save you some money and make this fucking ridiculous deadline of yours. Which I told you in the beginning was impossible."

"But you agreed," he insisted. His face was flushed with streaks of red, and each freckle stood out like an angry exclamation point. "You agreed that you would do it. And I've paid you a shitload of money for what? That *disaster* out there in my dove field?"

I leaned across the desk so that my face was only inches from his. All the frustrations of the week came flooding back. All the disappointments, the shock, the sorrow. My work had been my last retreat from all of it, and now that had turned to shit too. And he was blaming me. Me.

"I had nothing to do with that disaster out in your dove field," I said, enunciating each word slowly and clearly. "You wanted to keep your dove hunt a secret from your little girlfriend? Well, apparently she was planning a surprise of her own. Adam said she came out here yesterday to personally supervise the installation."

"Stephanie?" Will shook his head. "She wouldn't do something like that."

"It's all Stephanie," I said. "And if you weren't so fucking blind, you'd see that."

"No," Will said. "I can't believe—"

"Are you that pussy-whipped?" I cried. "She's turning this place into her own personal Versailles. The woman is a fraud. You think you're building this place so she'll settle down here and raise a family? Have you got your head totally up your own ass? You haven't even popped the question yet and she's already shopping for a house in Buckhead. With a swimming pool and tennis courts. How long do you think she's going to live in podunk Madison? She might stay out here at first, maybe on weekends. Then every other weekend. Then maybe just for parties. You won't even have Erwin around to pee on your shoes. The only company you'll have is those damn black designer swans."

"Stephanie isn't like that. She loves Mulberry Hill," Will

protested. "We're going to build Loving Cup together, right here in Madison. You're wrong. Dead wrong."

"No, you're wrong," I said. "She's already looking for office space for Loving Cup in her building in Atlanta. You don't believe me? Ask her yourself."

"You're jealous of her," Will said, his voice going suddenly icy. "Of her taste. Her success."

"Jealous?" Now it was my voice that was echoing throughout the room. "Of that money-grubbing social climber? Of her taste? My God, what a joke. Did you see that monstrosity of a fountain she installed out there? It looks like a reject from a New Orleans bordello. But that's perfect. I can see now that you are a perfect match for her. Because you are both just as shallow as that fucking pond."

"You're fired," Will said. He swiveled his chair around to show me his back.

"No sir," I told him. "I quit." I reached into my briefcase and brought out the thick file folder of invoices for all the furniture I'd just bought in High Point. I opened it and let the pages and pages go floating down over his head.

64

A cold front moved in overnight. Saturday morning I woke up at seven o'clock. I tossed and turned and tried to go back to sleep, but it was no use. I got up and looked out the window. The street downstairs was slick with rain, and standing that close to the drafty window, I could feel that the temperature had dropped.

While the coffee was brewing, I got dressed. Blue jeans, flannel shirt, thick socks, and hiking boots. Okay, they weren't actual hiking boots. I'd never on-purpose hiked in my life. But these boots were flat-soled and leather and as close as I came. I poured the coffee into a thermos and headed over to Daddy's house.

It was early, but I wasn't worried about waking him. My father has always been "up with the chickens" in the early morning hours, as he'd say. He'd be surprised to see me up this early, but I wanted to confess to him that I'd broken my promise and gone to see Sonya. I wanted to tell him about Mama's burial place, and get him to go with me out to Vince Bascomb's hunting camp. In short, I wanted to find Mama.

But when I pulled into Daddy's driveway, I saw that Serena's blue Hyundai was snuggled alongside his truck in the carport. I backed out and drove on.

This is a good thing, I told myself. *She is a nice woman. He deserves some happiness. It's time.* All the same, I was fighting back the tears. The early morning streets were empty. I felt so horribly alone. I almost turned back. I didn't want to face that desolate cabin by myself. It was too cold, too dark, too wet.

I went anyway. I drove right past the turnoff for the Jernigans' shack, and on down the road to the driveway to Bascomb's. As I turned in, a covey of mourning doves that had been pecking away on the broken asphalt rose up and scattered into the treetops. Fly away, doves, I thought. Fly away home.

The cold front had brought rain and high winds. The drive was littered with bits of broken tree limbs and blanketed with fallen leaves. More leaves were still sifting down from the treetops bent over the road. Here and there, bits of bright pink ribbon stood out from the tapestry of leaves. Survey flags. Had the property already been sold? And was Will the buyer? Maybe he would get his dove field after all.

I parked the Volvo in the same place I had on my last visit. I was glad of the boots and jeans this time around. It was copperhead mating season. I hesitated a moment, then rooted around in the Volvo's trunk until I found what I needed—a wooden yardstick.

At first I deliberately skirted the cabin, walking toward the water's edge, scuffing my feet and beating the weeds with my yardstick to chase away any lovesick snakes. Then I chided myself. If the well had been the only source for drinking water, the cabin would probably have been built as close as possible to the well.

I squared my shoulders and worked my way back up the gentle slope toward the cabin. I stared at it, trying to picture my mother out here. Had she sat on the glider on that now-crumbling back porch, with her lover's arm tucked around her? Had she walked in these woods, maybe picking up a stray leaf to bring me for my nature collection? Had Darvis Kane taken her for a moonlight ride in that red rowboat? Was this where she came to escape the drudgery of being a wife and mother?

I tried to reconcile my mundane memories of her, dabbing Joy perfume behind her ears, ironing my daddy's handkerchiefs, fixing my school lunches, with Sonya's version; Jeanine, young and yearning for the forbidden, for adventure and intrigue.

I felt myself tense as I got closer to the cabin, and resolved not to stare at it. She was not in that house. Not anymore.

Wielding the yardstick like a sickle, I whacked viciously through the kudzu vines and fallen leaves. Once the stick hit something solid, and I bent down to take a look. I'd found what looked like the remains of Bascomb's trash pile. With no garbage pickup out this far in the country, most folks simply burned their trash. Old charred tree trunks ringed the fire circle, and with my stick, I poked bits of rusted tin cans, beer bottles, and broken glass.

I worked my way around the house, whacking at random, torn between wanting to find the well and wanting to run far away from this place of ruined lives. But something kept me there.

After an hour I was damp and tired and thirsty. I went back to the Volvo and poured myself a cup of coffee. I was drinking it, savoring the heat between my hands, leaning against the hood of the car, when I heard leaves crackling underfoot, twigs breaking, and voices. Voices coming from the Jernigans' property line.

I had my car keys out, ready to flee, but then I recognized one of the voices.

It was Big Drew. "Been a long time," his voice boomed out. "He let the place go to shit. Not that it matters now."

As I watched, two figures emerged from the trees. Both men were dressed much the same as me, except that they wore vests of hunter safety orange, and baseball caps. It was Drew all right, and with him, his older son. A.J.

I could leave right now. Get in the car and haul ass out of there. But A.J. would recognize the car. There would be questions. Recriminations. It was too late to go.

The men grew closer, and I could see that Drew was puzzled by my presence there.

"Keeley?" A.J. called, when they were a hundred yards away. "Is that you?"

"It's me," I said grimly. I put the cap back on the thermos and stowed it in the car, and then I waited.

"Hey there, Keeley," Drew said as he approached.

"Hello," I said coolly.

"Whatcha doing out here?" he asked. "It's private property, you know."

"I know," I said. "It's Vince Bascomb's property. I'm sure he wouldn't mind my coming out to take a look around."

"What for?" A.J. asked with a laugh. "Ain't nothin' out here anymore. The house is fallen down. There's snakes and poison ivy. And spiders. You know how you hate spiders. Not even you could save this old place."

"I'm looking for something," I said. "An old abandoned well."

"Why?" A.J. wondered.

"Ask your father."

Drew's eyes narrowed.

A.J. looked from me to his father. "Dad?"

"I don't know what she's talking about," Drew said.

"Okay," I said. "How about I get to ask a question now? What are you two doing out here?" I glared at Drew. "It's private property, you know."

"It's ours now," A.J. volunteered. "Vince sold it to us. We own the whole cove now. We've got a buyer interested already." He grinned. "Sweet, huh? It'll be a gated community." He gave me a meaningful look. "I'm saving this lot for myself. Once I get it cleared, tear the old place down, it'll have the best lake view on the cove. Better than the shack's even. But what's this about a well?"

"Ask your father," I repeated. "It's a pretty interesting story. Kind of a mystery, I think you'd say."

"Dad?" A.J. asked, his sunny face now puzzled. "I don't get it."

"She's nuts," Drew said. "Bad news. If that scene she made at your rehearsal dinner didn't prove that to you, this should." He put his hand on A.J.'s shoulder. "Let's go, son. I told your mother we'd be back for breakfast."

"Was that part of the deal you made with GiGi over the years?" I asked Drew, keeping my voice light, conversational even. "That you could stay out all night, do whatever you wanted, with whomever you wanted, as long as you made it back in time for breakfast with her and the kids?"

"Keeley!" A.J. said sharply. "Cut it out."

"Ask him about the well," I said again. "He still hasn't answered you, you know."

"Dad?"

Drew turned his back on us and started tromping through the woods. "I'll see you back at the Jeep."

A.J. looked torn. "Why haven't you returned my calls? What's going on with you?"

"Tell him about the well," I hollered, running to catch up with Drew. "Go ahead, Big Drew. Tell him about all the parties out here at Vince's place."

Drew stopped, turned around, and took a step toward me. I thought for a minute he might reach out and slap my face. I could tell he wanted to. "Shut up!" he hissed.

Now A.J. was right beside me. "What the hell is going on between you two?"

Drew shook his head, as though to warn me off. But it was too late.

"They used to call this the hunting camp," I cried, gesturing toward the ruined cabin. "Hunting pussy is what they did. This is where Vince Bascomb brought his girlfriend. My mother's cousin Sonya Wyrick. It was private, out of the way. A perfect little love nest for married men. And Vince was willing to share too. Your dad had a key. He used to bring Lorna Plummer out here."

A.J. looked like he'd been slapped. "Paige's mom?" he whispered, staring at his dad. "You and Mrs. Plummer?"

Drew didn't bother to deny it.

"And my mother came out here with her boyfriend. Darvis Kane. The man she ran away with all those years ago, right, Drew? It was just one big old party for cheaters, wasn't it?"

Drew Jernigan stood very still. I remembered Sonya's description of him the night my mother was killed. "Like a statue," she'd said.

He was stone. He was granite. He was impenetrable. Nothing touched him.

"Vince Bascomb told me the whole story," I said now.

Drew flinched, just slightly, but enough so that I knew he did have a pulse.

"They were out here that night," I told A.J. "Your dad and Lorna. My mom and Darvis Kane. Kane had been drinking. He slapped my mother around, and then he left. When he came back, he had a gun. There was a struggle, and my mom was shot."

A.J. looked horrified. "Dad?"

But Drew was still a statue.

I jerked my head in the direction of the cabin. "She died. Right over there. They never went for help. They never called the police. They were too worried about covering their own butts. Your dad and Lorna dragged my mother's body out of there and they stuffed her down a well. They covered her with rocks!"

A.J. winced.

"And then they went back to town like nothing happened," I continued. "I bet you made it back in time for breakfast with GiGi that morning too, didn't you, Drew?"

I fell on him then, pounding his chest with my fists. "Didn't you? You and GiGi and your boys had breakfast together every morning. And I never saw my mother again, you son-of-a-bitch." He didn't move, didn't even try to protect himself from my blows. "You son-of-a-bitch," I cried, clawing at his face. "All these years she's been out here, and we never knew."

A.J. grabbed me by the wrists and pulled me gently away from his father. He wrapped his arms around me, but I tore myself away. I wouldn't, couldn't take comfort from him. Not from anybody. Not today. I wiped my runny nose on the sleeve of my shirt. "Show me the well," I said, my voice shaking. "We want to bring her home.

My father wants to bury his wife. You can at least have that much decency."

"Dad?" A.J. asked.

Drew just shook his head.

"Tell her where the fucking well is!" A.J. shouted. "For God's sake, Dad, show her. You owe them that much."

Drew sighed. He pointed toward the lake. "Out there. When Georgia Power built the dam to create the lake, all that land was flooded within less than a month afterward. She's somewhere out there, under maybe twenty, thirty feet of water."

"I don't believe you," I said. "You're just lying to save your own skin. I'll ask Mr. Bascomb. He'll tell me the truth. He doesn't have anything to lose anymore."

"He's dead," A.J. blurted. "He died Tuesday. The funeral was Thursday."

"Poor bastard," Drew said. He gave me a coolly appraising look. "Don't be so quick to judge others, Keeley. Your mother was a cheap little tramp. We did you and your daddy a favor keeping that quiet all these years." His smile was sardonic. "But don't worry. Your secret's safe." He turned and looked at A.J. "Coming?"

A.J. shook his head no. I watched Drew tromp off through the underbrush, back toward home and a forgiving wife, and I went to pieces again.

"Son-of-a-bitch," I screamed at him, sinking to the cold, wet ground. "You didn't have to leave her out there, you son-of-a-bitch."

"Keeley," A.J. said, kneeling down beside me. He put his hand gently on my shoulder. "Let me take you home."

I shook him off. "Don't touch me."

65

Saturday night I threw a pity party for myself. The refreshments were simplicity itself: chili-flavored Fritos squeezed with lime and a tub of frozen margaritas.

For entertainment, I turned on A&E and watched an old Shirley MacLaine movie called *Gambit*, where, through the magic of movie makeup, Shirley and Michael Caine managed to convince the world that Shirley was actually a reincarnated Asian goddess.

The phone rang half a dozen times, but the caller ID informed me that it was A.J., and since I was fresh out of understanding, I finally turned the ringer off so that Shirley and I could enjoy our evening without interruption.

I woke up around noon Sunday, with a mouth that tasted of dead cactus. A shower helped matters, as did some cheesy scrambled eggs and bacon. I was puttering around the apartment when the phone rang. I glanced at the caller ID to make sure it wasn't A.J.

Instead it was a woman named Tiara, who said she was with Ryder rental. "You have our van," Tiara said accusingly. "It was supposed to have been turned in yesterday. Miss Murdock, we have a reservation for that van, and it's supposed to be picked up at four this afternoon."

"The van," I said, slapping my forehead. "I'd completely forgotten. I'll have it there by four."

"Three," she corrected me. "It takes us an hour to clean and service it for the next customer."

I hung up and went to the window and looked out. The van was right out front where I'd parked it Friday. And it was still full of furniture. Furniture that belonged to Will Mahoney. Who was no longer my client.

"Crap," I said, dialing Austin. There was no way I could unload all that stuff by myself. I let it ring six times, then hung up. "Crap," I said again, dialing Daddy's number out of desperation. With a sister and a daughter in the interior design business, my father absolutely hated moving furniture. He'd declared himself out of the moving business several years ago, but he'd just have to break with policy for this one last emergency.

Daddy's phone rang four times before his answering machine picked up. I slammed the receiver down and scowled. It was probably his turn to spend the night at Serena's. This was plain pathetic. My fifty-something father was getting more action than me. Way more.

I went out to the van and climbed in. I would rather have taken a beating than ask Will for help, but that was just what I was going to have to do. Anyway, it was his furniture. Why should I kill myself unloading it?

When I got out to Mulberry Hill, the gates were open. As I approached the meadow, I caught my first break of the day. Two pickup trucks were parked at the edge of the pond.

I recognized the big silver Ford F-150 as belonging to Adam, as in Adam, the big strong construction foreman. I didn't know who the other truck belonged to, but it didn't matter. Chances were very good that it was a guy—a guy who could probably be sweet-talked into helping me unload the van, if I played my cards right.

I pulled up alongside Adam's truck and hopped out. I heard the chug-chugging of a motor then, and smelled the unmistakable scent of gasoline. As I got closer, I saw the source of the racket. A huge gas-powered pump sat on the ground, and a thick hose ran from the pond to the pump, with water gushing out of the discharge hose on the other side of the bank.

The men had had a busy morning. The rose bushes had been yanked out of the ground and tossed in the bed of the other truck, alongside the fancy wrought-iron furniture. There was a large wooden crate in the back of the F-150, and from the amount of hissing and quacking coming from it, I guessed the designer swans had been evicted.

Adam and another man were standing in the middle of the pond, wearing rubber hip boots and circling the fountain as though they couldn't decide whether to climb it or wrestle it.

"Hey, Adam!" I called, standing at the edge of the pond.

"Hey, Keeley," he said, turning and waving at me.

"What are y'all doing?" I asked.

"Ripping out this fountain and draining the pond," Adam said, grinning. "The boss's orders."

"The man has no appreciation for fine art," I said, giving him a wink.

"Guess not," Adam said. He cocked his head. "Hey, uh, I thought you were fired."

"No. I quit," I said. "But I've got one last delivery to make." I gestured toward the van. "That thing is full of furniture for Mulberry Hill, and I need to get it unloaded before three, when I have to return it to the rental place. Do you think you two could help me out?" I batted my eyelashes exaggeratedly. "Pretty please?"

"Sure," Adam said. "Soon as me and Jorge get this statue thing out of here. It'll take a while for the pond to drain. Then we got some truckloads of dirt coming to fill it in. We could get the furniture, right, Jorge?"

"No problem," Jorge said. "Soon as we take care of this horse."

"They're unicorns," I informed him. "And they're magical, you know."

"That's good," Jorge laughed. "Because we're fixing to make 'em disappear. You watch."

He clambered up on top of a thick concrete post that supported the statue, put his arms around it, and tugged. His face contorted with the effort of it, but the unicorns did not budge. "It won't move," he told Adam. "They must have cemented it on here."

"Well, we gotta make it move," Adam said. "The boss said it had better be out of here by the time he comes back. If you saw the look on his face like I did, you'd know he means business." With that, Adam waded out and climbed up the muddy embankment to his truck, where he fetched two lethal-looking sledgehammers.

"Now you're talking," Jorge said, grabbing one of the sledgehammers. He circled the unicorns looking for a likely place to start, and with no further ceremony, hauled off and gave it a mighty whack.

"Uuuuh," he grunted. A small chunk of concrete broke off the unicorn's flank.

Adam took up position on the second of the unicorns and proceeded to give it a whack. The two of them were hammering away, and the pond was slowly lowering. I sat on the tailgate of Adam's truck to watch the show.

Suddenly a white Porsche Boxster came speeding down the driveway. It screeched to a stop beside Adam's truck, and a woman in a set of white silk tennis warm-ups jumped out of the driver's seat.

I saw Adam look at Jorge. "Uh-oh," Jorge said softly.

"What's going on here?" Stephanie cried, surveying the scene before her. "What have you morons done to my beautiful pond?"

As if on key, Erwin hopped up on the Porsche's dashboard and started to bark. "Aaar-aar-aar-aar-aar." He sounded like a VW with a bad starter.

"Get away from my statue," Stephanie demanded, striding over to the edge of the pond. "Don't you dare touch those unicorns."

"Sorry, ma'am," Adam called. "It's the boss's orders. He wants his dove field back."

"Well, he can't have it back," she announced. "The fountain stays. Now, get out of there and turn this pump thing off."

Jorge put his sledgehammer down and leaned on it, waiting to see what his foreman would do.

Adam just shook his head. "Ma'am? I'm sorry as can be, but Will wants this fountain out of here. And the pond too. And he's the one who signs my paycheck."

Adam swung his sledgehammer and landed a blow on the unicorn's side, and Jorge followed suit.

Bravo, I wanted to cheer. Well done, Adam.

For the first time Stephanie looked around and saw me sitting ringside.

"Keeley," she said pleadingly, "Those idiots are destroying my statue. Make them stop."

"I can't," I said. "Haven't you heard? I don't work here anymore. I got fired. I'm not in charge of anything around here."

Her eyes flared. "Well, I haven't been fired." She clapped her hands. "You men. Stop that this instant. That is a very expensive sculpture. I had it shipped all the way from Italy. It's a signed, limited edition Vesuvio."

I thought it looked more like something from the Franklin Mint myself, but Erwin seemed to agree with his mistress, because he hopped out of the car and ran around now in little circles, barking and hopping with anger and energy.

"Sorry, ma'am," Adam said. "Boss's orders." He reared back with the sledgehammer and knocked out a good-sized chunk of the unicorn's nostril, which landed on the bank with a thud.

Stephanie screamed as though it were her own flesh being assaulted. "Stop it!"

Unwilling to let Adam outdo him, Jorge chimed in with his own sledgehammer, which Adam soon joined, until the two of them were playing their own version of the "Anvil Chorus." When a piece of the unicorn's plumed tail whizzed by my ear I ducked down behind the hood of the truck.

But Stephanie was fearless. "I said STOP IT!" she screamed. "STOPIT, STOPIT, STOPIT!" She was hopping up and down, and Erwin was barking in matching staccato, "Arfarfarfarfarf!"

When Adam's sledgehammer dislodged his unicorn's magical horn, this action seemed to have triggered Stephanie's panic button. Suddenly she was splashing her way into the pond. She launched herself forward, grabbing for Adam's sledgehammer, but he spun effortlessly out of the way, and she did an awkward belly-flop.

Total immersion did little to dampen Stephanie's fury. When she emerged, water streaming from every orifice, sputtering and spitting, Adam guffawed, a serious tactical error on his part. Without warning, she hauled off and socked him square in the crotch.

Adam howled, dropped the sledgehammer, and doubled over in pain, clutching his privates as though to ward off any further assault. Jorge, wide-eyed, backpedaled as fast as possible away from her.

Erwin seemed to be cheering from the sidelines, "Aar, aar, aar, aar, aar, aar," which, when you think of it, must be the dachshund equivalent of "Rah-rah-rah!"

Now Stephanie was diving for the sledgehammer, bringing it up and thrusting it menacingly at Adam, who, with no place else to hide, had positioned himself on the far side of the unicorn.

"Get away from my statue, motherfucker," Stephanie said, lunging at him with the sledgehammer. "I mean it! You get away from my Vesuvio, or you'll be singing soprano in the church choir in this god-forsaken hellhole. I'll chop your nuts off and feed them to these goldfish."

"Stephanie!"

The shocked voice cut through the cool morning air like a hot knife. All four of us turned to see Will standing behind us, hands on hips, a look of shock and disgust on his face.

As if on cue, Stephanie dropped the sledgehammer and burst into tears.

"Oh Will," she cried, wading toward him. "Look what they've done! They've chopped up my Vesuvio! I tried to stop them and then Adam turned on me. He actually threatened me with that axe thing. I've never been so terrified in my life."

She'd reached the bank now, and she was trying to climb out, but couldn't seem to get a proper toehold with her tiny designer Nikes. "Will," she whimpered, after sliding belly-first in the thick red mud.

The white silk warm-ups were caked with mud, her blond hair lay flat against her skull, and her melted mascara ran down both cheeks. She staggered back to her feet and held out her arms, imploringly. "Will?"

"Christ," he muttered. Then he turned around and stalked back in the direction of the house.

"Will," Stephanie cried. I couldn't stand it any longer. I got up and reached down and hauled her up onto the bank. She flopped on her back like a beached carp. Erwin trotted over, yipped, and tenderly licked her face.

66

"**All of this?**" Will asked, peering into the open cargo doors of the van.

"Yep," I said. "All for you. I believe you've already seen the invoices."

He glowered at me. "Where does it go?"

"Anywhere you like," I said. "It's your house."

"I mean, where do you want it all to go?"

"I don't work for you anymore, so it doesn't make any difference to me. Maybe you should ask Stephanie."

"Not funny," Will said. He chewed on the inside of his cheek for a minute, and then looked over at Adam and Jorge, who were waiting expectantly with the furniture dolly at the edge of the loading ramp.

"Keeley," he said, finally. "Could you step into the library, please?"

I glanced down at my watch. "Okay. But just for a minute. This van is due back at Ryder in half an hour."

"I'll pay for an extra day," Will said. He looked at Adam and Jorge. "Why don't you guys go out to the kitchen and get yourselves a sandwich or something?"

I followed him into the library and he carefully closed the door behind him. He gestured toward the only seat in the room, the leather wing chair behind the desk. "Would you like to sit?"

"Sure," I said. I sat down and folded my hands on the desktop and waited.

Will paced around the room. He reached down into one of the boxes stacked against the bookshelves and brought out a leather-bound volume.

"Keeley," he said, his voice low, his eyes on the pages he was thumbing through, "I've been an ass."

"That," I agreed, "is an understatement."

"I've been an ass in a lot of ways. About Stephanie, this house, blaming you for that disaster out in the dove field, all of it. I, uh, got caught up in some crazy fantasy, and then I was concentrating on getting Loving Cup back on track, and I guess I just lost touch with reality."

He looked up and smiled crookedly. "The only thing I did right since I moved here was to hire you in the first place."

"Probably."

He stared down at the book. "As it turns out, you were right about her all along. She, uh, didn't have any real interest in living in Madison full-time."

"Imagine that," I said. "How'd you figure it out?"

"A broker called me yesterday, wanting to set up an appointment to come out and list the house."

"This house?" Now I was shocked.

He nodded. "He was with some Atlanta real estate agency that handles what they call exclusive properties. He'd been showing Stephanie houses in Buckhead, and I guess she let it slip that I owned a plantation house over here, and that we'd eventually be selling it. I think he actually jumped the gun. I called her as soon as I got off the phone with the guy, and of course she tried to deny it, but I even had the guy's name and the name of the agency, so she couldn't really lie her way out of it."

"Ouch," I said. "I'm sorry you had to find out about her that way."

He sighed. "Better now than later. Anyway, I, uh, want to apologize to you. And I'd really like it if you'd come back to work for me. I want you to finish up Mulberry Hill."

Now he was standing directly in front of the desk, looking down at me. "Without any interference. Or outside influences."

I gave it some thought. "What about that Thanksgiving deadline?"

He reached in the pocket of his slacks and brought out a small black velvet box. He looked at it sadly, then put it back in his pocket. "No more deadline. Take all the time you need."

67

On Wednesday Gloria came back from the post office with a package, which she laid on my drawing table. It was wrapped in brown paper recycled from a Bi-Lo grocery sack and addressed to me in wavery black ink. "Open it," she instructed.

I slit the box with the edge of my scissors, and out slid a thick rectangle wrapped in a cardboard sleeve. I cut the tape on the sleeve, unfolded the flaps of cardboard, and found myself looking down at a formal black and white portrait of Jeanine Murry Murdock. She wore the same kind of black off-the-shoulder drape I'd worn in my own high school senior picture. Her dark hair was teased and flipped up at the ends, and her lips were parted, just slightly, into a smile that promised everything.

Gloria stood by my shoulder, looking down at the photo. "You like?"

I nodded. "Where'd you get it?"

"Sonya Wyrick," she said. "She called me, not long after you went to see her that second time. Said she wanted to do something to make amends. We talked. I told her how you felt. She hadn't heard about Vince Bascomb. I told her what Drew said—you know, about the fact that we'll never be able to recover your mama's body. She said then that if she could find it, she had something she wanted you to have. I think this is it."

"And I'm just supposed to forgive and forget, is that it?"

"That's up to you," Gloria said.

I turned around. "What would you do?"

"Me?" she asked. "I think I would want to lighten my load. Right now, Keeley, you're carrying around an awful lot of black muck. You hate Drew Jernigan. Hate Lorna Plummer. Hate Sonya. Hate Darvis Kane. And you know what? It's not doing you a damn bit of good.

Sonya feels bad, but she's apparently the only one of 'em who has a conscience."

"I want them to hurt," I said. "I want Darvis Kane found. I want him in jail for killing my mother."

She sat down at the conference table and started flipping through the rest of the mail she'd brought back from the post office. "Look," she said. "I wasn't going to tell you this at all, but I hate to see you spending all this energy making yourself miserable, so here goes. I talked to Howard Banks about Darvis Kane, and he's been doing some digging."

"Sheriff Banks," I said eagerly. "Does he know where Kane is?"

"No," Gloria said. "Howard ran one of those national crime computer checks. Darvis Kane did some time in the late eighties and the early nineties for mail fraud, auto theft, and bank fraud. He was released from a county jail in Bakersfield, California in 1997. And after that, there's nothing."

"He might still be alive," I said. "Daddy's detective could still track him down."

"No," Gloria said, sounding very definite. "No more detectives. No more digging. Howard says Kane is probably dead. Darvis Kane was a con artist and a thief. He ran with criminals most of his life, and the chances are one of them killed him. So that's it. End of story."

"Did you tell Sheriff Banks about Drew Jernigan's part in Mama's murder?" I asked. "Does he think something can still be done?"

"He already knew," Gloria said. "Vince Bascomb called him up and asked him to come out to see him at his house, just a couple of days after you saw him. I guess he didn't want to take his secret to the grave."

"Then why isn't Drew in jail?" I demanded.

"Because Drew Jernigan denied everything," Gloria said. "And without a body, there's no proof of any of it. Now, Keeley," Gloria said sternly. "I want you to stop obsessing about this. Your father wants it too. Jeanine has been dead for twenty-five years. It's over."

I propped Mama's picture up against the drafting lamp on my table. I would need a frame. Sterling silver always looks nice with black and white.

"So that's it," I said softly. "No justice. Sounds like a made-for-television movie. No justice for Jeanine."

"Well," Gloria said thoughtfully, "maybe just a little. Poetic justice, I guess you'd call it." Slowly that megawatt smile blinked on. "I passed Madison Mutual coming back from the post office, and I thought I'd check to see if the new console tables we ordered for the boardroom had been delivered. Guess who's sitting in the president's office starting today?"

"Drew," I said. "He's been sitting there every day for as long as I can remember."

"Not anymore," Gloria said gleefully. "It's Kyle's office now. According to the new head teller, there was a shake-up at the quarterly board meeting, and Drew was quietly dethroned by unanimous vote."

"How?" I asked. "It's a family-owned bank. The Jernigans *are* the board."

Gloria shook her head. "Correction. GiGi, A.J., and Kyle are the board. Together the three of them hold controlling interest in the bank. I guess having the sheriff pay them a visit to inquire about Vince Bascomb's story got GiGi's attention. Plus I hear she thought Drew was spending too much time with JoBeth, the old head teller. And the boys had apparently had it with their father screwing around on all of them. So now JoBeth is on the street, and from what I hear, Drew is too. Although it's a very nice street. GiGi has decided to keep The Oaks and the house at Cuscawilla. She's decided Drew can have the house at Highlands."

"So Kyle's president of Madison Mutual?" I asked. "A.J.'s in Chicago, learning how to be a mortgage broker. And Drew's out? For real?"

"For real," Gloria said. She reached for her Rolodex. "I think I'll give Kyle a call. That new office of his is going to need some work."

68

We held Mama's memorial service on the Saturday after Thanksgiving.

True to his word, Will had quietly bought up all the lots on the cove from the Jernigans, including, at his absolute insistence, Vince Bascomb's property. His first acts as new owner had been to burn down what was left of the old cabin, and replace all the planks on the dock.

And so, on that sunny autumn Saturday, at three in the afternoon, the five of us—me, Gloria, Daddy, Serena, and Austin—stood on the end of the dock and finally said our goodbyes to Jeanine Murry Murdock.

Austin had made a beautiful wreath of daisies, Mama's favorite flower, with a single fat pillar candle set in the middle of it, like a float, and after Dr. Wittish finished with the brief service, we lowered it into the lake and set it adrift.

After a while Dr. Wittish went off to work on his sermon for the next day, but the five of us stayed on. We drank some champagne, cried a little, and stayed out on the dock well past dusk, watching the gently bobbing wreath until finally a soft breeze came up and the candle's flame flickered and died.

Exactly one month later, on Christmas Eve, the five of us stood around another grouping of flowers and candles with Dr. Wittish.

Austin had outdone himself decorating Mulberry Hill. Two huge Della Robbia wreaths festooned with gleaming apples, pears, lemons, limes, and a single pineapple hung from red velvet ribbons on the wrought-iron gates to greet the wedding guests. He'd lined the driveway to the house with hundreds of glass hurricane lamps, inside each of which burned large red bayberry candles. All the tree trunks on the oak alley had been wrapped with tiny twinkling white lights, and on the porch of the house itself, miles of spruce roping were interspersed with the waxy magnolia leaves, holly berries, and dried hydrangea blossoms. More white lights covered the six-foot fir on the hanging balcony over the front door, and the door itself was flanked by a pair of eight-foot-tall hand-hammered brass figures of the angel Gabriel, whose trumpets crossed in the exact middle of the door.

And parked near the doorway, festooned with ribbons, stood Daddy's favorite touch, a gleaming white 1959 Cadillac Coupe de Ville.

With Stephanie off my back, I'd easily completed Mulberry's restoration by the first week in December. Will had been so pleased—thrilled, really—that he'd given me a very special Christmas gift.

All modesty aside, the house looked spectacular that night, lit almost completely by candlelight. A fire crackled in the fireplace in the front parlor, where we'd placed the big Frazer fir Will and I had driven to North Carolina to cut ourselves, and the mantel was lined with boughs of holly, spruce, fir, and magnolia, wrapped with wide cream silk ribbons.

I'd hired a string quartet to play in the back parlor, and they'd arranged themselves artfully around the room, where they were the perfect accessories to the magnificent furniture and paintings.

Miss Nancy had offered to hire the caterer for the event, and I, with a hundred other details to take care of, had gratefully accepted her offer. She'd dimmed the lights of the glittering Waterford chandelier, but the heavy mahogany table was covered with the Georgian silver candlesticks I'd bought in New Orleans, plus silver trays of the tiniest, most delicate canapés I'd ever seen.

It was an hour before the ceremony, and I'd been so busy all day, I hadn't had a single bite to eat. I was famished. When I thought nobody was looking, I snuck downstairs, barefoot, with only a thin satin robe covering my slip, and swooped down on the table and snatched up what turned out to be a morsel of crab cake. Miss

Nancy, dressed in a floor-length green velvet dress with a red ribbon wrapped around her walking cane, came into the room just in time to catch me at my thievery.

She slapped my hand smartly. "Get your mitts off the goddamn crab cakes," she exclaimed. "That's for company. And get your ass upstairs before the guests start arriving and catch you in nothing but your drawers."

"Ta-da!" Both of us whirled around to see Austin, standing in the dining room doorway flushed with excitement. He was still dressed in jeans and a white chef's smock.

Two men in white shirts and tuxedo pants stood beside him, staggering under the weight of the biggest wedding cake I had ever seen.

"Good Lord!" Miss Nancy said.

"Put it over there, on the sideboard," Austin directed. "And don't break any of those Steuben wineglasses."

"Do you like?" he asked, when the men had disappeared into the kitchen.

Nancy and I stood in front of it, turning this way and that to take in every detail. The cake was a three-foot-tall scale model of Mulberry Hill, accurate right down to the balcony with a tiny tree fashioned from a sprig of rosemary trimmed with silver dragees.

"It's amazing," I breathed. "How did you do it? Or did you?"

"All by myself. All it took was five years' worth of back issues of *Martha Stewart Living*," Austin said, preening just a little. "It's a lemon pound cake, with lemon curd filling and white chocolate ganache icing, and all the windows and doors are marzipan."

He turned from the cake to give me a disapproving stare. "And just what are you doing down here in your shimmy, little miss, when we have a wedding here within an hour?"

The three of us poured ourselves a glass of champagne, and then finally I ran upstairs to get dressed. I was upstairs in the master bedroom, brushing on some mascara at what should have been Stephanie's dressing table, when Austin knocked and then darted inside.

"Oh Austin!" I had to catch my breath. He'd changed into a black Armani tux, starched and pleated white shirt with black pearl studs and a red plaid cummerbund and matching bow tie—with black velvet monogrammed evening slippers.

"You like?" he asked, whirling around so that I could get the full effect.

"You're divine," I said, deliberately using his favorite adjective. "It's all divine. And you are the best best friend any girl ever had." I flung my arms around his neck and kissed him directly on the lips.

He wriggled out of my grasp and stood in front of the full-length mirror, turning this way and that, smoothing his hands over his waist. "Is the plaid too much? Too precious maybe? It's the LeFleur tartan, you know."

"Do the LeFleurs have a tartan?" I asked.

"They do now," he said, twinkling. "I designed it myself. Do you think it'll work for New Year's Eve, too?"

"In Madison?" I said dubiously. "I think it's a little formal for here."

"No, silly," he said impishly. "New Orleans. I'm spending New Year's Eve in New Orleans this year."

"With Robert?" I was jumping up and down with delight.

"Who else?" he said coquettishly. "Now please, Keeley, get dressed."

"Is everybody here?" I asked.

"Everybody who is anybody," he replied. "The house is full to busting."

"What about Daddy? Have you checked on him? How's he holding up?"

"He was kind of nervous. Until I gave him his gift. I think that cheered him right up."

"And what kind of gift did you give him?"

"A tee-tiny little sterling silver flask," Austin said. "Full of single malt Scotch. He took a swig of that and mellowed right out."

"Oh God," I said. "Go back in there and take it away from him. We can't have him passing out in front of Dr. Wittish."

"He'll be fine," Austin said airily. "You just worry about yourself. How are *you* holding up?"

"Me? I'm fine. No problem. Cool as a cucumber."

"Really? Then why are you *still* sitting here in your shimmy, when the cream of Madison society is sitting downstairs waiting for that string quartet to start playing Mendelssohn?"

"I've got time," I assured him. "I just want to sit here for another minute or two, and then I'll get dressed. I'll be down in five minutes. I promise."

"You're thinking about your mama, aren't you?' he asked.

I nodded, and a lump rose up in my throat so that I couldn't speak.

"See you downstairs," he said, and he kissed my forehead and left.

I sat down at the dressing table and took the tiny cut-crystal flask out of my evening bag. I shook the bottle vigorously, removed the stopper, and touched the last drops of Joy perfume to my wrists and earlobes. Then I slid my dress over my head, zipped it up, and stepped into the highest pair of Manolo Blahnik shoes they were selling that season. I gave my hair, twisted into Mozella's most elaborate upsweep, a quick spritz of hair spray, and then it was time to make my entrance.

I had to hold the dress's train bunched up to my knees as I took each stair slowly and deliberately. At the bottom of the stairs, crowded into the hall and parlor, I could see the crowd of glittering guests, and the mingled scent of the flowers and perfume and candles rose up and nearly made me swoon, and I hurried down to join them, gently working my way through the crowd into the parlor, where Dr. Wittish waited patiently in front of the fireplace.

Now the quartet was playing the first sweet strains of Mendelssohn, and there was a low collective "aaah" as Serena, radiant in a long-skirted ivory satin evening suit with a sweetheart neckline, made her way down the stairs, clinging to my father's arm.

The guests parted to let them pass, flashbulbs popped and motor drives whirred. Gloria stood on the other side of the fireplace, like me, dressed in black velvet, although my gown was sleeveless, with a deep plunging V-neck, while hers was a more modest long-sleeved number. We both held the bouquets of white stephanotis Austin had made for us, and Daddy, as he approached the makeshift altar, had a single white rose pinned to his lapel. He was beaming, and I thought he must be the most handsome man in the room.

Serena's dark hair was pinned off her neck that evening, to show off the diamond necklace Daddy had given her as a wedding gift. Daddy towered a good six inches over her, and looked down at her with such undisguised adoration that I was blinking back tears even before they'd begun to repeat their vows. I glanced over at Gloria. She was crying. I heard a sniffing off to my left, and sure enough, Austin was bawling like a baby.

Half an hour later we were all drinking a champagne toast in the dining room. Serena hadn't wanted much in the way of formality. No receiving lines. Just champagne, and good food, and wonderful friends.

She cut the cake and fed it to my father, who by the look of the glow on his face, had long ago drained the rest of the Scotch from his tee-tiny flask. I felt a warm hand on my bare shoulder and looked up into Will's dark eyes. He looked gorgeous in his black tux, and his red hair, which still needed cutting, gleamed like copper in the glow from the candlelight.

"Nice night, huh?" he asked.

"Perfect," I told him. I stood on my tiptoes and planted a kiss on his cheek. But he turned his face just slightly and my lips brushed his, for just an instant.

"Thank you for tonight," I told him.

"For what?" he asked. "You and Austin did all the hard work. I just stayed out of the way."

"You've done a lot, and you know it," I said. "Daddy and I can't thank you enough."

"How does it feel?" he asked. "Watching your father get married?"

"It feels right," I said simply. "He and Serena are so sweet together. They're like a couple of teenagers. She makes him happy. And I couldn't ask for any more than that."

"No regrets?" he asked.

"About what?"

"A.J.?"

I made a face. "What about you? Any regrets about Stephanie?"

"Christ!" he said. "When I think how close I came. If it hadn't been for that grotesque fountain, and the absolute fit she threw over it, if I hadn't walked up and seen it with my own eyes . . ."

"She turned out to be a real ball-buster, didn't she?"

"Literally," Will said. His hand was still on my back, and he pulled me just the slightest bit closer. "Mmm," he murmured. "You smell really nice tonight. I never noticed that about you before. Do you always smell this nice?"

"It's a special occasion," I pointed out.

"The first time I met you was a special occasion too," he said, grinning wickedly. "As I recall."

"When was that?" And then I remembered. The night of my rehearsal dinner. "Oh my God," I said. "When I think of how I must have looked that night I could still just die of embarrassment. There I was, covered with strawberry margarita mix, barefoot, and having just thrown the biggest hissy fit in my entire life. I can't believe you watched me vandalize A.J.'s car, without even saying a word. And then you pop up out of that ridiculous yellow Cadillac of yours, and point out that I can't even spell. That was a great first impression, wasn't it?"

"You were adorable," Will assured me. "How could I not hire you?"

My cousin Janey came running up just then. "Hey you guys, come on! They're about to leave. Serena's about to throw the bouquet." She grabbed my arm and dragged me after her, shoving me to the front of the crowd, where I stood with Gloria and a couple dozen other single women of various sizes and ages.

The white Cadillac was pulled up out front, with the motor running, and a big white silk bow tied respectfully to the hood ornament.

A cry went up just then, and Daddy and Serena emerged from the house in a hailstorm of birdseed.

"Bye, shug," Daddy said, spotting me on the porch and pausing to give me a big hug. "You be sweet, y'hear?"

Serena turned her back to the crowd and tossed her bouquet high over her head. The women all squealed, and reached overhead, but it was Janey who dashed forward at the last second and caught it on the fly.

I wandered back into the house and fixed myself another glass of champagne. The string quartet was still playing, and guests were lingering, seated on the sofas, or standing around, admiring Austin's decorations.

I went upstairs, to the master bedroom that the wedding party had commandeered to get ready in, and I was sitting at the dressing table, making repairs to my makeup, when Will walked in.

"Oh," he said, startled to find me there. "I'm sorry. I thought you were downstairs."

"It's all right," I said, dabbing at the corner of my eye with a tissue. "It is your house. And your bedroom. I'm just finishing up here."

I got up, turned with my back to the mirror, and adjusted my dress.

"I forgot to tell you earlier," he said, standing in the open doorway. "You look amazing. Incredible. Even better than the night we met."

"Thank you," I said, blushing at the rare compliment.

"There's just one thing," he said, walking toward me with a frown. "It's been driving me crazy all night."

"What?" I twisted around to look at myself again in the mirror.

"This," he said, standing behind me. He looped his finger under the strap of my black lace push-up bra, which had slipped down onto my shoulder. He bent over and kissed my shoulder, and then my neck, and then the hollow of my throat, and then my earlobes, and then, finally, he turned me around and his lips found mine.

With his arms around me, I forgot where I was, and who I was. And I think he forgot too. After a long time, his hand found the zipper of my tightly fitted dress. The dress had begun to fall off my shoulders when I sensed, rather than heard, someone else in the room.

"About goddamn time," Miss Nancy roared. And then she leaned in, flipped the lock on the doorknob, and gently closed the door.

Grits n' Greens Casserole

INGREDIENTS

   2 cups whipping cream or half-and-half
   8 cups chicken broth, divided
   2 cups grits—not instant or quick cooking
   1 lg. bag frozen collard greens
   2 sticks butter
   2½ cups parmesan cheese
   ½ tsp. fresh ground pepper
   1 cup cooked and crumbled bacon

Grease 13 × 9 casserole. Combine cream and 6 cups chicken broth and bring to a boil. Stir in grits and cook over medium heat until grits return to a boil, cover, reduce heat to simmer, and stir frequently to keep from burning, 25–30 minutes. Add milk if needed to thicken to proper consistency. If you're Southern, you know what that is, if not, think of slightly runny oatmeal.

While grits are simmering, cook frozen collards with remaining 2 cups of chicken broth till tender, about ten minutes. Drain well in colander, squeezing out remaining liquid. Add butter, parmesan, and pepper to cooked grits, and stir till butter is melted. Stir in cooked greens, and spoon into greased casserole. Top with additional parmesan, and crumbled bacon. Dish can be served at room temperature, or heated in 350° oven till browned on top.

A READING GROUP GUIDE
to
Hissy Fit

Introduction

Keeley Murdock's wedding to A. J. Jernigan should have been the social event of the season. But when she catches her fiancé doing the deed with her maid of honor at the country club rehearsal dinner, all bets are off. And so is the wedding. Keeley pitches the hissy fit of the century, earning herself instant notoriety in the small town of Madison, Georgia.

Even worse is the financial pressure A.J.'s banking family brings to bear on Keeley's interior design business. But riding to the rescue—in a vintage yellow Cadillac—is the redheaded stranger who's purchased a failing local bra plant. Will Mahoney hires Keeley to redo the derelict antebellum mansion he's bought. Her assignment: Decorate it for the woman of his dreams—a woman he's never met.

Only a designing woman like Keeley Murdock can find a way to clear her name and give her cheating varmint of an ex-fiancé the comeuppance he so richly deserves. And only Mary Kay Andrews can deliver such delicious social satire.

Discussion Questions

What do you think of Keeley's reaction to her fiancé's behavior at their engagement party? Does she do the right thing? How would you react in a similar situation?

Do you find it surprising that Will Mahoney is so determined to impress a woman whom he's never met? Why?

Is the picture that Mary Kay Andrews paints of life and business in a small town a realistic one?

When Keeley gets underneath the façades of some people she's known all her life, what does she discover? What does this novel say about how well we ever really know one another?

What part do antiques play in this story? Are Keeley's questions about her own past reflected in her search for enduring old furnishings and her wish to create beautiful homes for her clients?

Do you feel any sympathy for A.J.? Does he get the comeuppance he deserves? Does Stephanie?

What secrets does Keeley unearth in her search to find out about her mother's disappearance?

The novel, which begins with a broken engagement, ends with a wedding. Is the identity of the happy couple a surprise?

If you loved *Hissy Fit*,
check out

Savannah Blues

M ARY K AY A NDREWS

Turn the page for a preview.

Available in paperback from

Perennial
An Imprint of HarperCollins*Publishers*

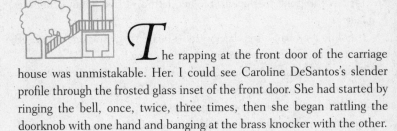

CHAPTER 1

*T*he rapping at the front door of the carriage house was unmistakable. Her. I could see Caroline DeSantos's slender profile through the frosted glass inset of the front door. She had started by ringing the bell, once, twice, three times, then she began rattling the doorknob with one hand and banging at the brass knocker with the other.

"Eloise? Open up. I mean it. That beast of yours did it again. I'm calling the dogcatcher right now. You hear me? I've got my cell phone. I'm punching in the number. I know you hear me, Eloise."

She did indeed have something that looked like a phone in her hand.

Jethro heard Caroline too. He raised his dark muzzle, which has endearing little spots like reverse freckles, his ears pricked up, and, recognizing the voice of the enemy, he slunk under the pine table in the living room.

I knelt down and scratched his chin in sympathy. "Did you, Jethro? Did you really pee on the camellias again?"

Jethro hung his head. He's just a stray, but he almost never lies to me, which is more than I can say for any other male I've ever been involved with.

I patted his head as a reward for his honesty. "Good dog. Help yourself. Pee on everything over there. Poop on the doorstep and I'll buy you the biggest ham bone in Savannah."

The banging and door rattling continued. "Eloise. I know you're home. I saw your truck parked on the street. I've called Tal. He's calling his lawyer."

"Tattletale," I muttered, putting aside the box of junk I'd been sorting.

I padded toward the front door of the carriage house. The worn pine floorboards felt cool against the soles of my bare feet. Caroline was banging so hard on the door I was afraid she'd break the etched glass panel.

"Bitch," I muttered.

Jethro barked his approval. I turned around and saw his tail wagging in agreement.

"Slut." More wagging. We were both gathering our resolve for the coming barrage. Jethro crawled out from under the table and sat on his haunches, directly behind me. His warm breath on my ankles felt oddly reassuring.

I threw the front door open. "Sic her, Jethro," I said loudly. "Bite the bad lady."

Caroline took half a step backward. "I heard that," she screeched. "If that mutt puts a paw in my garden again, I'm going to . . ."

"What?" I demanded. "You're going to what? Poison him? Shoot him? Run him over in that sports car of yours? You'd enjoy that, wouldn't you, Caroline? Running over a poor defenseless dog."

I put my hands on my hips and did a good imitation of staring her down. It wasn't physically possible, of course. Caroline DeSantos stands a good four inches taller than I do, and that's without the four-inch spike heels she considers her fashion trademark.

She flushed. "I'm warning you. That's all. For the last time. There's a leash law in this town, as you well know. If you really loved that mutt of yours, you wouldn't let him run around loose all the time."

She really was quite lovely, Caroline. Even in Savannah's ungodly summer heat, she was as crisp and fragrant as a just-plucked gardenia. Her glossy dark hair was pulled off her neck in a chignon, and her olive skin was flawless. She wore lime green linen capri slacks and a matching linen scoop-neck blouse that showed only a tasteful hint of décolletage. I could have gone on living a long time without seeing her that way, that day.

"Oh," I said. "Jethro is running around. Is that what's bothering you about my poor little puppy? But you're an expert at running around, aren't you, Caroline? I believe you and my husband were running around on me for at least six months before I finally wised up and kicked him out."

I'd kicked Tal out, but he hadn't gone far. The judge in our divorce case was an old family friend of Tal's daddy, Big Tal. He'd given our 1858 townhouse to Tal in the property settlement, and only after my lawyer raised the god-awfullest ruckus you ever heard, had he tossed me a bone—basically—awarding me the slim two-story carriage house right behind the big house.

Tal installed Caroline in the big house the minute the paperwork was completed, and we've had a running back-fence spite match ever since.

My lawyer, who also happens to be my uncle James, talked himself blue in the face trying to persuade me to sell out and move, but he knows better than to try to make a Foley change her mind. On Charlton Street I'd make my stand—to live and die in Dixie. Move? Me? No sirreebob.

Caroline flicked a strand of hair out of her face. She looked me up and down and gave me a supercilious smile.

It was Thursday. I'd been up at dawn cruising the still-darkened lanes of Savannah, trying to beat the trashmen to the spoils of the town's leading lights. I looked like hell. My junking uniform, black leggings and a blue denim work shirt, was caked in grime from the Dumpsters I'd been digging through. My short red hair was festooned with cobwebs, my nails were broken, and peeling paint flakes clung to the back of my knuckles.

The day's pickings had been unusually slim. The two huge boxes of old books I'd pounced on behind an Italianate brownstone on Barnard Street had yielded up mostly mildewed, totally worthless Methodist hymnbooks from the 1930s. A carton of pretty Occupied Japan dishes rescued from a pile of junk at a house on Washington Avenue hadn't turned up a single piece not chipped, cracked, or broken. The only remotely promising find was an old cookie tin of buttons I'd bought for two dollars at a yard sale I'd nearly passed up on my way back to the carriage house.

It was that box of buttons I'd been sorting when Caroline had mounted her assault on my front door.

Now there was a soft pooting noise behind me. Caroline literally looked down her long, Latin nose at me and curled her full-blown upper lip. "My God," she cried. "What is that wretched smell?"

I sniffed and looked over my shoulder at Jethro, who was slinking in the other direction.

"It's not Jethro," I said, leaping to my dog's defense. I pointed over at the wrought-iron railing in the entryway, where I'd draped the tattered hooked rug I'd been trying to air out before bringing it inside.

"It's probably the rug," I said. "I got it out of an old crack house on Huntingdon. I think maybe it's got fleas."

Caroline jumped back as though the rug were a live skunk.

"I can't believe the filthy garbage you drag back here," she began. "It's appalling. And it's no wonder I have to have the house sprayed twice a month. I told Tal, 'Weezie is infesting our house.'"

Behind me, in the vest-pocket living room, my telephone was starting to ring.

"Gotta go now," I said. "Got a business to run." I slammed the door in her face and turned the dead-bolt lock.

Jethro licked my toe in gratitude. "Ro-Ro," I said gently, not wanting to hurt his feelings, "that was bad. No more bologna sandwiches for you, little buddy."

I caught the phone on the fourth ring.

"Weezie, wait 'til you hear."

It was BeBe Loudermilk, my best friend, whose mother, exhausted after having had eight previous children in ten years, had settled upon the name BeBe, and the French pronunciation of "Bay-Bay," for her ninth and last child.

To BeBe, being last meant she was always in a hurry, always trying to catch up. She was a human hurricane who never wasted time starting a conversation with any conventional pleasantries such as "Hey" or "How've you been?"

"Go ahead and guess," she urged.

"You're getting married again?" BeBe had only ditched husband number three a few months earlier, but like I said, BeBe's a fast worker. And she never liked being without a man.

"This is serious, Weezie," BeBe said. "Guess who's dead?"

"Richard?" I said hopefully. Richard was BeBe's second husband, the one who'd had the unfortunate proclivity for phone sex. BeBe was still fighting with the phone company over all the bills Richard had run up calling 1-900-YOU-SKRU.

"Be serious now," BeBe demanded. "Emery Cooper called me this morning. You know Emery, don't you, darlin'? He's a Cooper-Hale Cooper, you know, from the funeral home? He's been pesterin' me to go to dinner for weeks now, but I told him I never date a man until he's been divorced for at least a year. Anyway, Emery's cute, but he's got children. You know how I am. And I don't like the idea of necking with somebody who works with the dead. Is that awful of me?" She didn't waste any time waiting for an answer.

"Anyway, Weezie, Emery let it drop that Anna Ruby Mullinax died last night. In her sleep. Ninety-seven years old, did you know that? And still living in the same house she was born in. Of course, Cooper-Hale is handling the funeral arrangements."

Jethro was licking my toes again. He wanted out. But I hated to have him pee on any more camellias until Caroline cooled off. I cradled the phone to my ear.

"That's nice, BeBe," I said. "Listen, could you call back? I've got to take Jethro for a walk right quick."

"Weezie," BeBe exclaimed. "Don't you get it?"

"What? Emery Cooper wants to get into your pants? Does he smell like formaldehyde, do you think?"

"No," BeBe said. "He smells lovely. Like money. But child, I'm worried about you. Didn't you hear what I said? It's Anna Ruby Mullinax. That house she lived and died in? It's Beaulieu, honey. Now what do you think about that?"

I felt a little tingle on my neck. Beaulieu. I looked down at my forearms. Goose bumps.

"You said she was ninety-seven," I said, my voice shaking. "Were there any survivors?"

"Not a living soul," BeBe said triumphantly. "And Emery says the house is jam-packed with old stuff. Now. Who's the very best best friend in the whole wide world?"

"You are," I assured her. "I'll call you later."

If you loved *Hissy Fit,*
check out

Little Bitty Lies

M<small>ARY</small> K<small>AY</small> A<small>NDREWS</small>

Turn the page for a preview.

Available in paperback from

Perennial
An Imprint of HarperCollins*Publishers*

I

Mary Bliss McGowan and Katharine Weidman had reached a point in the evening from whence there was no return. They had half a bottle of Tanqueray. They had limes. Plenty of ice. Plenty of time. It was only the Tuesday after Memorial Day, so the summer still stretched ahead of them, as green and tempting as a funeral home lawn. The hell of it was, they were out of tonic water.

"Listen, Kate," Mary Bliss said. "Why don't we just switch to beer?" She gestured toward her cooler. It had wheels and a long handle, and she hauled it down to the Fair Oaks Country Club pool most nights like the little red wagon she'd dragged all over town as a little girl. "I've got four Molson Lights right there. Anyway, all that quinine in the tonic water is making my ankles swell."

She thrust one suntanned leg in the air, pointing her pink-painted toes and frowning. They looked like piggy toes, all fleshy and moist.

"Or maybe we should call it a night." Mary Bliss glanced around. The crowd had been lively for a Tuesday night, but people had gradually drifted off—home, or to dinner, or inside, to their air conditioning and mindless summer sitcom reruns.

Bugs swarmed around the lights in the deck area. She felt their wings brushing the skin of her bare arms, but they never lit on Mary Bliss, and they never bit either. Somebody had managed to hook up the pool's PA system to the oldies radio station. The Tams and the Four Tops, the same music she'd listened to her whole life—even though they were not her oldies but of a generation before hers—played on.

She and Katharine were the only adults around. Three or four teenaged boys splashed around in the pool, tossing an inflated beach ball back and forth. The lifeguard, the oldest Finley boy—Shane?

Blaine?—sat on the elevated stand by the pool and glowered in their direction. Clearly, he wanted to lock up and go to the mall.

"No," Katharine said, struggling out of her lounge chair. "No beer. Hell, it's early yet. And you know I'm not a beer drinker." She tugged at Mary Bliss's hand. "Come on, then. The Winn-Dixie's still open. We'll get some more tonic water. We'll ride with the top down."

Mary Bliss sniggered and instantly hated the sound of it. "Well-bred young ladies never drive with their tops down."

Katharine rolled her eyes.

The Weidmans' red Jeep stood alone in the club lot, shining like a plump, ripe apple in the pool of yellow streetlamp light. Mary Bliss stood by the driver's door with her hand out. "Let me drive, Kate."

"What? You think I'm drunk?"

"We killed half a bottle of gin, and I've only had one drink," Mary Bliss said gently.

Katharine shrugged and got in the passenger seat.

Mary Bliss gunned the engine and backed out of the club parking lot. The cool night air felt wonderful on her sweat-soaked neck and shoulders.

"I can't believe Charlie gave up the Jeep," Mary Bliss said. "I thought it was his baby. Is it paid for?"

"What do I care?" Katharine said, throwing her head back, running her fingers through the long blonde tangle of her hair. "My lawyer says we've got Charlie by the nuts. Now it's time to squeeze. Besides, we bought it with the understanding that it would be Chip's to take to Clemson in the fall. I'm just using it as my fun car this summer. We're having fun, right?"

"I thought freshmen weren't allowed to have cars on campus," Mary Bliss said.

"Charlie doesn't know that," Katharine said.

Mary Bliss frowned.

"Shut up and drive," Katharine instructed.

The Winn-Dixie was nearly deserted. A lone cashier stood at the register at the front of the store, listlessly counting change into her open cash drawer. Katharine dumped four bottles of Schweppes Tonic Water down on the conveyor belt, along with a loaf of Sunbeam bread, a carton of cigarettes, and a plastic tub of Dixie Darlin' chicken salad.

"Y'all got a Value Club card?" the cashier asked, fingers poised on the keys of her register.

"I've got better than that," Katharine said peevishly, taking a twenty-dollar bill from the pocket of her shorts. "I've got cash money. Now, can we get the lead out here?"

The fluorescent lights in the store gave Katharine's deeply tanned face a sick greenish glow. Her roots needed touching up. And, Mary Bliss observed, it really was about time Katharine gave up wearing a bikini. Not that she was fat. Katharine Weidman was a rail. She ran four miles every morning, no matter what. But she was in her forties, after all, and the skin around her neck and chest and shoulders was starting to turn to corduroy. Her breasts weren't big, but they were beginning to sag. Mary Bliss tugged at the neckline of her own neat black tank suit. She couldn't stand it the way some women over thirty-five paraded around half naked in public—as if the world wanted to see their goods. She kept her goods tucked neatly away, thank you very much.

Mary Bliss made a face as she saw Katharine sweeping her groceries into a plastic sack.

"Since when do you buy chicken salad at the Winn-Dixie?" she asked, flicking the tub with her index finger.

"It's not that bad," Katharine said. "Chip loves it, but then, teenaged boys will eat anything. Anyway, it's too damn hot to cook."

"Your mother made the best chicken salad I've ever tasted," Mary Bliss said. "I still dream about it sometimes. It was just like they used to have at the Magnolia Room downtown."

Katharine managed a half-smile. "Better, most said. Mama always said the sign of a lady's breeding was in her chicken salad. White meat, finely ground or hand shredded, and some good Hellmann's Mayonnaise, and I don't know what all. She used to talk about some woman, from up north, who married into one of the Coca-Cola families. 'She uses dark meat in her chicken salad,' Mama told me one time. 'Trailer trash.'"

"She'd roll over in her grave if she saw you feeding her grandson that store-bought mess," Mary Bliss was saying. They were right beside the Jeep now, and Mary Bliss had the keys in her hand, when Katharine shoved her roughly to the pavement.

"What on earth?" Mary Bliss demanded.

"Get down," Katharine whispered. "She'll see us."

"Who?" Mary Bliss asked. She pushed Katharine's hand off her shoulder. "Let me up. You've got me squatting on chewing gum."

"It's Nancye Bowden," Katharine said, peeping up over the side of the Jeep, then ducking back down again. "She's sitting in that silver Lexus, over there by the yellow Toyota. My God!"

"What? What is it?" Mary Bliss popped her head up to get a look. The Lexus was where Katharine had pointed. But there was only one occupant. A man. A dark-haired man. His head was thrown back, his eyes squeezed shut, his mouth a wide *O*, as if he were laughing at something.

"You're crazy, Katharine Weidman. I don't see Nancye Bowden at all." She started to stand. "I'm getting a crick in my calves. Let's go home."

Katharine duck-walked around to the passenger side of the Jeep and snaked herself into the passenger seat. She slumped down in the seat so that her head was barely visible above the dashboard. "I'm telling you she's in there. You can just see the top of her head. Right there, Mary Bliss. With that guy. Look at his face, Mary Bliss. Don't you get it?"

Mary Bliss didn't have her glasses. She squinted, tried to get the man's face in better focus. Maybe he wasn't laughing.

"Oh.

"My.

"Lord."

Mary Bliss covered her eyes with both hands. She felt her face glowing hot-red in the dark. She fanned herself vigorously.

"You're such a virgin." Katharine cackled. "What? You didn't know?"

"That Nancye Bowden was hanging out in the Winn-Dixie parking lot giving oral sex to men in expensive cars? No, I don't think she mentioned it the last time I saw her at garden club. Does Randy know?"

Mary Bliss turned the key in the Jeep's ignition and scooted it out of the parking lot, giving the silver Lexus a wide berth. She would die if Nancye Bowden saw her.

"It's called a blow job. Yes, I'm pretty sure Randy knows what Nancye's been up to. But you can't bring yourself to say it, can you?" Katharine said, watching Mary Bliss's face intently.

"You have a very trashy mouth, Katharine Weidman. How would I know what perversion Nancye has been up to lately?"

"I guess y'all were down at Seaside when it happened. I just assumed you knew. Nancye and Randy are through. She moved into an apartment in Buckhead. He's staying in the house with the kids, at least until school starts back in the fall, and his mother is watching the kids while Randy's at work. Lexus Boy is some professor over at Emory. Or that's what Nancye told the girls at that baby shower they had for Ansley Murphey."

"I had to miss Ansley's shower because we took Erin down to Macon for a soccer tournament," Mary Bliss said. "I can't believe I didn't hear anything, with them living right across the street. The Bowdens? Are you sure? My heavens, that's the third couple on the block. Just since the weather got warm."

"Four, counting us," Katharine said. "You know what they're calling our end of the street, don't you?"

"What?"

"Split City."